DARK STORM

BARRY T HAWKINS

Other Ninth Precinct Novels by Barry T Hawkins:

Puppet Master

Dark Medicine

There Are Smiles That Make Us Blue

Gotham Books

30 N Gould St.
Ste. 20820, Sheridan, WY 82801
https://gothambooksinc.com/

Phone: 1 (307) 464-7800

Published by Gotham Books (August 10, 2024)

ISBN: 979-8-88775-998-2 (H)
ISBN: 979-8-88775-996-8 (P)
ISBN: 979-8-88775-997-5 (E)

TABLE OF CONTENTS

The ruler of the South Sea was called Light; the ruler of the North Sea, Darkness; and the ruler of the Middle Kingdom, Primal Chaos. From time to time, Light and Darkness met one another in the kingdom of Primal Chaos, who made them welcome.

—*Chuang Tsu*

We are, I know not how, double in ourselves, so that what we believe we disbelieve, and cannot rid ourselves of what we condemn.

—*Montaigne*

Chapter 1

"No goosebumps, Gil."

The shorter of the two men spoke, his breath puffing out a small cloud of mist in the frigid atmosphere, like a chilly version of the caterpillar in Disney's Alice-in-Wonderland, whose hookah smoke formed words in the air like sky-writing.

"No shit, Sherlock," his companion laughed. "Wish I could say the same." The first nodded in agreement, popping a jellybean into his mouth.

It was a bitter, blustery day—the kind of day most people lying on the chill ground would have plenty of gooseflesh. This individual was wearing nothing but a flimsy, tattered silk shirt, worked up under his armpits to expose pale bare skin. Then again, he was dead. Homicide detectives generally don't get called out at two in the morning to look at the living.

There had been plenty of hubbub surrounding the corpse for the last hour, but now it had died down . . . so to speak. The dozen patrol cars had thinned to four, their flickering lightbars creating dancing shadows, cooling engines still giving off an occasional plink or sigh. Unnecessary emergency services personnel had been dismissed, intrusive reporters diverted to a warmer command center, curious onlookers moved away by the uniformed cops like a flock of pigeons shooed from a seeded lawn. Numerous crime scene photographs had been taken and an initial search completed, the area protectively cordoned off by what seemed miles of yellow tape, proclaiming repeatedly, "Police Crime Scene—Do Not Cross."

Detectives Gil Beach and Frank Terranova waited, hugging themselves, slapping cold hands together, stamping on the pavement. There was no sign of someone from the Medical Examiner's office, who had to do an on-site examination before the body was moved.

"You sure he's on his way?" Beach, the taller of the two men, asked.

"Yeah," Terranova assured him, "I got a confirmation from the dispatcher. I wish he'd hurry his ass. I'm freezing mine off in this wind . . . uh, no wisecracks."

Beach grinned in reply, then grimaced, hunching his shoulders against the cold. A biting wind was whipping off the East River, swirling around the huddled figures. Now and then, bits of debris flew at them, hurled by the gusts. It felt to Gil like a storm was coming, the sky was dark and threatening, an armageddon sky. They stared down at the cause of their lost sleep and comfort.

The body was lying in a position only the dead could hold. The upper trunk was nearly face down, yet the spine twisted so severely that the hips and legs were nearly facing upward. A skinny hand peeked out from under the flat chest, bearing lacerations, as did most of the torso. The other hand was caught under the butt and combined with a dirty mound of ice to shove the pelvis upward in an obscenely frozen bump-and-grind. The corpse looked like a male, but it was hard to tell, because in places the wounds merged into an ambivalent red mess. It was similar to some industrial incidents (not accidents) Beach had investigated. The flesh looked grey and rubbery.

The snow was stained pink, though the small amount of blood on the ground did not match the massive wounds on the body.

“Must have been dumped,” Frank said, “Not enough blood.”

Beach nodded. He was thinking about the corpse, wondering if this man or anyone, for that matter, ever expected to end up under the FDR Highway overpass, like a poor stray, lying here in frozen mortality—broken, drained, and discarded.

“There’s Anton now.”

“Damn, it’s about time.”

An unmarked black Malibu sedan turned the corner, crunching noisily over ice, glass, and gravel as it pulled up to the curb. The headlights had a milky coating that diffused the beams, but they still put the scene in glaring light until the driver turned them off.

A cardboard sign on the dashboard read "NYC Medical Examiner's Office." The driver was Anton Krispnick, Assistant M.E. and one of the best forensic pathologists in the Northeast. Most locals knew that if he had been more of a politician, Krispnick might have been appointed Chief Medical Examiner, but he didn't have the desire, self-advancing style, or competitive instincts necessary to achieve, much less maintain such a politically demanding position.

The stocky man heaved himself out of the car, delicately picking his way over the patches of ice and litter cluttering the street. Krispnick wasn't prissy—his office usually resembled scenes in the aftermath of a tornado or other natural disaster. For some reason his weight had ballooned over the last year, so on the slick pavement he moved with a careful step. Gil had heard a rumor that his friend was overeating due to affairs of the heart but would never be so tactless as to ask him about it directly.

"Sorry about the delay, Gentlemen. What have we got?"

Terranova tilted his head toward the body; hands remaining plugged into the deep pockets of his overcoat. With a nod, the pathologist moved over to the bloody form and bent down for a closer look. The others moved around him, a trio of silent mourners gathered by the priest at a temporary grave.

"Umm. Umm," the Examiner mumbled, as he moved around the body, pausing occasionally to hunker down so he could peek from the side. Cars and trucks rumbled by on the highway overhead transmitting tremors to where they stood. The air was thick, smelling of smoke, asphalt, gasoline, East River, refuse and human waste. Flickering lights from emergency vehicles swept over them in red, blue and yellow flashes like they were at some grisly Mardis Gras party. Gil thought of the Mexican Day of the Dead.

"Okay, you can turn him over now."

Like Beach, Krispnick didn't refer to the man's corpse as an "it." Other Assistant ME's were not always as tactful.

"You mean completely over, or what?"

"Just push his legs all the way, so the face and chest are exposed. I'll do a more complete exam at the morgue, but I need to see the lividity and condition of the head."

The detectives motioned to a couple of uniformed men standing nearby, to indicate that they wanted the body moved. Beach and Terranova were not the type who avoided getting their hands dirty, but there are subtle divisions of duty and authority in the NYPD. At a crime scene, Detectives tell Uniforms what needs doing, and they do it. It isn't individual ego, but an accepted hierarchy. That's one reason a Gold Shield is something to be coveted. The privileges also create resentments at times, but then, so do a lot of things. Gil's "Rabbi", Bob Mabry, the officer who had sponsored and looked out for him when he was getting started, once said, "Show me a cop without a beef and I'll show you a crossing guard."

Between the natural rigor and the cold, the body was stiff as a frozen turkey in the supermarket freezer case, so it flipped over as a unitary slab. Part of the victim's silk shirt was frozen to the ground, tearing with a ripping sound when they turned him over. The chest was caved in, there was no face to speak of—just a crushed mass of bone and hair and blood.

"Well, initially, I'd say we got us a vehicular death here," the M.E. mumbled. "Looks like the guy got creamed by a truck. But since it doesn't look like it happened here, I guess you got yourself a homicide. Or at least a cover-up attempt. I can tell more when I get him back to the morgue. The lack of clothes is interesting."

"The only nude bodies that interest me are alive and female," murmured a uniformed man, craning to get a better look. His nameplate read "A. Sapio."

"Could they have been removed later . . . after the crash?" Frank asked, giving the man in uniform a glare. Sapio just grinned.

"Not really," Anton shook his head, "If he was wearing anything, it would've been pulverized into the wounds. Nope. The guy was just wearing that skimpy shirt when it happened. Not exactly dressed for the weather."

"Maybe one of the street people decided to walk around bottomless. Half of 'em are Bellevue early-outs," Terranova suggested grimly.

Beach was silent but shook his head slightly. Terranova turned to Krispnick.

"Whadda ya think, Doc?"

"It's possible he came from a psych ward, but he hasn't been living on the street. Look at this," the pathologist said, lifting one limb.

The hand was clean and well-manicured. As the doctor turned it, the palm appeared, soft and unsoiled except for the cuts and abrasions of whatever killed him. On the wrist, there was a visible tattoo.

"What is that?" Beach asked, "a flower?"

"Ah—ha," Terranova hooted, "and they say the eyes are the first thing to go."

"I always thought it was the mind that went first. I lost that a long time ago."

"Believe it," Frank nodded, "that's why we work so well together. Anyway, I think it's one of those yin-yang things—you know like a circle that's half white, half black? . . . which reminds me of a joke about this black guy who . . ."

"Now what have we here?" Krispnick interrupted the wisecracks, lifting his eyebrows and sniffing like a dog that just caught a scent. As he raised the body's hand his eyes were drawn to the rest of the limb. A shirtsleeve fell away to expose the upper arm. Just above the elbow, an uneven reddish colored ring circled the arm at the lower part of the bicep.

"What is it?" Frank asked, "ligature marks?"

"No, there's no abrasion. Can't say, for sure," Krispnick answered. "Looks like a stain, or dye. Not a standard tattoo."

The Pathologist checked the other arm, unbuttoning the sleeve this time, to push it up. The same red discoloration appeared on that arm.

"Umm-hmm," Krispnick now added, his attention returning to the crushed torso. Out of his pocket, the Assistant M.E. pulled a paper-wrapped tongue depressor, which he opened and used to probe gently in the chest area of the corpse. He wore latex gloves—standard practice, given the possibility of infection. A corpse could carry anything.

"It looks like homicide, all right," he nodded, pointing at the sliced flesh. "These are blade wounds."

"So he was stabbed to death?"

"Not necessarily, but these cuts weren't accidental. It looks like a very sharp instrument was used, maybe a razor blade or something like it. Might be one of those utility knives all the kids are carrying these days. When I get him cleaned up back at the morgue, I'll be able to tell you more, but it looks like somebody carved a little something on his chest before they ran him over. Looks like a letter Z."

"'Z'?"

"Yeah, or maybe an S."

"What have we got, some guy thinks he's Zorro?"

"Who's Zorro?" Sapio asked.

"You don't . . . oh, never mind. Maybe it's an S."

"Oh Jaysus," Terranova exclaimed in an imitation Irish brogue. "Sure and it must be the mad Slavic Slasher."

Krispnick, Croatian by birth, gave a labored guffaw to acknowledge the insult, but kept at his examination. He looked impatient to get out of the cold, glancing up now and then at the gathering clouds.

Though Gil had chuckled during the interchange, he wondered about the marks and their implications. He hoped this wasn't some kind of trademark; the chosen symbol of a killer who planned to use it again, or already had. That would be the style of a multiple killer. Most folks called them "serial killers," these days. It was as good a term as any, he supposed. Yet in his mind, the term "serial" didn't have the right ring. Gil had handled several cases in which a killer had multiple victims, and after a while, he came to think of them as "murder addicts." Killing, the experts said, was a kind of rush for these sick individuals—a "high" that they usually sought to repeat ever more frequently, like a heroin user's increasing habit. The last thing Gil wanted was another murder addict on his hands.

Then again, Beach didn't get to pick the cases that went down on his turf. During seven years with the Ninth Precinct, Gil had never had a homicide case that he liked. He didn't like death at all, and he didn't like most of what it took to find a killer. It was mostly boring work, or laborious, or distasteful, like tonight. But it could get worse. Sometimes it forced you to come face to face with the sickness that motivated a killer. Sometimes it made you find the seeds of that sickness in yourself, if that was the only way to understand and hunt him down. Gil especially didn't like that part. Still, sometimes it had to be done, and he was able to do it.

Beach had the qualities that make a successful detective. Fitness reports over the years had noted that he was methodical, persistent, patient and intuitive. If that meant that he was also sometimes rigid, bull-headed, and wrong, so be it. He was an excellent observer and noter of detail. He was cynical—which made him suspicious of what was on the surface of things, and underneath as well. That meant nothing was sacred to him, nothing was spared from examination, nothing was beyond suspicion, and nothing was safe from being linked to the matter at hand. The matter at hand was usually murder.

"Damn, look at that," Krispnick said, looking up at the dark banks of heavy clouds, gathering overhead. "Looks like the friggin' end of the world."

"After some of the shit we've dealt with—we could probably even survive that," Frank laughed. "Bring on the storm!"

The detectives returned to the PDU by way of Houston Street, cutting through the Wald and Baruch housing projects, where clusters of hard looking men eyed them as they passed. They went past rows of small businesses in the Bowery section - sweatshops, storefronts, and bodegas. The day was starting to clear, with only a scattering of high clouds. Once the sun rose a bit, the chilly temperature became tolerable, so Beach rolled down the window of the grimy Plymouth. The car was formerly a drug dealer's heap that had been confiscated and now belonged to the Precinct. The ones that didn't get sold at auction were often used by Detective and Vice Units for street work. As they drove through the streets, he sniffed the air like a cat, smelling traces of smoke, rotten garbage, curry and a waft of what he thought was probably sauerkraut. *God bless this stinking melting pot!* He thought.

Several new storefront businesses had sprung up in the last month, desperately clinging to a microscopic margin of profit. They were like flowers; some hung in there year after year, while others were annuals that blossomed for a time and then were gone, replaced in their season by new varieties. He thought of the NYPD Ninth Precinct like an ugly, unkempt garden, always changing, yet always staying the same. The exact ethnic content varied from time to time, like different crops, as new waves of immigration, or economic and political winds blew the seeds of different groups here and there. Still, the basic core was the same. The people at the bottom of the economic ladder carried the boxes and pushed the carts, while the upwardly mobile tried to start small businesses. Those who earned enough to spend became the consumers. If they earned a little more, they moved to a better address.

Right now it was the Koreans who were fighting with the Blacks about respect and a place in the scheme of things. When he was a boy, it had been the Italians in the shops, with the Irish fighting them. Although he had not grown up in this unique piece of Manhattan, he was still deeply bound to it. It may not have been love, but it was a relationship. This was his piece of turf. In a strange way, even though he lived elsewhere, this one square mile of carnival and chaos owned part of him too.

A major element in this personal connection had to do with another thing that didn't change. Among the vegetable stand owners and their customers, among the office workers and salesclerks; mixed in with the children and old folks, the Haitians, Cubans and Afro-Americans, the Hasidic Jews and Puerto Ricans and Irish and all the rest,

were people who killed other people.

CHAPTER 2

"You just kill me," Lenny Charles laughed. He was working with Sanford "Sandy" Pichel, a new guard with Double A Security Consultants. Sandy had the gung-ho attitude of most new employees, along with what Lenny recognized as signs of a frustrated cop. Give a guy a uniform, and suddenly he thinks he's on Brooklyn Nine-Nine.

"Look, I'm just gonna to do a visual," Pichel said, unfolding his tall skinny frame from the small and worn Dodge Omni they used to make rounds. The young man walked to the entrance of ManCo Petroleum's Plum Point Transfer Station, where he rattled the chain and heavy padlock holding the gates shut. Then he slowly scanned the area in a way that he probably thought made him look like Clint Eastwood or John Wayne. Lenny thought it made him look silly. Somehow the coke-bottle eyeglasses ruined the effect. Slowly, Sandy ambled back to the car like the sheriff in a spaghetti western, thumbs hooked in his belt, easy in the saddle.

"You sure we aren't supposed to check inside?" he asked as he climbed back in the Omni, his door creaking as he swung it open.

"Give it a rest, cowboy," Lenny chuckled. "For what ManCo pays, they're lucky they get two pass-byes a night. Besides, this is the Hudson Valley for God's sake, not Bed-Sty!"

The transfer station was in a remote area near Poughkeepsie, New York, on the east bank of the Hudson River. The station permitted massive oil tankers to remain at anchor out in the river, while pumping their black gold through a ten-inch steel pipe to the holding tanks on shore. There were eight such tanks in this depot, each capable of holding up to a half million gallons of petroleum. ManCo Oil was a small-to-moderate-sized operation, which used the transfer station for shipment to its only refinery, in Eastern Pennsylvania. Theoretically, the pumping operation could be reversed, allowing ships to fill up at the station, but that had never been necessary.

Heavy security had never been necessary, either. Except for the occasional graffiti "artist", or drunk teenager that wanted to pound on the tanks like they were huge drums, there had been few problems. In the sleepy Mid-Hudson valley, nobody seriously considered the possibility of terrorism or sabotage. ManCo had been able to get by with a part-time arrangement with AA Security of Hopewell Junction. "Double A" made periodic passes by this and several other facilities each night. "Periodic" generally meant twice a night. Lenny and his enthusiastic partner had just completed the first. There might be another in six hours or so, but even that was dependent on what they found at their other four stops, as well as how long a nap they had at their favorite scenic viewing point near Breakneck Ridge.

The Omni made a wide turn, little yellow light flashing, before pulling out onto route 9D heading north in a cloud of dust and spattering gravel.

A shadow detached itself from the brush neighboring the Transfer Station, gliding across the gravel berm to the security gates. The slack chain allowed a ten-inch gap between gates. That was all the man needed to slip through. No need to climb over or cut a gap. He wasn't the first to gain unauthorized access, as indicated by a line of elaborate graffiti on the side of one oil tank. He moved deliberately, unhurried. By the time the security patrol returned, his work would be done.

Dressed in ink-black clothing and dark cammo make-up, the man moved toward a complex intersection of large pipes and valves. First, he disabled an electronic monitoring device, as well as the system failure alarm. Somewhere at a distant office, a small green light blinked out on a large display of many. The dozing night engineer at a control room 50 miles away didn't notice. Even if he had seen the light fade, it wouldn't have registered as an emergency, which would normally show as a brightly blinking red light and would simultaneously trigger an alarm. In the unlikely event that the engineer noticed the failure in his next routine check and took initiative to act, it would be at least an hour before anyone could get to the site. That would be too late, anyway.

At the Transfer Station, the shadowy figure hefted a long iron bar, using it as a lever to turn one of the big valve wheels. After repeating this operation in several places, he placed a hand gently on the largest pipe—the one that led to the shore before disappearing under the waters of the great Hudson River. A thousand yards from shore, the conduit reappeared, rising to a docking rig, where tankers could anchor in deep water while they connected the tube to their holds for off-loading. The rumbling vibration of the pipe told him that the flow was proceeding as planned, out from the massive holding tanks into the river. Since the docking rig was distant, he couldn't see the gushing black stream that began to spew into the water. In the darkness, no one was likely to notice the spreading oil slick. At this time of night, few vessels navigated the river this far north. The gushing disaster would proceed unnoticed for some time.

He mused about a local history connection. During the Revolutionary War, the colonists had strung a barrier across the Hudson, made of massive iron chain links to prevent English ships from floating up the river. "There's more than one way to block a river," he thought.

Still, the meter indicated only seven-to-ten thousand gallons an hour. The flow would have to continue for several hours to create a truly significant spill. The man went to a low metal shed, where he was able to break in and locate a forklift. Designed to load barrels and equipment, the machine was small, but adequate for his purposes. The key was hanging on a nearby hook. After starting it, he drove to the first valve that he had opened. Inserting the forklift's heavy blades under the valve wheel, he pushed a lever on the control console to raise the lift mechanism. There was a creaking, straining, protest of tortured metal, then the wheel popped off like a bottle cap off a warm beer. He repeated the operation at the other valves, leaving a series of twisted sprung shafts that could not be closed. Finally, he drove the machine to a set of other tanks, in a neighboring cluster. Raising the lift to maximum extension, he butted into the smooth metal sides with the pointed blades until they punctured the metal. Streams of dark fluid spewed from the holes. Penetrating the tanks lower, might have sent a forceful gusher straight at him. At the higher level, the punctures created thick streams that arched over his head, like great black fountains. He knew that these tanks located away from the mangled valves would not affect the flow of his primary sabotage, but they would add to the confusion, difficulty in selecting priorities, and quantity of emergency equipment needed to get the situation under control. As a last detail, he ripped the battery out of the forklift, disabling the machine. He threw it into a deepening pool of oil, where it disappeared from sight in the dark ooze.

The man knew much about control. It was his accustomed role, his chosen position. He knew that he had just affected miles of a great ecosystem, as well as the lives of many species. As he reflected that one of the species most affected would be humans, he smiled.

Chapter 3

Ten hours later, and fifty-six miles south of what would later be referred to as the "Plum Point Spill," Gil Beach arrived at the Ninth Precinct NYPD, in lower Manhattan. Beach remembered when he first saw the Precinct Station a dozen years earlier, thinking it looked like a tomb. The blocky structure occupied the middle of the block on Fifth Street between Second and First Avenues, an anchor of solid stability in the middle of urban chaos. It was hard to tell the true color of the old sandstone walls. Perhaps the tone had begun as the ochre-tinged tan of an Egyptian temple when it was erected in 1946. Under the post-war Mayor there had been a building splurge that gave him the reputation of having an "erection complex." In the intervening decades it had been coated and cured by the murky urban atmosphere to a vaguely sooty color varying between charcoal gray and a muddy brown.

A weathered brass plaque to the right of the entrance memorialized two police officers who had been killed decades ago in the line of duty. Beach extended his hand to brush a finger over the raised letters on the plaque. It was a habit of his, maybe a superstition of sorts. Other cops had been killed on the streets more recently—he had even known a couple of them. But Officers Rocco Laurie and Gregory Foster had died the same day Gil had been sworn in as a rookie. Most folks wouldn't even remember the names. Like

Piagentini and Jones, two other cops that had been gunned down about the same time, their names had faded from public memory, but not the memory of this Detective.

A retired cop named Corey told Gil that he had been elected to 'fill a gap in the blue line.' Despite cringing at the cliché, Beach knew that he did have a sense of commitment and loyalty to the task. Corey claimed that there was a war going on in this city, and in some ways Gil could understand what he meant. This "war" cost lives at a terrible rate. Most people who weren't in immediate or obvious danger backed away from the conflict. Somehow, they believed that their role was a minor one, their contribution not worth the risk of getting involved. Unlike Corey, Gil could understand that feeling of wanting to distance oneself from the darkness and at times part of him felt the same way. Yet Gil knew that he had to take his place in the line, even if it put him in harm's way. If he didn't, he would be betraying Rocco and Laurie, and the others who had sacrificed their lives because they believed that was what it meant to be cops and men. It was certainly part of what it meant to be Gil Beach.

"Hey Gabby, you coming in, or you plan on standing out there all day?"

As the voice intruded on his thoughts, Gil realized he had been standing outside the station for a long time. The call was from Sedgwick, “The Procurer.”

Still in uniform, after twenty-five years on the force, Cassius “Cage” Sedgwick had foregone the route of promotion for the more immediate rewards of free enterprise. He had started with his wife’s Tupperware catalogue.

It happened after she walked out on the marriage one day, leaving him everything, including their son and a heavily mortgaged house. She ran off with a landscaper who had put in a rock garden for the people across the street, while apparently getting his rocks off with Sedgwick’s wife during break-time. In her hurry to split, she forgot to cancel a home party she had set up for the following week. Cage was watching the seven-o-clock news while fantasizing a sexual relationship with the woman TV anchor, when the doorbell rang. He answered it, as his story went, only to have two good-looking suburban housewives push their way into the house. One of them had a plate of delicious looking cookies, and the other had a set of equally delicious looking hooters, each of which distracted him to the extent that he decided to let the party take place, as scheduled.

Cage managed to find his wife’s product catalogues and order forms as well as a box of expensive perfume bottles he had recently confiscated from an illegal street dealer on Astor Place. The seven women who eventually showed up for the plastic-ware sales pitch were surprised and pleased to walk away with expensive designer perfume as door prizes. Sedgwick was equally delighted with over two hundred bucks in orders that were placed in his hands along with the telephone number of the foxy lady with the immense hooters. He still wore a fancy gold bracelet with a large black onyx stone and intricate, red-tinged gold detailing that the woman had later given him as a token of her affection. In time, the bracelet became more than merely a trophy of conquest. It grew to be a tangible symbol of the fateful day that his career in "procurement" was launched.

Soon Cage branched out into Mary Kaye Cosmetics. Then he started an Amway dealership, while somehow managing to distribute a competing line of Bestway products at the same time. Later he picked up jewelry lines, clothing, shoes, vitamins, lingerie and encyclopedias. It wasn't a big reach to start finding cheap gear popular with cops. Where there was a demand, Sedge delivered.

In time, Sedgwick's reputation became that of a man who could get you anything you wanted, usually at a deep discount. His resources now went far beyond home retail products. If a fellow cop needed extra firearms, a sap, tickets to a popular Broadway show or concert, deep discounts on new cars, a supply of Laetrile, or Madonna's home telephone number, Cage Sedgwick could get it for him. The rumor was that the man made at least double his police salary by way of these various enterprises. Yet he still put on his uniform, badge, and gun every day.

As the cop/cum entrepreneur stood before him, Gil couldn't help wondering what motivated Cage to stay on the force. Apparently, it wasn't financial need. Was it one of those cases where the uniform had become so much a part of his identity, that the man didn't know who he was without it? Was it just habit? Or did a man as materialistic as Sedgwick share any of that sense of commitment and loyalty that moved men like Beach?

Gil turned from his thoughts to stride up the wide slab steps of the Precinct, dark and beveled from the passage of countless heavy shoes. The entrance was gloomy despite the glow cast by old-fashioned lantern lights at each side of the door, but a few steps inside, the gloom gave way to startling brightness and bustling action. The large muster room enveloped him in a familiar cocoon of smells and sound. There was a constant undercurrent of noise made up of various conversations, the clump and scrape of heavy steps across the hardwood floor, the creak and jingle of Sam Brown belts laden with cuffs, holsters, and batons. Gil sniffed the permanent odor of sweat and floor wax, leather and wood, cigarette smoke and musty stacks of records. Night and day, the assembly area was awash in bright neon light, with a flicker from the ceiling fans that moved the fetid air around without changing it. The large institutional looking windows were never opened, the only new air coming from the front entrance, the doors of which seldom closed. He was swallowed up into a familiar world. It was oddly comforting.

Sedgwick moved beside Beach, with uncharacteristic hesitancy. He seemed to be working himself up to something. For ten months during Gil's early years in uniform, the two men had shared a Patrol Car. Though they had gone their separate ways, the two still kept a bond gained during those interminable hours in the RMP together—hours cruising the streets, responding to calls, gabbing, cooping, pursuing, searching, smoking, writing reports, arguing, eating, reading perps their rights, waiting, sweating, making collars, losing them, talking each other down from highs and up from lows, drinking coffee, making calls, reading reports, trying to stay sane and alive while guarding each other's back. Sedgwick had been the senior officer of the two, back then. Over the years there had been a reversal of roles. Gil had not only been promoted beyond his former training officer but had become the person Cage sometimes turned to for advice. This looked like one of those times.

"What's on your mind, Cage?"

"Yeah, well . . . see, it's about my kid. I really don't know what to do with him."

"You and ninety-nine out of a hundred other teenagers' parents. Which doesn't include me, `cause I never had any kids, as you may remember."

"I know, I know. But you've worked with kids a lot. Remember that I was your partner. I know about the Little League coaching and all that volunteer stuff you don't tell anybody about. Besides, you always had good sense. Parent or not, I could use your advice."

"What's the problem?"

Gil moved to a quieter part of the muster area opposite the huge wooden desk with its great protective brass rail filling the west side of the room, like a huge bar in a strange saloon. With all the general hubbub, there was almost as much privacy in a corner, as there might be in a separate room . . . a pool of relative calm in the midst of the human rapids. Cage followed, continuing the conversation in an embarrassed mumble.

"Well, Jimmy's seventeen now. There's only so much control I can have over him, I know. But . . . well, he's gotten into this heavy rock stuff so much that I'm beginning to worry. It's not the music, though damn if that's not enough to drive somebody crazy, but this kinda . . . weird uhh, blood and . . . death stuff. At first it was just black tee-shirts and ugly posters, but lately there's been some weird shit going down."

"Weird, like how?"

"Well, he disappears for days at a time, and comes back looking like he's been to war or something. I mean, like torn up and bloody, and acting very strange."

"Have you asked him?"

"Sure. And he says strange stuff, like he was 'making the earth more habitable,' or some shit like that. And like, maybe he's trying to jerk me off when he says it, but he doesn't smile or anything. One time I try to follow him, right? No luck, I lose him in traffic. He didn't make me, but you know how hard it is to do a tail with one vehicle. On the third try, I stay with him out as far as some woods in Massapequa. I see him head into the woods, and I follow. He goes into this sort of barn-like building, where there are other kids waiting. At first, I was gonna surprise him and show myself, but as I'm watching him and this group of real punky looking types, I see lots of knives and other shit that makes me think I'd better know what I'm stepping into here. A lot of these kids have shaved heads, you know?"

Gil nodded, not interrupting.

"So I stay back and watch," he continued, almost breathless in his rush to explain, "as they pass around some grass and start taking off their clothes. Guys, gals, everybody is getting nearly naked and ripped. There was drugs all over the place. Then they bring out a bunch of weapons, along with this weird cammo and leather stuff, like a cross between military and heavy metal, if you know what I mean. They also had this big mutt of a dog. The things they started doing, I hardly can tell ya. Like this one chick pours something between her legs, and they have the mutt lick it off!"

"You can see that kind of stuff on Forty Second Street any day of the week, Cage."

"Yeah, maybe, but it's different when your kid is on stage. Besides, that wasn't the worst of it. Sex I can handle, even if it's a little kinky. But then they all gathered around this big mutt, and they . . . they just ripped him to pieces!"

"They killed the dog?"

"Oh shit, yes. They just all went into a kind of frenzy, and cut him into a million pieces—stabbing, ripping, smearing blood all over . . . I mean it was real sick, Gabby."

"So what did you do?"

"I didn't do nothin'. What am I supposed to do—run in and tell a coupla dozen freaked out hopheads with knives that they're under arrest? Jesus, Gil, what am I supposed to do, call for back-up? Don't you understand, Gil? This is my fucking SON! I don't know what the fuck to do. God, this is one of the only times I wish Rita was still around. Since she left, Jimmy and me haven't gotten along all that good. I can get him any stuff he needs, but, shit, Gil, I . . . I can't talk to him."

"Have you tried counseling?"

"I sent him to some shrink in Great Neck for a while, but it just ate up my fucking savings account and . . ."

"No, I mean for you."

"What are you talking about? I'm not crazy. He's the one with a problem."

"Sounds like you've got a couple of things you could use advice about. You don't have to be crazy to talk to somebody. I mean, here you are talking to me, and there probably isn't anybody in the world that knows less about this stuff than I do. I'm sure Pilar could give you the name of somebody, if you're interested."

"Look Gil, I know your wife is a psychologist and all that, but you've got this thing all wrong. It's my kid that needs a shrink, or a jolt of electricity, or a jail cell or something. Me—I'd be fine, if he wasn't out killing animals and who knows what other kind of shit." Sedgewick's neck was turning red.

Sedge hadn't changed much over the years. Gil remembered that once after a record nine spilled coffees in one week, Cage still blamed the shape of the cups, rather than his habit of perching them on the dashboard. Not the kind of guy that spent much time bellybutton gazing. Eventually, Gil had seen that Sedgwick was mostly interested in conquests. Whether he called it sales, scores, or collars, the primary thing as far as Cage was concerned was win or lose, profit and loss. To suggest that he might have an equal part in the relationship with his son, would be like speaking underwater in Albanian.

"Well, whatever, Cage. I don't think I can be much help. If you want, I can put you in touch with Dick Ovens, a friend of mine. He's with the State Troopers and specializes in some of that stuff. Kids in trouble, gangs, all that stuff. He works in the troopers' EAP."

"What's that?"

"You know, Employees Assistance Program. We've got one too. Anybody on the Job can go there for free to get help. It's completely confidential."

"Oh yeah. Right."

Sedgwick made some polite noises about calling later, then walked away. Not, of course, before shoving a free sample of Nu-Skin hand and body cream into Beach's hands. Whether it was supposed to be payment for his advice, or a marketing technique, Gil didn't know.

Later that day Beach called Dick Ovens to suggest he bring his wife over for dinner the next evening. It was a way to catch up on a friendship, but Gil also hoped his former Academy classmate might feel like sharing some information.

CHAPTER 4

By evening a front of cold Canadian air had collided with the warm low-pressure system that had moved up from the south a few days earlier. The heavy laden southern air began dropping its moisture, washing the entire Mid-Atlantic region with a monsoon-like deluge. On Staten Island, without the benefit of adequate storm sewers, streets in the lower lying sections flowed like Venetian canals.

Higher up the hills of Staten Island, on Howard Avenue, Gil's wife Pilar sat on a seat built into the old box window, looking out at the fury of the storm. She was sipping at a glass of hot cider spiced by a dollop of Jamaican Rum. She had a large book open on her lap, the cover a glossy picture of tropical jungle growth.

"The rain's terrible. I can't believe I'm sitting here reading about rain forests, while we're having a deluge. Second day in a row. I wonder how the Deasons are making out?"

"Depends on how big a boat they've got," Gil mumbled, shaking his head, "their basement they can forget."

"I warned them about that contractor, too."

"I wish you had been wrong. That house probably represents everything they have."

"Watch out with those wishes, Cupcake. Especially when you start wishing I'm wrong."

"Not that you ever are, of course," Gil deadpanned.

"Well, except maybe in my choice of husbands," she laughed.

A crash of thunder shook the windows. Pilar shook her head, more serious now.

"It isn't just bad for the Deasons, it's terrible for all the other Brooklyn refugees who paid three times too much for cardboard houses built on top of swamps and landfills and underground streams."

"It's still better than living in the City."

"Come on Gil, I know you don't entirely share my concern about the environment, but don't you see how unorganized development has devastated the island? Greedy speculators, and ineffective politicians have raped this area."

"Rape is a strong word."

"Maybe so, but they've allowed the natural streams to be plowed over, flow patterns ignored, and huge subdivisions created where there are no sewers. They've destroyed the environment to build these developments. They're literally killing the earth."

"I guess I'm more concerned about people getting killed. A little more primitive, maybe, but then I'm a simple kind of guy."

He was reacting a bit to her speech-making, but mostly he was kidding. Pilar had been a strong influence on his awareness. They had often discussed how many working class families that wanted to flee the city were buying up thousands of hurriedly built modulars and row-houses. Higher up the hills that had once been the retreat of Carnegies and Vanderbilts, Gil knew that older homes had become prized possessions. Since New York City kept threatening to institute a residency requirement for the 37,000 members of the NYPD, many of them had crossed the Verranzano Narrows Bridge seeking housing that would lie within the city borders, while providing distance from high crime areas, congestion, and potential harassment. In most subdivisions, like New Dorp, Eltingville, and Great Kills it was an unusual block that didn't have a couple of resident cops.

Gil Beach had been ahead of the rush. He had leased the top floor of an old mansion on Grymes Hill from an elderly woman. She supported herself on the rental income from that house and two others her wealthy husband had left her when he died of a stroke ten years earlier. She liked Gil immensely, so when he married Pilar, the woman offered to sell the entire house to the new couple for a generously low figure. When they had trouble with a mortgage, she even agreed to hold the paper, accepting previous rent as the down payment. They still had to watch every penny, but over the first couple of years real estate values kept climbing so before the economy leveled out, they had enough equity to get a second mortgage that covered most of the medical bills not paid by insurance. They hadn't put all difficulties behind them by any means, but if finances were the only problem, Gil thought, they would be okay. Some other problems are harder to get at, like why their conversation was making him fidgety.

"I don't know why I bother," She sighed.

"Probably 'cause I'm so strong, intelligent, and handsome."

"Modest, too. Now if only you were rich!"

"Maybe in another life," he said wryly. Looking out the window, he saw the rain sluicing down the panes in solid waves, instead of drops. His thoughts turned to some of the wealthy contributors that his wife dealt with to raise money for her environmental causes. He wondered how she felt when she had lunch with some rich and handsome philanthropist. How did a simple cop look in comparison?

"What's going on in that mysterious mind of yours," Pilar asked. "You look glum."

There she went again. Though not exactly reading his thoughts, she sure as hell didn't miss a trick when it came to noticing his moods. Sometimes he didn't feel like opening his thoughts for examination.

"Oh, I guess I was just thinking that if I was rich, I might consider building an Ark for the coming floods."

"Oh?" Pilar responded, not convinced he was being honest, but deciding to let it go. "I hope Dick and Maggie can make it tomorrow—she doesn't like driving in the rain."

"This isn't rain, it's Lake Michigan dropping from the sky."

"Well, it's depressing," Pilar said, "I think I'll go to bed now, and hope for a better tomorrow."

"Sounds like an ad for a finance company." Gil snorted. He looked up from the book he was reading to see that his wife's robe had opened slightly. His eyes automatically moved to the swell of her partially exposed breast. She saw the direction of his glance, and grinned.

"You might not be rich, but perhaps you have certain talents. Would you care to give a demonstration?"

Gil had mixed feelings about her invitation, but he didn't know why. Sometimes the two of them could seem to be joking around, yet he would end up feeling uncomfortable. Was it because she got on her soapbox about the environment thing again? Lately, she'd seemed to be coming on awfully strong about that. Or was it the business about being rich? Gil liked his work, but every now and then he heard about guys his age that pulled down six figure salaries, and he got annoyed. What's more important anyway, running a company that makes drugs, manipulates other people's money, or the job of trying to make the streets safe for decent people?

"At your service, Ma'am," he said with a grin, but had to work to bring it off. They made love after that—but it was uninspired . . . more form than substance. They kissed and fondled each other in familiar, established ways, but there was no heat or urgency. All the silent communications that had come to be part of their sex life, seemed like small talk rather than news flashes. Eventually, Pilar moved on top of him, rocking until his body responded. There were times she rode him wildly, as if he was everything she wanted. Tonight, it seemed automatic. Still, the sight of her soft breasts hanging near his lips, was as irresistible as ever, the feel of her back and hips the same sensual pleasure it always had been. Eventually the stimulation brought him to a sexual edge, then pushed him over. After he climaxed, Pilar didn't seem interested in pursuing her own fulfillment.

"Something wrong?" he asked.

"No, it was nice . . . I just . . . I don't know, it just didn't seem like you were all there tonight. Are you feeling distant or something?"

He hated when she read him so well—the downside of being married to a psychologist. Instead of answering, which might have started a difficult conversation, Gil just kissed her on the cheek and turned over. After a while he could hear regular heavy breathing. He got out of bed quietly, pulling on sweatpants and a tee shirt, slipping into his running shoes. There was a soft "click" as the door closed behind him.

Gil shrugged into an old fleece jacket before descending the stairs to the framed glass front door. He stepped through onto the old wrap-around porch, wide antique boards creaking a familiar tune. Tonight, it sounded like a sad song. Rain pounded overhead in a depressing rhythm. The air was heavy and moist, even protected as he was beneath the overhang. Standing there he could see the water sluicing down the driveway and pooling in the back, muddied and foamy from its rushing travels. The dirty rain filled a wide depression in the back yard, forming a brackish pond. A small concrete figurine stood there, next to a spreading yew, as a bit of decoration for the low-lying area of landscape. Gil remembered placing it there as part of the preparations for their wedding.

They had decided to have the marriage ceremony at home, planning it for outdoors, with hopes that the weather would cooperate. A trellis arch had been constructed at the center of the large yard, as the site for the wedding ceremony. Gil and Pilar had spent a month prior to the festivities, trying to trim, prune and amateurishly landscape the area for the special day. In a garden center off Hylan Boulevard, Pilar had sighted the gnome-like figure, laughingly claiming it looked a bit like Gill. She insisted that he cart it home and include it in the yard arrangements. She called the statuette “Junior.” There was a bittersweet flavor to the reference, since they had not been able to have children. For a long time, they had made a habit of patting “Junior’s” head, whenever they passed the funny little figure. “Stick with me, Baby,” Pilar had always whispered, as she stroked the small smiling head. The frequent pats and touches had eventually worn all the paint from the gnome’s top, so now it had a little area of bare plaster on top. In earlier days, Pilar had claimed that it made the statue even more like Gil, matching the small bald spot, where his hair was starting to thin in back.

Gil stood listening to the incessant drumming of the rain and watched as the smiling little gnome gradually disappeared beneath the rising murky water.

Chapter 5

Eight hours later, Beach was watching the Statue of Liberty slide past from his vantage point on the top deck of the Staten Island Ferry. There were express buses he could take that crossed the Verranzano Narrows Bridge, then cut through Brooklyn, over the East River into Manhattan, but he preferred the slightly slower ferry trip with its temporary retreat from city insanity. He liked the foggy days best. While others dreaded the white shroud of mist, Gil loved the way it insulated the boat from the world, allowing him to ride a misty voyage pushing through the clouds with the melancholy accompaniment of distant foghorns.

Fighting against a head wind, the ferry took an extra few minutes to cross the harbor. It slid slowly into its slip on the other side, gently colliding with the pilings that creaked and groaned like tired old men in a soup line, not wanting to be bothered anymore. He waited until the main rush of people had surged off the ramps, before making his way through the Port Authority building toward the recently renovated train platform. The rail car shuddered and rattled through the short ride up to Astor Place Station. Gil didn't usually mind the subway, and was about to enter its maw, but today the escalator sucking people into the bowels of the city looked disturbingly depressing. The hazy darkness, the herd-like shuffling crowd, the smell of damp clothing and mushed cigarette butts underfoot was more than he was ready to take. Beach retreated to the street despite the rain. After three tries, he finally managed to grab a taxi.

“Where to, buddy?” the driver hollered from the front, leaning over the seat to open the rear door from the inside.

“Second Avenue at Fifth Street.”

“You got a’ address?”

“No, the corner is fine.”

“You got it, Buddy.”

Gil thought he was going to be saved from any further conversation, but no such luck. This driver was one of the talkative types.

“I know that corner. Sportline Bar, right?”

“Close enough. It’s the SportsPage.”

“Yeah, yeah. Sports-Page, Sportline . . . whatevah. The Astro Lounge is just down the street. Am I right, or what?”

“What are you, an expert on bars?”

“Oh, no man. I jus’ been pickin’ an’ droppin’ for fifteen years. You get a lotta calls from the bars. I know all the main intersections. On Fifth and First, you got your Stevens store,” he boasted, his accent making the street names sound like “Fift” and “Foist.”

"Ain't that right?"

"Not bad. I'm surprised I haven't run into you before. I guess there are a lot of cabs."

"You got that right. Gotta fight for every fare, 'specially wid these Uber and Lyft guys grabbin' so many. But whatta ya gonna do. By the way, buddy, my name's Tony."

Although his rider gave no name in return, the driver didn't seem to notice, continuing his attempt at conversation.

"So you live around here, or is it a job?"

"Job."

"Okay, don't tell me, lemme guess," the cabby cackled, glancing quickly at Gil in the rearview mirror. "You're civil service, I'll bet."

"You've gotta do better than that."

"Okay, lemme see. I'd say you're a cop. On your way to the Ninth Precinct," the words as he pronounced them, sounding like "Nyntt Precink."

"Am I that obvious?"

"Naw, not really," the cabby laughed, "but I'm a little nervous about guns, and I thought maybe I saw the edge of a holster. Besides, cops never wanna be dropped right at the stationhouse, even when it's rainin'. An' of course, I know the Ninth is right there."

"Anything else?"

"Well, don't take it personal or nothin', but most of youse guys got this sort of a look."

"A look?"

"Yeah. I don't know how ta say it, exactly. It's kinda like you're real tired, and sorta mad about something . . . like deep down inside."

"If you ever stop hacking, Tony, you probably could get a job as a psychiatrist."

"Look, I didn't mean nothing. I mean, I . . ."

"It's okay. Don't worry about it. It's true. You have a good eye. That's how I'd describe a lot of cops. I just never thought it fit me too."

"Well, it ain't bad or nothin'. I mean with what youse guys have ta deal with all the time, it's no wonder you get a little tired and all."

"What about you, Tony? You must see a lot in your job. Does it change you too?"

"Oh it ain't the same. Nah, it's different for us."

"Why? Why is it different?"

"Well . . . I guess 'cause we don't hafta do nothin' about it. I mean, sure I see all the shit—and it makes me sick, ya know, sometimes. But it's got nothin' to do with me. I can just drive away, ya know. And the way they been whackin' cabbies these days, that's just what I do most of the time. I get the hell outta there, if anything looks even a little bit dangerous. But you cops—you're supposed to make it better. When I would run, you guys go straight to it."

A dozen responses came to Gil's mind—mostly Departmental Public Relations kind of stuff, about the responsibility of the average citizen. Yet, there was something true about the cabby's simple conclusion. Gil glanced at the livery registration where he saw that the man's name was Anthony Giardini. It would have been easy to dismiss the man as just one more nameless, faceless, ethnic resident. But Tony had touched a nerve. In a way he was right—when others could walk away, a cop couldn't. If you accepted the job, you also accepted that. It was the "make it better" part that was the problem for Beach. There was a lot they couldn't make better. There was certainly a lot HE couldn't make better.

When the cab stopped at Fifth Street, Gil thrust the fare into the driver's hand, including a bigger tip than usual.

"Stay safe, Tony."

Gil jumped out of the cab, into a downpour. Although he started to run down the street, he slowed after a few yards, no longer trying to stay dry, figuring it was a wasted effort. A lonely line of trees was planted along the street. The gnarled old survivors couldn't flourish in the exhaust fumes and odd temperatures of the asphalt, concrete, brick and glass city, their roots burned by countless douses of dog and human urine. Yet the old creatures somehow hung in. It was a familiar ugliness that made Gil feel like he was returning to home base. Back to the urban garden with the rest of the gnarled old sentinels. Back to the weeding.

When he reached his desk on the second floor, he shed his damp overcoat, tossing his hat on the wide window ledge where it caused a poof of dust as it landed. The desk was so cluttered, someone who didn't know him would have been amazed at how he immediately spotted the message form amid the jumbled papers, files and miscellaneous stuff mounded on the surface. Gil claimed that despite the apparent chaos, he knew where everything was located. God help anyone who attempted to straighten up his personal un-filing system. His desk may have been a mess, but it contrasted sharply with his mind, which could organize, categorize, and analyze incredible amounts of seemingly unrelated information. He could bring order out of chaos. In fact, that probably is how he would have described his work. Many crimes had been solved because of his head for the job, but looking at his desk, you would think he was a slob. Beach would have said you were right.

The note said to "call Krispnick." The number was Anton's office at the Morgue. Gil moved a stack of DD5 activity reports waiting to be entered into the computer, settled back into a creaking office chair and punched in the pathologist's number. After some small talk with the secretary, he got the man he wanted.

"Hello, Anton? It's Gil. What's up?"

"Ahh, Gilhooley, it's you is it? Well, I got something for you on that John Doe."

"What'd you do, find a driver's license in his armpit?"

"No, but something almost as good."

"Okay, so what do I have to do, beg?"

"I'm tempted, but you can grovel for me some other time. Right now, you can start checking out urinogenital surgeons. This kid—looks like he's in his early twenties to me—had a vasectomy within the last three weeks. I'd say between eighteen and twenty-two days ago."

"Do you realize how many people get that little operation every week?" Beach asked. A brief thought darted through his mind like a trapped sparrow, about how unnecessary birth control had become for him and his wife, but he didn't let it roost. Some thoughts are better to let go.

". . . and he could have had it anywhere" he continued, "—not just locally."

"Yeah, but this one's different. Ninety-nine percent of these things are just slice and sew jobs. But this one was a special order. He got a faucet put in."

"A faucet?"

"Well, almost. It's a little valve thing. The idea is to make it easily reversible. The surgeon installs this little valve, closed in the `off' position. No little spermies get through, just as much as if the tube was cut. But if the patient ever decides he wants to make babies after all, it's a fairly simple procedure to make a tiny incision and open the valve again. Presto, sperm highway to heaven."

"Is it a pretty unusual procedure?"

"Well, it isn't that difficult, but not many U.G. boys do it, `cause most folks aren't willing to pay the extra bucks it costs. Figure it at four or five times the cost of a simple vasectomy. Insurance isn't usually gonna cover it because it would be considered elective. And there are some worries about complications caused by the implant, small as it is - rejection, and so forth. Besides, no U.G.

man is going to guarantee reversibility, even with the valve. Too many variables."

"Thanks, Anton. Maybe we'll get lucky."

"But there is more, my friend!"

"Yeah, like what?"

"A whole lot."

"Which I suppose you'll eventually tell me."

"All in due time. First, you should know about the message carved in our freeze-dried friend."

"A message?"

"Well, not in words. But that slicing . . . well you saw what looks like a letter of the alphabet? It's not a Z, or even an S."

"Okay, so do I have to pump you, or what?"

"Well, I don't want to get into much speculation here, that's more your job. But it looks like some kind of symbol was inscribed in the thoracic area. There is the double curved line—like the letter S. The line runs from his umbilicus to the sternal notch. It wasn't accidental."

He closed his eyes in thought. "You know I read about a killer they called the 'alphabet slasher' once . . ."

"Yeah, Thanks, Anton," Gil cut off the pathologist's story. Krispnick could get far afield if he strayed from the cadaver examination at hand. "Anything else about this one?"

"Yeah, well, I was getting to that. The cuts were a little more than a single letter."

"Like . . ?"

"Like the guy was so pulverized, I didn't make out the outer figure until later."

"Outer figure?"

"Yes, surrounding the other. It was a bit crude, of course, but the S shape was inside a larger circle. So the S really created two halves, woven together. If I make myself clear, the total effect was to suggest . . ."

" . . . a yin—yang symbol."

When the Assistant M.E. was silent, Gil responded.

"I get the picture. Doesn't necessarily mean too much, even if that's what it's supposed to be. It's a common symbol. In fact, the thing's overused. You see it on jewelry, tee shirts, whatever. Some kids don't even know what it means—they just see it and like it. They think it's a cool thing. Oh, was the head shaved?"

"Like if he were a Skinhead, you mean, or a Moonie? Well no, not really. But a couple of other things were missing."

"Missing? What?"

"The orbits . . . the eyes, and the tongue. I would have noticed at the scene, but you saw how crushed the face was, and the whole mess was frozen till we got him inside for a few hours.

"Ummm. What do you think, could it have been animals—rats or whatever?" Gil asked.

"Not this time. We see that a lot, of course. But where I can find the cuts, they're sharp and clean. No teeth marks—I guess it's a little cold for the little beasties to be out as quickly as usual. No, that stuff was done with a blade, too."

"I see," Gil said quietly, "Is that it?"

"Well, about those stains . . ."

"You mean on the arms?"

"Yes, those interest me. It's odd that they would be at that location. My guess is that the kid was handling some dye or something that color, wearing elbow-length gloves. Didn't quite avoid some getting on his upper arms. I took some tissue samples and sent 'em to the lab along with the other specimens. We got some good fingernail scrapings. You can check with the lab guys later. They can give you the toxicology report and so forth.

"So that's it?"

"Yeah, for now—but I'm not through looking yet."

"Okay, thanks again," Gil said, hanging up the receiver. He decided to wait on the lab information, since he preferred to get the direct observations of "Shig" Higawa, the Director of the Forensics Lab. Higawa wouldn't be in his office for another hour or two.

Chapter 6

On a pad of yellow legal paper, Beach began making notes. He turned the pad on its side, to draw several lines across the page, forming columns. Then he turned the pad upright again, and labeled each column at the top. He wrote headings of “facts”, “time”, and “people.” Another wider column was headed by a question mark. In this column he planned to enter issues yet to be addressed, questions needing answers. There were a lot more entries in the “questions” column than the others. The last column was titled, “To Do”, where he listed tasks he would have to accomplish or have someone else accomplish. In this space, he wrote “Call Shig” and “Check U.G. Dr’s.” Frank could get started on the second one. His partner and friend, the recently promoted detective had gotten good at research while sitting out a few months of “rubber gun squad” service; desk duty required while he proved that his treatment for a drinking problem had been successful. It had. His worst addictions now, seemed to be jellybeans and awful jokes.

If thoughts could mystically summon someone, this must have been one of the times, because just then Frank came in, balancing two coffee containers and a paper bag.

“I got a good one, Gil. Tell me, who’s the most popular guy in a nudist colony?”

"I don't know. Who?"

"The one who can carry two cups of coffee and five donuts at the same time!"

Gil thought for a moment, got it, and groaned. But Frank wasn't finished yet.

"And who do you think the most popular woman is?"

"Go ahead, tell me . . . I can't wait."

"It's the woman who can eat the fifth donut! Ha!"

"Good grief, Frank, I don't know where you come up with 'em. I don't think I want to know."

Beach outlined what they had to look for from the leads developed in the autopsy and set Frank to work making calls. Terranova strolled off, popping jellybeans into his mouth and humming an unrecognizable tune.

As Beach sat looking at his columns of words and phrases, Gina Esperoza walked past. She was a middle-aged mother of four and currently the only woman detective in the Ninth PDU. She was a little stocky, with a heavy chest and thick waist. The chest looked good on her, Gil noticed, filling out her blouse in a very feminine way. Gina had the rich colored Latin skin, with dark brown eyes that could sparkle or shoot fire. He decided that she had pretty good legs, and there was nothing wrong with her rounded, womanly rear end.

"What the hell are you looking at?" she suddenly asked him. "Is my slip showing, or what?"

Gil jumped, and quickly bent back to the work on his desk, mumbling.

"Geez, can't even stare into space anymore."

He was embarrassed by being caught ogling but put it down to simple horniness. The sex between him and his wife last night hadn't been very satisfying. Maybe that was his own fault, but it still left something that felt unfinished. Oh well, sex isn't everything. Look at the priests and nuns.

"Then again, I'm not a priest," he muttered under his breath. He crumpled up the piece of paper he was writing on, to throw it halfway across the room, missing the nearest wastebasket by three feet. He drew new columns on the paper, starting his lists over.

After writing "John Doe" in the column marked "people," he noted various items like the missing eyes and tongue as well as the tattoo under the column of "facts." He also added the detail that the body had been transported. He moved on to the column headed by a question mark. This time, besides "location of death?" and "red stains" he also wrote the words "yin-yang" and "carver" as unanswered puzzles. Mostly, he was just jotting down random thoughts at this point. "Revenge?" "Turf?" and "Red Herring?" were notes on possible motivations that he put in the row of questions.

When he got to the "To Do" column, he began by listing the telephone canvass that even now Frank was probably beginning, which would seek to identify the surgeon or urinogenital specialist who performed the vasectomy. There were some standard procedures he added to the task list, like running the fingerprints and name through the law enforcement files. He also made a private note at the bottom of the page, "Workout." It wasn't about the case, it was more about him.

Gil had a hunch about this case. He handled homicides all the time. It was his daily work. But sometimes there was one that required something more . . . that demanded every resource he could bring to it. Long ago he had found a way of coping with his feelings and frustrations when they threatened to overwhelm him. It was a physical discipline of intense exercise that consisted of running up and down numerous flights of stairs. It didn't matter much where the stairs were located, but he preferred ones without an audience, accidental or otherwise. Recently he had not kept to the discipline as much as he once had. Having Pilar to talk to had provided a new outlet. Many stresses seemed less burdensome, when he shared them with her.

In addition, HE had changed. He was no longer the same angry man who once had to drive himself beyond exhaustion to rid himself of demons. Yet he could feel a knot of smoldering heat inside again. Something was building. This case might be one of those exceptional ones that could again suck him into the mind of an insane killer. It wasn't a pleasant prospect, but he had a hunch that it was going to happen. He could feel the first licks of pressure again. It was the pressure of darkness and wrongness at large. He wouldn't come right out and say it, but he felt like evil was on the loose in his backyard.

That evening he was at the Wagner College Stadium, up on Grymes Hill, now deserted. He dressed in old sweats and tattered Asics running shoes, finding them less bulky than the type he had previously worn. The shoes were an old model Gel-Kayano that he had picked up cheap at a clearance sale, now worn to a frayed and dirty resemblance of their former appearance. Still, they were comfortable, and he hated to get a new pair, no matter what innovations the makers had come up with in the last few years. He just kept replacing inserts, hoping the shoes would last forever.

As he started up the stadium stairs, he felt a familiar tightening of his thigh and calf muscles. He was surprised at how soon he began to tire. It reminded him of how quickly conditioning falls off. As the fatigue turned to pain, he felt the old numbing effect, the natural anesthetic that came with the intense exertion. Enzymes and hormones, lactic acid, and adrenaline, mixed and fought with each other. His head tried to ignore them. Flight after flight of stairs he pushed himself, at times yelling out as he fought his own body and mind.

Up the north staircase he pushed, across the upper aisle of the stadium, down the south stairs . . . then a circle of the track to let his body regain some of its resources before heading up the steps again, gulping at air that carried the scent of poured cement from the raw concrete stadium walls, shadows lengthening in the late afternoon sun.

After several circuits, he found himself slowing on the upward climb. It wasn't just exhaustion. He looked up to see a portal, where the exit tunnel began. He stopped, staring at the opening.

This was where he had first seen Pilar years ago. She had been using the stadium for a quiet meditation place, and was fascinated by his discipline. Here is where they had begun their first awkward conversation—the first of many long talks and attempts to learn about each other.

There was no one there today. The opening looked dark and empty. Gil was surprised to find it reminding him of old emotions, also dark and hollow, which he tried to shake off. He had come here to exorcise his feelings, not be caught up in them. Still, this feeling shook him because he hadn't expected it to exist. He thought it was banished, a part of the past. The sensation was like having been cured of cancer, then finding a new lump, or struggling to rebuild your burned house, and waking in the night to the smell of smoke. He had overcome that awful emptiness, hadn't he?

He ran his hands over his face, through his hair, tugging at the sweaty strands for a moment. His eyes were shut and his mouth clenched, a muscle quivering tightly in his jaw. Then he dropped his arms to the side, looking up beyond the tunnel to the high rim of the stadium. He took a deep breath, as deep as he could, before slowly exhaling. His body gave a little shudder. Then he started up the steps again.

Chapter 7

Down far different stairs, many miles away, a hulking male figure stepped through a hidden door into a spacious dressing room enclosed by walls of old stone. A woman clothed in a diaphanous shift waited until he approached. With a sponge she gently wiped greasy camouflage paint off his well-defined features. His face became more recognizable, with strong chin and high forehead. The eyes were the most striking element, colored a deep bluish tint bordering on purple. The intensity of the gaze was not simply due to the color or setting of his eyes. A smoldering quality hung about the man, which seemed to flare out of his gaze like something burning. The woman was a moth to the flame.

He stripped off the rest of his garments as he walked to a roomy shower stall. She anticipated his moves, adjusting the spray of water for him. As the warm stream cascaded over his body, the water turned a muddy color, mixing green and black camouflage paint with the blood caked on his arms and torso. A dirty river sluiced into the drain . . . muck flowing to its sewer home.

He stood motionless, as if in a trance . . . legs spread, arms out at an angle, head tilted back. The water splashed over a muscular body, not tall but solidly built. He slowly tightened and relaxed the thick muscles in his arms, then he did the same with other areas of his body—legs, buttocks, back, stomach—in a languid, informal isometric routine. After a few minutes, he gave a low animal-like snort. In silent understanding, the woman stepped into the enclosure where she began smearing liquid soap over him. Except the one guttural sound, he didn't acknowledge her existence, even when she washed between his legs.

She was an antelope of a woman: dark and lithe, eyes darting at every movement, ready to bolt. Her modeled face had high cheekbones and clear skin, yet there was tightness around her mouth and eyes that suggested quiet desperation. A cloth band held long auburn hair back from her forehead, where a circular tattoo was located near the hairline. Her long legs and firm rear tapered to a slim waist. She had disrobed to only a brief silky loincloth. Small firm breasts with jutting nipples stood out enough to occasionally brush against the man's arm or back, but he appeared not to notice. After rinsing in the steaming spray, he stepped out of the enclosure into a thick terrycloth robe the woman held for him. He moved to a large soft chair, sat, and pointed with his finger toward a nearby table, where there was a boxy SAT handset, crafted of heavy impact resistant plastic with a military camouflage pattern. The woman handed it to him, then settled on the floor at his feet. She rested her head against his leg, dark sad eyes looking cheerlessly up at him. He smoothly punched in a number, then let his left hand rest on her head, fingers playing around the mark on her forehead as he spoke into the receiver. There was a symbol on the back of his wrist that matched the one on her head.

"It's me. Yes . . . I left something in room Three. Yes, the new one. Phil . . . Philomena, something like that. She became difficult. I don't need that. She won't be difficult anymore. Make sure you clean things up."

He glanced down at the dark-haired woman at his feet, seeming to notice her for the first time. Seeing his look, she spoke quickly.

"You won't get rid of me, will you Drang?" she whispered in a throaty voice. "I do please you, don't I? Let me please you."

His eyes remained hooded, though his lips thinned in what might have been a smile or a sneer. He reached beneath his robe to pull out a heavy brass key that hung around his throat like a necklace. She tensed, a cat seeing movement in the shadows. He held out the key, which she grabbed hungrily, kneading it in her hands as she darted to a small safe which was anchored to the floor of a hidden closet a few feet away. In a moment she was back at his feet holding a dark metal box. She hesitantly surrendered it to the man, who released the catch holding the lid and opened it. He removed a cloth packet, which he unfolded to reveal a syringe, short needle, and a small glass bottle of amber liquid.

Now she mewed in anticipation, settling herself in a practiced position between his legs. While he fitted the needle to the end of the hypodermic to extract liquid from the bottle, she reached out to open his robe. Leaning forward, she placed her mouth on him. In the same movement, she extended her trembling arm over his thigh. The arrangement seemed a practiced position. He removed a latex strap from the box, tied it around her arm above the elbow, and tapped a vein in the hollow of her arm until it stood out under the skin . . . a pulsing blue worm, asking to be fed. As he continued his efforts, she continued her's busily, as if urging him on. It was hard to tell what was exciting her . . . the sexual contact or anticipation of what was about to be done to her arm. The needle penetrated her skin on the forearm, a few inches above a circular tattoo matching the one on her forehead. As a scarlet drop of blood formed at the point of injection, there was a momentary hardening between his legs, the beginning of an erection. He eased back the plunger, breathing harder, as blood mixed with the liquid in the syringe. Moans escaped her busy mouth as she felt the puncturing jab. He pushed the shaft of the syringe to its hilt in the barrel while pulling the elastic strap loose, allowing the drug to surge into her circulatory system.

"Blood," he whispered. "Natural fluid of the body, and supporter of life. Without it we cannot survive. I own your blood, don't I?"

The woman shuddered and held a frozen posture for a long moment as the rush of chemicals pumped into her body, then slipped to the floor. His erection softened with her collapse. For him to climax, to be satisfied, required more pain, more struggle, more blood.

After a few minutes, he rose, stepping over the nodding form to rummage through his discarded garments. He removed a red-stained object, an old-fashioned barber's straight razor sporting an ivory handle inlaid with ebony figures that resembled astrological symbols. He washed it in the bathroom's white marble sink, before approaching the far wall where the natural stone surface was covered with dark wood paneling and a series of tall teak cabinets. Using another key, he opened one unit on the far left to reveal shelves cluttered with sharp implements—scalpels, razors, knives of various types, burnished edges glittering. On the top shelf there was an empty space in a row of similar razors. He gently placed the ornate instrument there, between two ivory handled blades, each with elaborate symbols carved on the age-yellowed sides.

Securing the first cabinet, he moved to a second. A low rumbling sound rose from deep within him, like the purr of a great cat. The cabinet doors opened smoothly to disclose a collection of lethal weapons—firearms and munitions, secured in leather and wood brackets, gleaming a dull blue-black and smelling of machine oil, bulbous canisters and shells, like eggs waiting to hatch death. It was only a matter of time, he knew, until the enemy would come for him. He planned to be ready when they came . . . more than ready. They would know the fury of the storm—for he was the

Storm and Fury. He pulled a heavy gun from the cabinet, running his hand sensuously over the barrel of the Colt AR-15 semi-automatic assault rifle. Now, at last, he smiled.

CHAPTER 8

"Somewhere, over the rainbow, skies are blue. . . ."

The child's voice was a clear penetrating treble that reached the audience without benefit of a microphone. She went by the name "Winnie", short for Winifred, one of the kids in the "New Start" program. Gil smiled at Helen Joseph standing nearby. The two of them had come up with the idea of holding a talent show several months earlier, but hadn't managed to bring together all the elements until now. The audience was mostly made up of parents, relatives, and people involved one way or another with Youth Bureau programs. Every kid that didn't have a parent to bring, was given an adult volunteer sponsor during the project. Gil was determined that none of the children would be without a fan watching and rooting for them from rows of well-worn folding chairs arranged in the basement room. Now the chairs creaked and groaned with a full crowd of well-wishers, but quieted as the performance began.

The idea of doing a show got started with "Hands" Belcher, a twelve-year old boy referred through the PINS, "Persons In Need Of Supervision" diversion program. Belcher didn't come up with the idea, but his talents made others start thinking. "Hands" had made money on the street by juggling for the money people would throw to him. He was a gifted juggler, able to keep multiple objects in the air at once, often picked at random from the onlookers. Unfortunately, he had supplemented his entertainment income with some part time work as a pickpocket. While borrowing objects to juggle, he often slid out a wallet or watch that failed to return to its owner. Still, "Hands" was so good at the juggling, Helen wondered if there wasn't a way to use his talent in a more positive way. She mentioned it to Gil, who was reminded of Angel Cardoza, a child he tutored in an after-school program. Angel was no "angel" in the usual sense of the term, but he was a natural with the harmonica and his melodies could seem almost heavenly at times. A few inquiries identified other talented children who had been sucked up into the Juvenile System. Eventually almost two dozen kids were recruited for the "First Annual Talent Show and Extravaganza" of the Youth Bureau. Some of the talent was little more than pantomiming to a recorded R & B song, but a lot of it was surprisingly skillful, and everybody seemed excited to be performing. Just planning for the event had been a positive experience for some kids, who had never felt part of a constructive group before. Gil knew that rehearsals had been as much social gatherings and support groups as they were labor. Work sessions to put together the costumes and scenery came to be a highlight of the week for many of the young people, and some of the adults too.

Gil noticed his friend Ahmed a row behind them and marveled to see moisture forming in the big black man's eyes. Ahmed Ali

Muhar was a ten-year veteran of the NYPD, who had a reputation for being about as tough as a cop could be. Gil had recruited him as a sponsor by convincing him that black youth needed African-American role models. There was no real discussion; Gil just laid out the whole idea to the imposing giant who listened impassively. There was a full minute of silence, then Ahmed said, "Awright." In the intervening months, Gil had often noticed him off in a corner with Raynell Washington, his sponsee, the two working together silently like there was nobody else in the world. It was a perfect match. Raynell had never talked much either. The expression of grateful awe on his face, whenever he looked up at Ahmed looming over him, spoke eloquently.

Ahmed's face had formed into an odd grimace when he watched Raynell performing earlier. At first Gil had wondered what the expression signified, then recognized it as the closest Ahmed got to a beaming smile. Together the two quiet souls had worked up a routine for the boy, using his well-developed skills as a break-dancer, then expanding the act into what was essentially an impressive display of acrobatic ability. Now Ahmed's eyes were moist.

Gil became aware of Winnie's song.

" . . . where troubles melt like lemon drops, away above the chimney tops, . . . that's where you'll find me."

Working with her as much as he had, Gil had almost forgotten that the ten-year-old had spent most of her life in a wheelchair. Gil had learned not to use the term "wheelchair bound" at Winnie's insistence.

"I'm not bound by my chair," she had explained, "it's the only freedom I have."

The chair had been decorated for the show in pink crepe paper and fluffy flowers made from tissue. Winnie was radiant, with her matching pink pinafore, and blonde hair woven with flowers. Where the lacy dress ended, just below the seat of the wheelchair, two spindly limbs extended—caged in metal rods and bulky hinges.

Gil thought about the fantasy of a place where troubles really melted away "like lemon drops." In his experience, troubles usually multiplied like a virus. As he watched the girl, he felt a deep sadness, but it wasn't because of her handicaps. It was because he knew the pain and loss she had yet to live through . . . pain her little optimistic heart didn't even know was coming.

Looking at the crippled child, facing the audience and life with such confidence, he hoped she had the strength and will to endure this stormy and difficult life. It would take all her courage and hope . . . items he knew to be very valuable, and very rare.

“ . . . Birds fly over the rainbow,” the small voice sang, “Why, oh why, can’t I?”

Chapter 9

"We've got an ID on the vic," Frank Terranova announced with a quizzical look, " . . . I think."

He stood leaning against Beach's desk, backlit by dirty beams of partial sun leaking through a gap in the big blue shades that covered the high PDU office windows. Gil raised an eyebrow.

"You think?"

"Yeah, well, it's a little strange. At first it seemed like we were going to get lucky. I had Myrna help me with the calls. I started with the City numbers, while she worked the outer counties. It seems there aren't many Docs who do this kinda snip-n-sew job. Myrna only made a half dozen calls before she found a sawbones in White Plains who specializes in it. He usually does twenty or thirty a month, but he's been on vacation in Florida and hasn't had anybody under the knife in the last four weeks except a half dozen just before he left. That made it easy to pare down the possibles to three guys. Only one matched the hair, height and weight we got for the vic.

"So the doctor had the name for him?"

"Well, he had a name, but it was a phony."

"I thought you said you had him I.D.'d?"

"So I did . . . but I never said it was simple. I guess, once in a while somebody up there likes us, 'cause the Doc's medical history just happened to mention the kid's dentist. Seems he had a bad reaction to anesthetic during oral surgery last year. They always ask about previous anesthesia problems before any kinda surgery. So, then we get ahold of the dentist, who faxes us the dental records, and batta-bing, batta-boom, we got a positive ID an hour later. I should've known it was too easy, but the name is William Paxton McSwain, the Third."

Terranova pronounced it "da Toid," exaggerating a Bronx accent in an attempt to be witty.

"Not <u>The</u> McSwains?"

"None other—as in "W.P. McSwain the Second," principal stockholder of Megamite Computer Systems, board member of the Knickerbocker Securities Trading Company and First National Metro Bank.

"Also reputed to be the power behind a certain New York Senator, who shall remain nameless, but never seems to lack for generous campaign funding," Gil added.

"Which fits the picture Anton put together," Frank agreed, " . . . somebody with plenty of bucks and soft hands."

"So what's the problem?"

"The problem is, then I call up the McSwains. I speak to some guy, name of Peter Granson, who is no less than 'Personal Secretary' to the Man, himself. Geez, I'm wondering what kinda guy wants to be a secretary? But this Granson does not seem impressed that I represent New York's Finest.

Beach sighed, "Frank, can you cut to the chase?"

"Okay, okay, so when I say that this has to do with the McSwain's kid, he says—and I quote: `I am sorry Detective Cassanova . . .' that's what he calls me, not Terranova. Casanova, he says. `I'm sorry Detective Casanova, but I am afraid that Mr. and Mrs. McSwain have no son."

"What?"

"Right. So I ask if that means there is no William Patrick McSwain the Third, and he hangs up on me. Believe me, Gil, I talked real nice, and everything."

"Okay, I get the picture. You have any idea if there's a William the First? Maybe we can find him, and he might have a grandson the secretary forgot."

"Well, if there is, but Grandpa won't remember either. The word is that he's the most famous vegetable at Mountain Ridge Nursing Home. . . . Alzheimer's or something."

"Okay, thanks. Let me make a couple of calls. We'll find out what's going on."

Beach reached in a side pocket for a dog-eared address book that he paged through until he found the number he wanted. The book was a holdover from before he used a cell phone, with some old contacts he had never gotten around to transferring. He punched in the digits on the phone with the same forefinger he used to hunt and peck his typed reports. The Detective was old enough to remember when The Department had first purchased push-button telephones, for years getting by with ancient rotary models, supposedly as a cost saving measure. Gil wondered how much time had been wasted with the old equipment. A lot of detective work was done on the telephone. Sometimes it took hundreds of calls to follow up leads. Initial calls were easier and faster with pushbuttons, but also countless redials could be made with the touch of a single finger, instead of the laborious redialing of the rotary dial each time. For years he had a callous on the first knuckle of his forefinger, built up from the abrasion of the dial and now he wondered how often he had given up after twenty calls, when the twenty-first might have uncovered vital information. Of course, he realized how much this dated him, so he didn't mention his reminiscences.

This call was to Grady Dickson, a reporter who covered the upper-class society affairs of New York City for the Eastside Evening

News and had known Gil for years. It didn't hurt that he owed Gil a favor or two. The reporter only took a few minutes to confirm that there was indeed a William McSwain III, but a falling-out in the family had ostracized the young man from the rest of the clan.

"The word is, that the kid was disowned," Dickson explained.

"That explains it. Thanks for the skinny," Gil said, preparing to hang-up, "Take care of yourself."

"Hold it, Hold it!" Grady protested. "Hey guy, this is a reporter you are talking to. How about a little tit-for-tat, here? Give me something. Are you on to a case involving the McSwains?"

"Nothing I can talk about."

"Oh sure. I'm just your handy free information service, right? C'mon Beach, gimme a break. What's up? Scandal in the making? The little weirdo into drugs? He didn't kill somebody, did he? C'mon, man. Off the record, what's the story?"

Gil knew the man was right. He couldn't ask the reporter's help, without returning the favor occasionally and this was not the first time he had sought information from Grady.

"Okay, but look, this is strictly off the record. We found a John Doe corpse last night. It looks like it could be the `little weirdo' you mentioned. Why did you call him that, anyway?"

"Oh hey, high society homicide! Love it, love it! Oh, that sounds terrible, doesn't it? Look, Gil I'm no ghoul. It's just that I haven't had a story worth spitting at in ages. I don't like anybody to die, but on the other hand, it could've been a worse loss. Billie-boy was a real wild one. I don't know everything he was into, but it seemed that anytime he wasn't doing something to embarrass the family, he was weirding out in Istanbul or calling from a jail in Tijuana. I think the family got tired of bailing him out, so finally they handed him a hunk of cash and told him to get lost. I guess he even overdid that, if you get my drift. Don't worry, I won't mention your name . . . "reliable sources" is cool. But thanks, Gil. This is big. I still owe you."

Two hours later, Beach and Terranova pulled up to the gate of the McSwain estate on a remote lane in the town of Oyster Bay, Long Island. The Long Island Expressway had been the usual jammed up mess. "Biggest parking lot in the world" the locals called it. You'd never know it, in this neighborhood. Stone and timber castles sat down long landscaped drives, behind hedges, rock walls or sturdy privacy fences. The classic wrought iron gate of the property was open, so they drove up a long oval driveway, rumbling over cobblestones, to a wide parking area in front of the immense colonial mansion. A few moments after they rang a bell, the massive oaken door was opened by a middle-aged woman in a simple dark housedress, apparently part of the house staff.

"Detectives Beach and Terranova, NYPD," they introduced themselves, displaying ID and shields, "We'd like to speak with Mr. and Mrs. McSwain."

"Are you expected?" the woman asked nervously, her hands flitting about, birds with no place to land.

"No, but I suggest that you let them know we're here," Frank responded coolly.

"I'm afraid the McSwains do not see people without an appointment, gentlemen. So if you would like to leave your card, I will be happy to . . ."

"Look, lady," Frank interrupted, "we're not your local vacuum cleaner salesmen come to call."

Gil stepped forward, touching his partner's arm, to slow him down a bit. Frank could be a little quick on the draw at times.

"Ahh, ma'am, this is police business," Gil said. "It concerns a homicide, and it is a matter we will have to discuss with your employers."

He considered a threat to haul her bosses down to the station but knew it would have been mostly bluff. Bluff works sometimes, but you'd better have a fallback position in case it doesn't. The truth is, no cop in his right mind would choose to pull a VIP in for questioning, except by invitation, even if he could. Not that servants needed to know that. But he didn't have to go farther. The woman had turned pale at his words.

"Homicide? You mean a murder? But what . . . who . . ?"

"We will be happy to discuss that with the McSwains."

The woman looked shaken, her neck and face now flushing, in contrast to the pallor that had preceded it. She seemed to have an effort composing her expression, but when she did, she straightened. Her hands came to rest in pockets, and her expression changed to a haughty air.

"Please come in, Gentlemen. I am Olivia McSwain."

It was the detectives' turn to feel uncomfortable. Frank was the first to speak.

"You are . . . uh, oh. Well, we didn't realize . . . I mean, we didn't mean to offend you or anything, it's just that we weren't expecting you to open the door, and . . . uh . . ."

Gil gave him the high sign to shut up before he put his foot more in his mouth than it already was. The woman just stared at Frank as he ran out of steam.

Moisture then began to form in her eyes. She spoke in a trembling voice, as if she hadn't heard anything Gil's partner had said.

"It's Billy, isn't it? My son?"

"Well, ma'am, if you'll pardon me, we're a little confused. . . Mr. Granson told us that you have no son."

"Oh God. He's dead, isn't he?" she blurted, her voice a sharp keening sound, nearly a wail.

"We have a probable homicide victim," Gil softly confirmed, "that has been tentatively identified as a William Paxton McSwain, the Third. I must ask you again, if you have a son by that name?"

"Of course we do! . . . we did. But it was because of that goddamn fanatic! He killed him, didn't he?"

"Which fanatic is that, Ma'am?"

"You don't know? Why that awful survivalist guru or whatever he is—Director of the Federation of Natural Selection, or something like that. The phony con-man, with the stupid name—Storm! He took our son away from us."

She paused, hands wringing a hanky, "I understand your confusion. As far as we were concerned, Billie was dead. He rejected us so completely that he might as well have been. But now . . . Oh God, I just don't know what to feel. My son is dead . . . again! And that bastard killed him. I know that fanatic killed him, whether you are aware of it or not."

"How do you know that?" Beach asked.

"Because he took away everything that made Billie a person! He turned my boy into an extremist like himself; a brain-washed, freaked-out drug addict. How about that for a so-called environmentalist? I could never figure how you could believe in nature, and the environment, and purity, and stuff your body full of chemicals."

"Yes, Ma'am," Frank said earnestly, trying to make up for his earlier faux pas.

"I finally gave up trying to make sense of it," she went on. "When you're dealing with addicts and weirdoes, why would it make sense? That freak who calls himself 'Storm' poisoned my son's mind. When he was through, my little Billy was completely gone. Anything that has happened had to be that bastard's doing. He's a storm alright—a terrible destructive storm, that blew in and ruined our son's life."

"What do you know about your son's recent activities?"

"Nothing."

"Nothing?"

"That's right . . . absolutely nothing."

"Are you saying . . . ?"

"They were very secretive, of course. But, the truth is, we didn't want to. You see, my husband felt we had no choice. He insisted that we consider Billie as already dead. He said we needed to stop letting ourselves be hurt. It wasn't our boy doing those things anyway, he said. Our boy was gone." Tears finally brimmed out of her eyes. She wept softly for a moment, before continuing.

"That's why Peter told you we have no son. He was instructed to respond to inquiries that way. You've got to understand, it wasn't because we didn't try. We tried everything. We found his bank accounts emptied out—over a million and a half, gone. There were other things too, it was so terrible. That monster took his money, took his mind, and now the bastard has finally killed him."

She stepped over to the side of the room, where she rummaged in a bottom drawer, finding a small photograph. It showed two blonde boys, arm in arm. The worn edges and fingerprints suggested many viewings.

"I don't have a current picture. This was a few years back. We lost his twin brother, Bobbie, too. That was three years ago—cancer. He's the one on the left, with the funny hat. Billie's on the right. Now we've lost them both. They were . . . all we had."

"I'm sorry for your loss, Mrs. McSwain," Gil said, but cautioned, "we have no idea yet, who perpetrated the crime."

"Oh it was him, all right!" she almost spit in the Detective's face, "You might not be able to prove it, but you can bet that bastard killed him. You want your killer? You get that damned survival freak."

The little control she had tried to maintain to this point finally gave way. The woman broke down into desperate gasps, groans and shudders. She reminded Gil of someone who had the wind knocked out of them, gulping for air, bent over in pain and gasping need.

Out of a hallway stepped a dark-complexioned girl, wearing a soiled apron. She rushed to comfort the grief-racked woman, darting accusatory glances at the men. After walking Mrs. McSwain into another room, she returned. The detectives explained the reason for their visit. Frank told her that someone would have to come to the morgue to identify the body. She still glared at them but promised to pass along the message. Gil left a card with the precinct telephone number.

As they walked to their car, Frank gave one last look around and sighed.

"Some digs, eh? And we bust our butts to earn enough for a handyman's special and a ten-year-old Chevy."

"Yeah, well it doesn't look like all that saved them much pain."

"Oh come on, Gil. You don't really believe that all the rich folks are unhappy do you?"

“No, maybe not. But then again, I wouldn’t trade with the McSwains right now.”

“I guess you’ve got a point, Socrates.”

“Well, let me see. As I recall it, Socrates died when he drank poison. So, in order to properly follow in his footsteps, how about I take us to the diner and get some of their famous rot-gut chili?”

“You mean Socrates poisoned his partner, too?”

“Who said I was getting you any?”

“Was Socrates cheap, too?”

“No Socrates was . . . thrifty.”

“Then you are not Socrates, boyo. Because you, Detective Sergeant Beach . . . you are definitely cheap.”

“If you think I’m cheap now, just wait till I borrow money for the chili.”

The men didn’t talk about the grief they had just witnessed. They joked and swore and avoided reference to what they had seen so often . . . the effects of murder, as its force spread out like a shock wave. Sometimes you just do what you’ve gotta do.

CHAPTER 10

A few hours later, Gil met the Director of "The Federation." The so-called environmental group's central headquarters was in a slightly dilapidated section of buildings near Second Avenue and Third Street. The main structure might once have been a synagogue or school but had apparently undergone various attempts at renovation and conversion. Now it was called the Federation Center. Whatever its previous disguises, the building was now vaguely Greek in architecture, with wide steps leading up to an arched door set in the center of a row of Imitation Doric columns. An artificial peak at the second story formed a triangular pediment, on the surface of which was inscribed the legend, *"salus mundi suprema lex esto."*

"What's that mean," Frank asked, looking up quizzically, "Wipe your shoes before entering?"

"Uh it's a bit beyond my high school Latin. Most of what they tried rather unsuccessfully to drum into me at La Salle Academy, I forgot ten minutes after the final exam . . . thank you Irish Christian Brothers very much. I think 'mundi' is world and you can guess 'suprema.' Whatever it says is probably a bit grandiose."

Leaving Frank outside in the car, Gil pulled open the Center's heavy front door, and found himself in a large open entrance room, with a high vaulted ceiling. The place was larger than it looked from outside. The expanse was impressive, with large arches rising to a distant ceiling; multiple passages extending darkly off the main hall. Gil felt like he was entering foreign soil, another country. He was reminded of and old TV advertisement for a lending institution in which a man stepped through the huge doors of a bank, seeking a loan, only to be transformed into a small child as he entered the interior. The ad was intended to show that the bank could appreciate how intimidated and dislocated most people felt in such surroundings. Here the intimidation was probably intentional.

The slapping sound of his shoes on the hard tiled floor, the odors of musty walls and spicy incense, the way sound echoed, the dim lighting . . . all combined to make Beach feel out of place, an alien, an intruder. He was also pretty sure that was how he would be received. A questioning cop was not usually greeted with open arms even in legitimate places. There aren't many places that a cop isn't an outsider. That's why 'Members of the Service' hang out with each other so much of the time. Unfortunately, Gil Beach sometimes even felt like an outsider among cops.

These half-formed thoughts and feelings were tugging at his attention, when a woman stepped from the shadows. She was dressed in a gauzy garment, similar to an East Indian sari. It revealed little of the woman's body yet was wound tightly enough to outline what could only be a splendid figure, swelling the fabric in just the right places. There was a veil on her head, only partially covering her dark hair, which fell in soft waves to her shoulders. Her features had a slightly eastern cast, suggesting mixed parentage. She was smiling with unusual brightness. That seemed to make her more attractive than merely the shape or color of her features, though these were attractive enough. Many faces would be just average, if it wasn't for a charming smile. For some reason Gil had images of a fairy, or water sprite flit through his mind. Maybe that was the intent, given the love affair these environmentalist type folks seemed to have with nature. He tensed, when he saw that the "sprite" had a symbol tattooed on her forearm, much like the one he had seen on a body under the FDR overpass—a divided circle with light and dark halves.

"Welcome to the Federation Center. I am Selene Windsong. Is there any way that I can help you?"

Gil felt an urge to smile, and almost chuckled, though he resisted the impulse. It wasn't just the sixties hippie-type name, but the warm greeting and smile that accompanied it. He hesitated to answer the question. He didn't really want to reveal his business there. People's attitudes had a way of changing when they heard the word "Police." He made a snap decision not to disclose his identity. It was more impulse than considered judgment, but once he decided to hide the real reason for being there, it didn't take long to come up with a rationalization. He could always reveal his identity later, after he had learned what he could from less guarded responses. Keeping this lovely woman interested in him a little longer had nothing to do with it . . . nothing at all.

So, though he didn't realize its extent at the time, this was when Gil Beach embarked on an adventure.

"Uh, yes, I guess so. I'm, uh, 'Daniel'—'Daniel Wiggins'." The lie came easily. He had used the alias before in other situations.

I'd like to know more about you—I mean, about the movement . . ."

"We call ourselves The Federation."

"Yes . . . I'd like to, well, know more."

"Do I sense that you are unfocussed, my friend?"

"Well, yes, I guess you could say that." *Not that far from the truth.*

"I thought so," she said softly, "Most people who come here to inquire, have been looking to commit themselves to something—to join a cause. Often, they hear about us from a friend or teacher who knows that we have found a path to security, serenity and union with the earth. How did you hear about us, Daniel?"

Oh the last guy you killed has these weird rich parents who thought I ought to bust you all.

"Well, gee, I found this little booklet. I found it at a street fair."

Gil pulled out a cheaply printed newsprint leaflet that Olivia McSwain had given him as an example of the organization's literature. The part about the street fair was an educated guess. There were always lots of aging hippie types and left-wing stuff floating around those scenes. It must have seemed reasonable . . . she didn't bat an eyelash.

"Of course. When the student is ready, the teacher appears. You were ready, so the teachings were delivered to you. You must be someone special, Daniel."

Special! He knew the praise was a gimmick. Anyone who walked in the door had to get the same basic rap. After all, they didn't know him from Adam. Despite that, she said it in a way that started a warm feeling tickling his innards. In fact, when that beaming face turned to call him "special", he felt warmth flood his face, and was afraid he was blushing.

She stepped closer to slide her arm into his, turning him to walk arm-in-arm down the hall, as if they had known each other all their lives.

"Come, you will want to meet our leader, Storm. I'm sure he'll be pleased to meet you, Dan."

So first it was "friend" then "Daniel" and now "Dan." How quickly you became part of the family. He felt a small shudder run up his back. He wasn't sure if it was anticipation, fear . . . or the pressure of this lovely woman's arm against his.

It had been a long time since he had felt that little thrill of excitement. The last time he could recall feeling the same electrical kind of rush was the day he and Pilar had celebrated their first wedding anniversary with a trip to Blue Pines Resort in the Poconos, walking together by a moonlit lake.

Gil used their passage through a doorway as an excuse to disengage his arm from hers, pretending to be chivalrous by allowing her to precede him through the opening. Instead of moving back to her side, however, he stayed a step behind. He didn't know what that little tickle of feeling was, but it made him uncomfortable. She said nothing, but turned slightly to stare into his eyes. An enigmatic smile played across her lips, then she moved on, leading him into a nearby lounge where he was asked to wait. He watched her rounded hips sway smoothly, as she moved out of the room.

His quickly manufactured lies made Gil more nervous that he would normally have been. 'Softclothes' work was nothing new, but it's one thing to do a planned, authorized undercover assignment. It's quite another to do it on your own, without adequate preparation or planning. Normally, he would be equipped with a "legend," of fake background information. Rather than sit down, he made a tour of the room, examining everything like a field slave allowed entrance into the planter's manor house, curiosity heightened by the differences between this world and his own.

The furniture was functional, but tasteful. Several couches and settees combined fabric and metal in a contemporary style that was neither flamboyant nor mechanical. The walls were a mute ivory color with a delicate border separating a patterned ceiling that he recognized as the antique tin material coveted by renovators. Recessed fixtures provided indirect lighting, except for two graceful floor lamps arching delicately over comfortable chairs. There was a profusion of potted shrubs, hanging planters, and vases of cut flowers. On a low rosewood table he found a collection of literature, mostly expensively printed versions of the same material found in the cheaper pamphlet he brought with him. Above the table a framed parchment was carefully printed in precise calligraphy.

"We owe our Earth the loyalty of children for their parent." read the ornately inscribed words. In smaller letters below the quotation was the name of the one who had presumably authored it, —"Storm." Gil wondered if it was a first or a last name.

If the wait had been much longer, he might have bagged the whole idea and just left, but soon he heard footsteps echoing hollowly in the corridor beyond. Gil's mind went through a rapid series of images, trying to visualize this guy 'Storm,' before his actual entrance. It was a little game he played with himself to see how accurately he could predict a person's appearance with limited information. First, he thought of and discarded the image of a national network weatherman who went by the name, "Storm Field." The next thought that came to mind was of a Disney style Father Winter, blowing clouds and wind. When he added the idea that this guy was into a survivalist mentality, the picture quickly deteriorated. Gil didn't have a lot of experience with survivalists, but those he had heard of, often expected society to collapse into chaos at some point. When that happened, they planned to be prepared for anything, and sometimes even formed military type forces and hidden enclaves where they expected to defend themselves from the apocalypse to come. His fantasy image of "Storm" began to take on the tones of a scene from the movie Deliverance—with filthy, ignorant, and desperately evil mountain people, clad in jungle camouflage violently attacking interlopers and led by a demented wild man.

Well, nothing like negative expectations, the real thing is sure to be a let down!

As if summoned by his thought, Selene appeared in the doorway, her hand grasping that of the man who had to be Storm. For some reason, Gil felt an irrational twinge of annoyance at that easy intimacy, though he had not been so annoyed at the woman's touch, earlier.

The man's appearance wasn't exceptional, though most observers probably would describe him as handsome. His face was partially covered by a neatly trimmed beard and mustache, yet seemed strong and open. He had a straight nose, high forehead, and a full head of hair—silvery gray that matched the beard. His eyes were his most striking feature, colored a dark blue, bordering on purple, which may have been part of the intensity that seemed to radiate from him. Standing about six feet in height, he was dressed in simple casual clothes—a well-tailored velour shirt and polished cotton slacks. In the habit of years as a cop, Gil mentally noted Storm's distinguishing marks—his striking eyes, hair, that same woven circle mark on his left wrist. Most notable was his manner.

Gil was struck by the presence of the man. Some people have an aura that accompanies them, a zone of personal power surrounding them. When certain individuals enter a room full of others, everyone knows they've arrived, no matter how loud or busy the party. Sometimes it has to do with the person's position, like the President of the United States, or the Roman Catholic Pope, but Gil suspected that only people who already carried some of that unique power got into those positions in the first place. In the military they spoke of “command presence.” In political circles they talked about those with personal “charisma.” Wherever you go, people notice these stand-out individuals and try to label the quality, whether the words are “royal bearing”, “the right stuff”, or “star quality.” Of course, it isn’t limited to the bright stars. There are dark stars too; insane people or monsters like Charles Manson, Hitler, and Saddam Hussein who have a type of charisma as well.

Whatever “it” might be, clearly Storm had it.

The man had a well-modulated voice in the mid-range. Not an announcer’s rich baritone, yet there was a melodious quality that made it seem gentle and musical. The tone was neither weak nor aggressive. Gil guessed that part of the man’s seductiveness was in an apparent lack of it. He spoke like you were already an acquaintance—even a friend.

“Hello, Daniel . . . if I may call you that?”

“Oh yeah, sure.”

“The man smiled warmly. He gave a little chuckle and asked, “What did you expect, dreadlocks and a machete?”

“No, of course not. I didn’t know what to expect,” Gil lied, wondering how well the guy could read his thoughts.

"Well, most people come to meet me with some sort of expectation, whether they are aware of it or not. It hardly ever matches. I don't mind. I like people, and it doesn't take long for most of them to sense that."

When the man lowered himself into a comfortable chair, Gil realized he had been prepared for Storm to sit on the floor or something.

"My given name is Boyd Stormer. I'm not quite sure when it got shortened to 'Storm', but I guess somewhere along the line, we decided it wouldn't hurt if the leader of our movement sounded like somebody unusual and powerful," he chuckled.

"Not that I take that too seriously!" he continued waving his hand like he was shooing away the idea. "I suppose the whole business sounds a bit pretentious to someone not used to it, don't you think?"

Gil smiled in spite of himself.

"Well, it was easy to picture someone up on Mount Olympus."

"Yes, I understand. I've often wondered what people would think if I went around in a Toga and carried a lightning rod or something. The truth is, it wasn't even 'Stormer' to start with. My grandparents were immigrants to this country. When they hit Ellis Island, my granddad told the clerk his name, which was

Sturmerzhinski, and got a blank stare. The clerk made an attempt, but only got as far as the first part. 'Sturmer-what?' he said, 'Well, two syllables is quite enough for good American name—let's make it Stormer, like barnstormer. Welcome to America, Mr. Stormer.' That was our family name from there on.

"The first name, 'Boyd' isn't much better. My folks never got around to picking out a name at the hospital, so the birth certificate just said 'Baby Boy Stormer.' Mom's English wasn't very good, so she thought she heard them saying 'baby . . . Boyd Stormer' and figured Dad had picked out the name. At least that's the story I was told. By the time anybody figured out what had happened, I was stuck with Boyd. Nothing wrong with that . . . just not a real choice. Only name of my own is my middle one—Roger. Nobody uses it, though. You can call me whatever you're comfortable with."

Gil found himself warming to the man, who appeared to speak with frankness and charm.

"I'm glad you had time to see me," Gil temporized.

"Well, to use a cliche that happens to apply quite well," Stormer said with a smile, "The pleasure is mine. Selene says you have a special quality about you. I can see that she is correct. I also see you have come a long way."

"No, not really. Just a few miles, really."

"I didn't mean geographical distance."

"No?"

"No. I think you have been on a long journey of the soul, my friend. Your spirit is tired. Part of you is very much in need of relief."

Goddamn. First the cabby, and now this local guru. Is my face a bloody billboard, or what?

"The Federation can offer you a new sense of dedication, my friend. Forgive me, if I say you look like that might be just what you need."

Gil recoiled. He didn't like the unsolicited analysis and he certainly didn't like the recruiting pitch. It felt like someone was doing a B & E,'break and entry,' on his mind, and he didn't like it. Still, you had to appreciate how the guy seemed concerned. Also, though he would never have himself used those words to describe his life situation, what the man said was at least partly true.

Chapter 11

"WE ARE KILLING OUR CHILDREN!" the speaker called out.

There was a roar of approval at his words, which echoed out over the crowd. At the raised podium, the speaker waved a finger, as if admonishing the assembled people, but they didn't seem to take his judgement personally.

"WE ARE KILLING OUR ENVIRONMENT!"

Another swell of cheering and applause followed the next phrase. Though he was a white man, middle-aged and dressed in an expensive suit, the rally had some of the atmosphere of a black Baptist revival meeting. There was even a scattering of individual praises, including "amen" and "right on brother" reflexively shouted by those with the habit.

"WE ARE KILLING OUR FUTURE!"

The volume and emphasis of this phrase, indicated to the crowd that it was the last line of the man's litany. On cue, the massed horde dispensed with any vocal inhibitions to explode in thundering waves of sound. Hands stretched skyward with screams and bellows; placards waved wildly. The signs bore color reproductions of the person on the stage, along with slogans like "MARK'S OUR MAN," and "DELUCIA: So we can all have a future."

Senator Mark Delucia knew that he could recapture their attention, if he needed to. He was ready with one of the long perfected and polished interchangeable public speaking segments he thought of as "speech mods." Most of the segments had been crafted to carry subtle underlying messages that would appeal to base motives, while permitting the listener to claim more high-minded ideals. The slogans about "having a future" were designed to play on insecurities and fears about what was ahead; the criticisms of "uncaring, uncontrolled, uncivilized people" could simply be translated into comments on certain ethnic groups, as could his linking of crime and the environment. He played the masses like a grand piano. Still, he sensed that he wouldn't produce any greater heights of enthusiasm from this crowd than he had already managed. Why waste further energy? He had two more speeches to make that day.

At the agreed signal of a tug on his ear, two bodyguards stepped forward, appearing to whisper a message. Senator Delucia nodded with a frown of concern, as if he had just received an urgent communication. He turned to the crowd, smiled a final trademark grin, and then threw his arms over his head, in a classic gesture of victory. A psychologist might have mused about this politician's choice of clenched fists as a symbol rather than other possible signs. The analyst might have pondered the potential significance of a fist, instead of an open hand. But there were no psychologists in this crowd.

There was an observer, however. Standing in the shadow of a large maple tree near the speaker's rostrum, was a man dressed in the mottled fatigues of a soldier. As the Senator descended, working the crowd, and pushing through the throngs toward a place of safety, the observer moved along with the knot of people, keeping about twenty yards away.

Senator Delucia was not expecting a group of aggressive reporters to be waiting inside the doors of the gymnasium where he had been seeking quiet, so he was caught a bit off-guard. His staff was not supposed to allow this unexpected encounter. The surprise, as well as the probing nature of their questions, made him less cordial than usual, when they swarmed around him.

"Senator—why are you suddenly pushing the environmental issue? You've never seemed so interested before."

"I've always been concerned about the environment." he reacted quickly. "There are other priorities that needed to be addressed. They have occasionally taken precedence, but it is time to tackle this urgent issue head-on, and I intend to do it. I believe in . . ."

Before he was able to segue into a familiar speech mod, other reporters jumped in, interrupting his prepared and TV-ready sound-byte.

"Aren't you trying to find a new issue because Forester's leading in the polls?"

"I don't pay attention to polls."

"Then why did you commission one?"

"I don't know that anyone did. It wasn't me. That's my campaign staff's responsibility," he snapped. "They have a job to do. I don't pay any attention myself."

"Is the environment a compelling issue for urban voters, Senator? Aren't city residents more concerned about crime, taxes, and transportation?"

"There is no more important issue than the environment, no matter where we live. The quality of our air and water are vital to the residents of New York City. Look at what recently happened at Plum Point. Milions of gallons of crude oil discharged into our beautiful Hudson River. It may seem distant from my district, but that spill will cost all of us—both in terms of expense and loss of our precious natural resources."

"Then why are you slipping in the polls?"

"I TOLD you . . . I don't pay attention to polls!"

Sensing that they had hit a nerve, the reporters rushed in for the kill, like hyenas when a satiated lion moves away to leave the remains of its victim available for picking."

"Forester says . . ."

"Nobody seems interested in this issue . . ."

"How can you claim . . ."

"Isn't it true . . ."

Delucia shrugged aside all the questions. He pushed through the group, shaking off the nipping carrion eaters. Still, he couldn't resist turning to throw out a final rebuttal.

"This city is an ecological disaster just waiting to happen. The people of New York City know that. They can elect me to stop the tragedy before it happens, or they can suffer the dire consequences. I believe the good people of this city know the choices, and they know what is good for them."

"That almost sounds like a threat, Senator."

"Don't be foolish," he snapped. "Of course it's not a threat. But I suppose you could say that it's a warning . . . a warning about the inevitable consequences of ignoring natural law."

Raising his eyes, Senator Delucia disengaged with the reporters, switching smoothly into his public media persona—smiling, waving, and staring over everyone's heads, while seeming to be looking at every individual. Among those included in his wide view and generic smile, was a man in fatigues, still positioned about twenty yards distant, in the shadow of a large banner.

Delucia turned away, moving toward sanctuary. The shadowy man turned that way also, but he did not seek refuge. He was not the sort of man who ever sought sanctuary. On the other hand, it was easy to imagine someone hiding from him. It was also easy to imagine that only an unfortunate or very unlucky person would need to.

CHAPTER 12

"I am quite capable of meeting my own needs."

Pilar said the words with such apparent ease, Gil felt put-off. She probably didn't mean anything harsh by the comment, but it sounded like a brush-off. He was from the old school that believed married folks at least to some extent, were supposed to meet each other's needs. What ticked him off, was that she was probably right. If it came down to it, she probably could get along without him.

While dressing for guests, they had gotten into one of their periodic disagreements over a subject that never seemed very clear but had something to do with how much attention they paid to each other. Gil always found himself getting hot under the collar and saying something he later regretted. Tonight was no exception.

"Sounds like masturbation to me."

"Oh Gil, sometimes you're so difficult."

His comment was a stupid remark, and Gil knew it. He didn't even know why he said it, or why he was so touchy. In truth, he was mostly proud of his wife's independence of spirit. It's just that there were times that he wished she needed him more. Instead of explaining that, he changed the subject.

"The Ovens have driven all the way from Queens to be with us. The Deasons are going to try to make it too. I'm going to go out and try to make them feel welcome."

He pushed open the bedroom door, walking down the hall to the kitchen, then out into the family room, where Dick and Maggie Ovens were nibbling on some crackers and cheese, looking uncomfortable. Gil wondered if they had heard any of the argument in the other room. They seemed relieved to see him. As he offered drinks, the doorbell rang. A bedraggled pair appeared at the entrance—Charlie and Denise Deason, with another couple that Gil didn't recognize.

"I hope you'll excuse our appearance," Denise apologized, "We haven't had hot water at the house for two days, since the flood. The water heater is caput, along with almost everything else in the basement. The furnace is shot, too, but we are heating with a kerosene heater. Charlie showers at work, and I run over to my sister's place when I can, but most of the time we just pretend we're on a camping trip and go grubby."

"I also hope you don't mind, but we brought some friends with us," Charlie interrupted. "This is Ted and Peg Gorman. Ted's a Member of the Service," he noted, using the insider's term for a law enforcement officer, "and Peg is a writer. They're neighbors of ours. They've been lifesavers during this mess. Hope you don't mind."

"Don't be silly," Gil protested, "the more the merrier."

"Peg writes for Human Services Press," Denise offered, "I know she and Pilar will have oodles to talk about."

Gil smiled. His wife never seemed to have difficulty finding things to talk about. He was the less talkative one.

"Right now, my conversation is mostly about sump pumps and drainage patterns," Denise continued, "not to mention the finer points of how to rough it in the wilds of Staten Island."

She had the talent to make it sound like a funny story instead of a tragedy, her speech accompanied by a collection of giggles and busy eyebrows. Charlie kidded her about her talkativeness, calling her "motor-mouth", but her enthusiasm was infectious. In minutes she had everyone laughing, while telling stories about flooded basements and other assorted home disasters. Pilar eased out of the bedroom a few minutes later and soon let go of her peeved look. She seemed to hit it off well with Peg Gorman. Gil didn't get a chance to talk much with Ted but learned that the man was temporarily assigned to NYPD Special Operations. That could mean many things from undercover work to politics. Since Ted didn't explain, no one pressed him. Sometimes it was better not to ask. He seemed to get along well with the other guys, and Gil decided the group was a good mix.

When the party seemed to be running on its own steam—with people moving about, touring the house and sampling the goodies, Gil found Dick, who was in a spirited discussion of his work. Ovens was principal member of the State Troopers Employee Assistance Program, "EAP" for short. He was called on regularly to intervene in crises, help troopers in trouble, give workshops on various topics, or make impromptu speeches at a moment's notice. He was always full of information, which made him a great resource and a good addition to a social event.

"Are you saying there aren't really that many Moonies?" Charlie was asking.

"Oh yes, the numbers are very limited, despite all the publicity. They never had too many in the first place—maybe a few hundred in the States, but now they've shrunk even more."

"I think anybody that runs around with a shaved head and cymbals needs a shrink."

"Very funny. Of course, the Unification folks are just one of hundreds of cults around."

"Jesus, there's that many of them?"

"Oh yes, not to mention the little ones. You've got huge ones like the Chinese Falun Dafa, but there are lots of small sects. There are minor sects within sects and cults within cults."

"Sounds confusing," Ted Gorman joined the conversation. The others responded with a general nodding of heads. Gil took advantage of the momentary lull, to work his way into the conversation.

"I don't think this case has anything to do with cults," he said, "But I'm curious about some fringe groups."

"Fringe groups? Like what? I've got some good stuff on the Branch-Davidians. They didn't disappear, you know, even after WACO."

"No, I'm thinking of an environmentalist organization. Or at least that's what they call themselves. I think they're more survivalists than anything. The name of the group is 'The Federation of Natural Selection.' I thought you might have something in your Hand-Out-Mobile."

"Ummm. Doesn't ring a bell, but it sounds like something to do with our old friend Darwin. I can run out and check."

Oven's car was a traveling office, educational branch, and resource center with boxes, files and sheaves of printed materials packed in the huge trunk. Whether it was the topic of stress reduction, religious cults, or Transactional Analysis, there was usually some resource in Dick's traveling stock.

"No, not now," Gil stopped him. "It's not that important."

Ovens was a really nice guy, who would do anything he could to help another human being. Pilar called him a "Helpful Harry." That's why he was so good at his job, though sometimes Gil thought he overdid it, driving himself to near burnout in his attempts to help others. Still, it was comforting to know there were still some people around who really cared.

"Maybe when you leave, I can walk out with you."

"Had any direct experience with the organization, Gil?" Ted Gorman asked.

"All I've got at this point, is a case where the victim had a yin-yang symbol on his arm, and a bigger one carved in his chest. The victim's parents think the killing is the work of a survivalist type, who heads this Federation."

"The yin-yang makes more sense for environmentalists than end-of-the-world types, but they wouldn't have anything to do with killing" Ovens mused. "Has this survivalist group reacted to the death yet? I mean, maybe they've offended somebody, or something, and this is payback on one of their people."

"No, they haven't responded at all. Maybe they don't know yet, but that doesn't seem likely."

"It could be intended to throw you off," Charlie added.

"Yeah, I'm keeping that in mind. Could be just a red herring. I'm thinking the victim could have been an insider, who got in over his head. Maybe he crossed horns with somebody or saw something he wasn't supposed to see. Whoever did him, did him good. The guy was smashed and slashed like a piece of chopped meat—only a kid, really. Oh yeah, the eyes and tongue were missing."

"Holy shit," Ted Gorman said, shaking his head. Then he got a funny look on his face, and added, "But if they figured your guy for a traitor, it sort of suggests a message about not looking or talking doesn't it?

CHAPTER 13

Sedgwick was having difficulty putting the brief conversation with Gil Beach behind him. Try as he would, he couldn't rid himself of an uneasy feeling—the feeling that things were not right. Not usually one for navel-gazing, Sedgwick couldn't pin it down better than that—something was just NOT RIGHT!

He didn't like the feeling. There was a rumbling in his gut and a sour taste in his throat. He reached in his pocket to pull out a package of Extra Strength Rolaids, popping three into his mouth, trying not to gag as he chewed the chalky tasting tablets.

How do you spell RELIEF?—Don't have kids!

In the basement locker room, he dialed the combination to his personal locker. Actually, he had six lockers in the basement, the rest of them filled with various special products. Locker space was precious, so it was a minor miracle and a triumph of negotiating that he had managed to snag five extras. Hanging on the inside of this one's dented metal door was a photograph of his son, Jimmy. He glared at it for a moment, then angrily flipped the picture around so only the back of the frame showed.

Sedgwick changed out of his rumpled uniform, sniffing under the armpits of the shirt to see if he could manage another day of wear without washing it. *No way*. He quickly stuffed the smelly garment in his canvas carryall, then slipped into roomy jeans, flannel shirt, scuffed boots and a well broken-in goose-down parka. Despite his reputation as a procurer, Sedgwick seldom wore anything new.

Into the top of the left boot, he shoved a small pistol, a Walther PK that only weighed a few ounces, but packed a lot of power. He had traded some tickets to a Knicks game for the little weapon after seeing a James Bond movie in which a PK was the favorite gun of the Sean Connery '007' character. In the pocket of his parka went a long-handled sap; a flexible leather club with a lead weight imbedded in its tip. Cage didn't want trouble, but if it came, he would be ready for it. He walked from the station to a nearby parking lot where he picked up his 2014 BMW, purchased last year from his off-the-grid sales profits. Sedgwick's thoughts were so focused, he was hardly aware of driving uptown, across the clogged Queensboro Bridge to his home turf of Rego Park. Negotiating the crowded roads was such a habit, he could do it without thinking. He hoped that Jimmy would be home. It would be worse if he had to go looking for the boy.

When Cage reached the house, he parked at the curb for a few moments staring at his hands like they belonged to someone else. After a while, he hitched himself out of the car, slamming the door violently. When Sedgewick let himself in the front entrance of the house, Butch jumped all over him, slobbering and knocking things over with his ferocious wagging tail. Such enthusiasm suggested that the dog had been alone for a while, and the house still seemed deserted. Sedgwick threw off his parka, moving to the liquor cabinet where he pulled out a bottle of Johnny Walker Black, one of many gifts he had collected last Christmas from grateful citizens and customers. He rinsed an old-fashioned glass from the stack of dirty dishes piled to overflowing in the kitchen sink, then poured it half-full. Potent fumes wafted from the amber liquid, prompting him to reach for the faucet to add water. Before he turned the handle, he changed his mind, taking a deep swig of the whiskey straight-up. He breathed through his nose to reduce the burning affect, but still felt his eyes watering. The second swallow went down easier.

Sedgwick stood in the kitchen, hands splayed out on the countertop, bottle and glass in front of him—an old gunfighter steeling his courage at the bar of the Last Chance Saloon. It took two more slugs of straight scotch before he was ready. Then he shook his head, trying to clear the fog and headed up the stairs.

Jimmy had installed a padlock on the room, but two drunken kicks easily broke the hasp loose from the doorframe. Sedgwick stepped into the space a bit hesitantly, considering his means of entry, not sure if he was more afraid of what he would find, or what he wouldn't. It might look bad, he realized, if he broke in and found nothing.

"Don' need prob . . . lubel cause," he muttered to himself, slurring the words, "not when it's my own fuckin' house!" He moved heavily into the room.

Glossy posters were plastered around the dark cubicle, alternating between pictures of weapons, armed services recruiting posters, and longhaired rock groups.

How the hell can he like . . . both . . . they're so different?

Next to a classic Green Beret-type "Lifer", and a scene from a Desert Storm tank battle were music posters in which Cage wasn't sure who was male or female. They looked more like grotesque creatures of the night, with bizarre make up, outrageous hairstyles and raunchy costumes out of some rank scene in Hell. Sedgwick leaned over a nearby wastebasket and spit. It was a reaction to the sourness eating away at his stomach, as well as a comment on the display. But the posters were not the primary focus of his interest. He was looking for something more damning than an exhibit of heavy metal freaks, as revolting as that might be to him. He looked past the obvious hiding spots.

He didn't expect it to be out in the open. Jimmy wasn't stupid. He might be crazy, but he wasn't stupid. Sedgwick began a methodical search. He'd had plenty of practice. You couldn't be a cop for as long as he had, without knowing how to do a thorough toss. There were copies of Playboy and Penthouse under the boy's clothes in the drawers. That almost brought a smile to Cage's tight lips. Maybe the kid had some normal impulses after all. He wasn't as pleased when he found a stash of marijuana behind the plate of the light switch, but that wasn't what he was looking for either.

Eventually, he flipped back the rug and found it. There was a pattern inscribed on the floor, probably done with felt tip markers. Pain seared through Sedgwick's stomach, and he sat down on the bed with a deep sigh, looking blearily at the picture.

He saw a large circle, about six or seven feet in diameter, divided into two roughly equal sections. One half was dark, the other light. Each section had a focal dot of the opposite color. The symbolism meant little to him. He was a concrete thinker, more at home with action than ideas, more with cash than concepts. All the symbols meant to Cage was that the boy was into something weird. Maybe a club, he thought, or a secret society.

Cage noticed an irregularity in the floorboards. He took out his pocketknife to clumsily probe at the cracks. First one, then a second board pried loose. Under them, he found military and survival gear. One olive drab shirt was emblazoned with a slogan "Clean up the Environment: Kill a Cop." That hit Cage like a slap in the face, more hurtful than some of the other strange things he found. His own son! The shirt had a pattern of faded brown stains. He had seen this kind of stain before. Cage had been on the force for many years and had seen countless crime scenes where beatings, muggings, accidents, and killings had taken place. He knew these marks. Bloodstains always looked the same.

A shoebox with the Reebok brand name printed on its side, was not full of shoes. It contained timers, wiring, paper wrapped hunks of gelignite and C-4 explosive—all the necessary elements for a powerful bomb. There was also a set of well-thumbed books on sabotage and terrorist techniques, including ways to interfere with public communications, the water supply, and mass transportation.

"Who the hell publishes shit like this," he said to himself. Wrapped in white silk, he found a spring-loaded, blackened stainless steel knife with the brand name "Black Magic" on the handle. There were stains and brown flakes of dried blood on the knife, too.

A manila envelope held several Polaroid photos. Sedgwick eased them from the envelope and spread them out on the stained floor. Jimmy appeared in some of the pictures dressed in pseudo military dress, in others semi-naked. In a few of the photos, Cage noted an older man, with silver hair and strange dark blue eyes that could be seen through the variegated camouflage face paint. In the pictures the man was brandishing weapons or engaged in sexual acts with various other participants. It wasn't always easy to tell the sex or age of his partners. Some looked like children. From a back view, one looked like Jimmy.

Another photo was of a person lying still on a bloody surface. The person was a small woman or girl. Cage was unsure of the age but had no doubt about the state of the subject. He had seen that look too often in his career. He was pretty sure she was dead.

Almost an hour later, fortified with several more shots of scotch, Sedgwick went looking for his son. He had an idea of where to look. In one of the terrorist instruction books, like a bookmark, Cage had found literature from the people who had sucked Jimmy into their craziness. The address was for the Federation of Natural Selection's Headquarters. He didn't expect it to be a pleasant visit.

CHAPTER 14

The most unpleasant part of police work for Gil Beach, was the paperwork. He still called it that, even though it was mostly data-entry on electronic forms. He had been punching away at the outdated desktop computer for the better part of an hour, struggling with the word processing program, trying to catch up on his reports. When Frank Terranova appeared, his oddball humor was a welcome interruption.

"Say Gil, do you know the difference between a terrorist and a woman with PMS?"

"I dunno. What's the difference?" he replied agreeably, with the expected straight line.

"Well, you can negotiate with the terrorist! Ha!"

"Don't pull that one on Gina, or you're liable to be up on harassment charges, Gil laughed, nodding at the woman detective on the telephone a few desks away. She raised her eyes in a "Give me a break" expression. Frank spoke a little louder to make sure that she heard his next line.

"Her ass ment? What in the world could her ass have meant?"

The woman detective flipped Terranova her middle finger, turning back to her telephone conversation.

"So now that you have interrupted me, not to mention lowering the image of New York's Finest while offending every woman within a city block, what can I do for you, Frank?"

"Not for me, Oh noble Detective Sergeant . . . Sir . . . not for your humble, nay, even subservient partner. I ask no boon for myself at all. But "Helen the Wholesome," to whom, it was implied, you might just owe a favor or three, would appreciate the courtesy of a telephone communication. I can't imagine why she would want to talk with someone like you when I am available, but women, as we know, occasionally have strange quirks. She said she can be reached at the Youth Bureau."

He gave a mock salute as he sauntered away, then threw a jellybean into the air and caught it in his mouth. Gil shook his head, smiling, as he ran his finger down a worn departmental telephone listing, until he found the entry for the Youth Bureau.

He had the irrelevant thought that Helen Joseph sounded like two first names. Her name used to be Helen Strudnick. She was an athletic, muscular, former army officer who had parachuted into Grenada, carrying a supply of personal health foods strapped to her back, and led a combat unit to occupy a strategic radio station four hours earlier than the battle plan had scheduled. The official story was that she saw no direct combat, but in truth she narrowly missed getting popped by a mortar round, and she captured two enemy soldiers at gunpoint. There and elsewhere, Helen gathered a few impressive decorations, but gave up a promising military career when her father became terminally ill. She resigned her commission to stay with him until he died. After that, she joined the NYPD, quickly rising to the rank of Detective. Currently, she was attached to the Youth Bureau.

Some of the guys figured her for a lesbian, until Max Joseph, an Assistant D.A., managed to marry her and get her pregnant, not necessarily in that order. After a six-month maternity leave, she was back on the job. Another six months and Max disappeared, off to the greener pastures of a law firm in Sausalito and his new lover. Apparently, Helen hadn't been masculine enough for Max, as the lover was a gay musician.

Gil knew how much she had been hurt by all this, especially how little support she got from the ranks of her fellow officers. Yet, as the finest people often do, this woman just became stronger. She didn't waste sympathy on herself, saving it for others. More than once, she had been the one to help Beach in a tough situation, rather than the other way around. Frank's comment was true—Gil did owe her, though it wasn't like Helen to call in markers.

Gil dialed the Youth Bureau Office, where she spent her time trying to save kids from the City's predators and soul sickness. It wasn't an easy job.

“Hello, Helen? This is Gil. What’s up?”

“Oh Hi, Gil. How’s Pilar?”

“Oh fine . . . fine.”

“How about you? I haven’t talked to you in ages!”

“Oh, I’m fine, too. Just fine.”

“Right. Well, where I come from, they say FINE stands for `Fucked up, Insecure, Neurotic, and Emotional.’ Not in your case, I hope.”

“Not that far from it, Helen, but what else is new?”

She read his reluctance to delve further and changed the subject. Gil was glad she didn’t press him. He didn’t want to seem unfriendly but didn’t feel like soul-searching. Nevertheless, her next comment caught him by surprise.

“I heard you were doing some checking into this Federation of Natural Selection group.”

“News travels fast around here. If Alexander Graham Bell had known about the cop grapevine, he wouldn’t have wasted his time with the telegraph.”

“Well, Gil, you and I have some friends in common.”

Then Beach remembered that she and Frank Terranova were close. He wasn’t sure how serious it was, but they had been seeing each other for a long time. When single people in their thirties spend most of their time in each other's company, you make certain assumptions. Then again, who knows? Max had turned out to be gay, Helen despite nasty rumors, wasn't. Storm turned out to be nice, Selene was . . . nicer. Gil found himself making fewer and fewer assumptions these days. Could a man and a woman be friends, without a sexual relationship? He remembered going with his wife to see a film called "When Harry Met Sally" in which Billy Crystal and Meg Ryan kept arguing that question. He and Pilar had kept coming back to the issue for days after going to the movie.

"It has to do with your definition of friendship," Pilar had insisted. Always the psychologist, she had used the term "boundaries" to describe limits you needed to set.

"You have to establish boundaries in every relationship, no matter which kind . . . even between husbands and wives," she said firmly. "You have to know what kind of relationship you want and set the appropriate limits for it."

Gil wished he were as certain about the subject. It was easier to accept the idea of him having a woman friend, than to picture Pilar being buddies with another man. He knew she'd call that a double standard, but he didn't think it was an opinion he could change. It was more like a reflex.

Lately, he had wondered about the "boundaries" that were rising in their own relationship. He missed the way things had been. He missed the laughter, the comfortableness of mind and body that they had shared. He wished she turned to him for comfort as often as she did to her social causes.

He found his mind turning to thoughts of Selene. Now there was a striking woman!

Not that he was really tempted.

The purely physical reaction he had to the woman was natural. After all, she was a knockout. Any man could see she had all the right parts in all the right places. Still, he knew he couldn't let his gonads lead him around. There were plenty of women who would be available, if he were the sort to look for "something on the side." Plenty of cops had gotten into trouble that way. Gil wasn't about to make that mistake. He reminded himself that he was there to do a job, and this Selene woman was just part of the background that he had to understand, as well as perhaps a link to the main players. He felt clearer when he put it like that. It didn't stop him from feeling a funny tickle in his groin . . . especially when he remembered the way she had taken his arm in hers; the gentle warmth of her breast through the gauzy wrap she had been wearing. A voice interrupted his thoughts.

" . . . and he'll be ticked off if they have a better record than the Jets, but still don't make it into the play-offs."

Gil realized that his mind had been drifting. Helen was continuing her chit-chat about Frank, so she hadn't noticed that his mind was elsewhere.

"What made you ask about the FONIES? he asked, trying to get back to business.

"Phonies? Oh, I get it—Federation Of Natural Selection—F.O.N.S.—`FONIES,' right? That's cute Gil, real cute. But shouldn't it be `FONS? Aren't they called the Federation of Natural Selection?"

"Yeah, well, it's close enough for horseshoes or government work. Look, Helen, it's nice talking to you and all, but is this conversation going somewhere?"

"Good old Gil Beach—always the sparkling conversationalist. Okay, I'll get to the point."

"But look, Gil, this may require a little tact on your part. 'TACT' I might remind you, is a common human trait seldom possessed by homicide detectives. When it operates, you see, persons generally do not say the crudest, most insulting, or insensitive thing that pops into their head. Instead, they make a slight effort to be nice, and even choose their words in a way that might convey respect and good will. This is not a trait that you have been accused of having in overabundant supply, Detective Beach."

Gil bristled a bit. He had been accused of some insensitivity on occasion, but it was less often saying something offensive than just not thinking of the right thing to say.

"All right, all right, So I'm not great at small talk. So, crucify me already. What needs so much tact, anyway?"

"Not a 'What,' Gil, a 'Who.' Her name is Nina, and she's only thirteen. Father Noonan over at Homewell House called us. You know, that's Francis X. Gentry's operation. They take in stray kids off the street. We work closely with the staff there, because so many of the kids are into drugs, prostitution, and other dirty stuff. The staff won't spill anything confidential on their own, but they will encourage a kid to tell us what's going down. Sometimes the kids give us leads to the big guys that do the supplying, and so forth. Of course, occasionally an imposter is hiding out at Homewell, trying to play the role of the homeless waif, with a big wad of cash in his pocket, a gun under the mattress and a few hundred grams of crack in a stash somewhere, ready for sale when the nobody is looking. Father Gentry tries to weed those ones out. He's the guy that founded Homewell House . . ."

"I know Gentry. Noonan, too. You can skip the history lesson."

"Geez, Gil. Give me a break. Was it something you ate, or is something eating you?"

"Sorry, Helen. I guess I haven't been getting much sleep."

"Either that or you've got PMS," she remarked dryly.

"I said I was sorry. Say, speaking of that, did Frank tell you the one about the difference between a terrorist and a. . . ."

"Yeah, I heard it."

" . . . Right. Anyway, go ahead, tell me about this Homewood House thing at your own pace."

"Yeah, well, I suppose I do get verbal diarrhea sometimes. I'll try and cut to the chase. What we've got is this real frightened kid—her name is Nina, who is telling us some very nasty stuff about somebody in your . . . 'FONIES' organization."

"Is it a guy they call Storm?"

"Didn't get that name yet, but she keeps talking about a "survivor" or something like that—and some guy with silver hair. This is some weird shit, Gil. I thought maybe you ought to hear it yourself. I was gonna record it, but if you're looking into these creeps' operation, maybe you have some questions you'd like to ask her yourself."

"Okay. I'll be right over."

"Listen, Gil. I was serious about the tact thing. This is one hell of a scared kid. We only get stuff out of her in dribs and drabs. Most of the time she just shakes and mumbles the same things over and over. We have a doctor giving her a light sedative now, so she can relax a little. I think she needs kid glove treatment for a while."

"I read you. I'll be gentle . . . and thanks."

"Well don't thank me, till you know if it's worth anything."

"No, I mean thanks for trusting me."

There was silence for a moment, then in a quiet voice she answered.

"I know you, Gil."

More silence. He tried to fill it with humor.

"That's what I'm afraid of."

"Make jokes if you want to, but there are a lot of creeps out there. I deal with 'em every day. I need a coupla guys like you around so I don't lose faith. Don't let me down, Hon., . . . don't let me down."

After they said goodbye, Gil slowly lowered the telephone receiver into its cradle. He wasn't sure he wanted to be an example for anybody. He wasn't sure he could be, even if he wanted to. The way he saw it, he had a tough enough time, just surviving.

Chapter 15

The Youth Bureau isn't exactly a place, although some of its operations occupy a building. It is really an ever-changing hodgepodge of programs. Every new City Administration, each new Police Chief, and various other powers, want to make points with parents (voting parents). This means they will always try to prove that they can do something about youth crime, youth problems, and youth solutions. Folks like Helen Joseph could tell you that nobody ever solves the complex issues contributing to alienated and criminalized youth, but new programs were always being formed and publicized as the latest miracle. So, a program for teen-age mothers got funded for a couple of years, then had its money slashed when the next political machine decided to push drug education in the schools instead. A year later it was storefront drop-in centers that were the answer, and later still, a "get tough" law enforcement effort or "scared straight." Recently, survival camps were the rage, complete with rope and ladder obstacle courses. Gil knew that the Youth Bureau worked with whatever funding it could get. They tried to keep good programs running, even if it meant sharing workers, offices, and supplies. Except for an occasional idiot that used the Bureau to advance his career or political fortune, most of the people there were as dedicated as you could find anywhere. Willing to work long hours and go to any lengths, the biggest problem of the staff was burnout, from caring too much.

Gil found Helen in her cramped office, a twelve-by-twelve room shared with three other workers, several file cabinets, and a stained coffee maker. Helen looked fresh and attractive in a simple white blouse and dark skirt. Her athletic frame, healthy complexion, and short blonde hair gave her the look of a Scandinavian Olympics competitor. No wonder Frank called her "Helen Wholesome." Gil decided that his partner had nice taste in companions, and wondered again about how far the relationship went. For a moment he began to imagine what Helen would look like without clothes, then mentally kicked himself.

What have you got, a one-track mind? he said to himself, shaking his head in wonder.

He was led to a room usually devoted to counseling sessions, where he could see the girl through a small glass insert in the door. She was lying on a decrepit fabric couch, lumpy and ripped in places.

"I see you're still using the best stuff the Salvation Army can offer," he noted.

"That's the Youth Bureau, nothing but the best," she agreed, then added wryly, "Castoffs for the Castoffs."

Helen gave him a few more suggestions about how to approach the girl, then led him through a heavy door into the musty room.

The child seemed to be sleeping, but when Helen touched her, the girl jerked and went rigid, eyes wide as goggles.

"It's all right, Nina. Everything is okay. Remember me? I'm Helen . . . this is Detective Beach. His first name is Gil, and he's a friend."

The girl's huge calf eyes swept back and forth between the two adults. Her body began shaking. Then her eyes went out of focus for a moment, the shaking subsided, and she sat up. She now seemed poised, smiling a gracious smile as she spoke.

"How may we help you, then, Officers?"

"Well, actually, we want to help YOU," Helen said, a little taken aback at the girl's quick recovery. "Now if you can just tell Gil here some of the things you told me, he might be able to help us."

"And just how could he do that?" the girl asked, the same smile held firmly in place.

"Well, perhaps we can stop the people at the Center from doing the things they did to you and others."

"The Center? Our Federation Nature Center? Why in the world would you want to do that?" the child asked, sounding quite reasonable and mature beyond her years. "All they do is help people understand the way of the Earth and our part in it. I miss them. May I go now?"

Helen looked like she had been hit with a bucket of cold water. After a moment of silence, she glanced at Gil with an expression of helplessness, and lifted her shoulders in a questioning gesture.

"But what about the children, Nina? What about the punishments and the . . . killing?" Helen pressed.

"Killing? Why whatever are you talking about?" the girl asked, as if they were speaking a foreign tongue. "Now, if you don't mind, we would like to go home. Our mother will be worried about us."

"Home? Where is that?" Gil asked.

"With our family, of course," the child answered, as if it were a strange question, "At the Center."

Gil glanced at her forearm, where he saw the same tattoo he had seen on the woman, Selene, a circle with merging halves of dark and light.

"What is your mother's name?" Gil continued, puzzled. "Euryale," the girl answered.

Helen motioned to him, and they stepped outside.

"You've probably frightened her," Helen whispered when they moved out into the hallway.

He started to protest, but she waved it off with a gesture of her hand.

“It’s not your fault. If anything, it’s mine for not thinking this through. From what she has told us, there’s been terrible abuse. I guess bringing in a strange man wasn’t the smartest idea. I suppose that introducing you as “Detective” didn’t help either.”

“She acts like she’s spaced out or something.”

“That may be the ‘trancs’ we gave her, but what she claimed to have seen and lived through would freak anybody out. Look, I made recordings of the interviews. You can take them with you, as long as you guard them with your life . . . and make a copy.”

“Okay. Thanks. I think I might also drop by to visit Father Gentry later.”

“That’s a good idea. Maybe he can fill you in on some of the other stuff that goes down around here. But I’m worried about this kid, Gil. Among other things she mentioned was, well, she told us that she’s PG.”

His face clouded.

“You said she’s thirteen?”

“Just barely.”

“Could she be making it up?”

"When the Doc examined her, he took a urine sample. She's preggo all right. Which means somebody knocked her up while she was closer to twelve. Before she clammed up, she told us it was a big guy with silver hair. Must be a real prince." Helen's teeth remained clenched as she spoke.

Gil lowered his head and slumped his shoulders. He placed his hands over his eyes, rubbing, as if to scrub out the image there. If that was the intent, it didn't work.

CHAPTER 16

The next day, Gil got a call from Helen. The girl, Nina, continued to deny her previous story and had returned to the FONS Center. Apparently, someone named Euryale was indeed her mother, who both worked and lived there. Since the child's pregnancy was presumptive evidence of abuse, Child Protective Services had been informed, but the mother was able to produce a witness who confirmed her explanation. She claimed that a teenage camp counselor had molested the child while on an otherwise well supervised field trip, then fled the city. The little girl supported the story, denying her previous allegations. So, they were forced to release her to her mother, pending further investigation. That was the recommendation of the Assistant DA, good old S.B. Randall. Helen described these developments in a tightly controlled voice, edged with anger.

As Gil tried to think of a decent response, he saw Frank waving at him from a desk by the windows. Asking Helen to hold, he punched the red button on the phone and raised his eyebrows, questioning.

"You're a popular guy today, Gil. The ADA is on line three. It's Randall."

Steven B. Randall was the Assistant District Attorney voted by the Precinct personnel as most likely to succeed—in causing nausea. The scion of a wealthy family from Hyde Park-on-Hudson, whose money came from a shadowy import-export business, "S.B.", or "S. O. B." Randall, as some of the cops liked to call him, seemed to be working in the Prosecutor's Office only until he could score the necessary points that would provide credibility on his way into a well-financed and waiting political career. Everyone was betting that when he moved on, he would also change his image. His shaggy brown hair hanging over ears and collar, expensively casual tweeds, and Dexter loafers gave him the appearance of a progressive intellectual, perhaps a graduate of social activism who had grown less radical, a hippie who had matured. For now, the longhair look suited his place and chosen pretense of a self-confident, committed public servant. He was, indeed, self-confident, but his only commitment seemed to be to S.B. Randall. When talking with anyone other than a potential political ally, he seldom paid close attention, constantly checking the large diver's watch he wore as if impatient to be elsewhere. Where he wanted to be was anyone's guess, since he seemed impatient no matter where he was. He also had a way of disappearing from public view for days at a time, then popping up just when you forgot he was still around to screw things up.

Gil promised to talk with Helen again later, switched to line three, and spoke his own name.

"Beach."

"Ahh . . . Gil, how ya doing? Randall here."

Gil didn't reply, choosing not to play the friendly game. He had never been accused of being too quick with a glib phrase anyway. That's partly why he was sarcastically nicknamed "Gabby." However, there were times his reticence could be used to advantage. He had also learned to use silence purposefully, as an important and well-established police technique. Keeping quiet, he knew, was one of the best ways to get people talking. In Randall's case, silence was also safer.

It was like the lessons his coaches had taught when he was playing football at Miller High School. He remembered Coach Audet telling an outplayed and overwhelmed group of linebackers that the best defensive players refused to let themselves get drawn out of position. "They hold their ground until the other player quits making fakes and commits himself to a direction," he explained.

When it came to Randall, Gil knew that good defense was the only way to play.

Sure enough, after only a few moments of silence, the lawyer blurted out his reason for calling.

"Say, Beach, are you intending some kind of investigation related to the Federation of Natural Selection?"

"What makes you think that?" Gil replied casually, though he was surprised that anyone could know about his embryo investigation.

"Oh, I have my sources," the lawyer said, slyly.

"Then you don't need to talk to me."

"Oh, you are cold, Detective. You are so cold! So, whadda ya say we cut the B.S. They tell me some freak got hit by a truck and the family is making wild accusations."

Gil was mildly surprised that the attorney had gotten information so quickly, but knew that once a report was filed, it travelled through all sorts of hands. That meant lots of possibilities for information leaks. He had often used that fact to his own advantage. There had been times it was in the best interest of a case to let some information slip, if it was possible to do so and still stay anonymous. The irony was that he seldom managed to keep his own paperwork up to date. And now, when for once he had been efficient with the forms . . . this was his reward. He wondered if the man also knew about the child, Nina, or the content of her early accusations. He hoped to hell that nobody knew about his impulsive visit to the Federation Center. For now, he chose to ignore Randall's choice of the word "freak" to describe the deceased boy, though that slur went into a back drawer of his mental files. He had a fat file in that part of his mind, labeled "stuff that might or might not be important someday." Every now and then, it was surprising what merited retrieval from that folder, as well as how useful it could be in the right situation.

"You seem to know a lot, Counselor. What exactly is your interest in this, anyway?"

"I represent the public interest, Detective, and the public interest would not be served by the unnecessary harassment of bona fide environmental groups."

"As opposed to what? Necessary harassment? But you haven't really answered my question, Counselor. ADA's generally go to great lengths to let us know how overworked they are with vital matters like undoing the stupid mistakes of street officers like me. It comes as something of a surprise that you would have time to become involved in daily police work, to the extent of suggesting how we should pursue an initial investigation."

"Ahh, the clever detective caught me in a poor choice of grammar. But nevertheless, Detective, you have put your finger right on the nut of the matter. The operative phrase here is, of course, `stupid mistakes.' It is precisely in the interest of preventing such stupid mistakes that I suggest you be very careful not to rush into ill-considered and unwarranted inquiries that might prove embarrassing to everyone."

"I am so grateful for your interest and willingness to take so much responsibility, Counselor. I can promise you that I will be very careful. Rest assured, that I will not rush into any `unwarranted inquiries.' Furthermore, if my actions seem like they will prove embarrassing to anyone, I will make every effort to see that the first one embarrassed . . . is . . . someone who deserves it."

Gil wasn't in the habit of these verbal duels, but Randall seemed to bring it out in him. Meanwhile, Beach's mind was racing along at another level than the oral fencing match. The ADA's intervention in this case was a noticeable departure from standard operations. Gil was curious about the reasons behind the heavy-handed action. He glanced at the lighted buttons arranged on the side of the telephone. All outside calls were automatically recorded, but Randall had apparently used the internal tie line. On the chance that the ADA didn't know these were excluded from taping, Gil decided to bluff a little. He tapped the phone hook lightly with his forefinger, so there was a momentary "click".

"So, for the record, Mr. Randall, exactly what instructions are you giving me?"

"No instructions, Detective," the lawyer responded smoothly, apparently falling for the ruse, "just some personal advice. I have the greatest confidence in your judgment."

"Well, thank you for your confidence and personal concern, Sir. In light of your helpful expression of opinion, I'm sure you won't mind if I return the favor. My advice to you, Mr. Randall, is to get your head out of my ass and go do your own job."

Realizing now that the Detective wouldn't be talking like that if he were recording the conversation, the ADA's tone changed.

"Don't fuck with me, Beach," Randall shot back, dropping the facade of politeness, "You'll regret it! Believe me, you'll regret it!"

There was a loud click, as the receiver was slammed down in the District Attorney's Office. Gil stared at the handset for a moment, wondering about himself and why he had chosen to cross the line from disguised hostility to open antagonism. He wondered if he was getting in too deep. Honesty wasn't normally one of the rules for dealing with the DAs Office. It was definitely not a good idea when dealing with this particular ADA. Like so many places in government, animosity could be acceptable, as long as it was disguised. You might hate someone and think he was a son of a bitch, but you couldn't just come right out and tell him that to his face. Randall was right about one thing. Gil might very well regret being on his shit list. The man had power. Even if he only used it to make life difficult for uncooperative detectives, that power was still dangerous.

Just last month, the two men had butted heads over a reduced plea offer. Gil had been one of the arresting officers for Joseph "Chee-Chee" Ciccicolli, a particularly nasty individual that they had on a righteous homicide charge. They had to use the term, "suspect," but everybody knew the creep was guilty. He had a rap sheet as long as the menu in a Greek diner, an IQ that barely qualified as human, and an attitude that didn't. Frank referred to Ciccicolli as a walking advertisement for the value of birth control.

Chee-Chee was the kind of animal that took whatever he wanted in any way that he could possibly manage, unless someone more ruthless stopped him. What little success he had on the street was not due to his intelligence, but rather his complete lack of compunction about any violent act. One of Gil's informants, "Snake" Snyder, said that in the streets Ciccicolli's reputation was for distributing "hot shots" every now and then. A "Hot Shot" is a dose of heroin that is deadly, either due to its unusual purity or because it has been mixed with one of various substances such as rat poison or the extremely potent fentanyl. Either way is usually fatal. This little trick convinced certain customers to avoid Joey . . . 'like poison' you could say. Still, if you understand addiction you know this could never eliminate his business completely. There are various types of addicts, but not many are motivated by fear of death. For some, the fentanyl was even an added attraction.

So, Joey continued to make his money off those who were too far gone to care if this hit might be their last—the desperate, the suicidal, or the naive who didn't know his rep. The little surprise packages were targeted at those who had earned Joey's resentment for some reason, big or small. You didn't badmouth Joey Ciccicolli, get behind in payments, or take something he thought he had a right to take first, without risking "Chee-Chee's" revenge. Apparently, it was easy to piss-off the little creep.

Joey was five-foot-three and weighed in at over two hundred and fifty pounds. With a high nasal voice, a habit of belching every couple of minutes, and a skin condition that gave him a perpetual flaking rash, Joey was not what you would call a lady killer. Or at least not in the usual sense. It was another, more literal sense of the term that had gotten the ugly cretin into police custody. Not one for subtlety, Ciccicolli decided that the strong-arm tactics that worked in his various activities as bagman, drug dealer, and general scumbag would probably work just as well with the opposite sex.

One time when he was feeling particularly horny, Joey waited outside Tony Bolla's place until a good-looking woman came out. The fact that she was already with someone was irrelevant to Joey, who dispatched her accountant type escort with a tap of the sap. He offered her the options of either giving him a blowjob or dying. The woman in question was not stupid and decided she would rather suck on Joey than the big black revolver he shoved under her chin. Joey, on the other hand, was stupid. As if to prove the fact, a few minutes later in the sweaty throws of his simple-minded ecstasy, he managed to drop his gun behind one of the garbage cans on which he was supporting himself in gasping pleasure. The woman who's anger now eclipsed her fear, took this opportunity to 'put the bite' on Joey, so to speak.

He was lucky he didn't lose his whole pecker, which they say wasn't that big to start with, but the incident and its humiliating aftermath at the hospital emergency room made him so vengeful that he had spent the next three months limping around the city trying to find the gutsy broad. She might have been home free, if she didn't decide to go back to Tony's place. For some unknown reason, she foolishly made a return visit. They do say that the clams oreganato at Tony's are rather special.

The woman's good fortune was that she lived through Joey's vengeance. Or maybe it was her bad fortune, as the doctors said she'd never be the same. Despite Chee-Chee's fearful reputation, too many people knew the story for it to stay hidden, and too many addicts would risk their sorry lives for the cost of a fix. So, some of the same gutter scum that tipped off Joey to the woman's whereabouts, also tipped off the police to Joey's role in her injuries.

It wasn't long before Gil had a case, and a witness who could testify to several telling particulars. Gil was able to make the collar a week later, with what he thought was ample evidence for a conviction, much less indictment. S.B. Randall disagreed.

Beach suspected that a deal had been made somewhere in the secret world of lawyer-land, but had no proof. When the ADA announced a plea bargain, Gil was amazed and mortified to learn that the altered plea was not for attempted murder, or an equally serious felony, but for simple drug possession, a misdemeanor. In twenty-four hours, Chee-Chee walked. It was an outrage, and Beach stormed into the DA's office to confront Randall. Ever since then, the ADA had treated Beach with all the courtesy and cooperation he would normally give to someone who had raped a nun. Yet, until now, Randall had never tried to interfere with the actual conduct of Beach's investigations. It was a significant departure, a sign that somebody was pressuring S.B. and a sure sign that somebody was worried.

Chapter 17

Later that day, in a deep basement room, the man with the fiery eyes wiped perspiration from his gleaming forehead, as he tightened a bench vice holding the Colt AR 15. He was converting it from semi to fully automatic fire. Once completed, he would have essentially the same weapon as the M-15 combat rifle. The legal injunction against private ownership of automatic weapons was no great obstacle. The conversion kit had been relatively inexpensive and easily purchased from a gun parts supplier.

First, he had completed a mail order course in gun repair from a correspondence school in Phoenix that advertised in American Rifle Owner magazine. He had filled out his student registration under a false name and used that pseudonym for a post office box. Soon he was on the mailing list of dozens of suppliers, and related businesses, as well as the predictable few rip-off outfits. Next, he ordered the conversion kit from a catalogue that carefully avoided describing the item's most popular function. The manufacturers would, of course, claim that they had no control over improper use, while knowing exactly why purchasers ordered it.

He wasn't sure yet, whether the converted weapon would be the appropriate means to silence the Detective. That pig was becoming an obstacle to his plans. Logically, therefore, the policeman would have to be eliminated. Normally, one man could not be terribly significant, yet this annoying detective was sure to be the vanguard of those who would come. “I know my responsibility,” the sweating man murmured to himself as he stroked the gun. “Someone must be out front in the operation. It is my role and my destiny to ‘take point’.”

It was like the other war he had lived through—the one in Viet Nam and Cambodia. There too, he had always been the first man out in front. He moved through the jungle like a wraith, a dark shadow of plague and death. After an NVA ambush of his LRCH patrol in which he was the only one to come out alive, they stopped using his name, just calling him “the Survivor.” It fit.

He survived but made sure that many others did not. His killing sprees were legendary. After he returned home from war, he quickly learned the truth. He was a destined leader of the strong, the determined, the survivors of the world.

Now that he had found that purpose, no mere cop would stop him. There were other enforcers of society’s laws who had stepped forward to join the conflict, but they had been dealt with. In Los Angeles, the chaos had allowed him to take down one cop under cover of the rioting. Still, this one felt significantly different. This Detective Beach had a distinctive aura. He was an adversary of note. His presence could only mean the final conflict was approaching. The automatic weapon the man fondled would be ready for whoever dared to enter the 'Point man's lair, the realm of shadow, the "Yin of Drang."

He had already ground out a space in the weapon's lower receiver to accept the new sear. Now he selected a 1/4-inch drill bit and began drilling above the letter "R" stamped above the fire selector switch. He had marked a point exactly 5/32nds of an inch down, where the hole for the sear pin had to be precisely located. He wiped his hands on a rag, for they were getting moist. His vivid eyes shone in anticipation, as he inserted a new M15 sear into the recess and slid the pin into place. He had already gently filed the secondary sear trip lever to fit. He knew better than to file the sear itself, as some morons did to attempt conversion to automatic fire. He didn't want to turn the weapon into a booby trap. If he wanted to make a booby trap, he was well aware of how to make one specific to the purpose, one that wouldn't turn on its maker. He had built a few such traps recently, and they were ready to greet those foolish enough to make him their quarry.

With a practiced hand, he reassembled the mechanism, put the safety on "Fire" position, depressed the trigger, pulled the slide to the rear, then released it. The trip lever disengaged, with a satisfying "clack", which indicated that the weapon was now on automatic. He smiled, but the smile didn't reach his eyes. They remained half-hooded, steely, and cold. Deadly cold.

Chapter 18

"I'll give him the message," Rita agreed, hanging up the phone as she typed notes into a file.

Rita Bravermann, a civilian employee of the NYPD, was doing phone cover today. "Phone Cover" didn't mean just answering calls, but the essential task of providing a number that could be called as verification for a covert operations fictional I.D. The PDU kept a couple of unlisted numbers available for any detective running a false identity. Often the target of an investigation got suspicious and asked the undercover officer for a telephone number, to confirm the covert operator's cover story. If they checked out the number, someone had to be at the other end of the line to respond in a way that reinforced the counterfeit identity, who backed up the 'legend.' Several index cards were tacked to the bulletin board above the phone, each with a name and brief description of the false I.D. profile. This old-fashioned method worked better than computer files. Everything was available and visible at a moment's glance.

The call that had just come in, was for a "Daniel Wiggins." Rita quickly eyeballed the cards and found the right one, semi-legibly scrawled in Gil Beach's handwriting. She responded as it directed, pretending to be another resident of the rooming house he had listed somewhere as his address. "No," she said, she didn't know when he would be in, but she would leave a message under his door to call “Selene.” Rita noted the caller’s number, along with the sexy tone of voice; she made sure to bring both to Detective Beach’s attention when he passed her desk later that day.

“Well, Gil, I mean, ‘Danny’ baby it looks like you been doin’ some heavy undercover work. Or is it work under the covers?” She waved the telephone memo at him like a hanky, fluttering from two extended fingers.

Beach didn’t answer. Rolling his eyes upward, he snatched the slip of paper and headed for his desk. His hand moved to the spot on his arm that earlier had come in contact with Selene’s body. He rubbed the area, absent-mindedly, as he flopped into his chair, a screech of old springs protesting the sudden weight. There were several other messages on the cluttered surface. It was surprising how many people didn’t trust e-mail messages and resorted to the old-fashioned notepad type. He looked at the paper Rita had handed him, but slid it under two others, as if it were a lower priority, resisting the impulse he felt to immediately dial the number.

The other notes included a message from one of his snitches, “Potsy” with no return number. One was from “Shig” Higawa at the lab, another from his wife to call home, and there was a slip with the words, “See Lou,” scrawled across it, with Frank

Terranova's initials underneath. "Lou" was the traditional title for an officer of Lieutenant rank. Since there was no time marked on the message, Gil figured he could put it off a while. He decided to answer some of the others, first. Potsy had probably called from a phone booth somewhere, so he wouldn't want Gil to call back, although the Detective knew where the C.I could be reached. Potsy wasn't anxious to receive calls from cops, being a petty gangster who was easily expendable should his "wise guy" friends learn that he was snitching.

Gil stared at the message from Pilar for a moment, chewing at his lower lip. Finally, he slid it to the bottom of the stack, took the last message of the bunch, and dialed the number of the Police Laboratory.

"This is Gil Beach, returning Shigura Higawa's call," he told the secretary who picked up the call. In a moment, the Lab Director came on the line.

"Top of the morning to ye," the Director piped into the phone.

"It isn't morning," Gil replied dryly, "and you are about as Irish as Emperor Hirohito."

"You're dating yourself, Beach. Hirohito hasn't been the Emperor since eighty-nine. As for the greeting, I am quite certain it is morning, somewhere in the world right now."

"Okay, okay, smart-ass. So why did you call, anyway?"

"Do I have to have a reason?"

"C'mon, Shig. You have called me about ten times in your life that you didn't have an ulterior motive. The last time, you tried to sell me some football tickets you couldn't get rid of. Usually, you call because you want to know something."

"You forgot about the time I called to invite you to the lab Christmas party."

"Yeah, only you failed to mention at the time that there was a twenty-dollar cover charge. I only found out when I arrived and was hit up at the door."

"What an ingrate! It was cheap at twice the price! But let us dispense with this unseemly exchange. I'm calling about the John Doe you found sunbathing under the FDR."

"He isn't a John Doe anymore. We I.D.'d him as William Paxton McSwain the Third, prodigal son of a hoity toity family of Long Island. Is that what you called about?"

"No, but thanks for the info anyway. I just wanted to know how far we should go with the work. We got some decent fingernail scrapings. Besides some blood and skin, there were a couple of other things. There was some oil with fragrant esters—maybe some kind of body oil, or massage oil—and then some animal hair."

"What, he got attacked by an animal?"

"Not likely. The blood and tissue are human. The good news is that the person who killed him is a secretor."

"What's the bad news?"

"The blood type is O positive . . . most common one around. Won't narrow things down a lot. We can send it out for DNA analysis, but that will take a while. And as you know unless you have a perp to match it with… well, you know. As for the animal hair, it's not from a living animal; probably a horse."

"Could it be synthetic?"

"Get a grip, Beach. You think we can't tell the difference between synthetic fibers and animal hairs? We're better than that."

"Right. So he was attacked by two guys in a stuffed horse suit, who then drove over him in a truck and threw him off the FDR. Who do you think was the perp . . . the guy in front part of the costume, or the guy who's the horse's ass?"

"Joke if you will, but the facts are the facts, and the evidence is what it is. So how much farther do we go on this? Do we need a DNA on the tissue? I gotta tell you, Gil, we are under a real tight budget . . . election year, you know. Mayor is trying to economize and that means Nussbaum is on my back. We're counting paperclips."

"Always was a bit of a tightwad," Gil commented dryly about Higawa's administrative superior.

"The test runs around a hundred fifty a shot," Higawa continued. "If you really need it, no problem. But half the time, we do these tests, no suspect is ever apprehended and with nobody to match, the results are just money down the drain . . . if you get my drift."

"Well, I got a feeling that I know who the perp is. I hope I'm wrong, because it may stir up a hornet's nest, but if I'm right, a DNA print may be the only way to get this guy. He's too smooth to give us very much."

"Okay, just had to ask. Nussbaum gets on my case. He says that if we did a full analysis of every specimen we logged, we'd be over budget by June. But don't worry, that's his problem. I've got some latitude. You'll have the results soon. I suppose you're gonna want a preview, too."

"A preview?"

"Yeah, most of the time, in this sort of situation, it's too dicey to pull someone in before you take a specimen for comparison, but the other evidence is too slim to justify that serious a step. Can't prove it without the specimen, can't get a specimen unless you've got some proof. You know—the old 'Catch Twenty-Two'!"

"So what's a preview?"

"Well, that's doing a test of some tissue that can't be used in evidence."

"Improperly obtained?"

"But my dear Detective, surely you're not suggesting that any of our fine officers would do something improper, are you?" chuckled the forensics specialist.

"Of course not," Gil agreed, smiling, "but I suppose that every now and then, you run samples of unrelated tissue…?"

" . . . just to test the equipment, check calibrations, that sort of thing. I'm sure you understand."

"If that tissue just happens to come in some mysterious way from the suspect, it couldn't be used for evidence, but it would tell the investigators if they were on the right track."

"You could call it a prediction of how a properly executed test would turn out. A prediction, or even perhaps a . . ."

" . . . a 'Preview.'"

That was when Beach knew that he would be going back to the Federation's Headquarters. Part of him wondered why that seemed so exciting a prospect, but he shrugged it off. After all this was clearly professional.

CHAPTER 19

"One day you will come to understand that saving the Earth and saving yourself are not unrelated," Storm spoke softly. Selene sat on the floor, a few feet away. She was close enough that Gil could smell her.

Storm and the Detective had been talking for a lengthy period. Gil assumed that much of what the man said in their long conversation was probably perfumed bullshit. Yet some of the sachet was very appealing. He had to admit that there was no blatant preaching or pressuring. Most of Storm's remarks were sharply observant, his questions penetrating, his conclusions intriguing.

"I've never thought of environmental concerns and survivalism as the same thing," Gil said.

"Think about it," Storm explained his philosophy. "The survival of the earth is necessary for the survival of any of us. Conversely, if things reach such a crisis point that society collapses or a great war decimates the population, some of us will survive. Those that do, must combine the twin priorities of personal sustenance and recovery of the ecology. Defense of our existence and defense of our environment are sister concepts. These are both ideas that the Federation espouses."

Although Gil found some of Storm's philosophy vague and inconsistent, he resisted voicing all his objections. His act as an interested learner seemed convincing enough to be accepted, because once he had given them that self-description, he had been treated to a carefully staged come-on. At least that is what he assumed it to be. His ingrained cynicism refused to accept it as unplanned.

Storm concluded the interview, or audience, or whatever it was, with an invitation to "unwind" in one of the "natural relaxation modules" before leaving. Gil was about to refuse, until Selene rose from her seat, holding out her hand to him. Uncertain, at first, if it was a parting handshake that was being extended, he raised his own hand to hers. Instead of pumping it in a goodbye gesture, however, she grabbed his arm while turning to walk away. He allowed himself to be led from the room.

Selene took him to a softly lit chamber where futon pads and cushions covered the floor around a sunken bubbling hot tub. Shrubs and flowers lined the walls. You didn't have to be a rocket scientist to figure out that relaxation meant a soak in the spa, so he looked around for a changing room. She caught his searching glances and smiled.

"I hope it doesn't shock you, but we try to avoid false modesty here. We think of our bodies as natural and beautiful gifts that need not be hidden from each other all the time. If it ever comes to the bottom line of survival, we won't be able to maintain the usual conventions of modesty. If this is offensive to you, I would be happy to obtain some bathing garments."

"Well, I am a little shy," Gil said, not anxious to reveal his scarred chest to the woman. There were other parts he wasn't anxious to reveal either. Not that he had anything to be ashamed of—just call it a certain need for privacy. He was the kind of guy who was a little uncomfortable peeing when someone was standing at the urinal right next to him in the men's room.

"Certainly. There's a garment over there," she smiled, pointing to a corner of the alcove.

Gil stepped over to where she indicated, finding a white one-piece garment hanging on a wall hook. He took off his outer clothes, put the long shift-like shirt, with his back turned to the woman, before slipping out of his underwear. When he turned back, it took a moment to realize that Selene had preceded him into the spa. He hadn't been expecting that . . . or the way she looked.

Although technically speaking, she had remained clothed, Selene was now revealed in a manner more seductive, as far as Gil was concerned, than being naked. The thin white fabric she wore had turned partially transparent, clinging to her body like shrink-wrap. Although most of that body was submerged, the part that he could see was terrific. In her case, the idea that our body is a beautiful gift, was easy to accept. His gaze loitered on her flawless skin, high sculptured cheekbones, graceful neck, delicate lanky arms, and the swell of heavy breasts bobbing at the water's surface. If she had blatantly exhibited herself, he might have found it less alluring, but there was no strutting, no display. She acted almost like he wasn't there. Maybe that was part of the appeal, invoking the voyeur in him, the part that stirred with desire as if he had come upon her unaware, watching secretly from a hidden vantagepoint.

He didn't know how to get out of the situation gracefully. So he wrapped the cloth around himself and dropped into the sunken tub. He didn't know whether Selene noticed that he had the beginning of an erection. She seemed to have her eyes closed. He let his close also. In a few moments the warm swirling water and soft lighting began to relax him. Soft instrumental music was playing - bells and strings in a delicate counterpoint. There was a strange, yet pleasant odor in the air that he couldn't identify, though it was vaguely spicy and flowery. He kept thinking, "I can't believe I'm doing this."

He must have dozed, because when he opened his eyes, the woman was gone. He imagined what her beautiful body had looked like when she came up out of the water yet was partially relieved that he didn't have to deal with it. His cynical side felt sure that this was all part of the Federation's come-on. Yet, another hungry part of him wanted it to proceed. He knew he would leave with an image of the attractive woman etched in memory. Maybe that's what they counted on to recruit guys into the movement. In a sense, it sure as hell was "moving." This might be the standard lure, Lorelei of the sea enticing every horny male onto the rocks. It was hard to know. So, the question was how to play it from here?

Gil climbed out of the spa, dried himself on one of the nearby towels, found his clothes and dressed. When he came out of the relaxation room, no one seemed to be in the area. He walked back through the deserted corridors, footsteps echoing in the uncarpeted expanses. He passed various doors, some open, although most were closed. Through one partially open doorway he saw a small office with a computer set-up alongside several file cabinets.

After looking around to see if anyone was watching and seeing no CCTV cameras, he made a quick detour into the room where he pulled open one of the file drawers. The cabinet was filled with hanging folders marked by color-coded tabs. The meaning of the colors wasn't obvious. He pulled out a manila folder that seemed to be a typical file. A data form described a building that could have been in New York or any urban scene. There were floor plans, notes about access, utilities, and other matters. Much space was devoted to the water supply, alarm systems, and security. The language was also a tip-off to something far removed from typical retail business or commerce. Some of the listed items included details of security schedules, alarms, and such, but used phrases like "occupying force in place," "time needed to breach," as well as "escape routes."

He was reaching for the next file drawer when he heard footsteps in the hallway. By the time the steps reached the door, he had closed the drawer, moved over to a desk and grabbed the telephone. A young woman entered the room, dressed in a halter and silk briefs, a flower garland in her hair. Not as striking as Selene, she still was attractive and the image of innocent sexuality in her minimal clothing . . . fresh, youthful, almost a child - another species of sprite or nymph. As she turned to face him, he spoke into the receiver, as if continuing a conversation.

" . . . and I'll be back as soon as I stop off for some coffee at Waldbaum's." He smiled apologetically to the woman staring at him, raising a single finger to indicate he would only be a minute. Blonde, thin, and oddly passive, she showed no obvious reaction to his presence or actions. She just stood eyeing him with a blank expression. He said "Goodbye" into the unconnected line, then raised his eyes to her opaque gaze.

"Gee, I hope you don't mind my using the phone. I couldn't find anybody to ask. I had to make this call, or I'd be in a lot of hot water. Hope it was okay?"

The girl/woman was silent for a moment, then nodded.

"Of course," she smiled a vacant smile, "If you are Mr. Wiggins, I have a note for you." She offered him a small envelope.

Gil noticed that when he reached out to take the envelope, the girl flinched. He wondered what kind of treatment she was used to getting.

"Oh. Thanks," was all he said.

The envelope contained a perfumed sheet with a woman's handwriting in looping swirls.

"We are so glad that you came," it read, "there are many other things for you to discover here. I think you have finally found what you have been seeking for so long."

The note was signed by Selene. He wondered what she meant by "other things." There was one particular 'thing' that came to mind, but he knew it would just mean trouble. He quickly squashed the thought.

He felt frustrated that he hadn't achieved his goal of getting a tissue specimen from 'Storm,' or 'Stormer,' the man he now guessed was responsible for Billie McSwain's death. Gil's reason for this visit had been to find something for the "pre-view" DNA test Shig Higawa had suggested. Getting a sample had turned out to be more difficult than he had hoped. At one point, Gil had asked to visit a bathroom, but found nothing useful . . . no comb with strands of silvery hair, tissues with mucus, or anything he could be sure was from the man. It was obviously a guest toilet. Storm didn't leave any hair fibers on the chair he used, or at least none that were visible to Gil in the moment he had to look. A good lab tech probably could have pulled out some evidence, with a few uninterrupted minutes to go over things, but that was out of the question. Gil had even planned a back-up ruse that involved spilling some coffee on Storm and vigorously wiping his arm to capture a few microscopic skin flakes. He wasn't sure whether or not that would have yielded an adequate specimen for the DNA test, but it didn't matter, because the guru took nothing to drink during their meeting. Besides, Selene was strategically placed to jump when he needed anything. Gil hadn't even gotten close. Probably just as well . . . the more he thought about it, the more obvious and stupid the ruse seemed. They would have seen through him in a second.

That was the downside. The upside was that now he would have to come back. Anyway, it seemed like an upside to Gil. He wasn't sure how anxious he was to end this little operation. At least not until he got to know the players a little better. Truthfully, some players he wanted to know better than others.

Chapter 20

". . .they'll take it . . . they'll take it, noooo, ahhnng . . .," a child's high-pitched tones pleaded from the recorder. The moaning of a wounded thing.

Even the player's small speaker transmitted the ragged fear . . . and something more. A mature female voice responded, low and soothing. It was Helen Joseph's voice.

"It's okay, Darling, it's all right. You're safe now. Do you want to tell me about it? I know you're scared, but it'll help to tell somebody. What is it that you're afraid they're going to take, Nina?"

The agonized child moans again, " . . . the baby, the baby. They're going to take the baby . . ."

There is a pause, a growling noise, then Nina's voice got hard and barked out a stern order, "She's not supposed to tell! No, she can't tell, no, No!"

"Who isn't supposed to tell?" Helen asks, but all she gets in return is gibberish, and long low keening sounds.

Gil stopped the sound, running open fingers through his hair. He had been listening for almost an hour, seated on the floor of his den at home, sometimes replaying passages a second or third time. He was still confused by the whole thing. Still, isn't that what madness is all about, a confusion of reality? Temporary insanity or not, she was making no sense at all. No wonder she changed her mind and went back to the Federation Center. Maybe it was all just a crazy fantasy.

. . . except for the fact that she was pregnant, wasn't she?

He caught a little movement out of the corner of his eye. Turning, he saw Pilar at the door, wrapped in her old chenille robe. There was a tilt to her head that looked like curiosity, an infrequently seen attentiveness in her eyes.

"Hi, Sweetheart," he ventured.

"Hi Cupcake. Where did that come from?"

"Oh, it's from one of Gentry's kids we got down at the Youth Bureau," he said, shaking his head, "Helen thought I might get something out of this, but the kid sounds like loony tunes. She doesn't even know who she is."

"You wouldn't either, if you were a committee."

"A what?"

"You know what you've got there, don't you?"

"Obviously not. And just as obviously, you are going to enlighten me, right?"

"Back it up a few minutes, then play it again."

Gil punched at the device again to go back on the recording and start it over. Again, the voice of the moaning child cried out, "they'll take it . . . they'll take it!"

Pilar reached over, then, pushing the "pause" control.

"Who are you hearing?" she asked Gil.

He was puzzled by her question but shrugged his shoulders.

" . . . a girl? . . . a little girl named Nina?"

"Right," Pilar nodded, then ran the fast forward control to skip Helen's response. She pushed the play button again.

" . . . afraid they are going to take, Nina?"

" . . . the baby, the baby . . . They're going to take the baby . . ." followed by that growling noise.

Gil could hear Pilar whispering "Yes, yes," under her breath, as the girl's voice spoke again, "She's not supposed to tell! No, she can't tell, no, no!"

"Now, who are you hearing?" Pilar asked, punching the pause button again.

"Uhh . . . same kid, acting weird?" Gil guessed.

"No . . . Don't you hear the difference in the voice?"

“Is that important?”

“You bet. That’s an Alter.”

“A what?”

“An Alter. As in ‘alternate personality’. I’d bet anything you’ve got an MPD on your hands.”

“I don’t suppose that stands for Military Police Department.”

“Oh Gil, come on. Haven’t you ever heard of Multiple Personality Disorder?”

“What . . . like ‘The Three Faces of Eve’?”

“You’re dating yourself, but yes. That’s one of the most famous ones—that and Sybil, because they made films about them. But it’s more common than you might imagine.”

“And you think our little Homewell House drop-out is one of those schizo’s?”

“I didn’t say anything about schizophrenia, Gil. MPD is a personality disorder, not a psychosis. I’d bet a byline in Psychology Today that you’ve just met your first case. Did you notice how sometimes she’s in the Executive, or ‘Master’ personality? That’s the only one that may be aware of the others, so that’s why she uses the plural pronouns like ‘we’ at times instead of ‘I’ or ‘me’. Who’s treating her?”

"Nobody that I know of. She bolted back to the group of fanatics with her mom."

"Oh Damn! What is it, some kind of secret group or cult?"

"I swear, I must be the stupidest sonovabitch in the world, or the slowest. Everybody seems to know the details of this case before I even tell them. How in hell did you know that?"

"Nothing very amazing, Cupcake," she said, smiling. "Nine times out of ten, a 'Multiple' can be traced back to some kind of severe or ritual abuse. When you said, 'fanatics' it figured."

"I wish you could have talked to her. Helen didn't have a clue . . . me either."

"How could you? You haven't been trained in this. It upsets me more when the trained professionals miss it or observe it but refuse to believe what they're seeing."

"Well, I gotta admit, it's a new one for me. It's hard to believe that somebody could be . . . that way, without knowing it. Or do they know?"

"Not usually, at least not in any complete way. In fact, much of the treatment for MPD consists of bringing the alters out in the open, then sort of introducing them to one another, in a therapeutic process."

"Too bad you can't see this kid, but she's hidden away in the FONIES Center."

"FONIES?"

"Oh that's just my name for this group. 'The Family of Natural Selection' is their version."

"I think I've heard of them."

"You're kidding."

"No really. Remember, environmental issues are a real interest of mine."

"How could I forget."

She raised her eyebrows at the remark. "Aren't we touchy? Anyway, don't they have a hot shot leader with a strange name?"

"Umm . . . 'Storm'—He says it was some Slavic name, but first it got changed to Stormer, then shortened."

"You know him?" Pilar's eyes widened.

"Well, actually, I did meet the guy, but I shouldn't say too much about it, on account of it being tied into the case I'm on.

God, how did I get into this? he wondered, realizing he wasn't anxious for his wife to know all the details.

"What's he like?" she pressed; interest obvious in her tone.

“Well, let’s just say, he’s different.”

Gil stood up and walked over to the bookcase, as if looking for something. Pilar knew that was his way of trying to end the conversation, but she didn’t back off.

“He’s certainly got some of the college crowd going,” she said, “They say he’s like a one-man Greenpeace, or Sierra Club.”

“I’m thinking more like Charles Manson, or David Koresh.”

“Do you have something to back that up,” Pilar said, frowning, “Or is this some kind of macho-man envy?”

“Geez, what did I say?”

“Just don’t be so quick to assume the worst about anybody with a cause, Gil. I’m very involved with the environmental movement, you know. Just because we don’t have children, doesn’t mean we don’t owe something to future generations.”

“Ouch. You really like to hit below the belt don’t you.”

Pilar straightened, a dark shadow passing over her face.

“What makes you think you can compare your pain to what I feel about not having a child?”

As tears started to form in her eyes, Pilar pivoted and strode out of the room. Gil watched his wife leave, unsure of what to say or do. He knew that their inability to have children was a real sore point with Pilar, even more than it was for him, but he was at a loss to know how to deal with her feelings. It didn't help that his job had put her in a position to be hurt so badly it ruled out any future pregnancy. The incident had been long ago, but the feelings were obviously still raw.

He stared at the voice recorder, wondering if Storm and his friends could come up with some herbs or natural remedies that could fix such things as barren wombs and wounded hearts.

CHAPTER 21

Senator Delucia was on a roll. He had just delivered a variation on his old "I am the new politics" speech, which had gone over like gangbusters with the Webster Heights Neighborhood Association. By the time he was finished, he had them thinking that he could save their neighborhood from becoming another "Love Canal." He knew that he had a gift, which allowed him to make a fringe cause sound like a grand cause and everyone's concern. With that gift, Delucia had made the environment a mainline issue that he could wave like the American Flag. He had taken Al Gore's shtick and improved on it. How could anyone not agree that we need clean air and water? With the proper spin, you could instill fear, while portraying yourself as the protector. It was one of his talents to manage that with a convincing appearance of sincerity.

Now he pushed through the jostling crowd, breathing in the smell of sweat and excitement, drawing energy from the urgency and longing he sensed in the common folk crowding around him. He knew that they held out a forlorn hope that their tawdry little lives would somehow be touched by greatness if only they could get close enough. Some of them called out "Senator Mark", as if he were a friend they could call on a first name basis. He encouraged that myth. On the podium, he was "Senator Mark Delucia, the Second," but had his staff spread the idea that he was really a down-to-earth guy, who thought of his constituents as friends. In truth, he thought of them as a vulgar horde, and he would have preferred even greater formality, like maybe …"Mr. President." Right now, his candidacy was just beginning to catch on, but if he could get the environmental thing going for him, he might get the big win over Forester that he needed to become a real contender for the next presidential nomination. At least it would position him for the second spot. Since the "Plum Point Spill" on the Hudson, he had been getting increased attention from the media. Not all the coverage was positive, but that would change. If the opposition got too strident, he could even take on the mantle of a victim for his beliefs.

Delucia was politically astute enough to know that the common riff-raff wanted to feel close to power. He grabbed an extended hand here and there, using just the right pressure, pumping, reacting with a big smile and affirming nod to each person that caught his eye. He paused for a moment to wave merrily at the folks in a balcony off to the right. Not every touch had to be physical. Sometimes just a distant gesture was enough. Two aides and a couple of burly security guards formed a line of interference to the exit, playing their assigned role of appearing to take him away from the mob he loved to touch. They seemed to be forcing him to forsake his ardent desire to mix with the "real people." In truth, the support staff people were only following his orders. They responded to his signal without question, only appearing to drag him off when he wanted them to do just that. The Senator's staff never did anything that he didn't clearly want them to do.

Finally, he slipped through a side door, down a short hallway into the private suite. The sound level dropped dramatically as he entered the lushly carpeted room. It was like entering the private lounge of a jumbo jet.

He glanced at his large watch. The timing was perfect. At a table in the corner, Jeannine Valopi, indispensable aide, clerk, administrative secretary, girl Friday and general gofer, was busily typing away at a laptop, the ticky-tic of the keys punctuated by occasional electronic beeps. Incredibly, she could manage this at the same time she was speaking continuously into a cell phone held between shoulder and cheek. Her current helper, Evelyn-something-or-other, was nervously sorting through stacks of paper, looking for some misplaced document.

Mark noted a length of exposed thigh, and skirt stretched tightly across a firm butt, as Evelyn bent down to pick up a dropped page. Rising, she saw him watching. A blush spread up her shapely neck, as she read the interest in his look. The distinguished Senator made a mental note to find out her name so he could arrange to follow-up to that star-struck reaction. She might make a nice bed-warmer on one of his longer campaign trips. Of course, Jeannine was always available, if he didn't have anything else set up, but Mark needed variety, and these camp followers were usually willing to satisfy his need. He knew that for his part, he gave them memories to carry away like a treasure they could hold forever. "My night with a famous man." Since Clinton, one had to be much more careful about who actually knew one's sexual habits, but with a bit of caution, it could be managed with adequate discretion.

Fred Valario, Delucia's campaign manager was satisfying another sort of need . . . his caffeine addiction, pouring himself one of countless daily cups of coffee from a stained urn that dripped thinly onto a soggy wad of napkins strategically placed below. DeLucia was sure that Fred would appear unflappable in a tornado, though his wrinkled trousers and bruised eye sockets were testament to numerous days of traveling and odd hours—often catching sleep in whatever bed, chair, or floor was at hand. The campaign manager tried to smooth down his tousled head of unruly brown hair. Fred seemed to treasure his unkempt look, mopish tresses and ponytail, as a last fragile link to the sixties. It was common knowledge that Fred maintained a fantasy that he was once a hippie of sorts. "Shouldn't flatter himself," Delucia thought, "just because he was a drug addict for a decade and slightly loony doesn't make him a hippie." On the other hand, a bit of the fringe look among his staff was good for the Senator's image as a liberal, and it didn't hurt with some of leftist groups to see a long-hair among his closest associates. Whether Delucia was really friendly with any of these characters was neither here nor there.

Several others sat in sectional sofas that had been arranged to form a separate area on the opposite side of the room. Steven Randall, the acerbic Assistant DA, was leaning over Sherri Cornwell the up-and-coming attorney who served as Delucia's Legal Counsel. She was seated, while Randall loomed over her like a bird of prey. If it had been Delucia, he would have been staring down the neck of her dress, but Randall seemed oblivious to the woman's generous attributes, displaying his usual intense manner and agitation. Randall treated every matter like it was a prelude to Armageddon, and had a permanent furrow frozen into the bridge of his nose. Delucia reminded himself that he had to keep a tight rein on that one.

Alone and silent, yet somehow dominating an area around him, was that other strange duck Stormer—"Storm." He certainly didn't have a furrowed brow. The guy was a cool one. At times Storm amazed Delucia, with his ability to seem like he stood above everyday concerns and hassles. The earth and nature stuff was bullshit, of course, but still there was a special quality to the man, a potency that seeped out of his eyes. They had a long history together, and a closer secret bond as well, but it didn't mean Delucia made the mistake of placing faith in such unstable types. Storm wasn't as crazy as some others, but he was too much of an unpredictable quantity, The Senator remembered a phrase in Shakespeare's account of Caesar's assassination "Yon Cassius has a . . . look. Such men are not to be trusted."

Delucia moved to a centrally located chair, where he gave a signal for the others to gather around him. It was a conscious power play. By making them come to him, he once again asserted his domination. Some scurried over to arrange themselves as close as possible, basking in the nimbus of power; fans granted onstage seats at a rock concert; compliant puppies competing for attention. Others moved more slowly, not disobeying his command, but resisting subtly. They were more like cats, those self-involved creatures that refuse to appear hurried, seeming to take some comfort in their small independence. Jeannine settled in a nearby chair, flipped open a steno pad, and jotted a heading on the page. She kicked off her high heels, slipping one foot under her other leg in a habitual pose of casual concentration. Then she raised her eyes expectantly, no other expression on her face—the neutral human recorder, ready for input.

An audio recorder might capture all the words, but Jeannine could capture the tone, the mood, the flow in a way no recorder ever could. Sometimes body language was more important than the words uttered. Evelyn hurriedly distributed some papers still warm from the photocopier. Randall pulled the window curtains shut and whispered something to Fred, who mumbled a low response and nodded before darting out of the room in his typical here-one-moment-gone-the-next style. The door narrowly missed closing on the end of his ponytail, as his long hair trailed him out of the room. Evelyn, the new girl, hung tentatively on the edge of the group, avoiding direct eye contact, her cheeks ruddy. Randall signaled his impatience by repeatedly consulting the elaborate watch he wore, crossing and re-crossing his legs, while sighing audibly. Storm merely turned, directing his attention to Delucia, without moving from his preselected position. This fact was not lost on the politician. Senator B. Mark Delucia, the Second, didn't miss much . . . not much at all.

Still, the meeting in the lounge was not as private as the participants assumed. Grady Dickson of the Eastside Evening News had left the rally before the main crowd exited the auditorium. When the Senator made his way out of the bustling mob, Grady watched him move toward the southwest corner of the building. Instead of following, Dickson circled the outside wall in the direction where he guessed Delucia was heading.

The reporter's guess turned out to be correct. He managed to find a position outside the window of the lounge, where the group of staff people was meeting. This room was designed with glass louvered panes set to form side panels for the larger picture windows. One set of louvers had been left ajar, apparently unnoticed because they were covered by decorative drapes. An occasional gust of air billowed the curtains enough to give a partial and momentary glimpse of the room inside. Mostly the flashes served as a tease, revealing little. Still, Dickson couldn't ask for a much better position for eavesdropping. A pseudo-colonial pillar on one side of the window and large bushy forsythia on the other essentially screened him from view of anyone walking along the street outside. If only he had thought to bring along his snoop mike—that amplifying device could pick up even the most meager sounds and boost them to seem as if the speakers were nearby. At least he had his audio recorder and a remote microphone. That would have to do.

The reporter plugged a blue-tooth dongle into his recorder, then inserted the small paired pick-up device through the bottom louver of the window, slowly letting it drop to the windowsill. He hoped that when resting under the bottom edge of the drape the sensitive microphone would pick up more than he was hearing outside. He slipped on a pair of light-weight headphones and plugged their mini-jack into a hole marked "monitor." It worked. He couldn't hear every word they were saying in the room, but he was understanding whole sentences now.

"I think we have a problem, Mark," a male voice said.

"I eat problems for breakfast," came a booming response that could only be the Senator. Grady wished everyone spoke up so clearly.

"What's Forester doing now?"

"Well . . . gaining in the polls, and . . . ridiculing . . . concerns about . . . environment."

"THE BASTARD! Damn, I thought that spill . . . trick. It's too bad the Exxon Valdez . . . this month. There must . . . problems to raise these issues . . . public concerns."

"Jeannine—what have we got on . . . and all that?"

A mumbled indecipherable reply from the woman.

"That's not enough! We must get something . . . We need press. Fred! Where's Fred? . . . Randall, find me an issue here. There's gotta be something.

"We've got another problem, too, Senator."

"Jesus H. Christ. Is this a campaign, or a feeding frenzy? What now?"

"There's this detective . . . getting too interested in The Federation . . ." the first man said, followed by something else that was inaudible.

Then another voice, not as loud, more difficult to distinguish. " . . . nnn worry, I can handle . . . ready started."

The conversation went on, but Grady paused in his listening, suddenly afraid that he would be discovered by the window, while his ears were otherwise occupied. He wanted to be able to hear anyone approaching. He kept looking back, to see if anyone would sneak up on him. The extra caution didn't accomplish much. He had just checked all the connections again, when the world exploded in a flash of startling color. Vaguely, he sensed that he had been struck from behind, but the force of the blow took away all power to respond. It also propelled the reporter forward so that his forehead slammed into the brick facing of the building.

After that was just darkness.

Chapter 22

Elsewhere, muted yellow light soaked a workbench in an amber wash. The scene it revealed thus had the sepia toned aspect of an old photograph, two-dimensional, seemingly not of this time. Yet the objects were frighteningly contemporary.

The Survivor knew that explosives required exquisite attention and meticulous handling. When funneled through a paper cone, the black powder poured easily into the end of the two-foot length of pipe. The tricky part was the initiator charge. The shipment of mercury fulminate had never arrived, so he was forced to make do with more gunpowder, emptied from individual shotgun shells. Fortunately, he had an ample supply from his cache in the damp basement. First, he sealed off the main charge with small pieces of modeling clay. Gelignite would have been better, but that was also part of the missing shipment. If he had more time, he would have gotten back some of the supply he had distributed among the youth squad, but he couldn't wait. He wiped the pipe threads thoroughly, then poured a few spoonfuls of the dusty black material onto squares of clear plastic wrap, which he folded into tight packets. He didn't want any loose powder lying around to be accidentally ignited. He had lost two associates that way, when the friction of screwing on a metal cap set off some loose powder in the threaded metal. That had been almost a quarter of a century ago when he had been doing work for the Central Radical Armed Student Hub, "CRASH." The acronym of the group had turned out to be prophetic. He had no intention of repeating that fall from power, that fall from grace. He also did not want to end as a splatter of gristle and red paste on the walls . . . at least not unless it had superlative significance—certainly not in the mundane act of merely constructing a bomb. Carefully, he inserted one packet into each pipe, on top of the main charge. With a pointed awl, he gently punched a small hole for the fuse.

The man of shadows wiped perspiration from his forehead, sighing. He had to talk to that other one again . . . the little shit who insisted on being difficult. It was that one's fault that the better ignitor chemical and precious lumps of brown gelignite hadn't come through. His brother was, and always would be a complete wimp, a soft pansy. That is why it was particularly frustrating to see the wimp walk away with all the marbles during most of their childhood. He had used derisive nicknames like "Bleeding Heart" for such a long time to describe his less intense, laid-back sibling, that now it came naturally to mind. Ironically, and annoyingly, his brother, the Bleeding Heart, always ended up with more friends, more fun, more success. It was that hokey act of his, pretending he cared about everything and loved everyone. It impressed the gullible, and gained him a following, while his brother had nothing. That would not continue. That was over.

"I am the point man for the next generation," he whispered to himself, "I am the cutting edge." As he spoke the words, his hand dropped to caress an SRK Combat knife strapped to his side. "When the Earth is destroyed by storm and fire, none will be left but those like me. Then I will take my rightful place. I will lead the battle, and THEY WILL FOLLOW!"

He reached out to touch a stained leather strap lying on the table. The smooth feel of it still sent a shiver through him. Every time he viewed the strap, it stoked his power. Long ago, it had been used as an instrument of his imprisonment, but now it had become a symbol of his fulfillment—his fetter and his fetish.

This sorry piece of worn leather was one of the very straps that had held his own ten-year-old frame for his stepfather's arranged torture . . . held him face down and bent over as a group of men forced themselves into him, one after another. They did not deserve the title of "men," yet they lived in the world as if deserving of all things. What each of them had really deserved was horrible retribution, and eventually he had dispensed it to them.

Yet the greatest anger was reserved for someone much closer. It had been his mother, who watched in stony silence at the travesty, ignoring his tearful screams and entreaties. It was she, he believed, who had betrayed him the most. Grossly humiliated, torn and bleeding, his hate was all that sustained him. With each driving onslaught of pain, his rage grew. He found that in the rage was power. The attackers and watchers were all drunken fools. They thought they were proving their metal, showing their wildness and rejection of societal norms, but they were only engaging in decadence. Even as they had tried to diminish him and his power, he was sucking their own energy from them, and planning their demise. Internally, He was able to transform everything. He would survive.

He could trace a gradual evolution in his reactions. When his anger began, it was all heat, dissipating as heat always does. But when there was no rescue, no quarter, the anger seemed to freeze into a cold fury. That rage finally crystallized into a frigid wrath that still held form within him today, so many years later. It was an ice sculpture with the shape of vengeance.

The hospital had kept him imprisoned for seven days, after he was dumped there, bleeding and mute, by the woman. She warned that if he contradicted her counterfeit story of a gang-related racial attack he would not survive coming home. So, he never went home. How much of him survived, was a matter over which there could have been differing opinions.

The number seven eventually took on symbolic power. Everything came out in sevens. He was hospitalized for seven days, the same number, he noted, that it supposedly took for creation by an all-powerful deity . . . all powerful except when it came to answering the desperate prayers of a child being tortured past all sane limits. A perfect seven years later, he carried out the oath of his covenant and exterminated all seven of them. Six men . . . and her. He arranged special treatment for her, as was warranted. The men were perverted cretins, with uncontrolled male impulses. She had no such excuses. She was supposed to be his mother, his protector and safe harbor. Children had to have faith in their mothers. There was no higher sacred trust. To break this trust was the highest order of betrayal, the ultimate sacrilege.

Yet she gave him up. She broke the bonds of motherhood and family. She sacrificed him to the vicious drunken animals. Her fear and weakness made her need the man more than anything—even more than her own son. She abandoned the boy to his degrading and humiliating torture. So that day, strapped to the stinking chair, he stepped away mentally and spiritually . . . away from this world and this horror long enough to make a vow and a take on an all-consuming mission. It was a bond of unbreakable strength, forged in the depths of pain and fashioned of pure rage. That day "The Survivor" was born, though it was years before he walked into the jungle with an M-16 in his hands and murder in his soul. It would be a long time until he learned his role as "point man" for a new race of victors and gained an honored and feared title from those who recognized his true nature. In his suffering and desperate anger, a creature of darkness and wrath was born that would grow to revenge himself upon the weak and uncommitted.

He spent the next seven years refining himself, purifying his resolve and honing his skills. While his simpleton of a brother was going to schools and parties and movies, The Survivor was crawling through sewer pipes and alleys at night . . . watching, learning. It was a course in human frailty, and how it could be exploited. Eventually he began striking out at the common mass. He took things. He took from girls and boys, men and women. He shattered their stupid trust in goodness and light. He took their sex, he took their illusions, and then, finally, when he was hardly fully grown, from one of them he took life itself.

When he stepped up to this new level, it was in response to an inner need for further stimulation. His rape technique was now so long perfected, he almost found it absent of challenge. Then he stumbled upon an opportunity. He came unexpectedly upon an old man in a deserted warehouse. The man was a nobody, a derelict, worth nothing. The remote building was seldom visited and far from any habitation . . . a place where no one would see or hear anything that happened. What did happen was a new level of letting-go—a release and exorcism. What happened was something much better than rape. The derelict must have been living in the fatigued old shell of a building for some time, but alcohol, sickness, or exposure had reduced him to a shivering, stinking wretch. When The Survivor chanced upon him in a nightly foray, the man elicited only disgust. Then, in some foggy-minded miscalculation, the sorry piece of refuse made the mistake of invoking God against the intruder. He called on the name of his divinity to guard him.

"Oh Jesus, oh Christ," the disgusting creature called out, vainly, "Oh God help me… oh God, oh God"

Instead of summoning protection, the bum's entreaty called up a small part of the rage that had entered the dirty shelter in the corporal form of The Survivor. How dare this piece of offal invoke a God against me? The Survivor did not acknowledge a Divine Being. If there was such a God, he would have answered the prayers of a tortured boy who called out to him in pain and anguish. In any case, any god that might exist had no power here. This was the dark side, the realm of The Survivor. He would show the dung heap of a human what power was . . . the very power of life and death. So that is what he did.

He used a baseball bat the first time.

Several more times during the next two years, he experienced his potency in this way, rehearsing the skills of death dealing, until he was ready to settle old scores. He was ready to find the ones who had first betrayed his childhood trust. He was pleased when he found that he could approach four of them together, drinking and playing cards. He found them and delivered their fate. This time he had a weapon much more effective than a bat. When the bullet-riddled bodies were found, the police and newspapers put it down to a war between drug dealers. He had helped that theory along by dropping several small bags of cocaine around the carnage.

He took out number Five by torching the man's house, watching the flames all night from a distant rooftop as they devoured the building and the mutilated corpse within. He felt great spiritual energy flow from the burning structure . . . a massive funeral pyre and beacon to the world. He finished off his stepfather, number Six, in a more personal hit-and-run, using a car hijacked for the occasion. He took pleasure in the paralyzed pose of terror that the man held, as the car bore down on him, mouth distorted in an almost comical grimace of horror. Hopefully, the man recognized the smiling face of his stepson before the collision. The rivulets of blood that streamed over the windshield were quite stimulating as well. It was so satisfying that the Survivor held the pleasure warmly in his chest for years. On one occasion, he was even able to partially recreate that stimulating pleasurable warmth. That occasion was quite recently, when he used a vehicle to crush the naked and powerless McSwain boy. The boy was too soft to join the cadre of survivors—a hanger-on and a whiner. It was also necessary to teach the aristocratic parents a lesson. They had been warned that generous political contributions were a necessary guarantee of their son's security, but they didn't understand. They didn't think it was a life-or-death imperative. They did not believe or put their trust in him. They should have trusted his power. Misplaced trust always pays a price.

That is why, years before, he finally completed the mystic number Seven by going after the woman who had once claimed the title of his mother. She had put her complete trust in a man, beyond the fuzzy boundaries of her own self and soul. She had put her trust so completely in her man and master, that she betrayed the sacred bond between mother and child. The price had to be paid for this travesty. No need for finesse, he just walked through her unlocked front door one day and dragged her off. Of course she didn't die until later . . . much later.

When he finally taught her the consequences of her betrayal, he was mindful to use the same straps that had held him as a youngster—those symbolic thongs of anguish and transformation. As much as possible, he wanted her to feel what he had endured that day long ago. Though he started by penetrating her with his enraged and engorged manhood, he knew that a simple sexual thrust was not nearly as destructive as the massive violation his own childhood body had endured, so he had to find instruments that could wound her as he had been wounded . . . tools appropriate to the job. He made do with a crowbar. When the blood was so bad he was afraid she would not live much longer, he carefully explained it all to her again, his face down close to her gasping, moaning face.

"Thus you reap what you have sowed," he whispered. Then he removed her heart. She didn't really deserve one. So it was that she died. And as was intended, he survived.

Chapter 23

Gil's heart was nearly beating out of his chest. If the current scenario was an intentional seduction attempt or not, he couldn't honestly tell. If planned, she was doing a great job . . . it was working. He had come back to the Center to get the sample he needed for the DNA "preview" Shig Higawa had proposed. That much had been successful, even relatively easy. During Gil's latest interview with Storm, a female assistant had been waiting on the man, attending to his every need. That included bringing him water, massaging his shoulders and at one point, even grooming the leader's striking silver hair. She returned the brush and other instruments she had used to a nearby bathroom. When the interview ended, the woman ushered Storm out of the room, down a narrow stairway to some lower level. Before she returned a few minutes later to gather her tools, Gil had stepped into the bathroom. He quickly located the implements in a glass cabinet, lifting some grayish tufts of hair from the brush. The vital, perhaps damning, fibers were now in an envelope inside his jacket pocket. He had remembered not to place them in a plastic bag, which the lab boys had told him could cause some types of specimens to deteriorate. They always used paper—even when bagging hands of a corpse.

What was more of a concern to Gil now, was that his jacket and the rest of his clothes were hanging in a distant closet. He was stretched out on a futon, nearly naked, while being stroked on the chest by one of the most beautiful women he had ever seen. It was Selene, of course.

The movement toward this state of . . . affairs, had not been all at once, blatant. In fact, he never had the feeling of making a real choice. He didn't remember everything, but there had been a succession of small steps that got him here. Selene had not invited him to have sex, or anything so obvious. It was just another "relaxation" session in the natural relaxation module. This time, he hadn't been quick enough in his change from street clothes to the robe. She had caught a glimpse of his scarred chest. He recalled her soft voice reacting.

"Ummm, you must have suffered greatly."

"It looks worse than it is . . . Shrapnel, is all. The war, you know," he lied easily, having used the story before.

Selene didn't answer, but the way her eyes drilled into him, was unnerving. Did she know he was lying? He was ready to blurt out more detail, but realized he was about to fall prey to one of his own favorite techniques. Silence was a great inquisitor. It hung heavy for a few long minutes. Then she smiled.

"Many of us carry scars. I too, have been wounded."

"I see you have a tattoo needle job on your arm there."

She frowned, at his attempt to avoid her obvious meaning.

"That is merely the mark of wholeness," she brushed aside his attempt to redirect her penetrating conversation. "Darkness and light joined together, joy and sadness, male and female."

As she said "male," her eyes dropped as if in modesty. Still, her gaze lingered right in the direction of his crotch. When she said "female" it seemed to him that her chest swelled, pushing the breasts forward.

"I have real wounds, as do you," she continued, eyes raising again, to lance him with their smoldering intensity.

Gil didn't know how to respond, but he felt like he had to say something. She had broken the silence. It was almost like she had made an offering. Up to this point, he had responded insensitively. For once, it was intentional. Now she was making personal disclosures, holding out a glimpse of her hidden self . . . more than he had been willing to do.

"Emotionally?" he asked, then regretted it, since it sounded so stupid when the words came out of his mouth.

"That too," she nodded. Then she undid something near her waist and opened her robe. Several patches of puckered skin on the right side of her abdomen, just below the rib cage, were evidence of major damage in the past—looked like bullet wounds. However, his eyes didn't center there for several moments, as pulling open the garment also exposed her body, naked beneath the robe. Despite their own shiny protest, the scars could not seriously detract from the impact of that stunning torso. To describe it, was to fall short of the experience. Every detail, from the way her graceful neck joined her body, to the soft curve of her stomach muscles, the swell of her breasts, the firm legs and gently rounded hips, each contributed to the effect.

Gil had trouble breathing.

Selene's hand brushed her scars, as if that was all she was exhibiting, letting the simple garment fall to the floor. In another context, it might have seemed more deceptive, a hypocritical display intended only to reveal her body. Given the Naturalist's belief about nudity, however, it was entirely possible that she was habitually uninhibited about stripping. She had said as much, earlier. He didn't want to be boorish, by overreacting or commenting on her nakedness. Yet he didn't know how to respond to her wounded torso, either. He hardly wanted to get into discussion of his own patterned chest and history, with all the potential traps that could blow his cover. It would take a lot of explanation to describe how those scars had been formed. Furthermore, any comment on her body seemed like it would, itself, be an intimacy; almost like verbally touching that extremely appealing body. Was that wrong? Before he came up with anything reasonable to say, she filled the silence with her soft voice.

"We have an herbal salve here, for this kind of blemish. It is rare to meet a Survivor without some marks of the journey. Storm says that the salve not only fades the external scars but has a soothing effect on the inner ones as well."

She moved to a wall cabinet, taking out a small round jar. Gil was so mesmerized by the movement of her lithe body, he didn't utter a sound. She came closer to where he sat, balanced on cushions beside the steaming hot tub. With a light pressure on his shoulder, she made him lie down on his back. Her breasts were firm and full, with large peach-colored nipples. He had trouble keeping his eyes off them, swinging slightly over him, as she reached to pull open his robe.

That's where he found himself now. You could also say he was finding himself over his head.

She leaned over him, dabbing the salve on his chest, rubbing it slowly into the skin. With each stroke of her delicate fingers, tingles radiated through his body and his resistance to her was drained another ounce. He couldn't believe this was happening. He couldn't believe he wasn't doing anything to stop it. It was like a fantasy made real.

Still, even in the middle of the dream, he knew it was an illusion. There were consequences to this course of action. Prices were waiting to be paid for this. And the repercussions were more expensive than he could afford. He knew he had to stop before it went further. Yet so far, he hadn't been able to act on that knowledge. He tried to get his logic to help.

First, he reminded himself that he didn't even know if this was truly a sexual come-on. Maybe a romantic response on his part would be a shocking faux pas. He really didn't know the rules in this place. There were whole societies where nudity was accepted, but promiscuity frowned upon. Maybe it was a "look but don't touch" situation.

Second, even if Selene was offering herself to him, it would be a very bad idea to accept. There was the investigation to consider. If he ever had to use his discoveries in making a case, a sexual liaison could really, well . . . screw things up, you might say. He could picture a courtroom scene, with a defense attorney cross-examining him. "And what did you do, after you obtained the evidence, Detective Beach? Isn't it true that you got your brains screwed out by a nubile groupie of the agency in question?"

Furthermore, Gil asked himself, should this scenario play itself out fully and the truth got publicized, what would it do to his marriage? All this ran through his head but didn't seem to result in any movement at all. Well, there was some movement, but all that was doing was making a little tent of the last flap of cloth still covering his crotch.

Get down, you traitor! I've got to get out of here, before life gets very, very complicated.

Selene was still leaning across his body, her naked hip near his groin. She brushed against the pesky erection, then directed her eyes to where it was pushing up eagerly. His face felt even more flushed than before.

"Don't be embarrassed, Daniel. It is quite natural, you know. I'm glad you are pleased. Surely, you know that I am attracted to you as well."

That did it. No question now, about her intentions. It was time to fish or cut bait. The only question was how he was going to field it. Would he do what he was supposed to do—get the hell out of there, or continue to let himself drift into sensual dream land? Would he let nature take its seductive course, even if it would come back to haunt him later?

And still . . . he did nothing.

Selene leaned over, touching her full lips to his. Smoothness, warmth, and the taste of spices clouded his thoughts. A small hand slipped beneath his robe to delicately touch him between the legs, as a soft and warm breast flattened against his chest. That is when it went wrong. If it hadn't been for her perfume, he probably would have simply pulled the woman over on top of him, letting inhibitions and body fluids fly. His pelvis ached in anticipation. The one discordant note was her perfume. That fragrance wasn't just any scent. It was "Marigolds."

Though not the most current fad in fragrances, this aroma was one of the few that Gil could recognize by smelling it. The reason this one was so familiar, was that it was his wife, Pilar's, favorite—her trademark scent, manufactured by Estee.

The touch of Selene's mouth, breast, and hand combined to send a jolt of sensation through his frame. The stimulation exploded into energy that had to be converted into movement. Gil could have moved toward her, wanted to move into her, but instead he moved away from the touch. It was one of those situations where you never know exactly why you choose the way you do. Maybe if she had called him by his real name, he might have been able to carry off the fantasy, but as it was, she called him by his alias, "Daniel." Then he smelled the familiar scent of that perfume—Pilar's perfume! His wife! Together, the two reminders were finally enough to break through the sensual pull. He rolled to the side and jumped to his feet. As he wrapped the robe tightly around himself, he couldn't help wondering if he was being very smart or incredibly stupid.

"I'm sorry," he stammered, "I'm . . . I'm not ready for this." His mind raced for a justification that wouldn't blow his cover. "My . . . my wife died recently, he extemporized. I guess I haven't quite let her go. Maybe another time. I don't know. I hope this doesn't offend you. You are beautiful . . . gorgeous . . . and kind. But I have to go."

"Don't be upset, Daniel. I understand. We don't judge people here. You are accepted as you are. If you want, we can be together in a physical way, but if you aren't ready, that's fine too. We can still share mind and spirit. And my body will always be here, if you should change your mind. Come back soon, Daniel. I knew you were special from the first. That's why I chose to share my scars with you. That's why I will share more if you want me to."

CHAPTER 24

"We've had a b-b-break-in!"

Helen sounded upset on the phone.

After leaving the Nature Center, Gil had driven up to the Bronx Zoo, where he walked around for an hour, lost in thought, fantasy, and a certain amount of frustration. It was a favorite place for him to organize his thoughts. Strolling along the winding paths, surrounded by various kinds of animals in and outside the cages, he was able to maintain a sense of detachment that he couldn't manage elsewhere. After watching the big cats for an intent half-hour, he felt better. Seeing the massively muscled tigers and lions quietly resting their powerful bodies somehow was soothing. He still wasn't quite his normal self, but somehow the sight of the powerful beasts calmed him. Gil could have gone home then but came back to the PDU instead. There was often an odd comfort in the grimy office, of a different sort than what he gained at the zoo. Here there was usually a secure feeling of familiar things and predictable activity . . . a sense of fitting in with the worn equipment, the bustling movement, the special language of the law enforcement fraternity. Still, even this didn't work to quiet the funny ache in his gut. If it had been a different place or time, he might have sought out a flight of stairs to climb doggedly until exhausted. That is how he usually vanquished his demons. But when his phone rang, he welcomed the chance to keep his mind busy. He hadn't expected it to be from Helen.

"Hi Gil. We got a little problem. Somebody broke into the Youth Bureau Offices last night.

"Yeah, so why are you calling me, instead of Burglary?"

"Because I think they were after the tapes."

"Tapes?"

"Well, not literally tapes. The voice recordings from our interviews of Nina. Do you have them?"

"Oh yeah. Well, Pilar has them," he explained, swallowing a vague taste of guilt at the thought of his wife and how close he had been to cheating on her. He had almost forgotten her suggestion about the psychology operating in this case. "She thinks the kid may be one of those multiple personalities—you know like Sybil? So I asked her to listen to the recordings, to see what she could make of them. That isn't a problem is it?"

"No, no . . . that's fine. Now that you mention it, the idea of the personality thing makes sense, doesn't it? But look Gil, whoever broke into the Youth Bureau office last night has to have s hell of a lot of chutzpah, right? I mean sometimes the place is deserted, but it is connected to the Department, right? A lot of the staff members are cops. Didn't stop `em—whoever they were. They made off with the old lockbox we got in the closet. It's basically a safe. Must weigh a ton. Took the whole thing."

"You don't think they were after money?"

"No way. No money in that old monstrosity but it was the only thing missing. If this was a standard B & E, they would have grabbed our electronic gear, the computer, and some cash I had in my bottom drawer. The safe even had a label that said, `no cash to be kept here.' The only things we stored in there, were a few records, mostly of interviews and interrogations."

"You think that whoever broke-in, knew that?"

"Yeah, Gil, I do. What else could it mean? And since there's only one set of recordings that we've made recently, don't you think maybe that's what they were after?"

"It's possible, I guess, but I'd hold off on jumping to conclusions. There are a lot of possible explanations for a break-in. Not every scenario is another Watergate. Don't assume you can guess exactly what the thieves knew or didn't know. Did you call in the techs?"

"Yes, but I don't expect much. Whoever did this, took most of the evidence with them. We have a report of a repair truck parked outside last night, so they probably did it that way."

“Right. I guess the big question is who `They’ are. Well, anyway, thanks for letting me know. I’ll get those sessions back to you soon. Keep me posted.”

“Right. But Gil, if you haven’t done it yet, don’t forget to make an extra copy before you give ‘em back.”

CHAPTER 25

Larry "The Hump" Shamel had expected an easy trip.

He'd been jockeying eighteen-wheelers for a dozen years, so appreciated an occasional milk run when it came along. There had been a lot of the crappier jobs, the nut-busters. This truck wasn't literally an eighteen-wheeler, it was an eighteen wheeler, it was a twenty-two-wheel rig, with an extra axle and four tires to carry the additional weight, but it was still an easy job. As long as you follow procedures, a truckload of radioactive waste isn't much more trouble than an empty rig. No loading, no off-loading, no sweat. Running the barrels from the nuclear power plant was the best paying job he got. It wasn't steady, but whenever he picked up a load from Indian Point, the job added a nice piece of change to the weekly check. It had already helped pay for Larry Jr.'s braces. His wife, Sally, didn't mind the extra time he was away from home, since it was only occasionally, and made a big difference with the bills. Larry wasn't aware that she had other reasons for appreciating his absences.

The only drawback for Larry, was that he wasn't allowed to work alone, as he would have preferred. It was uncomfortable having another driver that he didn't know well, but those were the regs for nuke hauling. Hoagy Benson was no prize either, smelling up the cab, smoking like a chimney. Luckily the run was almost over.

"Shee-it, Hump, I could use a beer right now," Benson complained in his nasal Tennessee accent, chucking a butt out the window, despite the dry grass along the roadway. Larry didn't like the man using his nickname. It was a play on the idea that 'Shamel' sounds like 'Camel,' which has a…hump. That familiarity was reserved for friends, but he decided not to get into it at the moment.

"Not on this run, Hoagy. But we have to stop up ahead for a D.O.T. check. Our log is good. While their scratching their asses with the paperwork, we could at least grab a Coke."

"Fuck the Coke. I already done my leg, bud. I ain't drivin' no more on this trip. So you drink the fuckin' Coke, I'm gettin' me a nice cold Coors."

Larry was surprised at the other man's strong reaction but didn't press the point. He knew that if anybody caught him, Benson's ass would be in a sling. The whole idea of the extra driver was to be ready as a back-up in case of emergency. They called it "riding shotgun" like in the old west. There was no real shotgun, but it amounted to the same thing—somebody awake and ready to handle emergencies. Then again, he wasn't about to get in a fight with the redneck asshole. It looked like the man loved his beer so much, it might come down to that. The guy looked all flushed and uptight. Larry had no time for such nonsense. At least he was glad Benson hadn't hit the bottle before his turn at the wheel.

"Well then, Hoagy, I'm takin' first break at the checkpoint. One of us is always supposed to stay with the rig, and I'll be damned if I sit on my tuckus while you get snoggered."

"Shee-it, it'd take more than a coupla beers to get me tanked. I kin hold my likker. But suit yerself, bud, I just wanna wet the old whistle a bit."

When their twenty-two-wheel International Eagle truck pulled into the Department of Transportation checkpoint before the Mid-Hudson Bridge, Larry headed for the restroom, while the other driver started to check the rig. Hoagy glanced at the greasy plate-like metal slab called the "Fifth Wheel" that formed the connection between trailer and cab. The trailer's king-pin was firmly locked into its jaws. Last week Hoagy had hit the pin high when he was connecting another rig. The foreman had caught the error, or Benson would have driven out with the trailer just balanced on the fifth wheel, instead of being locked in place. That could have been a disaster. But no harm, no foul, Hoagy believed. As soon as Shamel was out of sight, the flushed and jittery man opened a side utility case, from which he extracted a pint bottle of Old Kentucky sour mash whiskey. Draining the half-filled container in two long swallows, Hoagy chucked the bottle over a fence and headed for the restaurant. He was supposed to wait for Larry, but he couldn't understand why he should wait on a powerful thirst, just so the Yankee bastard could sip pisswater soda pop.

In the ten minutes that the rig was unguarded, a furtive figure slipped up to the truck, tools in hand. He had followed the truck for hours, waiting for just such an opportunity. His work didn't take long. All he had to do was to connect a thin cable. He fastened one end of the cable to the loop-shaped handle that allows a trailer's kingpin to disengage from the fifth wheel's locking jaws. At the other end, a small hook was welded. Laying the cable loosely in place, he knew it would only be a matter of time, before it jostled loose, allowing the cable to drop and the hook to find a place to catch on something. He also had time to back off the air pressure on all of the brakes except the first axle.

When Larry returned to the rig and found Benson missing, he was so angry that he didn't think to make his own inspection of the rig before they headed out again. The added piece of cable had no immediate effect, nor did the reduced braking power. Things started to come apart just as they hit the Cross-Bronx Expressway. The newly attached line worked free, dropping the grappling hook to bounce along under the trailer, a wild and snapping snake looking for somewhere to bite. Soon it flipped around the second axle. There was a screech and twang, as the axle wound up the line like a massive fishing reel. The taut cable then yanked the pin handle out of its place with a sound like a bullet being fired from a rifle.

The conventional long-nose cab continued to move forward at forty-seven miles an hour, as the trailer's kingpin disengaged, bouncing off the large flat fifth wheel. The service lines snapped like tiny, coiled threads. Unhampered by forty tons of haulage, the International Eagle model 9370 was propelled forward by its 425 horsepower engine: a workhorse suddenly free of the plow. Behind it, the nose of the trailer dropped to the pavement. Trailers generally have two bracing columns or jacks, jutting down near the front end of the trailer, used to support and lift it, as necessary. Drivers call them the "landing gear," as if they were the wheeled mechanisms that airplanes used to hit the ground and taxi to a stop. In this case, the trailer could have used that kind of gear, but the standard equipment was not equal to the task. The four-inch diameter supports are actually just simple jacks, with small metal coasters or no wheels at all. They are not designed to support a loaded trailer traveling at high speed. Instead, they burrowed into the asphalt surface like twin plows through a soft spring field. As they dug in, the tremendous force and weight immediately caused them to collapse, dropping the nose of the trailer onto the pavement. This created a great cascade of sparks and contributed to a wildly unpredictable path of travel. The automatic air brakes played practically no role, since their pressure had been released earlier.

The loaded truck body slewed ponderously to the side, smashing into a median divider. The nose drove into a low concrete pylon. A vehicle weighing over eighty thousand pounds, does not stop easily. Jammed down and caught at the front, the truck bed continued forward, momentum lifting it into the air, as if it were pole vaulting. The huge metal box flipped completely over to crash upside down on the road surface. The corrugated metal trailer split open, spewing heavy lead-lined barrels across the lanes. The containers bounced and rolled in weighty slow motion until they smashed into other vehicles like oversized cannonballs—the radioactive metal inside heavier than lead. Radioactive waste containers are manufactured to withstand great stress, so despite the stunning damage they inflicted, few of them lost their own essential integrity. Only three vessels sustained cracks to their outer shells, though five automobiles and their human vessels were not as fortunate. Eighteen vehicles were wrecked, twenty-seven persons injured, and eight died. One of the dead was Larry Shamel. He hardly saw it coming.

When he felt the jolting lurch of the separating trailer, Larry had managed to stop the truck cab. A few hundred feet along the road, he stepped down to view what happened, only to see great heavy barrels skipping in his direction. Although he avoided being taken out by the barrels, Larry couldn't get out of the way of a Chrysler minivan that seemed to come out of nowhere. The boxy vehicle had arrived at the scene just as it's driver, Earl "The Pearl" Maggowski, had decided to light a cigarette. Due to this moment of inattention, Earl didn't notice the pile-up directly in his path, until he was only fifty yards away, traveling at sixty-eight miles per hour. A vehicle traveling that fast, covers almost exactly a hundred feet per second, so Earl had less than three seconds to understand the situation, make a decision, react, and take evasive action. It wasn't enough. The minivan hardly slowed, before plowing into a low sports car and two heavy barrels, flipping three times before it came to a stop with Larry underneath. He and Earl were two of the eight that died.

Hoagy was unhurt. Although his drunken state led to accusations, Benson claimed that he only got inebriated later, as an emotional result of the accident and the loss of a friend, not prior to the incident. There was so much confusion at the scene, his story held up. Which is to say it couldn't be disproved. Most folks found it hard to believe that Benson had any friends.

Several blocks of the Bronx had to be evacuated, while federal officials inspected the three cracked barrels. In that section of the city, the displacement was limited, since most of the adjacent buildings were abandoned structures. There are those who would like the entire south Bronx evacuated, but in this case, it was only a few blocks, and temporary. The closing of the Cross-Bronx Expressway for twelve hours was also a disruption to the lives of many New Yorkers. Traffic tie-ups and rerouting cost thousands of work hours, numerous missed appointments, and lost tempers.

If you wanted to find a positive note, the net loss of life due to the incident was reduced by one, when a child was born to Minnie Colon-Sanchez as she sat in her Chrysler station wagon a quarter of a mile from the Parkchester exit, locked in the traffic jam on her way to the hospital.

In the papers, the incident was portrayed as a near nuclear disaster, though ultimately no radioactive contamination occurred as a result of the crash. The three cracked barrels were sealed on site, then rushed to a federal disposal center. The other containers continued their journey in a new truck. It was days before the sabotage was identified. Federal officials managed to keep that part quiet, while they conducted a lengthy investigation. As sometimes happens in politically difficult cases, nobody in New York ever heard the results of the inquiry. A citizen's action group was formed," Citizens Against Nuclear Transport" (CAN'T), to protest the trucking of radioactive waste through populated areas of the city. They demanded and duly received a meeting with their elected Senator, Mark Delucia, who vowed to represent their concerns in Washington. The next public opinion poll concerning the senatorial race showed Delucia, the outspoken environmentalist, gaining a welcome one and a half percentage points over his rival.

Chapter 26

A week after the incident, in an Upper East Side restaurant, two powerful men with connections to the Senator were having an intense discussion.

"This guy Beach is getting too curious."

"It's no big thing. I can squash the whole thing. I have an appointment with a Deputy Inspector today."

"Which one?" Randall questioned, chewing a toothpick rapidly so it flicked up and down around the edges of his mouth.

"What's-his-name, you know . . . the big Mick that supposedly cleaned up the Ninth a couple years back."

"You mean Mabry? Clean up? What is he, a straight arrow?" The toothpick was being gnashed to fuzzy splinters.

"Naw, it was just politics. Remember that asshole Lincoln? He screwed everything up, trying to score points. Fell on his butt, and Mabry was in a position to look squeaky-clean. Somebody always benefits from a fall. But what Irish cop came up from the ranks and doesn't know the game? I say stick with the Mick." The man chuckled at his own wit. "He'll play."

"You need to find out where Beach is getting his information. There's a leak somewhere. The Senator doesn't want to get tied up with damage control after the fact."

"What about Roger?"

"What about him?"

"You and he don't always see eye to eye."

"That's not your concern. Just follow your orders and leave internal matters to those who can handle them." Randall was glancing at his watch again, a standard signal that he was anxious to move on to other affairs.

The other man narrowed his eyes. His mouth opened, as if he were about to speak, but apparently thought better of it. He said nothing, picked up his attaché case, and left the room.

Then Randall moved to the telephone, spitting out the mashed toothpick, punched in a number, and waited, fingers drumming where they rested on the wall.

"Hello . . . Yeah, it's me. I want it taken care of. Uncle agrees. Find out where the cop is getting his information. Find the leak and seal it."

Chapter 27

Pilar looked up at the expansive facade of the Federation's Central Headquarters, noting the Latin phrase there. SALUS MUNDI SUPREMA LEX ESTO.

"Let the . . . welfare of the world be the . . . supreme law" she translated, trying to remember which philosopher had written the phrase. A noble enough motto, she mused, but wondered how many interpretations there could be for the phrase "welfare of the world." One person's welfare might be somebody else's loss.

"I suspect that the Ayatollah might have a slightly different reading than the Pope," she mumbled to herself.

Pilar's optimism was not what it used to be. Her "accident" had been a part of that change. It hadn't actually been an accident at all. It was an intentional attempt on her life, by a killer that was really after Gil. A bullet aimed at her forehead had glanced off her skull, but another intended for her belly had found its mark. That one had done so much violence to body and soul, she had wondered at times, if she would ever be the same. The wounds had finally mended, but her view of life had darkened. Out of her mental shadows, a half-formed thought appeared. If she had never fallen in love with Gil Beach, Detective Supreme, Challenger of Maniacs, and Confronter of evil, things might have turned out . . .

Pilar shook her head, to derail the thought. It wasn't a useful type of thinking. It stirred up too much inside. Psychologist or not, she resisted that turmoil. She didn't want to feel angry; she didn't want to feel wounded, and she didn't want to feel dependent. That was part of the motivation for her work with environmental causes. When she followed her heart in this area, she felt effective, independent, and confident that she was making a positive contribution.

The Federation represented something of a departure from her mainline environmental concerns—a dalliance in new and tricky waters. This guy Storm had ties to the radical right, the survivalist movement, which at its extremes could approach a millenialist psychosis. Environmentalism and Survivalism—where do bird watchers find common ground with gun collectors? How welcome are the defenders of the snail darter's habitat in the enclaves of the those who have been known to even resist the rule of society's law?

Her trip to the Center was not fully planned-out. The audio recordings of the girl had intrigued her, but not as much as the stories about the Federation's leader. Her social worker friend, Rosemary, talked about this guy Storm like he was some incredible cross between Ralph Nader and Kevin Costner, with a little Jean Claude Van Damm and Jacques Cousteau mixed in. Roe had practically squirmed in her chair when she was describing him.

"Those eyes . . ." she crooned, "those eyes!" Pilar felt her jaw clench, as she thought about Gil meeting the famous man.

She admitted to herself, that she resented the fact her husband could come and go wherever he wanted without explanation. All he had to do was claim it had to do with a police investigation. That gave him almost unlimited options, and as much secrecy as he chose to have. Not that she didn't trust Gil, but much of the time she felt shut out. It felt unequal, it felt unfair. Still, instead of sulking, she was determined to take action. It wasn't like Pilar to back off from life, or from a challenge. The Federation's link to environmental issues, however tenuous, was only one rationale for her decision. There was also the matter of the child, Nina, who might be an unrecognized and untreated multiple personality. If Pilar got a chance to meet a certain notable charismatic figure in the course of her inquiries, so much the better.

There was plenty of talk around campus about the Federation and its larger-than-life leader, yet the man didn't seem to be capitalizing on the notoriety. That was reassuring. The notoriety probably could have brought him droves of volunteers and plenty of donations, if properly exploited. Apparently, no such effort had been made. The so-called "Public Information Gathering" that she was about to visit, was not really public at all. You attended only by invitation, which required an interview by the Center's permanent staff. Whatever else, she had to admit, they didn't seem interested in gaining numbers alone.

The 'interview' had been strange. She was used to formal job interviews, certification panels, and oral examinations. She wasn't prepared for a handsome man dressed in Eddie Bauer flannel shirt and khakis, talking to her over coffee as they lounged on futons, being relaxed by gentle music and spicy odors of incense and unidentified fragrances. On the other hand, it had been a very pleasant experience. The man seemed genuinely interested in her and her life, which seemed a nice change. As much as possible, she steered the conversation away from her husband's profession, which she described as "government research." In a way that was essentially accurate. She found herself being remarkably open, however, about her history and hopes. It made her realize how long since she had been to see her counselor, a savvy woman she had turned to often over the years. She was surprised at how much was lying just beneath the surface. Maybe she hadn't been coping as well as she would like to think.

"You've been on a long journey," the man had perceptively remarked. He made reference to "wounds" in a way that it could have meant either the ones her body had suffered, or the traumas that had blemished her psyche. She knew that both were permanent . . . just as permanent as the yin-yang tattoo she saw on his arm.

The man's assertive attitudes and self-assurance were striking. Pilar left the interview with determination and energy she hadn't felt in some time. When he placed his hands on her shoulders and looked straight into her eyes, she had almost felt his energy pouring into her. My goodness, those eyes! She also felt a stirring in her lower belly that embarrassed her. It was exhilarating in a way she could never tell Gil. Not that she intended to pursue anything forbidden—just that there were some interesting fantasies that she wasn't ready to share . . . or give up. She was looking forward to the Public Information Session that promised greater understanding of the "Way of Natural Selection," and how to be part of a "whole New World order." She hoped the same man would be there. She had assumed she was talking to the man everyone called 'Storm.' Only after she left did she realize that he hadn't ever mentioned his name. She wondered how many men were that humble or that self-assured.

Now, as she approached the marble stairs, she was less confident about her own plans. Gil probably would be upset with her. Usually, the two of them discussed things more than this. Lately though, there had been a puzzling reserve. Up until now, she had to admit to herself that she had taken some comfort in blaming him for the distance, though she recognized it was a bit unfair. The guys at the PDU called him "Gabby", as an ironic comment on his usual closed mouth style, but he had improved in his ability to communicate since getting labeled with that nickname. In their years together, she had taught him a lot about feelings and ways of expressing them. Still, the ability to communicate was different from the willingness to do so. It seemed like he would rather look at her with those sad hound-dog eyes, waiting for her to break the ice. Lately it had been as thick as a glacier. Pilar wasn't much interested in Arctic expeditions. She shrugged heavily, then entered the ornate entrance.

CHAPTER 28

"You went where?!" Gil exploded.

"Why are you upset?" Pilar countered.

"Because I'm involved in an investigation there! What in God's name do you think you're doing at that place?"

"I don't think God's name has anything to do with it. Why shouldn't I attend one of the public information sessions? I have as much right as anyone. I have many contacts and interests in this area of knowledge. Frankly, I have some interest in finding a greater personal wholeness as well. What if they could help me?"

"You've got to be kidding! You don't really believe all that natural healing bullshit, do you?" Gil realized from her look that he was crossing some line he shouldn't pass, so he tried to crank down the intensity.

"Look, Pilar. I suppose you're right; I don't know everything you need or what you don't. I'm glad you want to grow. But please, not at this sleazy place. We're talking about a very strange guy here, and something is definitely not kosher."

As he spoke, Gil was picturing his last visit, with the compromising situation he had been in; the seduction he had narrowly avoided. His mind conjured up images of Pilar walking in on him and Selene during a naked embrace, then his active imagination quickly created other mental pictures. In one, a heavily muscled, bronze skinned male was offering the same things to Pilar that Selene had offered Gil. Was it standard procedure to seduce the newcomer? He had been within a hairbreadth of succumbing. Would Pilar resist as he had? As it was, the incident had been a close call for him.

"I wonder if you realize how rigid you sound?" She continued, a set to her neck and shoulders that he recognized as her professional pose—stepping back and psychologizing him like one of her clients. No exposure of her own soft spots, no chinks in her armor for him to reach through and touch her.

"I suppose that's to be expected from someone with a family background like yours. It seems that your opinions of the path to wholeness are similarly prejudiced. I'm not a child, Gil. I'm perfectly capable of seeing through fakery and assessing the potential benefits or dangers of a relationship."

"Oh, it's a `relationship' now, is it? How far have you gone with this, Pilar?"

"Oh Please! Could you hold down the paranoia, just a little? I use words differently than you. To a psychologist any interaction is a relationship, even a negative one. I can tell you this much, I went far enough to strike up an acquaintance with your little friend, Nina."

Gil was stalled by this revelation. After a moment to cool down, he grudgingly asked her to tell him more about what happened. Pilar described meeting in a small group for the "Information Session." It had been a relaxed, social kind of gathering, she explained, with unusual drinks and refreshments that put everyone at ease. Nina had been one of the servers, though it took a while to identify her. When it dawned on Pilar that the girl was the same waif she heard on the recordings, she made an effort to introduce herself, hoping to develop the beginnings of rapport with the girl. Pilar was sure that the child was in one of her "alters" at the time, because there were signs of anxiety, combined with willingness to link with a stranger. That didn't match the behavior you would expect from what was probably her 'Master' personality's closed defenses.

"Honestly, Gil, I think I might elicit some new disclosures, perhaps even sneak her out of the Center at some point. What do you think about that?"

Gil had to re-evaluate his opposition in light of this development. His wife was right. The chance connection could be a real break if it was handled right. Personal problems aside, he knew that Pilar's psychological training could be invaluable. Besides, as she discussed this, she was displaying an attractive animation and new energy. He liked seeing the lively attitude returning to his wife.

"Okay," he capitulated, "You win. let's see if we can't cooperate on this."

She smiled, leaning over to give him a peck on the forehead.

Chapter 29

The next morning, Gil got up early, intending to make a stab at fixing the plumbing before he had to leave for work. The pesky toilet had been running continuously for days. He had finally finished installing a new valve—one of those simple jobs that ends up taking three times the effort you expect, when he heard the doorbell. Gil wiped his hands on a rag as he walked to a window, where he could view the stoop. Two men were at the door, dressed in cheap topcoats, opened to reveal dark sports jackets and conservative ties. They stood slightly to the side of the door, watching intently. The look gave them away. *Have to be cops.*

He glanced around. The place was a mess, but what the hell. Curious, he went to the door and opened it. The men smiled thinly while showing their I.D.

"Warren Schultz, I.A.B. This is Gary Benowitz."

A cold shiver knifed down Gil's spine. IAB meant Internal Affairs, the so-called "watchdogs." An IAB investigator called himself a "Field Associate." Some cops thought of them as rats and were likely to call them names like "Ben," or "Willard" after the rodent stars of certain horror movies. There is a tremendous allegiance among law enforcement personnel, forged out of shared duty, honor, fear, responsibility, and a feeling of being misunderstood by almost everyone else. That led to a strong sense of loyalty to their fellows in arms. Cops who would go after other cops were often considered traitors.

Gil tried not to have that knee-jerk reaction. He knew there were cops that needed to be investigated. He had worked with a few, and their corruption angered him. Still, a wave of revulsion swept over him when he heard the Division's title. Maybe it was partly fear. There was certainly a clutch of dread in his gut now that they had appeared at his door. Everybody knows that life is too complex to always have easy and obvious choices. Being a cop is even more challenging than most vocations. It is fraught with ambiguous situations and choices that are less often between good and evil than between the lesser of several equally distasteful evils. Somewhere along the line, everybody in this business did things that he or she would rather not have publicly examined. When the IAB knocked on your door, there was a distinct possibility that it might come to that.

"What's the problem?"

"No problem. We would just like to ask you a few questions."

"Save the B.S. for the civilians. IAB doesn't come on social calls. Tell me who you're investigating and why or get the hell out of here."

"We don't have to tell you jack shit, Beach. It's your duty to comply with our investigation, or you can be shit-canned for obstruction."

"Look, you're not dealing with some stupid jerk citizen, or a rookie here, Schultz. If you want information voluntarily, you make nice. If you want information by force, you can wait till my lawyer gets here."

"Check it out, Gary," the man called Schultz laughed, "another guy with a personal lawyer. Funny how most folks suddenly have a private lawyer the minute their ass is in a sling. Okay, if that's the way it's gonna be, Beach, then you tell your asshole shyster to find a break in his busy schedule of evictions and ambulance chasing. He can meet you at our office. You can come with us."

"Not unless I'm under arrest, I'm not, Gil barked, backing away. There was a moment of tense silence, the two men staring each other down like gunfighters on a dusty western street. The other Investigator finally broke the tension.

"C'mon, Warren. Let it go. And you . . . Beach. Bring your lawyer and be at our office at ten tomorrow morning." He grabbed lightly at the other man's sleeve. Schultz finally turned to stride stiffly out the door. Benowitz dropped a card on the table, with the notorious address, 71 Poplar Street, formerly home of the 84th Precinct, now the base of Internal Affairs.

Gil slammed the door behind the two investigators, to stand in frowning thought. Then he grabbed his phone, entering a familiar number.

"This is Beach," he nearly shouted, when the call was answered, "Gimme Mabry!" Bob Mabry had been Gil's "Rabbi", and he couldn't think of a better time to have a friend higher up in the Department. They didn't see one another that often since Mabry had been promoted but remained friends. As a Deputy Inspector, Mabry wasn't too entrenched in the corridors of power, having ascended more by good work and longevity than by connections and ambition. Still, he certainly had better contacts than Gil did, and was at a completely different level of access to information. Right now Gil needed some information badly, and it was information he could not get directly.

Mabry wasn't immediately available, so Gil left a message, spending a nervous twenty minutes waiting for the return call. When it finally came in, the conversation was brief. Mabry hadn't heard anything specific but said he would do some checking. He told Gil not to panic.

"Don't let the reputation of these palookas throw ya," the older cop advised him, in the characteristic loud voice that had earned him the nickname "Boom-Boom."

"They wear the badge just like everybody else, and aren't out to bring down a good cop. Like I always told ya, Gil, if you're clean, you got nothin' to sweat."

Somehow, Mabry's attempt to reassure him didn't do much to relieve Gil's anxieties. He had seen more than one case where political needs had dictated that somebody had to take a fall, and it ended up being some cop who didn't deserve that kind of finish. He thought of Pete Patowski, a good cop who went gaga over a secretary in the local Assemblyman's office named Adele. He really thought he was in love with Adele and the feeling was mutual. One thing led to another. They were discovered playing 'hide-the-salami' in the supply room one day. The spotlight of the resulting scandal revealed that there was something akin to a prostitution ring operating out of the office, with the Assemblyman's clear knowledge and participation. It had nothing to do with Pete and Adele, but it came to light in the process. The politician's part in the scandal, however, never saw the light of day. The whole thing got completely reversed, with the crooked Assemblyman spearheading an investigation of the local precinct instead of being held up to the light of criticism himself.

Pete and another cop without VIP connections got selected as the sacrificial lambs. They were suspended, then finally terminated, supposedly for purchasing the services of a prostitute during work time. Pete hadn't believed that the politicians could do it. He loved the girl, for God's sake, and he loved his job. His biggest objection to the whole process was that she had been characterized as a whore. Sure, they had been a little outlandish to make love in the office, but it wasn't exactly a crime. When the brass took away his badge, Pete had this funny look of disbelief for weeks. Then his partner got a call. Pete had "swallowed his gun". It took three coats of paint to cover the stain where his brains had splattered.

Gil liked Mabry but didn't see things quite the same as the Administrator. He knew that as far as Mabry was concerned, the N.Y. Police Department and the Catholic Church were pretty much of the same status. You stood by them. They might have problems, but it was practically an unforgivable sin to lose your faith in them. Beach respected this attitude but wasn't able to give his pure trust that easily. He made a couple of calls, managing finally to get the name of a PBA lawyer by the name of Langfield. The lawyer wasn't in his office, so he left a number where he could be reached. He wondered why it was so easy to find an accuser, but so hard to find a defender.

CHAPTER 30

Pilar felt as if Nina was getting less defensive and beginning to relax with her. Of course, that only meant whichever "Nina" she was dealing with now. The puppy had been the real breakthrough. There had been several breakthroughs—and as it turned out, they weren't only for the girl.

Pilar had returned to the Center to continue her observations. This required her to assume the role of a volunteer worker. As an initial step of her volunteer service commitment, she was allowed to perform some of the duties around the place, including cleaning the nature displays, serving organic meals and doing maintenance of the relaxation modules. When she found herself working alongside Nina, she used the occasions to nurture what seemed like a building level of trust. With the ruse of needing guidance to find a local delicatessen, she managed to get the girl outside the Center for a few minutes. As fate or God or coincidence would have it, depending on your point of view, a young man was set up outside the deli with a cardboard box full of adorable puppies to be given away. The little fuzzballs whined for attention, licked anything that got within reach of their tiny pink tongues, and nearly wagged off their tiny furry butts, with the blur of energetic miniature tails.

Nina was infatuated. Her girlish gasps of delight and bubbling laughter were the first natural display of emotion that Pilar had seen from the child. It only took a moment to decide which puppy to purchase. One of the cute pups had little marks above its eyes that looked like eyebrows, curving inward to create an appealing sad expression. The pup never seemed to take its eyes off the child, or vice versa. When Pilar pulled out the twenty dollars that seemed to be the going rate for a mixed breed mutt, however, the girl had a strange reaction, showing a complex transformation. Her face registered surprise, amazement, longing, then flattened into blankness. Pilar could see what was coming.

"Ohhhh. Uhhhh . . . that is so kind of y . . . Ummmh," he child struggled to say. Then, after a brief pause, in clipped tones, "She cannot have a domesticated animal. They are not allowed in the Center."

"I can tell that you don't want her to get in trouble," Pilar tested the new personality that had taken over the girl. "You take care of her, don't you?"

"Yes, of course," replied the child in priggish tones, "Someone has to."

"I'm sure you are very capable," Pilar agreed. Then she took a risk, asking the troubled child, "What do you call yourself, dear?"

There was a critical moment of hesitation, the girl staring penetratingly at the woman, before she spoke. Finally, with a small sigh, she said, "I am Theodora."

Pilar nodded, “That means ‘Gift of God,’ doesn’t it?”

“I don’t know. Why?”

“No reason. But I think Nina is very fortunate to have you.”

“She is not a fortunate girl.”

“But of course she is, Theodora. She has you. And now she has a puppy, too. If it isn’t allowed in the Center, I can keep it for her . . . for you. It can be yours. I mean Nina’s, but I’ll take care of it when you aren’t able.”

After a long silence, the personality named Theodora nodded. She ignored Pilar’s somewhat clumsy merging of two identities.

“I suppose then, that she can have it.” She closed her eyes as she turned away. The child shuddered like someone after a relieving urination, lowered herself to a kneeling position for a moment, then turned back to Pilar. Now her eyes were wide and her mouth open in gape of awe. Nina had again emerged.

“Oh! Oh! He’s so darling! What shall we call him?” Grabbing up the furry wiggler, she hugged and nuzzled it as if there would never be enough.

“Well, he’s yours, Theo . . . Nina. What would you like to call him?”

The child frowned in concentration. She thought for several minutes before announcing her choice.

"We shall call him 'Genny' I think."

"How nice, Nina. Where did you think of a name like that?"

"Well, Genny is short for General. I think that Generals are more important than soldiers, isn't that right? We mustn't ever let the soldiers see Genny."

"The soldiers?"

"Yes, the Troops. They are the important ones in the Federation. They are the chosen leaders who are close to The Survivor. As the earth is being destroyed by criminals, industrialists and politicians, the Troops will resist. The survivors will hold out through the difficult times, until they can emerge as the leaders or a new age. My mother is one of them, as I will be too."

It sounded like rote memorization—adult words unlit by the light of internal understanding. How much had they brain-washed the child? Pilar looked at the child's tattoo, wondering if the intertwining dark and light halves had anything to do with the mythology she was hearing. The symbol had an ancient history with ties to Buddhism and Taoism, she recalled. Certainly it must carry some other meaning in this group's usage.

She thought Nina's phrases sounded like someone's radical and fatalistic distortion of real environmentalist ideas. How much of it was a defense the girl needed to survive? She decided to take the chance of another question.

"But if you become one of the soldiers, the uhh, Troops, well then, what will become of Genny?"

Obviously, the girl had not yet considered this eventuality. She looked stricken. Her face clouded as she started shaking her head in a negative gesture. Then the shaking became more and more severe, until she was violently throwing herself from side to side, screaming.

"Noooo . . . Eeeeeahhh . . . Nooooooo. . ! She cannn't! Ahhhhhhhh! Unnngh . . . But He's mine! Ahhhhhhheeeeee."

The fit became uncontrolled, wild, almost like a seizure. Pilar threw her arms around the thrashing child, holding her against the most violent of the exertions, until her motions slowed. Finally, the girl's body sagged, and tears began to flow. Pilar felt badly that she had set off such a reaction. The exaggerated response was probably because the girl was merging intense feelings that were unconsciously tied together—fears of losing her baby tied to feelings about the dog.

"There, there, darling. It's all right. I'm here, and you are safe. Nothing bad is going to happen."

Pilar hoped that she was telling Nina the truth. She wished that someone could hold and comfort her, the way she was trying to hearten the girl. Reassurance wasn't always that easy to come by as an adult. Still, it was hard to connect the horror in the child's expression and the nightmarish visions she seemed to experience, with the strong, intelligent, and seemingly compassionate figure of Storm. Something was strangely off-kilter here. Pilar felt that some vital piece of information was missing. She hoped that she would be able to discover it.

They returned to the Federation Center, after purchasing a pet carrying case at a local store. Pilar promised the child that she would only bring the puppy as far as the front lobby of the Center but carry it away with her as soon as she departed. Fortunately, the animal cooperated, remaining quiet after a few desultory whines. Pilar waited in a lounge with the dog at her feet, while Nina went to change her clothes and wash up. Pilar just shook her head, as she watched the child waddle away, holding her swollen belly, carrying the burdens of a woman, a mother, and much more.

She curled up on the couch, feeling the relaxing effects of the surroundings. The Center itself had a mellowing effect on her, as she smelled that sweet spicy smell on the air and was lulled by the gentle music. Before long, Pilar found herself drifting in a pleasant mental fog. She wasn't sure at first if she was daydreaming when she felt the gentle pressure of hands on her shoulder. But a familiar man's voice was added to the gentle massage, and she knew it was real.

"So much weight on those lovely shoulders, so much weight. No wonder you have been so tense."

"Oh, it's you. Should I call you Storm?"

"No."

"But . . ."

His hands softly kneaded the muscles in her shoulders, neck and rubbed the tension from her temples. They were warm and gentle hands, his touch seeming to send electric pulses into her.

"If you must call me something, call me your friend."

The warmth of his body seemed to flow out into hers, pooling at her middle, tingling. Her skin was incredibly sensitive. She shifted in her seat, unable to sit still. The man moved around the couch to take her hands, raising her to her feet. He said nothing but stared into her with those vivid purple eyes. The subtle smile on his lips seemed to tell her that he knew every thought, every feeling, every need. As he gazed into her soul, she found herself moving closer.

She had never been so much "in the moment". Nothing existed outside the space she occupied with this compelling man. There was no home, no husband, no context . . . just the thrill in her stomach and the glow in his eyes. Arms intertwined and their lips touched—gently, ever so gently. She was a girl again, so confident, so alive, unencumbered with the worries and burdens of a long life. She was the homecoming queen, the Belle of the ball, Cinderella with Prince Charming. The kiss went on and on, becoming more urgent as lips and tongues moved in passionate harmony. She felt his muscular body through the thin robe, hot and strong. As he moved his palms down her back to her rear, she imitated his movements, like a choreographed dance of love, done to the mystical beat of music in her brain. As their arms pulled each other closer, hips came together, until she felt a pulsing hardness against her. Now part of her became frightened. Her mind fought to pull back, but there didn't seem any resulting action in her muscles. She couldn't seem to stop. She wasn't sure she wanted to stop.

Just then, there was a small sound, like a gasp. Pilar managed to pull herself away enough to look behind the man, where she saw Nina standing in the doorway. The girl's expression was entirely blank, but even through the mental haze, Pilar felt the small eyes tunneling through. She pushed free from the arms and busy hands, her mind reeling, sensing that she had been out of touch with reality for the last few moments.

"I must go!" she blurted out, dashing from the room.

As she bolted out of the Center, the fresh air began to clear her head, and she realized with embarrassment that she hadn't been thinking clearly at all. Was there something in the air? Obviously, some rather immature fantasies had played their part. They had played entirely too large a part. As she looked back at the Center, she paused. The welfare of the world was appearing more and more like the welfare of a certain man who sometimes liked to be called 'Storm.' She knew she had to talk with Gil but didn't know exactly how she would describe what had amounted to an intimate encounter. She shook her head, walking away with her thoughts whirling. She didn't look back.

If she had looked behind her, she might have seen a man in army fatigues appear from a side exit of the Center. He waited until she was nearly a block ahead before he followed.

CHAPTER 31

When he started feeling a dim awareness, Grady Dickson wasn't sure whether or not he was hallucinating. Although he seemed to be regaining consciousness, his senses were distorted by a throbbing pain that ricocheted from ear to ear, making clear thought almost impossible. Grady sensed that he was seated in some kind of chair, with his head flopped forward on his chest. Hazily, with great effort, he raised his head to look around. What he saw was a disconcerting sight. A grotesquely made-up figure hovered over a large table nearby. The strange man's head was large and shiny, its hairless surface wet with perspiration. Smears of black, green, and red distorted his appearance, as well as a wreath of twigs and leaves lashed to his temples. The reporter thought giddily, that if the New York Giants could draft the man, he might scare opponents off the field. He sure as hell scared the shit out of Grady Dickson!

The surroundings were also macabre. Yellow lights dimly lit the room. It was more like a cave than a room, dark and dank with rocky surfaces dripping moisture. Against one wall a grotto was framed by drapes, tied back at the sides. The opposite side of the area was filled with an odd assortment of containers, gas cans, water cooler bottles, plastic jugs—clustered around a table of what looked like chemistry equipment. Dickson's reporter instincts immediately raised thoughts of illegal drug production, though he didn't recognize any of the paraphernalia most commonly used for the narcotic or amphetamine refining process. There was also a collection of deadly looking objects, guns, blades, shells, and canisters arranged around the area. Some articles had bright warning symbols stenciled on olive drab backgrounds.

More eerie, was the mural-like construction that provided a backdrop for the creature. Great swatches of ocher were splashed across a dark alcove. In huge letters, scrawled on the facing surface, was the word "SURVIVE." Poster size pictures hung here and there, featuring grim men in military clothing, clutching weapons and survival gear. A thin sheaf of papers was tacked to one relatively flat surface, the top sheet bearing a large number "3." Crumpled pages on the ground, suggested it was some kind of tear-off pad. The walls of the grotto were decorated with crude markings and hunks of meaty material arrayed on protruding spikes, dripping syrupy liquid, dark and viscous. In the shadowy recess, the light wasn't sufficient for Dickson to tell what the lumps of stuff were. Maybe it was better not to know.

The deep voice droned on, mumbling or singing to itself. A broken safe with a missing door stood to his left. On top of it was a heavyweight industrial drill, coated with grime, that must have been used for opening the thick lockbox. A whitish dust was scattered near and around the safe. To Grady's right, on a small table, several sharp instruments, knives and blades were arranged. Dickson tried to move, only to feel pain shoot through him—not just his head, painful as that was, but also his neck and shoulders. His torso didn't turn or rise when he wanted it to; he couldn't move his arms or legs. He couldn't budge from his seated position, except to lift his head and turn it from side to side. *Am I paralyzed?* It took a moment for Grady's fuzzy brain to realize that there was a strap or belt tightly fastened around his neck, while others secured his chest and limbs. It seemed he was lashed to a heavy steel chair. The bindings gave off a rancid odor. An acrid metallic smell, like sweat, blood and decay swirled about the area. Between the pain, the smell, and the pressure on his throat, his stomach roiled with nausea. He couldn't help gagging.

The sound caught the attention of the grotesque man, who rose to move toward Dickson. Even in this muddled mental state, the reporter noticed a blade dangling loosely from the big fist. It looked like a straight razor. There were full bandoleers of large caliber bullets slung over his chest, a ghastly Rambo. On the back of one arm was a divided circle tattoo, one half light, the other dark.

The sound that came from the man could have been called a voice, but it was a coarse and scratching voice, grating out human words in a harsh inhuman whisper.

"Foolisssh, foolisssh," it hissed, "You do not know what POWER you have offended. You have insulted the Point Man, the Leader of the new age, The Survivor."

Despite the dank atmosphere, Grady's throat was dry and strangled, so his reply came out hoarsely as well. Yet it was a weak protest that sounded, even to his ears, far too much like a frightened whine.

"I'm a reporter. I didn't do anything to get so pissed about. I was just following Delucia." The madman stared silently at him. The eyes seemed to glow, with a malevolent gleam. Grady felt like they were piercing his skin.

"Who are you? What are you going to do?" Dickson croaked, even as his gut told him he didn't want the answer. But the figure spoke again.

"For you, I am the power of life and death. I am the life giver and the life taker. The sower and the purging fire. You followed Delucia, but you thought you would spy on us all. You were not intended to hear certain conversationssss, but you did not concern yourself with our privaceeee. You are another lackey of the corrupt political powers, flattering yourself that you ssseek the truth, but the truth is not in the rules of your decadent society or your perverted pressss. I could give you great things to write about, but they would never appear in the words you puppets are allowed to print. You will never file the greatest story of your putrid little life. You have met the Survivor. But soooo, your future is also sssealed."

"Ah . . . uhh" Grady choked out weakly, "Wha . . . whoever you are, you'd better let me go. I'm a reporter for the Evening News! My Editor knows exactly where I'm supposed to be, and she's expecting a call. If she doesn't hear from me, she'll have every cop in the city out looking. And they'll find me, too!" There was as much wish as conviction in his words.

"Oh yessss . . . they will find you. Some of them will find me, too. I have prepared for that! But then it will be too late. They will only arrive to reap my vengeance. The weak do not continue—only the strong survive. You will learn that those who attempt to violate me shall be violated!"

The fear grew inside Dickson like a swift-spreading cancer, sending a numb feeling into his arms and legs, a cold dizzy wave as the blood drained from his head. The cave-like surroundings started feeling less like a shrine or grotto and more like a burial crypt. In his mind, the word "violation" had always been associated with rape. Maybe the term could be used for other things, but none of them were very pleasant either. He was not wrong in this assumption.

CHAPTER 32

After completing his work, The Survivor wiped his hands on a towel already marked with rust-colored stains. His chest heaved from the exertions. At the end, the reporter had even clawed at him, like the McSwain boy had done—that foolish, spoiled son of the decadent establishment. He shuffled over to his private sanctuary, where the calendar hung on a moist wall. It was a tear-off style, with a single number on each sheet. He had made the Register himself, arranging the sheets in descending numerical order, so it could serve as a count-down device. The pages, however, did not record days. Each represented an enemy to be dealt with. The numbers were the remaining targets, the decreasing number left to terminate.

Long ago seven of his torturers had received retribution. They were long gone, but there were new adversaries. The number was sacred. He had selected precisely seven of his newest enemies. When they had been annihilated, it would be time to release the chemicals and retreat to his enclave. He knew that the previous warnings had been too tame. They had resulted in only limited loss of life. His enemies could ignore that. This would be different. He was almost ready to test the potent mixture he called "Scarlet Dispatch." The test would serve as a true warning of the conflict to come, and the consequences that would ensue, should he be opposed. All the preparations had been made; the procedure determined. He had selected the Police Station for the initial trial. Some might think that foolhardy, but he saw it as a challenge. Furthermore, this first shot might even trap the adversaries' leader, the obsessive Detective Beach. The Survivor didn't really think he would be so fortunate as to end the threat this soon. He sensed from the man's aura that it would not be an accident that brought him to his end. Still, he would eventually be delivered to that final destination, and The Survivor would be conductor of his agonizing trip to oblivion.

Using his forefinger as a brush, the man dipped it in a puddle of red pooled on the floor, then scrawled the letters of the reporter's name on the top page of the register. He ripped the sheet off, to tack it to the wall of his grotto where others hung in dripping disorder. Earlier, he had just thrown them down on the ground, but the last ones were more useful as icons. The number Three was now torn off and posted. There were only two more pages on the register of confirmed kills, the countdown calendar to the final days. In the end, all the pages would be gone; the last enemies would be gone, while he would survive. Soon, the final events would take place, …soon. Two more pages . . . then nothing.

Two more pages … then everything.

Chapter 33

Maybe Gil was right. He figured that he had good reason to return to the Federation Headquarters. He didn't believe it had anything to do with feeling lonely and deprived. He was sure it had nothing to do with wanting to get seduced by an alluring woman, though she had practically jumped him the last time he was there. Maybe he was right. Sure, and maybe politics didn't screw up police departments, and maybe the only reason the Gambino family got charged with crimes was prejudice against Italian Americans. Maybe there really was a tooth fairy.

So shortly after managing this rationalization, he shouldn't have been surprised to find himself in a relaxation module of the Federation Center, trying to soak away a ton of guilt in the whirling waters of the hot tub. He should have known.

The sex had been good. No, the sex had been great. Selene was not only a work of art, but she was also an artist. Most of his life he had assumed that erotic fantasies were just that - imaginary ideas that couldn't ever be matched by reality. In this case, he had to admit that the actual lovemaking was just about as good as the best of his imaginings. In fact, the real episode had included a couple of surprises that hadn't even been in the fantasies.

The trouble came afterward, when his mind and body detoxed from the drug-like effects of the woman and sexual athletics. Something they had sipped out of crystal cups had undoubtedly helped his flight from reality as well. The Center's scent-infused air even seemed to affect him, though it wasn't the only enchanting odor. Selene hadn't been wearing Marigolds this time. Whatever scent she had used was alluring, along with her looks, her touch and her whispered promises of pleasure. Eventually the invitation had proved too tempting. As the last whiffs of her perfume and body fluids seeped from his nostrils, a heavy rush of remorse and guilt now flooded him. He had trouble believing what had just occurred, but he knew it had.

It wasn't the first woman he had been with other than Pilar, but it was the only one since she had become his wife. As old fashioned as it might be, Gil took his marriage vows seriously. He didn't make them until he was ready to keep them and had never put himself in a position to break those pledges . . . not until now. There were always temptations, from the cop groupies who had a fixation on guns and anything else a policeman could shoot, to the occasional nympho or prostitute who suggested a quick screw or B.J. to get out of an arrest or summons. He had always managed to put even the best enticements into practical perspective, to recognize the folly of risking so much for a mirage . . . to be grateful for what he had.

Now a three-sided conversation went on in his head. One side was the voice of a street-hardened and jaded cop who had seen everything there was to see, who couldn't understand what the fuss was all about. Hey, things happen. If every man who gave in to a temptation was doomed, it would be a pretty sparsely populated world. A second voice was more like a teenager, the ego, the part of him that still wanted to prove something. Wow, I just got laid by a woman most guys only dream about! But there was a third voice, which was really messing him up, and unfortunately, it seemed the one he heard the loudest. That voice said he was fooling himself.

Come on, Beach, grow up. What in the hell do you really think you're doing? You fucked up, big time.

For a moment he thought perhaps he could understand the multiple personality thing that had claimed Nina. In a way he had different parts of himself that were fighting with each other, too. Somewhere along the line, he had become a committee. Gil wondered how long he could handle the conversation going on between his ears.

CHAPTER 34

An hour later, Gil was having another kind of conversation with himself. He had asked the other detectives and support staff who were currently working homicide in the Ninth to cast a net, looking for any cases that involved unusual wounds, an environmentalist connection, or John Doe murders. Now he was realizing how much work he had made for himself. Copies of investigation reports were piling up on his desk and his computer inbox, leading him to mumble curses to himself. He started sorting out the sheets by date, made pasty notes for the emails, then wrote small letters and symbols to classify them, a code he had created for himself years before to make sense out of a jumble of documents. He was sure an electronic data whiz would have ways to better organize the information, but he didn't have the computer skills or inclination to manage that. Instead, he stuck with the method and code that he had always used. A little exclamation point meant he thought there might be a connection to the case he was working. A "13" meant violence was directed at a cop, which he took from the "ten-thirteen" code used on the police radio for "officer needs assistance." A large asterisk meant the report contained particularly sensitive material. Depending on the circumstances of the report and the skills of the detective making it, he drew one of three circles in the upper left-hand corner. A circle with two crossing lines through it meant that he considered it a very solid piece of information. If the circle had only one line across it, the data was less reliable. An empty circle meant you couldn't place much confidence in the report. He marked this information in code, in case one of those reporting officers ever saw the marks. It wouldn't create many friends, if one of them saw his submissions marked as unreliable. But some of them were just pro-forma junk, generic words and phrases to satisfy the needs of the bean-counters.

That was a funny thing about some cops. There were those you could trust with your life on the street, but you couldn't trust their paperwork for anything other than toilet paper. Gil understood—sometimes it was just a problem with writing ability. You only needed a high school diploma to be a cop. Not everyone was strong in the writing department. Other times it was an attitude thing, where they considered reports a necessary evil that you filled with any garbage you could think of, just so the brass couldn't bitch that you hadn't done it. That meant some accounts of interviews, searches and surveillances were useful. Others were exercises in fiction. As he methodically went through the avalanche of information, making marks and taking notes, the telephone rang. Since he wasn't expecting an outside call, Gil answered with a standard PDU reply.

"Ninth Precinct, Detective Harrigan, how may I help you?"

'Harrigan' was the generic "Detective" of the unit. There were plenty of nuts that dialed the PDU, so it wasn't unusual for a crackpot to file a complaint, just because the officer on the other end of the line hadn't jumped to his neurotic tune. A complaint against "Detective Harrigan" couldn't go very far. Besides, the fewer people that know a detective's real name, the better. Being unknown and invisible was an advantage in the work. Occasionally a good investigator had to be moved to another job, just because he got his name in the paper too often.

On the other hand, the identity of the caller was often important information. Some of the unit's telephones were equipped with "Caller ID" screens that flashed the number of the originating call. The old movie cliché of trying to hold someone on the line for long enough to trace the call, was a quaint relic of the past. Even when Caller ID wasn't in effect, current technology allowed a local phone trace in seconds rather than minutes. The break-up of the Bell system had made long distance a very different matter. In this case, the number appeared on the little LED screen, 212-660-3287. As soon as he heard the peculiar voice coming out of the receiver, Gil quickly pulled over his keyboard and called up a digital reverse-directory. It was a directory that listed telephone numbers in numerical order, so he could look up the number to identify the person it had been assigned to.

"Thissss is your executioner," hissed the threatening voice, "and I know you."

The Detective felt tension pull at his shoulders. He scanned the reverse directory without much optimism. He wasn't surprised to find the number assigned to a pay phone at the Port Authority Bus Station. No chance of sending a mobile unit in time to corner the crank—if that what he was.

"We've met, haven't we?" Gil asked, hoping to get the man to make a mistake, an admission—perhaps say something that would be a clue to his identity.

"Oh yessss!" the grating voice replied, followed by a diabolical laugh. "And we shall meet again, Oh most dogged Detective, but you won't know when or where. You have already met some of those who were not willing to follow me to sanctuary."

"Like who?"

"They have been marked, so you would not mistake them. Another package will soon be delivered. The one who wanted to tell the world about secret matters has been silenced. Those that violate the laws of Natural Selection will be violated."

Now Beach knew it wasn't a crank . . . or at least not a harmless one. He didn't like the part about a package. And the phrase,

"Those that tell the world . . ." sounded like somebody pretty public.

"You must be calling for a reason," Gil said, trying to keep the conversation going. He didn't have much doubt about why the man was calling.

"You will only be part of the vanguard to fall before us. But you will know the agent of your demise, for you have made the error of opposing me. You have hurt my cause before, and you have insulted me, but now you dare try to pursue me. You are not of the usual common horde; you should know better. You could have been one of the survivors. You chose to put your trussst in other things. Your stubborn commitment is missssplaced."

"What do you think my commitment is?" The question was mostly to keep the killer talking. Still, Gil wasn't sure he could answer the question himself. Part of him was curious enough to wonder what someone else thought, even if it was a deranged murderer.

"To fantasies, to fantasiezzz," the voice answered, "to myths of goodness and courage and love and all that pap. Survival is the only reality! We do what we must do to survive. It is the basic law of nature. Anyone who fails to follow that law is foolish. Survival will be for the fittest, and to the ssstrong come the spoils. Power is the ruling principle. You can run from the truth and die or embrace it and fly!"

The caller hung up.

Beach stared at the phone, puzzled by the apparent references to insult and opposition. Those terms implied he had interacted with the caller before. Could this be someone he knew, someone he had gotten convicted? He did a quick mental review of the killers he had put away, and the type of M.O. for each. He tried to remember if there were any recent or pending releases but didn't come up with much of anything.

He found himself affected by the man's distorted comments about life. Despite Gil's conviction that the man was crazy, it was hard to put the ideas out of his head. He knew that he could never accept what the voice had declared. He didn't think he could live in a world where survival was the only reality, power the only law. He was damn sure that he didn't want to. Fortunately, in his world there were other kinds of strength. There were people with courage, like his partner Frank, who had faced his addiction and his own demons. There was little Winnie, who accepted her crippled body and challenged the world to stop her from making life beautiful. He knew there were folks like Helen Joseph, and the priests Gentry and Noonan, whose goodness gave energy, hope, and opportunity to hundreds of kids that would have been grist for the evil mill the killer helped turn.

Gil also knew there was love in his world, because no matter what had happened or not happened between him and his wife, he knew he loved her and she loved him. His guilt about what had occurred at the Federation Headquarters was itself a kind of testimony to what he really believed . . . that real love was worth giving up something. Sometimes he believed that love was the strongest force on earth. He hoped that it was.

On the other hand, there was a kernel of truth in the caller's statement. It was one reason Gil went to work every day. The man had said you opposed his idea of truth, or you embraced it. Gil might not have used those words, but he figured that part was correct. As far as the consequences, however, he didn't agree. You might die fighting the other side, but everybody dies. Gil had a job, and a greater commitment too. It was certainly more than survival. It was a responsibility he had chosen to make sure those who did embrace the dark side, found themselves at a dead end. If they followed the strange leader's way, expecting to "fly", Gil intended to see that they had a very short flight.

Chapter 35

Only one more flight of stairs stretched ahead, hard, steep and unyielding. Gil fought the sick feeling of overexertion as he pushed up the final steps to the top of the stadium. The relief of reaching the highest level gave him enough will to trot around the upper walkway and start down the other side. He knew there was a kind of compulsion that drove him to punish his body this way, but he thought mostly it was a healthy drive. He didn't look like a man in his forties, except a little gray at the temples. His body was trim and in excellent condition. Most men ten years younger couldn't match the strength his legs had developed from years of this discipline. The truth was, he did it as much for his head as for his muscles. Once an outlet for the raging anger that had driven him, the workout was still his favorite way of dealing with many tangled feelings. Today it was also a way to avoid going home. He was going to have to face Pilar, and the guilt was clinging to him like great gobs of wet tissue paper.

Pilar was waiting at the door when he got back to the house. He saw an appealing welcome in her eyes, along with another subtle expression he couldn't identify. He almost forgot his remorse, until she reached out to embrace him—offering a kiss with warm, open lips. She seemed hungry for him, and he felt a deep sense of shame that someone else had sated his own appetite.

CHAPTER 36

Despite his guilt, Gil knew that life goes on. So does death.

The next day in Manhattan, an empty gurney cart rattled down the tiled hall of the City Morgue, propelled by a dark-skinned attendant with three earrings in one earlobe, a dragon tattooed across his forearm in three colors. He hardly acknowledged the two men who walked silently down the long corridor. The Detective and Pathologist were on familiar ground. Most people never saw this part of the morgue. Visitors coming to identify remains were kept upstairs. They could ID the person by Polaroid snapshots, or if the photos weren't conclusive, by a more direct, yet not brutal method. The corpse could be brought up in an elevator to a windowed alcove, where the family member could sit on a couch to view the body behind a window, almost as if they were viewing an exhibit in a gallery. Only if they insisted, would a viewer be allowed to come close. They weren't in a funeral parlor. The remains were often not pretty.

Detectives, however, often visited the bowels of the building, to observe an important autopsy, or just view a cadaver as part of the data gathering process for a case. A body could tell a story, even in death. After enough visits, it was easy to get accustomed to the morgue scene, no longer seeing the bodies as real people. There are close to seventy-five thousand deaths each year in New York

City. Almost half are referred to one or the other of five county morgues, over fifteen thousand examined. Thousands of autopsies are performed each year, more at the Manhattan site than anywhere else.

This time death was personalized. Krispnick had contacted Gil as soon as the body was tentatively identified. The two men pushed through swinging doors into a large room that had eight large stainless-steel tables anchored to the ceramic floor. Overhead neon fixtures saturated the area with a brightness almost painful to unprepared eyes, and the absence of shadows added to the surrealistic atmosphere. Some of the tables were strewn with knives, huge syringes, saws and drills. At the first station, another pathologist was bent over a bloody carcass stretched out on a steel mesh surface, murmuring observations into a microphone dangling near his head. Water bubbled from a hose and sluiced down grooves to a drain. It was a very different sound than the happy gurgling of a woodland brook. A heavy smell hung about the scene; a mix of harsh chemicals, putrefying flesh, and sour fluids, all overlaid with the odor of institutional disinfectant and floor cleaner. They moved on to the second table where Anton pulled back a thick plastic sheet from the face of the still form lying there.

"Is it him?"

"Yeah, that's Dickson," Beach nodded, an invisible weight slouching his shoulders. "I feel like asking who could do a thing like this, but I know the answer. The city is full of scum that could do this. Some of `em would do it for a dime bag."

"You know it wasn't like that, don't you, Gil?"

"I don't know anything except a friend of mine is lying here on a slab, and the creep that did it, is out there someplace, walking the streets."

"Well, I don't know if this is bad news or good news, Gil, but it's obvious this wasn't a random thing. And I don't think it's one person's work."

"What are you talking about?"

Anton looked thoughtful, then pulled the plastic down further, exposing a massively wounded torso. Gil grimaced, looking away from the remains of his friend.

"So, he's been sliced up. What's your point?"

"Look again, Gil. This is the same pattern I found on the boy with the fancy vasectomy—McSwain, wasn't it?"

The Detective turned back, to look closer at the wounds. He was silent for a moment. "Another warning," he mumbled, eyes narrowing.

"Could be," Anton agreed, " . . . mean anything to you?"

“Yeah,” the Detective replied tightly, “It means I may have to put out a warning of my own.”

CHAPTER 37

Gil's immediate plans had to wait until he made a trip to the IAB headquarters as directed. His nerves were being pushed to the limits. Ralph Langfield, a well known lawyer retained by the PBA, had agreed to go with him. The attorney was not a lightweight. Often his name was mentioned when talk turned to important judgeships or elected political offices. He looked like a page out of a men's magazine—two-dimensional perfection. Always impeccably dressed, he usually seemed to have just walked out of the hair stylist's salon, his chic razor-cut showing just enough gray at the temples to make him look distinguished, not old. He had bushy eyebrows that set off his clear blue eyes, as well as a perfectly trimmed mustache in a thin style that reminded Gil of the old-time actor David Niven. The attorney stood six foot four, which didn't hurt his imposing courtroom image. As a rule, Langfield tended to win.

Whether they knew his reputation, or not, the IAB Investigators tended to be more courteous in the presence of a legal expert. Schultz and Benowitz, the two who had come to Gil's house, were nowhere to be seen. No specific charges had yet been filed, the front office types assured Gil, but an investigation was in progress concerning police harassment and improper acceptance of gratuities. Until more information was developed, they couldn't specify if anyone would be charged or indicted.

The second accusation, about receiving gratuities was a common one, because it was relatively easy to pin on somebody. Even most straight-arrow cops had at least once let somebody buy them a cup of coffee or accepted free tickets to a game. That was enough to get nailed if they really wanted to get you. It was no small irony, since the earning and dispensing of political favors was not only allowed among the brass, but absolute S.O.P. That meant some higher ups could accept major gifts of influence and privilege, but real cops weren't supposed to get a free cup of coffee. If you happened to be the targeted victim of a political purge, cover-up, or diversion, they didn't need much to blow you away. Receiving gratuities was on the list, just in case they couldn't prove anything else.

Ralph took Gil aside to speak in a confidential whisper.

"I think this is all bullshit, Beach."

"Tell me something I don't know."

"I mean, I think this is one of those message things. You know, like a kind of insurance or protection."

"Protection for who? . . . or what?"

"I don't know, but probably somebody with connections. C'mon Beach. Can't you figure it?"

"What? Like if I get intimidated by the IAB, some hidden player gets me to back off from whatever I'm doing to threaten him. If I'm a good boy, the charges against me never get proven."

". . . or maybe not even officially filed," Langfield inserted, raising his eyebrows in a wry grimace.

"But if I don't get the message now, they will eventually find something that they can make stick. Joining in a toast at a neighborhood street wedding will get turned into a charge of drinking on the job; riding a few blocks to catch up on the latest from a cabby who is one of your snitches will get turned into coercing free rides from a local businessman."

"I think you got the picture, Beach. The thing is, it's not all bad news. The good news is I don't think they really want to take official action against you. There was a real 'only if you're a bad boy' kind of flavor to some of the conversation. If you get their message, I don't think anything will come of it."

"That sucks, Ralph. That really sucks."

"Look, it isn't pretty, and it isn't fair. But it's the way things work. That's life. Remember what they say: 'There really is no gravity, the world just sucks!' Power has its privileges, my friend, and we try to get along despite it."

Gil wondered about the "we." The lawyer's attempt to picture them on the same team didn't work for Beach. Somehow, he had the feeling that a well-connected successful courtroom attorney with the backing of various unions and the PBA, was not as powerless as a simple precinct detective.

"I seem to be getting a lot of warnings lately."

"Oh?" Langfield asked, "Maybe that says you are doing something wrong."

"I don't think so. It usually means I'm doing something right."

"Oh?"

"Yeah, it means I'm close enough to something important to get a few folks real uncomfortable."

When he got back to the PDU, Gil scrolled through his contact list until he found the number of the Eastside Evening News. He called the office of Lucille Sitra, the City Editor. He had known her for years, so the operator put his call through to her desk. In five minutes, Beach gave Sitra enough information to change her attitude about Grady's death from grief to aggression. The woman was glad for an opportunity to channel the sadness she was feeling for her former reporter. She was able to quickly convert it into positive and angry action. Gil knew from experience, that the media are almost as protective of their own as cops are. He had a feeling that police were going to increasingly become targets in this affair—especially a cop named Beach. He was going to need some allies.

Chapter 38

Senator Delucia was boiling. He had been in the middle of a private moment with Evelyn, her skirt hiked up to the waist as she leaned over a table. With his pants around his ankles, he was moving against her from the rear, enjoying her gasps of pleasure as he built to a climax. Then they were interrupted by an insistent knock on the door. He felt himself go limp. As if that weren't bad enough, the outside intrusion was a dose of very bad news.

When Delucia unlocked the office door, pants half-buttoned, he found Fred standing there, holding out a copy of the Eastside Evening News. When he saw what was printed on the front page, the Senator finished buckling his belt, and stomped into the next room, where others were sitting, looking uncomfortable.

"Son of a bitch!" Delucia exploded, flinging the newspaper at a nearby table. It landed with the offending headline face-up. "RADICAL ENVIRONMENTALISTS IMPLICATED IN REPORTER MURDER"

"Son of a fucking bitch!" he yelled. "Did you read this?"

Fred just nodded. Jeannine lowered her head to stare at her steno pad. Evelyn joined the group and busied herself with some papers, face still flushed from their coitus interruptus. Only Sherri Cornwell responded. After years of dealing with aggressive lawyers and flamboyant politicians, she had grown nearly immune to both sexual high jinks and the Senator's verbal outbursts.

"Somebody's playing hardball" She noted.

"Goddamn, Forester must be happy as a pig in shit!" Delucia ranted. "Damn article makes it look like environmentalists are all crackpots."

"Sir," Jeannine ventured, "what about . . ."

"Who the hell asked you anything? Take notes and shut up! What the fuck is going on around here, can't anybody follow simple orders? I told those jackoffs to find an issue, not create a fucking scandal in my face! I thought we lucked out with the Cross-Bronx radiation scare. I figured that mess would get me some positive mileage, but not with this kind of shit on the front page!"

"There's grounds for a defamation suit in there," the Senator's legal counsel suggested.

"Jesus H. Christ, no. That would just add to this mess. It's too public now. The last thing we want are more fucking investigations. The only one that is going to do us any good is the Internal Affairs thing on this detective, Beach. I know he's behind this. They even quote the asshole. Obviously, the shithead doesn't know what's good for him. He's giving us the finger; flipping us the fucking weenie. Well, he is going to find out that you don't fuck with real power."

The Senator strode angrily to the telephone, where he stabbed at the buttons.

"This is Delucia. Get me Randall!"

CHAPTER 39

While Gil Beach was running down leads and Senator Delucia was cursing out his staff, the Precinct Detective Unit was having a relatively quiet day. Rita Bravermann filled a cloudy glass carafe with water from the Great Bear water cooler, then took it back to the makeshift kitchen where she emptied it into a cheap Proctor-Silex coffee maker. She ladled coffee into the basket, adding an extra scoop to make sure it was the hearty brew most people in the PDU liked. In minutes hot black liquid was sending a familiar odor into the offices. Rita waited the four or five minutes the machine took to fill a pot, so she would be sure to get a fresh cup of the pleasantly addictive stuff. The aroma of fresh coffee would soon draw cops like flies to horseshit. She could end up making it for everybody but herself if she wasn't right there when it finished, a few minutes later. Sure enough, as soon as it completed brewing, the first sniffing cop poked his head in the door like a dog when you open a can of food. Rita poured a large mug of the steaming liquid and took a sip before returning to her desk. She felt her mouth water, as the sharp nutty aroma filled her nostrils. The coffee was a decent brand for a change, not just the generic store variety, and she had just opened a fresh package.

The bulletin board above her phone was crowded with slips of paper. There seemed more than the usual amount of soft-clothes work going on this month, so she'd been busy keeping up to date on the cover stories. She swallowed twice, as saliva filled her mouth. *Odd reaction*, she thought, swallowing again. But the dark brew tasted good, with just a slight bitterness, sort of like french roast or espresso even though it was a standard grind. That extra scoop really must have made a difference.

Rita turned to the keyboard, where she started tapping out a regular rhythm. The data entry was going slowly today. She frequently grabbed the mug, as saliva kept flowing. Once she scanned the area to see if anyone was looking, then spit into the wastebasket, embarrassed, but unable to stem the flow of juices. Bending over the bucket, she felt nausea flood through her, until, surprising herself, she gagged. When cramps grabbed at her belly, she grimaced. *Damn PMS. I shouldn't have my period for a week yet.*

There was a moment of relief, then the pain came back, more severe this time. *Woo—eee! This is going to be a tough one. Haven't had cramps like this for years.*

Perspiration broke out on the Rita's forehead and temples. A tremble ran down her spine, then she felt herself shaking. Saliva kept flowing, her heart was thumping heavily and rapidly. It soon became obvious that this was more than a pre-menstrual episode, though she still assumed it was nothing worse than a case of the stomach flu. By the time she recognized it as something more serious, she couldn't communicate the fact to anyone, because she was doubled up on the floor, retching convulsively and flopping about in spasmodic jerks. Before anyone found her, she had passed out from lack of oxygen, her throat completely constricted by muscle spasms and mucus. By the time help arrived, it was too late.

Chapter 40

Ambulances crowded the sidewalk outside the Ninth Precinct, as stretchers were carried in and out of the building. Plain-clothes and uniformed police milled about in clusters, their faces registering shock by remaining blank masks. The usual banter and jovial conversation were notably absent. Stretchers went in unoccupied but came out with silent covered forms. So far, the count was three dead, plus two in critical condition. Others looked ghastly pale. It was hard to tell whether from toxins or emotions.

Gil Beach stood outside, slumped against one of the many police cars, marked and unmarked, pulled up onto parts of the street and sidewalk. He wanted a cigarette. He had quit smoking five years ago, but the old habit called out to him as he tried to absorb the enormity of what had happened. The wide figure of Anton Krispnick stepped out of the precinct entrance and moved to his side. For long moments they stood in silence, staring at the dirty pavement. Finally, the Assistant M.E. spoke.

"Dirty shits used the water cooler."

"What was it?" Gil asked.

"Won't know till we run some tests. Looks similar to botulism, but I don't think so. It worked too fast."

"Rita?"

Krispnick just shook his head slowly.

“What did she do? Get coffee water from the cooler?” This time Anton nodded in reply.

“I’m always too lazy for that. I just fill it from the bathroom faucet. What about Wilson?” Wilson was the D.O.D., Desk Officer of the Day. He was known for his frequent trips to the water cooler and coffee pot.

“Depends on how fast we ID the toxin. He’s on his way to the hospital, and they’re pumping his stomach. This is bad stuff, Gil. Don’t get your hopes up.”

“I want to know how they got it in the water.”

“That was easy. Those water cooler jugs. They aren’t glass anymore—plastic. We found needle holes in two of `em.”

“Right here in the building?” Gil looked incredulous.

“Well, yeah, sort of. The bottles get delivered. Driver leaves `em outside, in the alley. Sometimes they sit there for a day or two before they get brought inside. Just about anybody could get to them.”

“Somebody got to them, all right. Somebody got to us.”

CHAPTER 41

The Police Laboratory found lethal levels of Sodium Fluoroacetate in the water from the cooler.

"It's a type of rat poison or 'rodenticide' as the technicians call it. The stuff is relatively easy to obtain," Shig Higawa, the Lab Director, explained to Gil. "It can be found in hardware or garden stores. They label it as 'Rodent Killer 1080' or 'X-Rat Max.'

Higawa had called Beach directly to tell him the results of his analysis. "I've got so many things, Gil, I had to make a list."

"I'm listening."

"Ever the charming conversationalist. Anyway, here goes. First, more about the poison."

Higawa went into detail about the toxic substance they had identified.

"Actually, it was a mix of two chemicals. There was also a phosphate ester that's used in insecticides. Those darling Nazis invented them during old `WW - II'. Normally, a lethal dose of the Sodium Fluoroacetate would be in the one-gram range, but the esters are stronger. The ingenious part was that there was so little taste or smell. That's partly due to the dilution ratio of course, but fluoroacetate is similar to the standard fluoride we put in our water supply on purpose. Folks don't realize it, but the fluoride levels in their water are quite variable, so most people wouldn't notice the slight change in the taste. Unfortunately, it was very effective."

"Are we talking a chemist, here?"

"No, not necessarily. Could'a been an amateur who accidentally mixed the wrong amounts—or bad luck. Common poisons, small quantities. Maybe they didn't even plan on killing anybody. Maybe it was some nut that just wanted to make some cops sick."

"I don't think so, Shig. The planning is too good. I think this was meant to be fatal, and if you want the truth, I think it was meant for me. At least three people have died—four if you include Grady—and I think all because this creep wanted me."

"Now don't get grandiose on me, Gil. Even if it was meant for you, don't take on the guilt for this thing. It was the asshole who adulterated the water that deserves that. Anyway, let me finish my list. Or wait . . . will you be anywhere near the lab today? I could show you some of what I have, better than tell you."

CHAPTER 42

It took Gil twenty minutes to reach the Laboratory. He was glad for an excuse to get out of the oppressive atmosphere that currently hung about the Precinct. Death scenes are often subdued after the event, but the death scene is not usually located directly in Police headquarters. The Precinct is normally such a vibrant place, the contrast was striking—and depressing. When he reached the lab, the Director was waiting. The room was cluttered with instruments, gauges, and glassware.

"I found something interesting in Dickson's hair," Higawa said, waving Gil over toward him, "take a look at these."

At the Lab Director's gesture, he bent over the microscope.

"Okay, I see some little doodads, look like hats or flying saucers or something."

"Those are diatoms."

"Diatoms?"

"Right."

"Okay, act brilliant and tell me what that is."

"Well, actually, they're fossils . . . tiny fossils of ancient sea life. There are thousands of different types, so if we had a matching sample, we can distinguish the exact batch of diatomaceous earth from which they came,

"They're from earth . . . dirt?"

"Well, not just any dirt, but yes, a certain kind of earth. That's where it starts getting really interesting."

"You saying that you can tell where he was?"

"Well, it's unlikely anyone would be hanging around the few chalky areas where this stuff occurs naturally. Some folks use it in certain types of pool filters, but that's out of season now. I even heard of sprinkling it around your garden to combat slugs. But again, not the season for slugs. Besides, the stuff also had fine fragments of Portland cement mixed in with it."

"So? Something to do with Oregon?"

"No. That's just the name of the substance. It has certain specific uses. In this case, it means he broke into a safe. Or at least was around when somebody cracked one."

"Pardon me?"

Higawa smiled. "You see, many safes built before 1936 used an inner insulating layer made of diatomaceous earth and natural cement. From the thirties to the eighties, companies used vermiculite and Portland cement. Some manufacturers have used gypsum, even sawdust and gypsum. Modern safes get into exotic polymers and all, but this had to be an old safe. No way you'd get this combination of fillers any other way. Diatomaceous earth is also used for some other purposes, like swimming pool filters, but not with the other stuff mixed in."

"You're saying we got ourselves a reporter who moonlights as a safe cracker?"

"Well, he had to be around one that actually got cracked. Not just opened, cracked. It had to have been cracked in a manner that penetrated the outer walls, releasing the filler stored in the walls."

"I think you've got to be a little cracked to do forensics," Gil offered with a grin.

"No question about it," the lab specialist laughed. They both appreciated a little humor to relieve the heavy mood of recent events. There was a lot of heaviness going around.

Gil told Higawa about the missing recordings and lockbox from the Youth Bureau Office.

"I'm sure Dickson was killed at the place wherever they opened the YB safe, and I think that is most likely to be someplace in the Federation Center."

"So does that mean you have a link between Nina's handlers and the killing?" Shig suggested.

"Yeah, only it isn't good enough. We know the FONIES had to have done the Youth Bureau break-in. Who else would be interested in the Nina interviews? But if anybody thinks we're going to convince a judge to issue a warrant on that guess, they're living in Disneyland. A judge, even a friendly one, is going to ask for a lot more reasonable cause."

Still, Higawa looked happy, proud of his work.

"Did you get a look at the phone call I recorded—run a voice print or anything?" Gil asked.

"No. It's been a trifle busy around here the last couple days. I have to send it out, anyway. We don't do audio analysis here. You need sound techs to do that. But I'm not to the end of my list, yet."

He opened a file, from which he extracted several narrow strips of shiny thermal paper, like they use in hospitals for electrocardiograms and other instrument read-outs. Higawa shoved a sheet into Gil's hands. It looked like a row of stripes down the page, that varied in darkness from light gray to almost black. There were graph marks and other numbers, also handwritten scribbles, with arrows pointing here and there.

"I'm not finished checking these yet, but according to the Hardy-Weinberg equilibrium assumption, we've got a match on at least one spec. The VNTR gene loci are parallel, and . . ."

"Whoa, hold on a minute Einstein. What am I looking at, and what the hell are you talking about?"

"Oh, sorry. I get carried away. What you've got is an analysis of the genetic material from the first specimen I fixed from that hair sample you brought me—what you'd call a DNA fingerprint, at least if you are Cellmark Diagnostics, who are making big bucks off the name, since it's copyrighted. And this . . ." he held out another sheet of gray bands beside it, "is from the fingernail scrapings of the McSwain corpse."

"They look the same to me."

"That's because they are! Of course, I could probably show you a picture of piano keys next to this, and you'd think they looked exactly alike. Fortunately, we don't even trust our own eyes. We use a photo scanner to get accurate reads on the grayscales, then feed the numbers into Max, our computer, for a match/binning statistical manipulation."

"If you say so. How reliable is this, anyway?"

"Pretty damn reliable—at least 99 percent accuracy. There's been some controversy, like with any new technology—nobody believed in fingerprints at first. But the problems have to do more with a particular lab's quality standards than the test itself. We're careful here and I did this one myself. I corrected for band-shifting, background interference; everything. There are some experts who think the likelihood ratio method is better than the match/binning one, but even the ones who argue about technique agree that it's a reliable tool when carefully applied. Most courts accept it as evidence with an exceptional degree of accuracy."

"But not perfect."

"Geez, Gil. Of course it isn't perfect—nothing is. You know that. But it's better than almost anything else we have. And if you want, I have the software to do the likelihood-ratio comparisons too."

"And these stripes says that my guy is the guy that killed McSwain."

"Okay, if you want us to be scientific, we'll be scientific. Tests don't talk, but if this one did, it would say that whoever managed to get his hair and tissue jammed under the fingernails of the deceased was the same person who got his hair jammed into the brush from which you obtained a specimen. It doesn't say he's the killer, but it puts him in a struggle with the deceased immediately prior to death."

"Fair enough. It's enough to take to Tyrone."

"Judge Tyrone? Aren't you forgetting that this was just a `preview'? You don't have any legally obtained evidence at all."

"I know, I know. But Tyrone's real people, not one of those idiots that play-act their life all the time. I think I can talk him into a warrant with this. Then we can get what we need."

"Sounds like wishful thinking to me, but you're the Detective. Oh, and there is one more piece you might find interesting."

"Like what?"

"The fluoroacetate cocktail. I had a feeling I'd seen that combo or something similar recently."

"Did you?"

"Well, not exactly, but close. I kept scratching my head till the fleas begged me to stop, then it came to me. It was McSwain's post-mortem too. But a later specimen."

"The kid? McSwain? I didn't see anything about poison in the cause of death."

"Because it wasn't the cause. I wouldn't be surprised though, if the kid was sick when he got run over."

"How so?"

"Well, it was those colored rings on his arms. Anton sent me tissue samples for analysis. The epidermal tissue was impregnated with the same chemical mix. It looks to me, like the kid was mixing the fluroacetate cocktail. He wore long protective gloves, but they weren't long enough, so he got some of the substance on his upper arms."

"Okay. That might help. I'm on my way to Judge Tyrone."

"Well, uhhh, just don't mention my name, and don't tell Nussbaum, okay?"

Chapter 43

"So the lab just happened to be calibrating their instruments and found this?" Judge Tyrone raised one eyebrow. "You can't be serious, Gil."

"Well, look Abner. . . I mean Your Honor, we don't need to use this DNA stuff as evidence, if we can have a warrant. Then we can go in and get everything we need. This just shows that it won't be a waste of time."

"It would be more than a waste of my time if I grant a search warrant and it turns up nothing. What am I supposed to use as reasonable suspicion here? You know I can't even consider that evidence. Just be glad I'm not the sort to press you on how you got it." The Judge chuckled, running a hand through his frizzled salt and pepper hair.

Abner T. Tyrone had been close to real world for too long to have many illusions about the niceties of law enforcement. His father had been a cop in the Nine-Oh, Williamsburg, for twenty-five years. Abner had lived there himself, until he went off to George Washington University in D.C., then he came back to New York City to study law at Columbia. If it was a matter of an official trial record, he could split hairs and demand proper procedure with the best of them, but he had some appreciation for what it meant to work the mean streets. That's why Beach went to him whenever he needed a court order or warrant that needed careful handling, or a supportive ear.

"I'd like to help, Gil, but this time I can't do it. You've got nothing solid. This is stuff I can't possibly consider." Tyrone gnawed at the unlit cigar he kept in his mouth whenever he was in his chambers. He claimed to hate the smell of smoke but love the taste of Cuban tobacco leaves.

"What about the poison on the kid?"

"What about it? The only connection you have is a questionable report by his parent. How could you prove that the chemicals came from the Nature Center?"

"By searching the place! That's why I need the warrant."

"C'mon Gil, you've been around long enough to know that it doesn't work that way. You don't get a warrant so you can find something to prove criminal activity unless you have a good reason to believe it is there first."

"But I do, Your Honor, I do."

"Stop sounding like you're the groom at a wedding. Sorry, my friend, but this just isn't good enough."

Gil clenched his fists several times, before he started pulling his papers together. When there was a knock, Judge Tyrone opened the door, allowing Frank Terranova to step in. Not the typical image of a serious and dedicated law officer, Frank was rather unconventional in his clothes and interests, more likely to crack a joke than ask for 'just the facts.' But he also had good detective instincts, he had guts, and he lived every day like it was a gift. They had been thrown together accidentally in a previous case, and Gil had spoken to his superiors about making it a more permanent partnership. He wouldn't have done that unless Frank was a good detective. Beach was thankful his partner had not been in the Precinct building when the poisoned water had done its work.

"Sorry to butt in, Your Honor," Frank panted, out of breath, "but I knew you were deciding about the Federation Center warrant, and something came up that you might want to hear. I know Gil would." He grinned a goofy smile and offered jellybeans to the others.

The Judge refused the candy, shrugged his shoulders, then flopped in a large leather upholstered chair, ready to listen. He had the look of a huge dark buzzard, glowering in wait. Frank looked over at Gil, got a nod to go ahead, took a breath and began in a tumble of words.

"Well, it's like rush hour at the morgue this week. So many bodies, they almost cut up an M.E. who fell asleep on a cart." His grin told them he was joking. "So we didn't get anything on this one right away. However, it seems they found a floater a couple of days ago, down at the river—caught on a support for the Canarsie subway bridge. I always thought that was weird. Doesn't 'sub' mean 'under'? How can you have a 'sub-way' on a bridge?"

Beach waved his hand in a circular motion to suggest Frank should hurry up and get to his point.

"Anyway, it was a Jane Doe—some woman that had drugs in her blood and semen in her tubes. She also had a tattoo, a lot of knife cuts and was naked as a jaybird. None of that means she was a hooker, but it all would fit, so that was the working theory, at first. There are plenty of working girls that end up that way, so it didn't set off any alarms until later. She was put in cold storage until they could get to her. So today a Mr. Dunlop shows up, looking for his old lady. Me, I was glad when my wife disappeared, but some guys don't know when they get a break, I guess." Frank's humor fell flat. The Judge just stared stonily at him.

"Sorry about that. Anyway, he identifies the Jane Doe as his wife, Filomena—that's Fil with an 'F'—and he is far from pleased when he hears what they thought about her profession. Not that anybody told him right out, but I think one of the dieners hollered something to another guy, like 'did you bring up the hooker' or something like that. I hear the guy got pink-slipped for it."

Tyrone was beginning to frown and tap his fingers on the arm of the chair. Again, Gil waved his hand, signaling his partner to get on with it.

"Okay, so here is the important part. This Mr. Dunlop says his wife has been involved with the FONIES for a long time . . ."

"PHONIES?" the Judge asked, looking over at Gil.

"That's what we call the group sometimes, your Honor," Beach explained. "It's sort of a pun, seeing as the initials of the Federation of Nature Selection are F.O.N.S."

"I see," said Judge Tyrone, his face a frozen mask.

"So, this guy's wife has been missing ever since the last time she headed for the ol' Federation Center," Frank continued. "That was four days ago. He waited a couple 24's before he sent out the hounds. When he called the FONIES place, they said she never arrived, but he knows she did, `cause he has been real suspicious of the whole scene there. She was a real groupie, it looks like, hot to trot for the Federation's frontman. Mr. Dunlop found an unfinished letter written by his wife, where she said stuff about giving herself to the cause as 'Nature's Concubine," or some garbage like that. So this time he follows her to the Center. He says he waited a long time, but she never came out. Now she shows up as a floater."

“Whatta you think now, Ab?” Gil blurted, reverting to the first name basis he used when he and the Judge shared an occasional lunch or round of golf.

The Judge sat thinking for a moment.

“Well, I think your case is still weak. If you have a good lawyer facing you, it might not hold up. But I guess it’s good enough for a warrant,” he agreed, stepping over to the massive oak desk where he began filling in the blank lines of some documents.

Papers in hand, the two detectives hurried from the dark-paneled office and worked their way through the maze of the courthouse to the street.

“So why didn’t you just call?” Gil asked his partner, “It would’ve been a lot faster.”

Frank grimaced and rubbed his neck with a hand. “Yeah, well there’s some other news, too, that I didn’t want to mention right away. First, you got a message from Nussbaum, at the lab. It says to hold off on everything, the DNA test was wrong.”

“What? That doesn’t make any sense. Shig said he checked the test himself and he even told me all kinds of technical junk to explain why he was sure about it.”

“I dunno about that, but I figured if you had the Dunlop guy’s story, it wouldn’t matter too much.”

"Maybe not for the warrant, but it shoots hell out of the case I thought we had against Storm, or Stormer, or whoever the hell he is."

"So, what are you gonna do?"

"I'm going to go back and talk to Nussbaum, for starters. Then we're going to execute that warrant. I don't care what that test says, I know there's a smell coming off this Guru like the underside of a latrine, even when he's sitting in a patch of daisies."

"Oh yeah, well there's another thing, too. A couple guys came lookin' for you. I think . . . uhh, I think they're IAB. I figured it wouldn't hurt to warn you before you got back. They didn't look friendly."

"Two guys named Schultz and Benowitz?"

"Schultz, yes—Benowitz, no . . . the other guy was named Gorman—Ted, or Fred, I think."

"Gorman? Why that S.O.B!"

"You know him?"

"If it's Ted Gorman, the creep came right in my house and ate my food. That's a new low. The rat was vetting me at my own damn party!

"Well if he's IAB, what do you expect? One of those creeps would stab somebody in the back and then arrest him for carrying a concealed weapon."

"But that's disgusting, man, real foul," Gil grumbled. "He comes into my own house, eats my food, talks to my friends and family, then uses it against me."

"He crashed the party?"

"Just about,,,wangled in with our friends. Now I feel like he walked into my home and stole the silver."

"Yeah, or maybe something more important."

CHAPTER 44

As Gil and Frank spoke, another event was taking place that could have been described as a theft. It was the theft of something priceless and precious. It was a monstrous larceny, but the one who committed it did not see things that way. In the mind of the Survivor, it was a celebration of life and death, not in mere theory, but in reality. In the catalclysm to come, he knew that death would come for many. So, after the purge, the Survivors he led would need to refill their own ranks. They would need new bodies, new replacements. In his distorted view, he, himself, the movement's leader was the only proper source of a gene pool for the new age. He had already begun the process, in fact had been developing the elements for years.

A breeder was finally ready, a direct product of his loins giving birth to another generation of his offspring, also out of his seed, doubling his DNA in the offspring. The female's small body was even now struggling to discharge a new addition to the ranks of Survivors. He had no thoughts of the girl's feelings. All that mattered was that her body had reached sufficient age to bear a child.

Now held hostage deep under the city, the impregnated child was terrified. Despite preparation and teaching, she was like a tortured animal, trembling in panic and pain, gripping her distended belly from each side as if she could hold back an explosion. Sweat beaded her forehead and upper lip, as her large childish eyes darted around looking for help that would not come. A small, worn teddy bear was wedged under one arm.

The girl's thirteen-year-old body was not ready for the tremendous stresses it was enduring. Her mind was even less prepared. She screamed as contractions surged through her. They came frequently, because an earlier injection of Pitocin triggered the instinctive muscular reactions.

Prowling the area during slow times in the process, snuffling and snorting in anticipation, was the sweaty, painted figure of The Survivor. His head and clothing were wet, matted from perspiration and the heavy humidity of the dank cave. He didn't notice because he was too involved in what he was doing. The drug's effect on the gestating child pleased him. A follower by the ludicrous name of Pearl had easily obtained the stuff from the obstetrical ward where she had been employed as a nurse. The woman would do anything he asked. She said that she would die for him. She meant it figuratively, but as it turned out, that is just what she had done. He couldn't have anyone know her role, and she was expendable.

Now he watched one of the first births from a personally chosen and generated breeder. The offspring should have been perfect, since it had a double portion of his genetic material. His biological offspring was bearing his offspring. Unfortunately, when the squalling baby was discharged from the breeder, there was a problem.

He wasn't as pleased. It had flaws. That was unacceptable.

CHAPTER 45

"You gotta look at this stuff, Gil. It's from the Cross-Bronx highway radiation incident."

Frank was holding a sheaf of papers with the letterhead of the New York State Patrol.

"The accident with the waste truck?"

"It was no accident, Gil. It was sabotage."

"Okay, but what does that have to do with us? They may eventually get somebody for manslaughter, but it isn't a homicide case, is it?"

"Normally it wouldn't be, but they found a note. Somebody intentionally rigged the truck to separate as it traveled—with a metal line and hook. The truck cab itself wasn't damaged. It's been sitting at the impound lot, until the investigation is finished."

"It's still not homicide's responsibility, or Ninth Precinct business," Gil said, puzzled. "I didn't hear any report on that crash being sabotage."

"There won't be one, probably. Or at least not a public one. The feds aren't anxious to publicize terrorism in our backyard. Especially, when it involves nuclear threats."

"Terrorism? Is that how they figure it?"

"Yeah. That's what they're thinking. Then this was found."

Terranova handed Beach a photocopy of a hand-printed note. Extra lines and shadows through the copy, indicated that the original had been crumpled and grease stained. As he handed it over, Frank added an explanation.

"Uhhh, it looks like it refers to you, Gil."

"So why haven't I seen it before?"

"Well the Feds had no idea who 'Beach' was. They didn't even know it as a name for a while. It went from the Feds to the State Troopers, then Downtown. It could have gotten lost in the bureaucracy down there, but some gal in document analysis spotted it—said she knew you. Her name's Deanna Van Noyes. Ring a bell?"

Beach couldn't hide the pink tinge that spread up his neck and cheeks. He didn't tell Frank about the brief and intense affair he had gotten into with Deanna. It wasn't immoral, but was before his marriage to Pilar, when he had different motivations and tastes in his relationships.

"Ummm, yeah, I guess I know who that is," he muttered, focusing on the page.

The note was a strange fatalistic warning:

"The CRISIS for the earth is upon you. I am the POINT MAN of the new world."

The words "point man" were printed in larger letters, with such a hard stroke, the pen had gone through the paper in spots.

"To save the world, it must be PURGED. Send out your champions, and they will be vanquished. Beach is not worthy of me—a waste of time. I will persevere. I am the SURVIVOR."

"Damn," Gil cursed, "this has to be related to the FONIES thing. What is he gonna do, destroy the whole friggin' city to make his point? And Goddamnit, what IS the reference to 'The Point'?"

Maybe you should ask WHO the point is, since in this note he calls himself—'the Point' and 'The Survivor,' Frank added. "Doesn't sound like he knows who the fuck he is."

"It has to be Stormer, I guess," Gil replied. "But I'm having trouble seeing him operate this way. He seemed a little different, eccentric, maybe, but not crazy. This note sounds like a certifiable fruitcake."

"Maybe it's one of his supporters," Frank suggested.

"Maybe. But whoever this is, he doesn't sound like a follower-type to me."

"Whoever he is, it looks to me like he's following YOU!" Frank said with a funny expression. "And it doesn't sound as if he likes you a whole lot, Partner."

Gil didn't reply. He just stared at the sheet of paper, trying to imagine the kind of person that would write it. He didn't like the picture that formed in his mind.

Chapter 46

An hour later, Gil sat in the office of the Forensics Sciences Administrator, staring at another shiny sheet of paper. This page had two rows of variegated stripes running alongside each other, similar to the stripes he had seen in Higawa's lab.

"That's what we call an `autorad match' around here," Nussbaum explained. "It provides a direct side-by-side comparison of the bands."

"So what was wrong with Shig's version?"

"Well, we usually use the DNA Print Test here, which is a trademark of Lifecodes, Inc." The Administrator replied stiffly, hands clasped behind his back, a professor lecturing his class. "The genetic material is extracted from the sample, then mixed with a restriction enzyme that cuts the DNA chain at specific sites. After that, the segments are sorted by a process of gel electrophoresis . . ."

"Yeah, Shig threw some of that technical stuff at me before," Gil interrupted, "and I don't understand it any better now. Can you simplify it a little for a layman? What's the point?"

Even as he used those words, the Detective wished he hadn't. They reminded him of the man who called himself "The Point,"—a strange mystery man who apparently was out to destroy the city, the environment, and Gil Beach. Gil's comment also drew a reaction from Nussbaum, who raised his eyebrows, with a little smirk. Gil felt like a stupid schoolchild. Once he and Nussbaum had been friendly—trading wise-cracks more often than lectures. He wondered about the change, since he preferred the old relationship. Now Nussbaum acted like it was part of his duties to make everybody else feel like an idiot. Some people just didn't wear the mantle of authority well.

"Well, the `point' is that the usual test uses length polymorphism for its analysis, and that requires a decent sized sample. When the sample is small, like the fingernail scrapings in this instance, we sometimes use a simpler test from the Cetus Corp. that identifies alleles in a minimal specimen. It's not as reliable."

"Shig told me it was ninety-nine percent accurate."

"That depends on which test, and more importantly, on the quality of the lab work."

Beach didn't respond to the implied reproach to Higawa's work. He knew Shig was a technical genius, and extremely careful. Nussbaum was usually far too critical, especially considering his own reputation to buckle under to politics. Still, Gil didn't want to get in the middle of their internal department conflict.

"The other thing, is that what you saw were two separate reports," Nussbaum went on, "A parallel Autorad provides a much more precise comparison of the two autoradiograph readouts."

"So what's the bottom line?"

"The bottom line," Nussbaum replied archly, "is that the two samples don't really match. I don't know where you got that hair, but it isn't from whoever killed McSwain."

CHAPTER 47

Nina sat frozen in the dim light, appearing to stare at the dark grotto awash with spilled life fluids. Yet her eyes were not focused. She had what combat veterans call "the thousand-yard stare," a distant look born of overwhelming pain, numbness and resignation, looking to some far away reality, beyond the sight of innocent mortals. It is a look that people get when they have seen too much ugliness, too much horror, too much death.

Her child's body trembled with the aftermath of tearing tissues, chemically induced spasms, and gross blood loss—but she had lost more than that. Her child, flesh of her flesh, was gone, taken for reasons Nina could scarcely understand. The infant had been born with a birthmark and a slightly withered foot. It was not perfect, so it had been killed. Those who were to populate the new age, He said, had to be perfect.

A ripple of pain passed across her face, then she stiffened. Straightening, she rubbed teary wetness from her cheeks with the back of a small hand, and mumbled a few words, as if a different person.

"She wasn't supposed to have it . . . it wasn't hers . . .," then rose and limped slowly out of the grisly chamber. As she shuffled away, she pulled a crumpled piece of paper out of her pocket. On the torn sheet was a telephone number.

The hulking figure of The Survivor hardly noticed her departure. He too, was focused on a distant reality. Still panting from his exertions, he moved as if in a trance toward the wall, each movement slow and measured. Using a bloody finger, he marked something on the top sheet of the register, tore off the leaf and skewered it on one of the spikes jutting out of the sanctuary backdrop. It hung with other crimson-splashed pages and lumps of flesh in a fetid display of butchery.

Where he had torn away the page, only a single piece of paper remained, marked with a large number one. He stared at the final page. Normally he waited until the termination was over, before he wrote the name, but there was only this last sheet left now; only one obstacle, one enemy in his way. The body count had almost reached the mystic number. He dipped his finger again, and in a shaky hand scrawled the name of 'Beach.'

CHAPTER 48

"They want your shield, Gil."

Bob Mabry spoke loudly, but compared to his normal bellow, it was the equivalent of a whisper. He stared down at the top of his desk as he spoke, avoiding eye contact with the Detective, who stood fidgeting a few feet away.

Gil's eyes narrowed.

"The IAB creeps told you to do it, because they didn't have the guts, right?"

"Yeah, well, not exactly, Gil. You know something like this has to be signed off by the Commissioner himself. I said I'd tell you. I figured it was better if it came from a friend. Sorry, Gil. Captain's gonna put you on restricted duty until this thing plays out."

"I know," Gil nodded. "It's not your fault, but it still ticks me off. I've got an idea of what's going on. I'm too close to something, I'm making people uncomfortable, so they want me out of the way. Look, Bob, can you cut me any slack on this?"

"I tried, Gil. Honest I did. It sucks, but I can't get you out of this one. They said to reach out for you `forthwith' and all that. I can keep you on the Job for now, but you know the drill—every detective only `serves at the pleasure of the Commissioner'."

"Okay, okay. But can you just give me a little time? What if I hadn't showed up for this meeting? What are they gonna do, put out an all-points on me because I missed an appointment? I need a few hours. Let's say till tomorrow morning. Can you run interference that long?"

The Deputy Inspector raised his eyes. He stared at the other man for a moment, then nodded.

"Uhmm, okay. Ten a.m. tomorrow . . . here. But that's it, Gil. Don't leave my ass swingin' out in the breeze." He turned, staring out of the window until he heard the door close.

Back at his desk, Beach examined a telephone message. After the poisoned water incident, the Department formed an internal task force to launch an investigation. There were many different faces around and a new civilian employee, Harriet Batewell, who was handling the phone. She hadn't yet learned the finer points of screening out unwanted calls or getting sufficient information from the person on the other end of the line, so the note didn't give him much to go on. This looked like a straight message, but Gil knew it wasn't.

The message was from "Mr. Pointe." It said, "He has something of yours, and will be waiting for you."

Gil crumpled the pink sheet in a tightened fist before shoving it in his pocket. From the note they had found on the sabotaged truck, he knew this had to be the leader of the terrorists. As Frank was coming out of the men's room, Beach caught him by the arm.

"Grab a couple of guys, Frank. We're going into the Federation Center, and I don't want to have to wait for back up. I've got an ugly feeling about this."

Frank jerked his head around to stare at his partner. He opened his mouth to say something, then closed it. After a moment he nodded.

"You got it," he murmured, heading for the stairs. As he left, he dropped a hand automatically to the gun holstered at his belt.

Seeing Frank's gesture, Gil's hand went to his back, where he kept his Steyr GB. He had switched from a regulation police issue weapon after nearly getting blown away by a crazed gang member several years earlier. The lunatic had kept coming, still firing after Gil had emptied his six-shot pistol without apparent effect. He had survived that incident, but quickly chose a different weapon to carry. The gun was a little large, but he liked the fifteen round magazine and hitting power. When he went into really hot situations, he sometimes even strapped another small gun to his ankle for insurance, a Hungarian manufactured Browning 7.65-mm pocket pistol. He had only needed to use the second gun once, but that was enough to justify carrying it.

“I’ll meet you downstairs,” he called to the retreating figure of his partner. Then more quietly, “We’re coming Mr. Point, we’re coming!”

CHAPTER 49

Moving canisters to the valve set-up was a simple matter. The Survivor did it himself, caressing the smooth metal as he shifted them to the floor opening. Obtaining the toxic liquid had not been difficult. Each volunteer had been instructed to buy only one container of the poison, and then only as part of a larger mixed order of common garden supplies. Even his troops had no idea that he had accumulated such a large stock of the lethal substances. It was better that way, since some of the less dedicated would eventually have to drink it themselves. Everything was planned. After the poison was introduced to the general city water supply, there would be a ceremony for the peripheral followers, the hangers-on. Then it would be time for the central core to follow him to the end—to put their trust and very existence in his hands. The soldiers of the coming conflict, the loyal Troops, would follow. They would survive with him, or they would not survive at all.

First, however, there was the enemy to deal with—one enemy in particular. He intended to start with that adversary's woman, who thought she had entered the Federation secretly. He had been aware of her duplicity all along. She was just another traitor woman, another betraying bitch like his mother. The Detective's wife had been ready to rut with him, when they had been interrupted. Her willingness confirmed his evaluation. She was another woman that cared more about being screwed, than about her family. This one was in for a big surprise. She was in for several big surprises. He reached between his legs to fondle himself.

Sex had never been as much pleasure, as a tool for him. It had been used against him to dominate, and he learned to use it the same way. Long before he honed his skills of capture and captivation in the streets of the city, he had found that sex could be a weapon. His first carnal experiences, other than being violated himself, were the times his stepfather and sick friends had made children perform for them. He was still a small boy, when he was put with a girl and told to do things to her—things that made him feel used and sick inside. At first he couldn't do it. His little organ would not cooperate. But then they did things to make sure he followed their orders. Once again anger came to his rescue. In those terrible moments he grew to hate the girl, whose name he couldn't even remember anymore. But he remembered how angry he was, that she could get away with just lying there, as his mother had gotten away with it, unresponsive, uninvolved, while he had to perform, while he was being persecuted. He wanted to slap her, to hit her, to wake her up from the clouds in which she had taken refuge. That is when he realized that in a way he could stab her. He could use his own body to do it. He could stab her with his male organ. He could hurt her; he could dominate her the way the men were dominating him. With these thoughts, his erection had swelled and hardened. Then he was able to do what they asked . . . and more. The girl became no more than meat for him—meat that eventually gave forth blood.

The touch of a cold metal canister against his leg reminded him of where he was, bringing him back to the present. He continued his work, looking at the valve construction with pride and pleasure. Access to the NYC water supply had been a primary factor in selecting this building for the Federation's Headquarters. There were three major freshwater conduits in Manhattan, pipes seventy-five inches in diameter, just over six feet wide. Each channeled water to a third or more of the city. The route of the huge tubes was easy to determine from diagrams available at the City Planning Board office. Since the pipes were buried deep underground, no one worried about the possibility of terrorist access. The authorities arranged security for reservoirs, but not these. The powers would have worried, if they realized that from his deep basement, the Survivor had only needed to excavate a few feet further down to uncover the City's aorta, the vessel that carried life-giving fluid to its members.

Unwilling to take the chance of a spy in his midst, he had studied principles of aqueducts and plumbing until he could install the access valve himself. The pipe was ancient, so cutting into it had not been difficult. Without the option of shutting off the normal flow, however, he had needed to construct an elaborate pressure chamber that kept the water from flooding back into his lair when he finally screwed the access valve through the side of the conduit. Ironically, he had found the final parts in the storage shed at ManCo Oil transfer station on the Hudson River during his destructive visit there earlier. He felt tickles of anticipation, as he prepared for the disaster he would visit upon this evil city, as the inevitable confrontation approached. He knew that Delucia wanted a crisis, an environmental issue to catapult him into power. He was going to get one. He was going to get more than he bargained for.

On the surface streets above, a police car drew closer to the Federation Headquarters. Gil Beach sat in the passenger seat, willing to let his partner drive while his gut did an anxiety number. Pre-operation jitters. It didn't show much in his expression, but he twisted the ring on his finger over and over. In that, he was typical. The tension and fear before an operation tended to show in cops' behavior more than their faces. Gum got chewed a thousand times a minute, cigarettes sucked to the filter in seconds, drum solos tapped on steering wheels. But faces were usually veiled. Even the few crazy cops that grinned the whole way in, were wearing a kind of mask.

Gil was not grinning.

CHAPTER 50

The damaged child, Nina, lay on a couch, drawn up in a fetal curl, her head on Pilar's lap, softly moaning. The girl's puppy, Genny, once released from its carrier, had inserted itself into the grouping, cuddling into the curve of Nina's stomach. Pilar slowly stroked the girl's hair, trying to be comforting, although she wasn't quite sure what the child had experienced since last seeing her. Nina had called, inhabiting her manager 'alter', to remind Pilar that the puppy was still in its carrier at the Federation Headquarters. In the confusion and turmoil of her last visit, Pilar had forgotten to take the animal away with her. Something in the child's voice suggested that her call was only partly about the puppy, but in her alter personality of Theo, she would not reveal anything more.

When she arrived at the Federation building, Pilar was met by a slimmer Nina. Obviously, she was no longer carrying the baby. Yet references to the pregnancy and its apparent termination, produced only evasions from the girl.

"Not here."

Pilar knew that the child had been through some deep trauma, perhaps there had been a miscarriage. She wasn't sure whether to be pleased or saddened that Nina needed to turn to her for support.

Despite her suspicions concerning Nina's mental state and wellness, Pilar was not anxious or upset. In fact, she was a little surprised at how relaxed she felt. Still, she enjoyed the sense of well-being. As they sat quietly, she could tell that the child was loosening as well. The spicy smell of the Center seemed particularly strong in the air today. It was a pleasant odor, taking Pilar's mind to early memories of pies baking in her mother's kitchen.

When a man stepped into the room, Pilar looked up dreamily. He looked familiar. It was the same man who had placed his hands on her shoulders before. The one that sent tingles up her belly. 'Storm,' wasn't it? His hair was strikingly silver, the eyes a penetrating purple. Yet if she ignored those distinguishing, and distracting traits, he looked like someone she had seen before. He looked like . . . like . . . The thought would not pull together. His gaze was mesmerizing.

He reached down to lift the pup from its human nest, then sat next to Pilar on the couch. In his hand, he held two glasses of murky liquid.

"You have great kindnesss and compassssion," he purred, holding out his pronunciation of the s's in an almost sensual manner. "You are very special. I wisssh to toast your loving heart."

Her ability to concentrate at the moment was unaccountably weak. With the distraction of his muscular leg pressed next to hers, Pilar hardly knew how the glass appeared in her hand. Yet, when he raised his goblet in a toasting gesture, it seemed natural for her to respond in kind. The sweet-tasting liquid felt warm and glowing as it went down her throat, the warmth spreading quickly from her stomach out into her entire body. She hadn't had a pain killer for ages, but this feeling reminded her of how she felt when she had once taken prescribed opiates during a episode of severe physical pain after being injured. Like that time, there now seemed to be a layer of invisible insulation between her and the world. The man rose, offering his hand to help her up. She stood unsteadily, then unthinking, moved easily into his arms. As before, without any conscious decision, it smoothly turned into an embrace. She pressed her lips to his, now knowing what thrilling feelings that could produce. Surprisingly, the kiss wasn't gentle this time. It almost bruised her lips, causing her to quickly pull back. Was something wrong? Yet she knew she was unsteady. *Maybe I'm just being clumsy.*

So as he led her away, she ignored the brief uncomfortable moment the same as she would ignore an accidental bumping of elbows at a dinner table. She moved forward in a mental cloud, the man's strong arm snugly around her waist. Another man walked not far behind them, dressed in military type clothing, Nina's limp form draped over his shoulder.

Chapter 51

There were six police officers in the quickly assembled team—five men and Gina Esperoza. Three were from Robbery Division, two others from Homicide and "Stubby" Kinnear from Narcotics, who was staying out of his current anti-drug operation until they could check a rumor that his cover had been busted. Meanwhile, he was temporarily available for odd jobs.

They drove to the Federation Headquarters in two cars. Ralph Bunger and "Red" McCormick, detectives from Robbery, took one of them to the back of the building to cover the rear escape route. The other four officers moved through the colonnaded entrance on foot. Gil felt his heart racing, as he told Gina to secure the lobby while the others divided and spread through the building. There were many rooms, many places to hide. T There were a lot of places for surprises.

The results were anti-climactic. In a few minutes, a small group of FONS volunteers were rousted and herded into the lobby. Stubby had interrupted a minor orgy, which got him some nasty remarks from one of the naked participants who had been caught in a particularly interesting position. Other than that single protest, there was little resistance. Not even from Storm, who appeared a few moments later from some hidden area, looking as if he were in a trance. He looked different. A "FONIE fog", Gil thought, noting the generally passive behavior of the Center's workers. Then he sniffed the odor-laden air. He directed officers to throw open as many doors and windows as they could get to, allowing a fresh breeze to blow away the spicy aroma. He wasn't sure, but those fragrant scents might have a mood-altering effect. No one interfered with the police's actions as they attempt to air-out the space.

Too easy, he thought, and didn't like it. Something wasn't right; the raid was overly simple. Beach felt unused adrenaline coursing through his body, which drove him to give a frustrated slap to a nearby marble column, the impact stinging his hand. He was tight as a drumhead. Hitting things wouldn't help . . . he needed to calm down.

"Back in a minute," he said, walking to the rear of the building. He made a restless tour of the rooms, until he found the lounge where he had first seen Storm, noting a downstairs exit. He descended the narrow staircase to a simple basement room, unfurnished except for storage cabinets and two food freezers. A large column occupied the center of the room, with strange dark paintings decorating each side. The murals pictured strange scenes of conflict with small bands of defenders, holding off massed attackers. It looked like survivalist propaganda in pictures.

The cabinets were unlocked. They should have been searched already, but he still opened each of them vigorously, his every movement energized by frustration. All he found were supplies of paper goods, dishes, and other dietary goods. Raising the lid of the first freezer with a bang, he saw plastic bags of vegetables and other side dishes. The second freezer was set aside for entrees, apparently, as it was mostly filled with paper-wrapped packages of meat, labeled with black marking pen. There was enough to feed a lot of people for a short time, or a few for a long time. He was about to slam the lid down, when his eye caught a discordant note. He looked more carefully at the packages, with their titles "Chicken breasts," "London Broil," and "Chopped Beef." One package caught his eye. He felt a lump in his throat.

The other officers had probably missed the message. He supposed that the letters looked a lot like the word "Beef." But this package said "Beach."

He gingerly removed the small packet from the freezer. A thin plastic coating on the paper allowed him to unwrap the icy contents, despite the cold. Inside was a partially frozen hunk of fleshy material. The clump was several individual bloody pieces lumped together. Gil could make out what appeared to be a couple of human ears and at least one eye in the bloody collection. The flesh must have been put there quite recently because it had not fully hardened. Also stuck to the tangled lump was a piece of metal, silver, in a familiar shape. Across the metal were the letters NYPD, with a number at the bottom, 22622. It was a New York Police officer's shield.

Gil stared at the grotesque sight. As his thoughts cleared, he recognized the number on the shield. He had seen it often, because that number was scratched along with the initials "C.S". across the front of half a dozen lockers down at the Precinct. Only one cop had that many lockers.

Gil turned back the wrapping paper, to confirm that it was labeled with his name. He felt something hot and dark surge through his torso. He dropped the package back in the freezer, then stood rigidly, hands clenching white at his sides. He moved back to the staircase he had used to enter the basement room. It connected to the floor above by way of several turns and landings. There were only four flights of stairs between the two floors, nothing like the many sets in the stadium where he usually worked out, but that arena was far away. He was here, and the firestorm was here in his gut. He needed to calm down now. Helplessness and frustration were melting into anger, and it was seething at an intensity he didn't need. Not only did it get in the way of clear thinking, but also it was an old demon—one that had almost beaten him in the past. But he had come to terms with the demon long ago.

The deep anger was not nearly as raw and potent as what had driven him years ago, but it would never be completely gone. He had learned to see the signs so he could take steps to control it. In fact, he literally "took steps." Running up and down flights of stairs had become a regular habit; a means of exercising, and exorcising—driving out his personal demons.

The combination of the fruitless raid and grotesque message left for him, turned his insides into a churning cauldron. Now he needed release. He practically leapt up the four flights of the rear stairway, returned to the bottom. Then he repeated the process several times. He didn't stop until he was out of breath with trickles of perspiration running down his back.

As he leaned against a large central column in the basement room, panting to regain his wind, he realized he was touching one of several dark murals, or frescos, painted on the plaster of the structure's surface. He pulled back, avoiding touching the strange column. After a few moments of deep breathing, he felt a little better. At least he could return to the others now with some appearance of calm.

Apparently, Beach hadn't been missed. When he reappeared, officers were still milling around, talking in low tones, making notes in little pads or on electronic devices, questioning a handful of detainees. He went up to Stormer, who didn't seem to recognize the detective as one his Foundation's newest "volunteers." Gil stared straight into his face, but there was no response, other than a gathering of moisture in the man's eyes. Was it the beginning of tears? There was an odd off-center appearance to the man's pupils. It was a moment before Gil realized what he was seeing.

"I'll be damned!" he exclaimed.

"What is it?" Frank asked quickly, still alert to danger.

"It's just contacts!" Gil explained, "He doesn't have purple eyes at all." Now the liquid brimmed, rolling down the man's cheeks. Since the tears were not accompanied by any other outward sign of emotion, it was hard to tell what he was feeling. It could be anger, fear, or both. Between the drugged-out stare, the slipping contacts, and the tears, it didn't make for a very charismatic appearance. Then the man spoke.

"You don't want me—you want Him."

"Him?"

"Yes . . . the Survivor."

Gil blinked in recognition of the name.

"The Survivor. Okay, so where is he?"

"In the bunker."

Before he could be interrogated further, Stormer slumped. His eyes rolled up in his head, and he went completely limp. That effectively ended the conversation, but the little that had been said needed to be pursued. It was too intriguing to let drop. Gil tried getting more information from some of the other gathered disciples, but they were either too drugged and frightened to answer questions, or really didn't know anything about the "Bunker." Repeated questions got no useful information.

Police officers combed the Headquarters top to bottom, but after an hour of frustrated searching and more grilling of the unresponsive detainees, the team was forced to return to the Precinct with their limited catch. Before they left, Gil went to the office he had stumbled upon days before, to gather several boxes of papers from the file drawers and desks for later examination. He hoped there would be something in the documents that would justify Judge Tyrone's warrant.

He was silent as they drove back through the streets of the city. The car tires hissed on wet pavement, seeming to taunt him, the wipers thumped out a mocking rhythm.

CHAPTER 52

When they reached Fifth Street, a police unit and barriers blocked off the road. Gil rolled down his window to speak to the Uniform standing his post there. The nametag said "C. Pordero" and Gil recognized the young man as a recent Police Academy graduate, already getting noticed because of his poise and willingness to learn.

"What's up, Cesar?" Gil could feel tension in his neck and shoulders. He didn't want to hear about another water cooler poisoning.

"There's a bomb in a car, up near the Precinct, Sir."

"For real, or just a scare?"

"Oh it's real, Sir. They've cleared the area."

"Where's the Bomb Squad?"

"I guess the containment vehicle is stuck somewhere, Sir. They said they would be a while, so everyone should keep clear from the car and the body, until they get here."

"Body? What body?"

"Well . . . there's a guy in the car, Sir. Looks pretty messed up. They figure he's dead. There's a pipe bomb sticking out of him."

“Out of him?”

“That’s what I hear, Sir.”

“No I.D. yet?”

“Naw, but I saw his arm hanging outta the window, and I swear I’ve seen that bracelet before. Kinda different, with a big black rock in it.”

“Was it gold, with some reddish designs around the stone?”

“Gosh, I’m not sure, but yeah, I think so.”

Beach pushed the door open to jump from the car, accelerating into a sprint after a few steps.

“Wait, Sir,” the surprised rookie called. “We’re supposed to keep everybody . . .”

Frank stepped out of the car’s driver side, hesitating.

“Gil . . . ?” he called uncertainly.

“It’s Sedgwick!” Beach called back over his shoulder. “I know that bracelet.”

Frank sighed, then jogged past the barricades following his partner. The rookie, Pordero, looked around helplessly. When he realized that he couldn’t control a couple of determined detectives, and probably wouldn’t be expected to, he shrugged and resumed his guard position.

Gil reached the car, puffing. There was a hand hanging out of the window as described, the bracelet on the wrist could be seen clearly. It was the one worn habitually by Cage Sedgwick. The jewelry was a trophy of his first post-marriage conquest and symbol of his entry into a career of procurement. He was lying across the seat, a large metal pipe protruding from his chest. Blood was caked on his shirt, neck, and what was left of his face. Gil almost wondered if he had made a mistake, until he realized the man's appearance had been altered. Where his eyes and ears should have been, there were bloody cavities. Gil's stomach gave a flip-flop as he figured that the missing parts must be what he had held in his hands a few minutes earlier—the contents of the grisly package he had found in the freezer at the Federation Center. He was about to make the most likely assumption that his old acquaintance and former partner was dead, when he saw a few bubbles form in the red wetness around the broken man's nose.

"He's breathing!" Gil shouted, running quickly to the opposite side of the car, where he slowly eased open the door.

"There's a bomb!" Someone shouted from a distance.

"Screw the bomb, we gotta get him outta here." Gil bent down over the bloody face to speak where an ear had once been. "Can you hear me, Cage? It's Beach. We'll get you out of this."

"Noooo . . ." in a soft moist whisper, "no time."

"What? What do you mean, Cage?"

"Timer . . . go off . . . any minute," the mutilated man gurgled through the blood puddling in his mouth.

Gil looked at the pipe protruding from just below Sedgwick's breastbone. About six inches of metal were showing, with a screw-on cap fitting over the end, pierced by a drilled hole. A plastic-coated wire extended through the hole, running downward to disappear under the car seat.

This was the Bomb Squad's jurisdiction, Gil knew, but a few moments' delay could mean death for Cage. He tried to remember the basics of "Bombs and Arson" he had gotten at the Academy, but could recall his armed service training better. Whatever explosive was used, he knew, there had to be an initiator of some sort, probably at one end of that wire. The launching charge would be under the metal cap, so the wire probably led to a battery and switch of some sort. It should be a simple matter to disconnect the wire. That's the way it appeared. Still, he hesitated.

Despite a lack of specific demolition training, Gil was an experienced cop. Part of his success as a Homicide Detective was because he wasn't content to accept the obvious. His many useful skills also included the ability to think like a perpetrator, even if that meant seeing the world from the distorted viewpoint of a killer. More than once, he had asked himself if this skill was a gift or a burden. Whatever it was, it made him good at his job. Unfortunately, it also made for some sleepless nights.

It was that quality that now made him decide the wire was a trick. He could already sense the way this "Survivor" thought. It was no accident that the bomb was jammed into the body of Gil's friend. The killer seemed to place great stock in commitment and trust. Beach imagined the man was counting on Gil to risk himself for his friend. The bomb was meant for Beach, the wire was there to fool him. He was supposed to be so distracted by his concern for Sedgwick, that he lost objectivity. He was supposed to thoughtlessly assume that outward appearances were true—that the wire was the solution. Gil was certain that it was a trap. If he traced that innocuous looking wire to its source, he was sure there would be a lethal surprise. So he ignored it. Or more accurately, he looked beyond it.

He tried to center his mind—to focus on the small area of space he occupied, the thick greenhouse warmth of the auto, the metallic smell of steel and blood. He noted the zinc-coated surface of the tube, the smeared blood, the faint scratch marks of a vice on its side. He focused on the heavy metal cap, under which the actual initiator charge probably resided. It too, could possibly be booby-trapped. The bomb squad didn't usually mess with this kind of thing at all. They just put it in a containment vehicle and took it to their firing range where they detonated the tricky thing. Usually, however, they didn't find these lethal devices sticking out of a living person's chest. At that moment, Sedgwick took a shallow breath, causing a rivulet of blood to seep out along the side of the tube, thick and dark.

Gil's mouth felt dry, despite the sweat on his upper lip. There was moisture on his palms, too. He pulled a handkerchief from his pocket, dried his hands and gingerly wiped blood off the surface of the pipe, then carefully slipped his left hand around the tube, below the cap. Sedgwick moaned and shifted, as the pipe moved slightly in his chest. His broken mouth continued to whisper, "no time . . . no time."

Gil tightened his grip on the pipe, grasping the threaded cap with his right hand, the cloth wrapped around it to improve his hold on the slippery surface. Unfortunately, the fabric was already soggy so it didn't help much. Gil almost jumped, when an arm suddenly appeared through the side window, holding something. It was a clean handkerchief. He looked up to see Terranova leaning into the car, an embarrassed grin on his face. He didn't grin back.

"Get outta here, Frank. This thing could go up any minute."

"Yeah, well, I ain't got anything better to do right now."

Terranova reached in a pocket, pulled out one of his ever-handy candies and popped it in his mouth.

“Want a jelly bean?”

Gil smiled in spite of himself. He declined the candy but took the clean handkerchief and turned back to his work.

Beach hoped that the metal cover of the bomb had been hand-tightened. Applying tools to metal filled with explosives was a recipe for disaster, so most bombmakers liked to work with their hands. It seemed he was right, because when gripped with the dry cloth, the cap moved without much force, loosening easily. He slowly turned it, trying to ignore the sweat trickling into his eyes. If he had the power to see inside the tube, he would have sweat even more.

When The Survivor was putting this killing instrument together, he had not been perfect. When he had pressed a packet of explosive into the end of the pipe, tiny particles of powder had leaked from the punctured plastic wrap, working their way into the pipe threads. The bomb had almost exploded as the man was assembling it, but at one point, he had paused briefly for a sip of water. That unintentional brief pause had allowed the grains of explosive to cool just enough, so that when the cap was secured with another turn, they had not quite reached kindling temperature. There was no such pause today. On the fourth turn of the cap, these same particles were heated by friction to the exact heat level required to ignite them. They flared for the briefest of moments, just long enough to ignite the packet itself, which in turn caught fire. It expanded with force and heat adequate to ignite the major explosive charge loaded into the steel tube. All this happened in microseconds. Gil had no warning when the bomb exploded.

Chapter 53

The Survivor heard a loud "whump" and felt a tremor in the pavement. Then he saw flame and smoke rising from where he had left the car and the cop's body as bait for his trap. Less than a block away, he lowered the binoculars he had used to view the street from a safe distance. He was in his normal disguise now, and could have walked right up to the scene, without danger of being recognized. Still, there was no use being too visible. He glanced at his watch. All was going according to plan. His mouth slowly shifted into a lazy smile. So much for the smart-ass Detective.

Minutes later he was in his lair, camouflage makeup and bandoleers of ammunition in place. He quickly glided to the wall, where the Register still hung, with its single remaining page. He might have preferred to use actual blood from the adversary, for the delicious symbolism, but he couldn't do that unless he went to where the man's flesh was now splattered all over the street. There were cop pigs everywhere—agents of the rich and spoiled, guardians of the status quo. Sometimes the law agencies were known to examine photos of onlookers in an attempt to identify a perpetrator. He was not afraid of them, but it was too soon for him to be revealed. Their meeting would come later. The best he could do for now was to take care of the enemy's woman, lashed onto the holding device, helpless and completely under his dominion.

She lay, unmoving, stunned. Her hair was disheveled, make-up smeared. Her alleged beauty was exposed for the facade he knew it to be. She was just a dirty whore like all the others. Her flat belly moved rapidly in and out as she breathed shallowly. She had been unprepared for his change from lover to torturer. While she was confused and slowed by the drugs, he had been able to strap her down before she realized what was taking place.

He took an antique straight razor from his pocket, opening it with a "snap." Now he carefully removed her clothing, piece by piece, cutting the resisting cloth with his razor. First the outer garments - the stylish slacks and blouse -"snick, snick, snick." Her eyes were so wide, he could understand how people spoke of eyes "bugged-out in fear." Soon she lay in only her undergarments, exposed and vulnerable. He smiled, humming a tuneless melody, then he leaned down to lick a spot on her stomach. He could taste her fear as he inserted his tongue into her navel and mouthed her skin. He rose, smiling, saliva dripping from his mouth then moved again with his razor. He snipped away the brassiere—"snick, snick," watching the breasts flatten out on her chest, nipples contracting into tight knobs, as if shriveling to hide themselves. Sometimes women reacted this way to sexual excitement, sometimes to fear. He believed that the two responses were quite similar. Thinking about this similarity, he felt a growing hardness in his groin. Next came the panties, "snick, snick." Her body trembled like she had a raging fever. Her breathing came short and fast. He thought she looked like a virgin on her wedding night, waiting to be ravished for the first time—apparent fear hiding her real eagerness. It was so tempting to take her now. Still, he waited. There would be time later for that. The waiting would only increase his anticipation and her delicious reactions. Besides, once he had dirtied himself with her, she would have to die. It was too soon for that concluding act yet. There were other matters to be completed.

Now he added a mental element to her suffering. He moved a monitor and video player to where she could see the screen. Then he played a recording of her husband that she wasn't expecting. The video showed her man during his betrayal, rutting with Euryale. In the darkened relaxation module, it had been relatively easy to hide a camera. As his captive viewed the scenes, he enjoyed seeing the twitches and jerks of her body, the display hitting her as solidly as physical blows. She didn't know yet that her detective husband was dead, so she could still feel betrayed and abandoned. He then set the machine on automatic replay, a continuing loop, so she would be forced to see it again and again.

Oblivious to pain, he stroked his arm with the sharp edge of the blade, seeing red blood welling up in the slit it formed. He went to her side, making a deep cut in her arm, similar to the one he had carved in his flesh. He ignored her screams and tears. Placing his arm in position directly above, blood dripped down and mixed with hers, pooling on the floor below. He caught some of the syrupy liquid in the cup of his hand, held it over her nude form, and let a few drops fall onto her breasts, her stomach, and between her legs. He felt his excitement growing, again wanting to pounce on her but knew there was an order to things and were other tasks that had to be completed before he took the pleasure of violating her body.

He walked over to his lair, dipping a finger again into the liquid still cupped in his palm, so he could trace Beach's name once more on the final page of the calendar, where he had written it earlier. His finger moved in trembling strokes. Knowing the end was near, he had been living on nothing but liquids and drugs for days. He had no need for food. He could survive on air, and water, and hate. It would not be long, now. He reached for a bottle of capsules, swallowing four of them. They would provide enough energy for the rest of what he had to do.

The woman was strapped in position, struggling vainly. The younger girl, the failed breeder, was tied to a chair, immobile in the stillness of deep shock. The dog whimpered in a corner, tied in place with a rope around his neck.

"I will have my way with each of you," he warned. "But first I am going to set free a wave of death for the ignorant hordes. They will know the reality of environmental disaster."

Pilar stared at him in horrid fascination. As she took in the situation, she was certain that she would not live much longer. So she threw aside caution and verbally questioned the building blocks of his insane reasoning.

"Don't you see any contradiction in your willingness to destroy great numbers of people, while claiming to love the world?"

He paused, sneering, for a long time, as if not deigning to answer. But then spoke.

"Not at all. The cataclysm is inevitable. I am only hurrying along the necessary steps. My most faithful followers will survive with me. There will be a new order of things, in which we will reappear as victorsss."

He wished someone could see his great achievements, marvel at his elaborate arrangements. Even this woman, face-to-face with him, did not understand. Impulsively, he released her from her fixed position, leaving only the bonds on her wrists. Holding this tether, he dragged her along as if on a leash, to watch his work. He stepped through a narrow door, pulling her with him, up a flight of steps to where he opened a panel that led into the basement chamber. The framing borders of a mural disguised the edges of the panel. A few feet away, the secret floor hatch was already open, and the pressurized canisters were in place.

After tying the woman to a standing pipe, he tugged at the spokes of the metal valve cover, straining to unscrew it like the wheel of a watertight door in a submarine. The locking latches swung aside, allowing him to remove a shiny cover plate. He paused for a moment, engrossed by the turbid water pushing past the clear viewing aperture. The water pressure was still contained by an elaborate watertight attachment, topped by a brass fitting. Then he reached for the first metal canister, hoisted it into place, and connected it to a thick rubber hose. The hose had brass fittings at each end; one end attached to the metal tank, the other end going into the conduit's added valve mechanism. Once the connector was tightened, he placed his hand on a red colored metal lever, then paused again, turning to his prisoner.

"This is the end," he told her. "Or at least the beginning of the end. The world will never be the same after this. Soon multitudes of the common mass will die. I will increase in power for every one of the weak horde that dies, choking on what they think is the water of life."

"Why?" whispered the woman. "If you care about the earth, how can you do this? How can you destroy its creatures . . . poison its waters?"

"The earth will be cleansed. Millions of people will no longer pump sewage into the rivers, chemicals into the air, and use up the resources of the earth."

Despite her distress, Pilar's mind suddenly made a terrible connection.

"This … this is connected to Delucia somehow, isn't it—another environmental disaster will boost his campaign?"

The Survivor laughed.

"You have some primitive intelligence, don't you? Perhaps there was such a connection at an early stage of the process. But not any longer. Delucia is weak. He wouldn't go far enough. The clown owes much to me, but he doesn't understand the enormity of the problem. Delucia thinks he can become President and control society. That's a joke. Politicians only have the power to maintain the status quo. They are little more than lackeys—figureheads of the decadent powers." He paused to spit on the ground. "The only way to truly save the Earth, is to kill off those who despoil her."

"But you are increasing the pollution, the destruction."

"Temporarily. Yet for our small cadre of Survivors, the natural resources of earth will retain an inexhaustible supply. In time, she will cleanse herself. In the meantime, only the strong will survive, to inherit the Earth and all her riches."

Desperately, Pilar fought to keep from collapsing in fear and resignation. She searched for something that would provoke him . . . anything to interrupt his thinking, his dark fixation.

"What if, . . . if someone is stronger than you?"

"Such a one does not exist. I will remain, because I am the Survivor. I have always survived, and I always will."

A glazed look was in the man's eyes now. He stopped talking, turning now to his tubes and valves. Pilar had run out of things to say. She felt frozen in fear and dread.

In panting obsession, the crazed man turned a large handle. Although it was slippery with blood, he managed to wrench the lever open. With a gurgle, the canister began discharging its contents into the city water supply. His prisoner gave a gasp, then quietly watched in horror as the poison was released. She couldn't hold back a scream of powerless terror and dismay, which slowly ebbed to helpless groans and sobs.

The process was slow, his patience hard to hold in check. When the first container was finally empty, he reached quickly for another. It took a long time to empty the perfect amount, ***seven,*** cannisters. He could barely stand the wait, but managed to endure, knowing that even now, as he still worked, the first victims would be drinking the lethal liquid, a lovely orange-red in its concentrated form. It was now flowing onward, spreading through miles of conduits, invading the entire New York City system, carrying the message of retribution and reminding all that they were but leaves of grass in the grand scheme of Nature as well as the plans of her ultimate Survivor.

He put the woman back in restraints, leaving her with a final terrible message.

"Oh, by the way. Your man is dead, too. His physical form no longer exists, except as small fragments mixed with the earth. I blew him into pink mist and bits of meat."

Surprisingly, she didn't appear shaken. He realized that she didn't believe him. She had great confidence in this husband of hers. A tickle of doubt crept into his mind. Was it possible this is not a normal man with whom he was contending? Could he be more than a mere mortal, and somehow survive even a bomb blast? It was a shaking thought that he did not want to entertain. Yet in the ultimate battle, the power to survive could itself be part of the final competition. That is why he had taken on his own title of Survivor.

He went upstairs to where a separate supply of canisters had been set aside for another purpose; preparing a special beverage for his less-needed followers. Those who could not serve as shock troops were expendable. As he mixed wine and the poison in a large vat-like bowl, an onlooker might have been struck by the resemblance to some childhood nightmare of a witch stirring her cauldron of evil brew. The similarities were not so terribly off target.

The pernicious idea had taken up lodging in his mind. The idea that his adversary might not easily die, preyed on the Survivor's thoughts, until he decided he had to confirm the kill. He went to a telephone and punched in the number for the Ninth Precinct, NYPD.

CHAPTER 54

As it turned out, his doubt was well founded. Miraculously, Gil Beach survived the bomb blast. Two factors saved him from being blown to fragments. First, the bomb's raw materials were old. Though it is not well known, exposure to air and moisture has a decaying effect on most explosives. If they still work after such exposure, they may have only a fraction of the blasting power they once possessed. Stored for some time in the damp basement of the assassin's lair, these aged explosives had lost much of their power. Yet, the amount packed into the pipe would still have been sufficient to blow the Detective away, were it not for the second factor.

Explosions are really just examples of rapid burning, i.e. combustion. Their blasting power comes from the initial containment of that quick burning and the rapidly expanding gases it produces. Wrapped tightly in layers of paper and glue, a few grains of powder will produce the ear-shattering bang of a firecracker. Yet, if you open one end of the fireworks wrapping paper, the act of lighting the powder merely produces a briefly fizzling flare.

Held back by an eighth inch of steel tubing, even the deteriorated explosives of the bombmaker's handiwork would have built to immense pressures, rupturing the metal in a lethal blast of fire and steel shards. However, as Gil turned the threaded cap, he not only created the heat to ignite the powder, but he also loosened the end enough so that the combustion forced it off the last thread, stripping the small metal flange with minimal resistance.

So instead of a killing blast, the igniting powder produced a loud pop, along with a flare of burning material similar to a large Roman candle. The threaded cap flew off, like a deadly champagne cork, blasting through the thin metal of the car roof, to land several hundred feet away, at the feet of a surprised rookie cop named Pordero, who would never forget this day. Smoke and flame belched out of the now open auto window frame, throwing Gil back with singed hands, smoking eyebrows, and a face scorched like he had been sunburned. The booming sound that everyone heard, was not from the primary bomb at all, but from a boobytrap that as Beach suspected, had been attached by the inviting dangling wire. Located under the car seat, that smaller charge made a big bang, and lifted the car seat a couple of feet straight up but did not produce a significant sideways or lateral blast to take Gil out where he fell alongside the car. Frank who was out of the line of both flare and vertical blasts, merely found himself sitting on the pavement covered with lumpy particles of fragmented safety glass and seat padding.

Sedgwick was not as lucky. He was already near death when the propelling force of the vomiting flame acted on the tube like the thrust of a rocket, driving it even deeper into his tortured body. Like a huge blow to his chest, it was more than Cage's depleted system could take. Then the booby trap lifted him and the seat forcibly enough to smash his head into the roof. When he came to rest, a few final bubbles formed at his mouth, and he was still.

Gil shook his rattled head, eased his way over onto his knees and rose shakily to his feet. For once, his face was easy to read. Even without the singed eyebrows he would have looked hot. He was infuriated.

The anger was still smoldering, but less visible when he walked into the Interrogation Room an hour later. After being debriefed, and getting a quick check by the doctor, Gil returned to the Precinct where he found two people waiting. They presented quite a contrast. One was a young man, though the unisex style he affected didn't aid in that classification. "Punk" as a style was past its prime, but there are always punks of one sort or another, Gil thought, whether they call themselves punks, or head-bangers, or skinheads, or whatever. They always dress in a way to broadcast the fact. This one wore an outlandish costume of black silk and leather, decorated with numerous studs and rivets. His hair was slicked down in a greasy style that didn't keep oily strands from flopping into his eyes. In the one ear that Gil could see, there were five separate earrings. Several others punctured one nostril.

The only surprising thing was the boy's expression, which was not the predictable sullen pout or disdainful conceit. The face seemed more open and vulnerable than usually seen in these types, the individual's sallow cheeks marked by tears.

The other man was older. He wore the simple black suit and hard white collar of a priest. His appearance didn't quite fit the priestly stereotype though—he was one of the few Roman clergy Gil had seen who sported a full beard and mustache. He chomped steadily away at a hunk of chewing gum, which didn't exactly match the image either. The cleric reminded Gil of a big lumberjack or mountain man, with a chaw of tobacco in use, or maybe a Hutterite farmer in his Sunday go-to-meetin' clothes. Still, he was a priest . . . a good one. He was the kind that was more interested in the needs of people than in his image. Gil recognized Father Noonan, the Assistant Director of Homewell House. The Founder, Father Gentry was his boss and handled most of the public relations-type activities. Noonan handled the day-to-day operations of the place. Gil wondered what had brought him down to the station from his normally hectic schedule running the shelter. The gum, he knew, was Noonan's attempt to break a heavy cigarette habit.

The priest rose, spreading his arms. He was a hugger. Gil wasn't. Not that he had anything against it, it just wasn't his style, especially in the middle of an interrogation room with a punk-type kid looking on. It seemed specially inappropriate right after he had seen a man die. Before the priest got within hugging distance, Gil quickly launched into conversation.

"Father Noonan," he nodded, "excuse me if I seem abrupt, but how urgent is this? One of our officers was just killed."

"Yes, I know." Noonan responded, dropping his arms. "That's why we're here, really." The Priest waved his hand in the direction of the young man who accompanied him.

"James came to me, but I told him that you would want to hear what he had to say."

"He's from Homewell?"

Father Noonan looked uncomfortable, appearing to search for words, when the boy intervened.

"I guess I've changed a little since you saw me last. I'm James . . . Jimmy Sedgwick."

Beach squinted at the young man in front of him.

"I didn't recognize you at first. It's been a long time."

"Yeah, two or three years, at least."

"Look, Jimmy, I'm sorry about your father."

Gil struggled for the right words. He felt helpless as tears slid down the boy's cheeks again.

"Look kid . . ."

"I'm not a kid," the boy objected, snuffling and wiping his nose with the back of a hand. "And I can help you."

"Help me? How's that?"

"I know who killed my Dad."

Gil recoiled at that. He looked over at the Priest, who nodded.

"Okay. Tell me what you know."

"It's the 'Point man' . . ." the boy began. "That's just one of his names. I've heard him called The Survivor, Drang, Leader and other stuff. When there was no response from the detective, he added, "You know, the leader of the survivalists—the loyal troops.

"You mean 'Storm', right?" Gil asked, puzzled.

"No, No way. Storm is just a wimp. Look, I'm in . . . I mean I *was* in "The Circle." I saw The Man do stuff . . . uhh . . . bad stuff, with kids, girls, I mean like, you know. We used a lot of drugs, I guess. The special wine drink and all, and like they put something in the air system at the place, this aerosol stuff with a sharp smell. Sometimes, afterwards, ya know, we didn't even remember what had gone down. That's why some of us younger . . . uh, troops did our own thing in this other place—a barn in the woods sometimes. It was like an acid trip, ya know, or somethin', like we would get really ripped and . . ." the boy's voice had become excited, until he realized it sounded like he was enjoying the memory too much, so he stopped at that point, lowering his head.

"Sorry. Look, I wish I'd never gotten into it, but like he said and did things that kinda hooked us, ya know, and kinda scared us about telling anyone, too. If you ever saw this guy's eyes, you'd understand. And like, he made these girls do it with him, until they got like knocked up, ya know. So he could, like keep the babies . . . I know you're gonna think I'm crazy, but I'm telling the truth, honest. He said, like civilization is gonna fall apart, and they're gonna like retreat to defensive positions, an' like hold out, ya know. I guess it sounds crazy now, but it sounded good when he said it, ya know? He said that if we learned to be hard and put aside the values of a weak society we would be the ones that survived. I mean, like there were a couple of guys that were scared an all, and like . . . well, they're gone now."

The boy was blubbering while shaking his head in apparent disbelief at his own story. Gil was tempted to ask exactly what role the boy himself played in these activities but decided to save those questions for later. Right now, he wanted other information.

"You think this . . . 'Point' man, killed your father?"

"I know it, man!" he shouted. "Dad came to get me. They stopped him, and they took him away, and, and . . ." he choked and broke into sobs. "Jeez, I was so shitty to my dad. And he just wanted to help, and like . . . oh shit, I know it's my fault!"

Father Noonan moved close to put his arm around the boy. He was a hugger, all right. Gil waited a moment, until the boy's sobbing had lessened enough to continue questioning.

"You're sure it wasn't Storm?"

"Shit, yes. That ass-wipe? Sorry. He's just a figurehead for old ladies and the cocktail set. All that "Federation" stuff is just a front for the real inner circle—the loyal Survival Troops. I told you. I was inside," pulling up a sleeve as he spoke, to reveal a yin-yang symbol inscribed on his forearm. He held it up, like an emblem.

"This is the sign. It's like, to show that you must have darkness to have light, ya know. We were supposed to be the darkness part. I guess that sounds bad, but like he said we were making the light possible. I'm telling you, The Survivor is the guy you want."

It sounded like a slogan or chant. Gil felt sickened at the revelations. He couldn't work up much sympathy for the young man, despite feelings of loss about his father, Cage's death. It was a little late for the loving son routine, and it didn't even begin to explain the grotesque actions he had just described. Horrible stuff had been shared in a way that pretty much indicated the boy had, himself, participated in the sickness. As Gil tried to think of an appropriate response, Frank Terranova stuck his head in the door, motioning for Gil to join him outside.

"Rancid Randall is here. He wants your ass, but I think he'll settle for springing the good Brother Storm . . . at least for the moment.

When Gil found the Assistant District Attorney waiting in an adjoining office, he didn't think he had ever seen the man so upset. Apparently, the A.D.A. had come without notice or time to groom himself. He was pacing around the perimeter of the room, his jacket buttoned wrong, hair mussed, and generally disheveled.

When he saw Gil, he stopped to look closer, as if not quite sure who he was seeing. Then he seemed to recognize the detective.

"Beach!" he nearly shouted, "You are up shit creek without a goddamn paddle. What the fuck do you think you're doing, violating the privacy of a community center, a service organization, a fucking headquarters for positive action? What the goddamn shit did you have in mind, dragging innocent people out like they were some common street criminals, and holding a respected community leader without a charge?" Specks of saliva flew from his mouth as he shouted.

Gil didn't reply. Partly because he suspected that part of what the lawyer said was right. There was a distinct possibility at this point that they had the wrong man. The other reason he didn't respond was because he didn't want let loose his own emotional chain reaction that he might have trouble controlling. He was barely holding his temper in check as it was. His revulsion for the attorney combined with anger at the recent events might lead to mayhem. There were times in the past when Beach's anger had not been under control. Fortunately, his partner read the signals and moved in at that point. Terranova stepped forward in a way that conveniently separated the two angry men, like cutting a steer out of the herd. He started talking to Randall, ignoring Gil. His partner took the opportunity to exit the room.

Grudgingly, Gil went to tell Father Noonan and Jimmy that they could go. He didn't tell them there would be no consequences, but right now, he had other priorities. After they left, he sat in the deserted Interrogation Room, alone at the table. A pack of Marlboro's lay on the scarred surface, with a book of matches tucked in the flip-top package. He took out one of the cigarettes, struck a match and touched it to the end, inhaling deeply. The hot acrid smoke choked him, so that he broke into a spasm of coughing. He stubbed out the thing like it was poison, wondering what the hell he was thinking about to actually breath it in.

While Gil was reminding himself of why he didn't smoke anymore, Jimmy and Father Noonan walked out through the office where Randall was still haranguing Frank.

After the shouting subsided, Beach returned. Randall was gone, taking Boyd Stormer with him. Steven B. was right, they couldn't hold him on anything . . . yet.

Chapter 55

Beach slumped in a chair, frustrated. Frank perched on the desk beside him, popping a jellybean into his mouth.

"Boy, that guy was really freaked. He scared the shit out of Jimmy, while he was at it."

"Jimmy? What do you mean?"

"Well, Jim came out with the priest while Randall was going crazy, looks at the guy and turns the color of a sheet. Maybe he got an idea he might have to go to court and face a creep like S.B. if we get a collar. I dunno, but anyway the kid turns to me, and like he's making a public announcement says he retracts everything he told us. He says we can't force him to testify to anything, and he doesn't know nothin' anyway."

"Just like that?"

"Just like that. I guess we blew it, Gil."

"Yeah, only it was me that blew it. It was a doozy, too. How do you figure it? How could this all go on without Storm being somewhere in the middle?"

"Well, the DNA thing kinda ruled him out, even before we knew about the other guy."

"But there was something funny about that, too. First Shig tells me he's sure it's the same guy, then Nussbaum says it's all a mistake. Now Jimmy bares his soul, then does a reverse five minutes later. Even Nina did a complete about-face. Is this as insane as it sounds? Could so many connections just be a series of mistakes?"

Beach walked out of the office, shaking his head.

A few minutes later he pulled into the NY Medical Examiners parking lot, entered the building and mounted the stairs, heading for his friend's office.

Gil had decided to forego a telephone call, intercepting Shig at the lab after six p.m. when the techs were usually still at work but the Director, Nussbaum, was seldom around. Beach preferred dealing directly with Higawa without the Administrator's interference. He was also having a hard time sitting still. His gut was a knot of fire, so he figured it was better to keep active.

As soon as he found Higawa, he marched up to him and blurted out the apparent mix-up.

"Nussbaum told you it was a mistake?" The scientist looked incredulous.

Higawa went to the files where he pulled out several sheets of paper, with the now familiar grayish bars arranged on them. He studied one, then another, then the first again.

"Well, he's right," eyes squinting at the markings.

"You did make a mistake."

"No, I'm right, too."

"What? C'mon Shig, don't be cute."

"No, I'm serious, Gil. We're both right. It's just that we were looking at different samples. Look!" he said, shoving the papers across a counter toward the Detective.

"See that little code number up in the top right corner? It's a sequential numbering system for specimens. The parallel auto-rad that Nussbaum showed you is from one sample, mine is from another specimen entirely."

"Do you think he didn't know?"

Higawa raised one eyebrow and the corner of his mouth.

"Well Nussbaum has been accused more than once of screening out data for political reasons. All I can say, Gil, is that the hairbrush you plucked, had more than one kinda hair. One of `em matches."

"Can you tell me anything more about the one that matches, like for instance the color?"

"That's easy. It's silver gray."

"Oh great."

"Bad news?"

"Well, it's good and bad. The good news is that I was right after all . . . Storm checks out as the perp. The bad news is that we had him, and we let him go."

Chapter 56

"If your girlfriends are going to send you love letters at the Precinct, you could at least give them the right address."

Helen Joseph smirked, as she dropped an envelope on Beach's cluttered desk. She was a frequent visitor to the PDU these days, ever since she and Frank had been seeing each other. Though she was currently assigned to the Youth Bureau, she was a seasoned detective and easily took part in the banter that was a favorite pastime at the Precinct. The small envelope was the size to hold a note or greeting card, with a flowered border. It was addressed in whorled, looping script to "G. Beach, Youth Bureau." He opened it to take out a single sheet of lined paper, covered with a childish scrawl.

The words were misspelled, disjointed—not even parallel with the lines. Some weren't legible at all. The ones he could make out, sent a shiver up his back. They were words and phrases about dead babies, hurt and pain—all written in a child's handwriting. Splotches of color on the paper could have been paint or could have been blood. The word that jumped out at him, was one that kept appearing repeatedly between the other marks and words. At least six times, the writer had managed to scratch out a legible word. You might say it was a four-letter word. The four letters spelled "HELP."

The margins contained several carefully printed remarks, like commentary on the text. The neat block letters said things like, “me too,” and “they are hurting us.”

At the bottom of the page, in the fancy style of the outer envelope, still another hand had written, “Pilar, I thought you ought to see this,” with a signature, “Theo.”

Gil flipped back to the front of the envelope, to see that both he and Helen had misread the loops and curls of the ornate script. The name “Beach” was relatively clear, but on closer examination, the single initial that they had naturally assumed to be a “G” could easily be a “P”—for “Pilar.”

“Why would someone write to Pilar, here?” he asked out loud, “And who the hell is Theo?”

He handed the note to Helen, who took a sharp breath when she saw the contents. She examined the paper for a few moments, before speaking.

“What about Nina?” She squinted in concentration. “She was with us at the Youth Bureau, she met you there. You said Pilar has been talking to her. Maybe it was the only address she knew.”

“But who’s Theo?”

"Didn't you say that Pilar had figured Nina as maybe a multiple personality? So maybe the scrawls are from Nina, and the printing is another personality. Maybe Theo is a third."

Gil shook his head skeptically.

Nina didn't know about our relationship, as far as I am aware. How would she connect us?"

"I don't know, Gil. It all seems very strange to me, but I'm no expert. Probably be a good idea to call Pilar?"

"Right," he answered, reaching for the phone. There was no answer at home. He tried two other numbers, including Wagner College where she taught part-time, but didn't have any luck. He decided to try again later, but meanwhile, he had to figure out this baffling crazy-quilt of a case.

He thought for a moment, then scrolled through his numbers to find the one for Dick Ovens, at the State Police EAP. This time he was lucky enough to find Ovens at work. After exchanging pleasantries, Gil got to his questions. He wanted to know more about the multiple personality thing. Dick assured him that MPD was a real disorder, one that was being diagnosed more often, as professionals became more familiar with the symptoms.

"Typically, the severely affected individual has anywhere from six to a dozen distinct personalities, though as many as a hundred have been reported in a single person," he explained, "though I have reservations about that one."

"Many legal precedents are being set," Ovens added, "including a criminal case where MPD was tried out as a defense. The defendant claimed that one of his 'Alters' committed the crime, but that his other seventeen were not aware of it and couldn't be held liable. He lost, because MPD is not accepted as true insanity. Psych experts testified that, as opposed to psychosis, it is an effective, if odd, character disorder that represents a childhood coping method gone to extremes."

"How common is this?" Gil asked.

"That's not so easy," Ovens told him. "There are maybe twenty thousand diagnosed cases, with more being identified all the time. Some think it is very widespread—much more common than we used to think. Others challenge that. There was a seminar at Harding Hospital recently, where somebody suggested that there's a group conformity process in the psychiatric profession that makes a lot of practitioners kind of gullible and too ready to accept uncorroborated accounts. Anyway, nobody denies that it's around, they just don't agree how common it is."

"Look, Dick, we're dealing with a fanatic, here. He talks environment, but he's more of a survivalist . . . sick fringe-type, with an unknown number of followers—troops, I think he calls 'em. It's pretty certain that we've got a kid with . . . uh with multiple personalities, or whatever. But the thought just struck me that the leader of this movement is still hard to figure. What are the chances that he could have the same thing? I mean, is it reasonable to think you could have two people like that in the same group?"

"Actually, it's probably more likely in a tight knit incestuous group than anywhere else. You probably know that ninety-five percent of MPD's report severe childhood abuse, often ritual sexual abuse."

"Yeah, Pilar said something like that."

"We know that generally, victims of abuse are much more likely to become abusers of others. So it makes a certain amount of sense that a victim of abuse could grow up to be both a Multiple, and an abuser. Then, because abuse also increases the chances of MPD, it would certainly be in the realm of possibility for the MPD Abuser to produce another MPD."

"Especially in a fanatical group where abuse and kinky sex stuff might be going on?" Gil asked, frowning.

"Yes. There might even be a modeling effect. You know—people learn from what they see. I read about a documented case, where both kids in a set of twins were diagnosed MPD. One had six personalities. The other had six others that were `twins' of her sister's."

“I don’t know, Dick. This stuff is pretty far-out. Could this all be a put-on; an act?”

“I suppose somebody could try. They might even succeed with an extremely gullible and poorly trained shrink, but it would be a rare exception. This is for real, and pretty much impossible to fake. They’re finding that sometimes alter personalities even have different allergies, reactions to anesthetics, and vary in whether they are right or left-handed.”

“It could fit . . . it could fit,” Gil nodded, “Storm could be the Survivor and the Point man too. He might not even know it himself. The problem is, do I know it? And even if I knew it, how would I use it to arrest him, and how would I manage to prove it?”

CHAPTER 57

"You're losing it," the Senator said, staring angrily at the phone, directing his words at the device like the person he was talking to was inside the instrument itself. "I don't know how he survived, I don't know how you screwed up, but I think you're losing it again." He listened for a moment, then repeated the refrain.

"This is getting too crazy. Either you are losing it, or you've already lost it. I've backed you as far as I can. You screwed up the McSwain thing, so I get nothing from there anymore. Now even Chee-Chee is getting nervous. I need money from his people. I need their political influence, too.

If I don't win this election, you won't have a power base with me anymore. I never wanted anything like what you've been doing. I must distance myself publicly. The environmental thing is my core issue. I can't let you screw it up for me."

After another moment of listening, he spoke bitingly.

"Don't threaten me, you bastard. You've gone too far already. It's crazy now. People have died. Those weren't accidents—they were planned. If they ever find out, they're going to call that murder. I think you are losing it, and I don't intend to go down the tubes with you. If you want to do something useful, get this cop, Beach, out of my life. Don't mess it up this time. And keep me out of it. If anybody asks, I don't know you from Adam."

He turned his face from the telephone.

"Evelyn, come in here! I want you."

He slammed down the phone viciously, knocking the entire table over with a crash

Meanwhile, a slightly different crashing noise was happening at the Ninth Precinct.

A worn leather wallet flopped loudly on Captain Schorno's desk. It contained Gil's Detective Gold Shield.

"I'll need your weapon, too," the Precinct Commander said in a controlled humorless voice, clipping off each word like he was biting them.

Beach reached to his back and pulled out a gun, which he laid on the desk beside the wallet.

"Is there anything you want to say?

Gil just shrugged.

"Okay, have it your way. You are on suspension for the next two weeks, then you will be reassigned to alternative duty."

Bob Mabry stood to one side of the room. He moved forward a step, spreading his hands in a feeble gesture.

"Look, Gil, I'm sorry. I tried to put `em off till tomorrow like you asked, but I couldn't do it. This is coming from very high up."

Beach just stood impassively in front of the desk. Mabry looked at him, then dropped his eyes. Captain Schorno waved Beach out of the office. Gil pivoted to walk silently through the door, along the hall and down the iron staircase, sliding his hand along the rail worn shiny by thousands of unconscious grips. The muster room was as empty as it ever got, with a cluster of blue uniforms huddled in one corner, a young officer holding a protesting derelict against the brass rail in front of the desk. It could have been a kid supporting his drunken dad at the bar. Flannery, the new Desk Officer, loomed over the huge wooden expanse like the bartender, ready to serve up a cold one. He waved at Gil.

The water cooler had been avoided for a few days but was now back in operation. Like soldiers trying to put a lethal ambush behind them, some were already using graveyard humor to distance the fear and anger, joking about the tragedy and calling it the "Killer-Kooler." Extra water bottles were now stored inside a locked cabinet. Every now and then, you would see an officer looking closely at the plastic water bottle, as if checking for punctures. The machine gave a loud gurgle as Gil passed, which was swallowed up in the swirl of voices, squeaks and jangles of police gear, crackle of two-way radios, and ever buzzing, fluttering, overhead circulation fans.

He left the warmth and familiarity of the Precinct for the frigid street, taking a subway to the South Ferry Station. Thirty minutes later he walked down the swaying ramp of the boat onto Staten Island, where he caught a taxi that took him up the steep slope of Howard Avenue to Wagner College. Quickly he changed clothes in the locker room, use of which was a perk from school officials who appreciated having a cop regularly on the premises. It probably would end up on his list of violations, he thought cynically, as another instance of that catchall, "Accepting gratuities."

Dressed in a set of sweats and his Asics, Gil walked out onto the oval track, then broke into a jogging pace. Then he turned to climb the series of stairs that reached to the roof of the stadium, pushing upward with steady strides. He crossed over the walkway to the next aisle, descended to the bottom, and trotted one circuit of the quarter mile track, before starting up the stairs again. This was the routine. He didn't stop until every muscle fiber, every gasp of his lungs, every pump of his slamming heart told him there was nothing left in him to use. Only then, could he be sure that the feelings were under control. Finally, spent, he sat on the steps, hanging his head as the last light faded from the sky.

Chapter 58

The house was dark when Gil got home. There was no note tacked to the fridge, nor any message on the answering machine. It wasn't like Pilar to leave no indication of where she had gone and it made him very nervous. He tried a few calls to locate her, again without success. *Is she mad at me? Is she trying to make me worry?*

He started imagining explanations, thinking about possible connections. Gil's mind always put two and two together, even though it occasionally added up to five. He thought about Pilar and Nina, a relationship important enough for the distressed girl to write to his wife, asking for help. Pilar's attraction to the Federation of Natural Selection was something that he didn't fully understand, but it could have led her to make another visit.

Then Gil slapped his head with the palm of his hand. He ran to the bedroom, where a wastebasket stood next to his dresser. That's where he dumped each day's accumulation of gum-wrappers, out-of-date notes to himself, gas receipts (he knew you were supposed to save them, but never did), and other assorted junk that had cluttered his pockets. He dumped out the container on the floor, to paw through the junk, pulling out anything that looked like a message slip . . . nothing. He had probably chucked it at work. Then he saw a pink corner jutting from behind a ripped envelope. A message reminder was stuck to the gummy edge of the closing flap. He pried apart the two pieces of paper, to find what he had been looking for. It was from "Mr. Pointe," according to Rose's spelling. He had been sure that it was from the killer but hadn't paid close enough attention to the rest of the message. It had said the man was "waiting" for him, which was what he had reacted to. But there was another part, which he read now. It said, "He has something of yours . . ."

The telephone rang before he could decide a course of action. He grabbed the receiver, hoping he was just being paranoid. Maybe it would be Pilar, calling from somewhere safe. Instead, it was the voice of Frank Terranova.

"Geez, Gil. The whole place down here is going to hell in a handbasket. Some wacko claims to have poisoned the entire City water supply. He says he's the agent of retribution or something. Called himself the point man, or . . ."

" . . . The Survivor."

"Yeah, that sounds like him. We think he's at the FONIES Headquarters. There seem to be some dead bodies there. I thought we cleaned that place out already, but I guess it's like roaches in the Projects, they keep popping up, no matter how many you squash. The first officers on the scene are holding tight until the situation is clearer. Looks like some of his folks did the old Jonestown Kool-Aid bit or something. The wacko's been on the horn, telling us to come get him. But well, he says he wants . . . you."

"Yeah, and what does Schorno think about that?"

"You know him, Gil. He wouldn't admit a mistake, if he was up to his neck in shit and sinking. He probably knows you're right, but what's he gonna do, come apologize? So he's putting together a whole assault force, Rapid Action Deployment, Emergency Services and all that. I got a feeling he thinks he's Norman Schwartzkopf or somebody. Say, didn't they used to call the General, 'Stormin Norman'? And here we are with this Storm guy…."

"Damn! Listen, Frank, I'm on my way. Don't say anything about me, but if there's a way to slow down the operation, do it. I have this awful feeling that the wacko has got Pilar."

After disconnecting with a hard jab, Gil went to the closet, where an old ditty bag hung behind the door. Until today, it had held his first service weapon, an old thirty-eight-caliber "Police Special." When asked for his weapon, he had turned in the thirty-eight to his Precinct Commander. No one had noticed that it wasn't the sidearm he usually carried. In its usual place at the bottom of the ditty bag, was the Steyr GB that he really used. He switched it this morning for the old gun, expecting pessimistically that he would be asked to give up his weapon. Lately, pessimism worked better than optimism.

Now he retrieved the fifteen-round automatic from where he had left it in the morning, slammed a clip of bullets into it, then slipped it into the holster at his back. It nestled in the leather pouch like it was glad to be home. Gil opened the top drawer of his dresser, from which he removed a small box. As he opened it, his grandfather's badge glinted as if it were looking up at him, winking a grandpa wink of understanding. He took it out, weighing it in his hand, then squeezed it like the old man used to squeeze his hand before a ball game to give him confidence. Gramps had kept him on track as a youngster and had been his reason for choosing a police career. The old man's death had been more of a blow to Gil than the loss of his parents. He shoved the well-worn badge into his coat pocket. He probably would never use the badge, and would, in fact, be getting in more trouble, if he did. Still, he didn't feel so naked anymore.

Chapter 59

Emergency vehicles crowded the street outside the Federation Headquarters Center, dozens of flickering lights giving a strobe-like effect to the scene. Unmoving forms, covered by tarps, were being loaded into ambulances. Gil recognized Father Noonan striding from stretcher to stretcher with his version of the last rites for those who needed them, a few words of comfort for others.

The rescue operation involving removal of the sick and dying from inside the building, however, had come to an abrupt halt. That was because minutes earlier a cop and two EMTs had been shot, trying to help someone out of the building. Vehicles had been hurriedly aligned to form a wall of protection, behind which various police and emergency personnel crouched nervously, weapons drawn. Gil tried to keep a low profile, not as much due to the danger of gunfire, as to avoid being seen by the police brass who had put him on suspension.

He caught sight of Frank scurrying over to him, hunched in a crouch as he ran. Gil smiled as his partner dropped to a knee beside him.

"I figured this was too crazy for you to miss, Gil. What is it about you and trouble, anyway?"

"Just lucky, I guess. Does anybody know where he is?"

"Who, Mr. Stormy Weather? No, but there's a knock-out of a lady that's been asking for you, even though she's got one foot in the grave, and the other one on a banana peel."

"Pilar?" Gil asked, breathlessly.

"Oh, no, not Pilar. I mean, don't get me wrong . . . she's a knockout, too, but this is one of the Federation groupies. Serena, Sabrina, something like that." Frank started to point the direction with his unholstered gun, but realizing he was waving a loaded weapon, he lowered it and used the other hand to indicate a stretcher nearby. Gil worked his way behind cover to find Selene lying there, waiting to be lifted into an ambulance, her face a deathly waxen color. Periodically, she drew herself up to jerk convulsively; blood and saliva dribbled from her mouth and nostrils. Gil wasn't sure how conscious she was, as her eyes fluttered behind the lids. Moans eked from quivering lips as her head flopped about listlessly. Yet she seemed to notice him standing over her, and mouthed his name, "Beach."

He blinked. How did she know that? She was supposed to know him by his alias of "Daniel Wiggins".

"You know who I am?" he sputtered in surprise; wondering the extent to which his cover was completely blown.

"We . . . always knew," she gasped weakly, "It was my job to keep you . . . busy . . . to compromise you. There are photos from our time together . . . videotapes."

Gil took a deep breath.

"I gotta admit, you are a gutsy lady, Selene, making threats even now." He almost ended the sentence, saying "with your last breath," because as far as he could tell, she looked like she didn't have much longer to live.

"No . . . no threats from me. He forced me . . . said he would kill . . . my daughter." She jerked into a rigid pose, with a grunt of pain. Gil thought it was the end, but after a moment of vibrating tension, her muscles relaxed a little, and she continued.

"I broke the rules for you. I betrayed them …for you. Please, you've got to help . . . my dear little Nina."

"Nina is your daughter? But isn't her mother named. . ?"

"Euryale. Yes, that's just another name He uses for me . . . when he wants me for his pleasure. Nina is his child too, but he doesn't care about her… except for his own fantasies…. She probably wouldn't still be alive . . . if I hadn't protected her," she choked out the string of words before the next spasm racked her frame. "But then he made her a . . . breeder. His own daughter."

Tears were now mixing with the blood on her face. After another long convulsion, she lay silent for several minutes. A medical tech crouching behind the next vehicle looked at Gil and shook his head slowly. Gil was about to cover her face when he felt a hand grasp feebly at his wrist. Her eyes no longer opened, but she whispered a few more words.

"He's got her. I think he's got your woman, too . . ."

"Where? Where are they!?"

There was no answer. Her jaw loosened and the grip on his wrist went slack. Selene the sensuous, Euryale the maternal, - he was getting giddy with all the names and personalities flying around - she . . . or they, were gone. Another victim, another one that wasn't one of the chosen survivors in this insane man's campaign of tragedy and travesty. He stared down at the once nearly perfect face, now sagging, colorless, ravaged.

When he heard the crunching sound of a car pulling up, Gil turned to see a dark limousine come to a stop. A driver and guard got out of the vehicle first. They glanced around nervously before the distinguished figure of Senator Mark Delucia emerged. He walked to a van around the corner, where Captain Schorno had set up his command post. There was some muffled talk, followed by the sound of shouting. A few words drifted across the street.

"Fuck that . . . gone too far for that now . . ."

Then in Schorno's tenor. " . . . tell that to . . ." "Shooting goddamn real bullets!"

There was an unintelligible reply from Delucia, whose strident voice then declared in assertive finality, "I'll take care of it!"

The Senator reappeared from the Command Center, walking to the front line of vehicles, accompanied by a cop with a hand-held bullhorn. You could see the politician was nervous, but still playing to the onlookers and television cameras. He took the bullhorn, and after a couple of unsuccessful attempts, managed to get it turned on.

"ROGER! IT'S ME, ROGER. I HAVE THINGS UNDER CONTROL OUT HERE NOW. IT'S SAFE TO COME OUT. DON'T WORRY, YOU'LL BE OKAY. I WON'T LET ANYTHING HAPPEN."

There was a long silence, then the Senator repeated his message, and waited again. The tension was electric, as they waited and watched.

"Heads up, someone's coming out!" a hoarse voice shouted, followed by a clattering of metallic action, the sound of cocking mechanisms on dozens of police weapons.

"Hold your fire for my command!" A nervous looking lieutenant yelled. No mere lieutenant would dare actually give the order to open fire, when there were higher ranks around to take responsibility, but it reminded the quick trigger types to not jump the gun . . . or fire it. Another voice, thin and reedy, called from the direction of the Center.

"Don't shoot! I'm coming out. I'm not armed."

Gil wondered if this was the man who the Senator was calling "Roger." He might not have recognized Storm, if it weren't for the silver hair and the flowing homespun robe he wore. The beard and mustache were gone, giving him a younger appearance—and a troubling resemblance to someone else, someone Gil felt he had seen, but couldn't place. Storm must have discarded the purple contact lenses after Gil had noticed the fakery, because even from a distance, you could see that his eye color was some rather normal shade, rather than the intense hue it had been. His manner had changed, as well. He walked in a hesitating shuffle, no longer cocky and assured.

Gil considered what he was seeing and hearing.

Maybe this is just another 'Alter' personality . . . And why did Delucia call him Roger?

If Gil remembered correctly, Storm had revealed this as his middle name. Was he truly a "Multiple" and now using it for still another personality?

Wearing an off-white dressing gown or lounging robe, the man made a strange figure—almost like a biblical character, or hermit coming out of the desert. He had his hands raised in surrender, still protesting his innocence. His words also had odd religious sounding elements.

"It's not me, it's my brother you want. I changed the wine into water, like Jesus . . . I changed the wine into water. I didn't know about the rest. I . . ."

His words were cut off suddenly, as the front of his robe billowed out sharply in jutting puffs. There was a crackling sound as crimson splotches blossomed on the plain cloth. He was pushed forward by an unseen force, an invisible blow from the rear. The robed figure struggled to keep his footing. His eyes dropped to his stomach in surprise, a hand clutching at each side of it, like a virgin shocked to find her belly swollen by instant pregnancy. Then he pitched forward, the crackling sound now identifiable as gunfire. The location was less clear, as the sound echoed from the walls of surrounding buildings. Apparently originating from behind the man somewhere, the rapid staccato of a single automatic weapon was then joined by a crash of answering fire from the line of police vehicles. The Federation Center entrance and upper windows nearly disappeared in a cloud of dust and fragments kicked into the air by the massive fusillade. Along with the rest of the façade, the Latin motto was pulverized to be nearly illegible.

"Who the hell fired those first shots?" Frank wondered out loud. "It wasn't one of our guys, not from that direction."

"Well it sure as hell wasn't one of his 'alter' personalities!" Gil replied, wryly. He heard a noise behind him and turned just in time to see Senator Delucia climbing out from under his limousine, stumbling forward, and falling in the vehicle. He was still having trouble closing the car's door, when the limo peeled out in a screech of smoking rubber and flying gravel.

"There goes another summer soldier," Gil remarked wryly, "the ol' survivalist army sure ain't what it used to be."

He did a double take, however, when he noticed Captain Schorno standing a few feet away, looking sternly at him.

CHAPTER 60

"I thought you were on suspension," the Commander growled.

"Uh, yes Sir. I just happened to be in the area and heard what was going down. Nothing wrong with a citizen watching from a safe distance, is there?"

"Knock off the bullshit, Beach. You didn't just 'happen-by', this isn't a safe distance, and you sure as hell ain't no friggin' average citizen. C'mon, Beach, my mother didn't raise no idiots."

Gil remained silent. It was just as well, because the next words from the Precinct Commander were a surprise. They were about the closest that man ever got to an apology.

"Damn politicians are screwing everything up. Friggin' parasites. I don't know how you got here, but I can guess," he growled, giving Frank Terranova a glare. "Well, since you're around, you might as well stay and be useful . . . uh . . . Detective Beach."

Apparently, whatever pressure had been on Schorno was gone now, along with any esteem still held for the retreating politician.

The sun had been down for over an hour when the first units re-entered the building. They were members of the Rapid Response Team, (RRT) or Rapid Action Team, (RAT) who preferred the latter, so they could call themselves "the City RATs," or sometimes the "C RATs." Sometimes mistakenly called a SWAT Team, they were extensively trained in assault tactics designed to rescue hostages.

First, a two-man team of C RATs tossed concussion grenades through the door before going in. The "Flash-Bang's" were supposed to disable any waiting gunmen, the awesome blast of light and sound interfering with their sight and hearing long enough for the entering shock force to subdue them. The team charged through the entrance, in a carefully choreographed rush, weapons in firing position. The strategy turned out to be unnecessary, because the entrance and lobby were empty other than a couple of still bodies. Apparently these were some remaining Center 'volunteers', the last of those who had been poisoned. In fact, a thorough search failed to uncover anyone still alive. A vat of something that looked and smelled like wine sat in an assembly hall, half-empty. A quick assay of the contents by one of the lab boys hinted at a chemical combination similar to the poison cocktail found in the Precinct water cooler incident.

"Fleuroacetate and other favorite flavors," Frank wisecracked. A few minutes later, an excited officer called the others to the basement, where they found an elaborate valve set-up giving access to the city water supply, now exposed in a previously hidden recess below the floor. There were also seven empty poison canisters.

"I don't get it," Terranova shook his head, "Why aren't we getting reports of people dying all over Manhattan?" He up-ended a canister, pointing to a few drops of orange-red poison that still dripped out. "Just a little of this stuff in the wine upstairs killed dozens of the FONIES."

"Maybe we were too quick to judge Stormer," Gil murmured.

"Whatta ya mean?"

"Well, you tell me. I'm not real up on religious stuff—but when Jesus did his thing at the wedding, he was supposed to have changed water into wine, right?"

"Yeah, I guess so," Frank agreed. "What's that got to do with anything?"

"Stormer said something just before he collapsed. He said he changed the wine into water. That's 'wine-to-water', not 'water-into-wine'. Maybe what he meant was that he did a reverse switch on this stuff."

Frank called a lab technician. A few moments later, it was confirmed. The liquid in the basement containers was the same orange-red shade as the poison upstairs but was merely water tinted with harmless food coloring.

"I'll bet we find Stormer's fingerprints all over the containers," Gil mused. "But will there be another set, too? I still can't figure if this is all the work of one madman working against himself, or not."

"You mean like one personality fighting another personality inside the same guy?"

"Right. I mean, could the good Stormer have tried to undo the evil of the bad Storm? Or is there somebody else behind the scenes?"

"Stormer sure didn't shoot himself, that's a fact."

"Yeah, but was it the "Survivor" character that pulled the trigger, or some dissatisfied follower? Damn if I can tell if there even is such a person as this Survivor. Maybe Stormer just played that role sometimes and played Storm other times. There's still no way to explain the parallel DNA autorads, unless we discount Shig's work. I know Higura isn't a sloppy guy."

"I know what you mean—Shig's a real whiz."

"So who am I supposed to believe—Nussbaum?"

"He never impressed me as the type who'd put anything ahead of politics, Frank said. "I'm not sure I'd trust him, or at least not more than Shig."

"Exactly," Gil agreed. "But unless I have more information, it seems like all we have are question marks."

While all this was confusing him, Gil was also distracted by his anxiety about Pilar. He had run from stretcher to stretcher, body to body, to see if his wife was one of the dead and dying. He didn't find her but wasn't sure if that was bad news or good. He still didn't know where she was, or in what condition. She might be safe and far away, or dead and still hidden somewhere, a lifeless corpse. Worse, she might be somewhere injured or poisoned, and depending on help arriving quickly in order to survive. Stormer was the only person he could think of that might have that information.

He got briefed over the radio that the man was still alive, but barely holding on. The report said he wasn't conscious. They rushed him off to New York University Hospital in an ambulance, IV fluids running, oxygen mask clamped on his head. Nobody knew if he was going to make it. The mask over Stormer's face kept Beach from getting a close view of the man, minus beard and mustache. Between that and the medical personnel bustling around, Gil couldn't get a better look before the man was loaded into an ambulance and driven away. Gil was still bothered by a vague but nagging memory of someone else who resembled the critically wounded leader.

Beach walked to a coffee truck that was attracting a bumper crop business from all the police and other professionals who could now relax from duty. They were scattered loosely about the area, decompressing, talking, and eating. Father Noonan sipped at a cardboard container of coffee while he munched on a donut, leaving crumbs in his beard. Gil tried to picture the priest without facial hair but couldn't. He was sure that removing his beard and mustache would radically alter Noonan's appearance, as it had Stormer's.

"I saw you giving the rites to the Guru," Gil said, "I don't think he's Catholic."

"Couldn't hurt," the cleric replied pleasantly. "Did you see that symbol on his arm? The yin-yang thing? He had another one, smaller, just at the hairline. That mop of his covered it `till I pushed the hair back off his forehead, to anoint him. It used to be an eastern religious symbol, but I guess a lot of people use it these days."

"Yeah, the so-called Inner Circle of this outfit all have it someplace on `em. We may have another wacko out there wearing it—whoever shot Storm. Probably the same one who killed a kid named McSwain that we found under the FDR last week."

"McSwain? That wouldn't be Billy McSwain, would it?"

"The same. You knew him?"

"Yes, I did. Homewood House was a frequent stop on his journey to find himself. Guess he never did – find himself, I mean. Tough on the mother—both boys dead like that."

"Yeah, I forgot he had a brother. The other one died young, right?"

"Yes, he was Billy's twin."

Gil's head jerked up at that.

"My God, I wonder if that's it?" Gil spoke his thought out loud, "Storm said something about his brother, just before he was shot, but I thought he meant, like a fraternal thing—a fellow-member-of-the-group-type `brother.' I never thought of a real brother. But even a brother wouldn't have the same DNA."

"Not unless they were twins."

"I don't know, is that true? Would twins have the same genetic fingerprint?"

"Well, I'm no forensics specialist, I'm a priest. But I think a Medical Examiner is over there, by the ambulances. You could ask him."

Just as Noonan said this, the familiar figure of Anton Krispnick hove into view, heading for the doughnuts undoubtedly.

"Hey Anton."

"Hey Gil."

"Say, I know you're kinda busy, but you're the only person I see around here, who could answer a medical kind of question."

"Well . . . if you keep it short. . . I'm a little…."

"Sure. I just wanted to know if twins have the same DNA."

"Not exactly my area, but as far as I remember, twins—at least identical twins—come from the same fertilized egg, so they would have exactly the same genetics. Their differences would all be environmentally determined."

"That could be it! That could explain some of this craziness. Storm isn't a multiple personality, he's a twin."

"Maybe that's why all the symbols," Father Noonan added, picking up on the Detective's excitement.

"Symbols? Educate me."

"If I remember my comparative religions correctly—Father Cristianus at the seminary would never believe it, he claimed I slept through his whole course—the yin yang thing is from Taoism."

Noonan pronounced the term as if it started with a D, like "Daowism."

"The symbol is really called the T'ai chi T'u—the diagram of the Supreme Ultimate."

Beach looked blankly.

"Okay," the priest went on. "…anyway, the idea of that philosophy, is the duality of nature and life. That's why one half is black, the other white, but sort of merging into each other. There's a complementarity in all life, they say."

"You know, like a balance," he explained further, seeing Gil's vacant look.

"Male is necessary to complete female, darkness is necessary to complete light. Twins were often considered epitomes of that complementarity—very mystical and all."

"Well, whoever's behind this, is crazy about symbols and weird names," Beach agreed. "For sure. Half the time I don't know what to call him—Cage's son listed off a whole bunch of aliases—The Survivor, . . . uhh, The Point, Drang, The Man . . . maybe others."

"Did you say 'Drang'?"

"Yeah, I think that was one of the names, why?"

"Just that it goes with Storm, kind of neatly."

"How's that?"

"Oh, it's part of a German phrase really—'Sturm Und Drang.' It's from a play that kind of became the description of a period of eighteenth-century literature. It loosely translates as 'Storm and Stress,' but like catastrophic.' I'm sure it's irrelevant. Just occurred to me, is all. Sturm is the German word for Storm."

"I don't know, but the 'dark and light' stuff sort of fits. "I think Jimmy said something like that," Noonan agreed. "He said the group believed they had to be the darkness, in order for there to be light."

"If I follow all this, what if it worked out like this: Maybe in their perverted thinking, Storm was the light, but he had a brother who was the darkness."

"If so, the other guy cut his own throat, as far as Taoism is concerned," Noonan added.

"Why is that?"

"Well like I said, they believe that you can't have only one side. Only the combination of seeming opposites creates the whole. Male requires female, strong needs weak, heat is meaningless without cold. In other words, by killing the one who represents one side of the circle, he guarantees the end of his side as well. It's supposed to be an unchangeable law."

"Something tells me these guys have a very loose idea of what law is all about," Krispnick said, shaking his head.

"I don't think they mean the law of society, Doc. Look up there." The priest pointed to the building's facade.

"The phrase up there is pretty pulverized from the shooting, but it's supposed to say, 'salus mundi suprema lex esto '" the priest explained, tracing the words in the air with his finger. "It's like a commandment, to let the health of the earth be the ultimate law.

Actually, it could also mean the welfare of the world, if you read it that way," he explained, "My mythology may be rusty, but my Latin's pretty good."

"Well, these yo-yos may think they know the supreme law," Gil said, eyes narrowed. "But the law in this city happens to be my responsibility. As far as they're concerned, I'm the law, and I intend to let them know just what the law requires."

"I guess that's your wu-wei."

"Woo Way?"

"Yeah, it sort of means like your natural path. Everybody has a natural course, and if you want any peace, you have to go with it."

"You mean like 'Go with the flow' right?"

"Yes, I guess you could say that. But everybody has their own path, so the flow for you isn't the same as the flow for this guy you're trying to catch—Drang, or whoever."

"Well, I'll tell you this: if I have anything to say about it, his 'flow' is gonna end up more like a 'flush'."

Noonan nodded, smiling slightly. Then added, "So it isn't over?"

"No Father, I'm afraid not. In fact, I think they may still have my wife. Until I have her back, it'll never be over."

"Someone has Pilar?" Anton said, wide-eyed.

"I'm certain of it. It could be Storm's twin brother, if we're right about all this."

"You really think Storm and this killer are twins? The other brother died."

"So we've been told. But we've been told a lot of lies. Isn't that what all this stuff seems to point at? As a theory, it will do for now. I'm sure Storm has a lot more that he can tell me. Besides, I know I've seen that face before."

"Well, I've got work to do," Krispnick sighed, gobbling the last of a doughnut.

"I guess we all do," Noonan agreed.

As the Assistant ME hurried off, Gil motioned Frank over to join him. They climbed into the battered Oldsmobile that his partner had signed out from the Precinct earlier. During the drive back to the Station Beach shifted in his seat impatiently, anxiously reviewing what he knew . . . and what he didn't.

Unfortunately, there was more that he didn't know, than what he did.

CHAPTER 61

At the PDU, Gil dropped into the creaking office chair and grabbed his telephone. The first call was to Cale Jefferson, a friend who worked at the Bureau of Records. Another was to Lucille Sitra, at the News. He asked each to do some digging in their respective archives. Gil knew he wasn't just calling in markers now, he was signing a few new "I Owe You's" of his own, which would have to be paid off later . . . if there was going to be a 'later'.

Within the hour, a long folding table at the PDU was covered with curling sheaves of architectural blueprints. Beach stood over the display, eyes searching the lines and boxes. Cale Jefferson had come over from the Bureau of Records armed with several rolls of drawings. Cale's smiling appearance would normally have been enough to cheer Gil up from any bad mood. The man's face was like a male version of Whoopie Goldberg, expressive, irreverent and appealing in a homely sort of way. Nobody could chuckle like Cale, and most conversations that involved him were seasoned with the happy sound.

Beach's concern about his wife kept him from fully enjoying Jefferson's pleasant manner today, but he was glad to see him anyway. Gil gave his friend a brief summary of the situation, including what he needed in the way of structural analysis, or at least observations for Cale to include in his evaluation.

The blueprints Gil had asked for showed the old Telephone Company Building, which had been the first identity of an aging building that over the years had also housed a museum of fine arts, a private school, and was now the Headquarters of the Federation. Page by page, they examined the sketches, while Gil tried to remember from his visits, how well the present structure matched the old diagrams. He was looking for recent alterations, or unexplained departures from the original plans. After a few minutes of examination, Jefferson focused in on a portion of the layout.

"What about this?" he asked, pointing to a box-like shape near the center of the drawing at the bottom floor. "There's no structural reason for this that I can see. It might be what you're looking for."

"Not if I have my proportions right. I've seen that in person. It just looks like a big support column. It's got paintings on it. That's only a few feet wide, isn't it?"

"Yeah, but it's no support column . . . not weight bearing at all. From these drawings, I'd say it could be hollow. It's big enough for a ramp, or stairway."

"A stairway? Where would it go?"

"No place for a stairway to go here, but down," Cale laughed. Gil looked at him silently, then back at the drawing.

He checked the markings at the bottom of the page, confirming that it was a diagram of the basement floor. If that was the case, there shouldn't be a stairway leading down. There weren't supposed to be any levels below the basement. Still, there were many things at the Center that weren't supposed to be the way they were.

"It might not be such a far-out an idea," Jefferson cautiously agreed with the Detective's unspoken thoughts. "I don't know if you are familiar with this area, historically, Gil, but it's not far from where construction crews have found some remarkable things while they were digging foundations. In one place, they found an ancient boat preserved underground, like a real Viking ship. In other areas they've run into old sub-basements, foundations, even tunnels. They accidentally found a lot of stuff during the work on the Second Avenue Subway."

"You mean the one that never happened?"

"Well, it happened, sort of. It just never got finished. Hundreds of millions on the project, and it'll probably never get completed. Make that never. The costs of construction are so astronomical today, and they just keep getting higher. Besides, they'd have to re-do a lot of it, after all this time."

"How much was done?"

“Well, a lot in Queens. In Manhattan there are still holes. People call ‘em the ‘Tunnels to Nowhere’.”

“Now the works are abandoned?”

“Some of it, yeah. Sections are deteriorating, so even what was completed would have to be cleaned up if the project ever got started again. I saw part of it, once, when Mayor Beame was still using it for political purposes. In 1974 he had a big groundbreaking ceremony for the fourth section. Lots of media hoopla, V.I.P’s—the whole works. I was just a punk kid engineer right out of college, working for the Feds. I’d got an inspector’s job with UMTA—The Office of Urban and Mass Transportation Administration. They were understaffed as hell, so they used a few guys like me who didn’t cost much and, frankly, didn’t know a lot.

Something like eight hundred million dollars of federal money had been sunk into the project by that time, which would be the equivalent of billions in today’s terms. People were beginning to ask questions—like is this thing all smoke and mirrors? Some of it was. Mayor Abe Beame apparently pulled some real fast ones. They even got to calling it the `Beame Shuffle’ when he managed to borrow federal construction dollars to cover unrelated City operational costs. Of course that was strictly against the rules, but somehow Abe did it. He managed to keep the transit fares down but pulled the plug on the subway project a few months later.”

"Some real tunnels got built?"

"Oh sure, but not until decades later. There was finally a big push in 2007, and some of it was even completed. But there are still sections that will never be finished. You ought to see them—they're a mess. Eventually, I got a look underground. Check out YouTube. There's one video a guy made, who snuck in and filmed a lot of it. They're big excavations, with rusting equipment all over. Water is several feet deep in places, stuff hanging from the ceilings. It's more like being in a cavern than a subway. There's so much oil and chemical junk down there I hate to think what would happen if the EPA ever did a real inspection. The Feds pulled out when they found out what was going on with the tricky financing. I guess my reports may have had a little to do with it, but then you could say I sort of 'went over to the enemy'. . . . I met some folks with the City Administration and got myself a job with the Office of City Planning. From there I moved on to the Bureau of Records."

"That's a change."

"Yeah, well, I didn't want to walk around in a hard-hat and boots any more, hoping that something I approved wouldn't cave-in or fall over and kill a lot of people. I never did get back to engineering. Don't really miss it, either."

"Can you get a map of that project?"

"Should be no problem, though the problem would be if it is completely up to date. You don't actually think someone might be using that space, do you?"

"Call it a hunch, but I have no problem picturing this creep right at home underground."

CHAPTER 62

The next morning, it didn't take long for Gil to figure out that this was not going to be an easy day.

He hadn't slept all night, worrying about Pilar. It was more like a few fitful hours of restless thrashing. Eventually, he gave up and started making calls. Without much hope for success, he made several more attempts to locate her. Nobody had seen his wife. Nobody had heard from her. He nearly smashed the phone in frustration. If he thought his wife's situation was separate from the thing he was working on, he would have dropped the terrorism case right then, focusing on Pilar's disappearance instead. But he was certain that they were related. If he solved the riddle of this case, he was sure it would also lead him to his wife. So, he kept with the case, but never worked without part of his mind looking for clues to where she had vanished in this mess.

The whole question of the DNA analysis still bothered Beach, but when he called the lab to speak with Shig Higawa, they told him Shig wasn't there.

"When do you expect him?" Gil had asked.

"Mr. Higawa is no longer employed here," was the surprising answer. Requests to speak to the Forensic Sciences Administrator, Arnie Nussbaum, were fended off by the stonewalling secretary, who insisted that her boss could not be reached. She would only take a number for him to return the call. Gil left his number but expected that he had about as much chance of getting a call-back from Nussbaum as from the folks at the Publishers Clearing House Sweepstakes. He made a call to the hospital to see the current status of the man they called 'Storm', but found that the enigmatic character was still unconscious, listed in critical condition.

Beach's rotten luck continued, when he tried to round up some personnel for a return trip to the Federation Headquarters building. Schorno may have reinstated him, but the Captain's tolerance only went so far. You could say his support for Gil, was a little less than Donald Trump's support for Mike Pence. He was barely civil when he heard Gil's request. As far as he was concerned, the site was clean and therefore better off forgotten. Politically speaking, an operation in which there were one officer and two EMT's shot, not to mention a lot of dead civilians, could not be advertised as a failure. The great and mysterious gods of public relations required that the whole thing be written up, and written-off, as successful . . . therefore complete. Go back in with a significant force, as if there had not been good reason for the first trip? On a hunch? Dream on, children.

Therefore, it was just going to have to be Gil and any other fellow loonies he could talk into coming along. Frank didn't need any convincing. Terranova also called Helen, who agreed to join them.

"Stubby" Kinnear was still loose from Narco, and the kind of guy that was game for anything. Dwight White, "Jimbo" West, and Gina Esperoza, the other detectives of the Ninth PDU, all begged off for one reason or another. Gil wasn't sure whether they were legit reasons, or excuses to avoid the trouble they were sure he was about to bring down. He couldn't blame them.

Gil let Terranova try to twist some other arms here and there but didn't really expect to end up with more than the four bodies they had. While they were waiting for Helen to come over from the Youth Bureau, he made several telephone calls, punching out the numbers like he was jamming an accusing finger into the chest of a sleazeball drug dealer in a street bust.

The first call was to a number from the back of an old address book pre-dating his newest cell phone. The number used to be the home phone of Shigura Higawa. The technician had moved, but ferreting out follow-up information was an old and practiced skill for the Detective. A few minutes later he was dialing Shig's new number. Higawa answered, but went on the defensive, as soon as he realized who was calling.

"You know I can't talk to you," he said, tersely, "That's why I got canned in the first place."

"Damn, Shig, I'm sorry. But maybe I can do something, if you let me in on what's going on with these tests. I mean, what can Nussbaum do now, fire you?"

"Very funny. I might laugh, if I wasn't so pissed and, frankly, scared."

"What are you scared of, Shig? Remember, this is me, Gil Beach, the guy who introduced you to Mae Ann . . . the guy who ruined all your steaks with a fire extinguisher when the flames got too high."

Higawa chuckled, in spite of himself, at the memory of Gil's disastrous helpfulness at a holiday barbecue held years earlier.

"Okay, look. If I tell you some shit, you've got to keep my name out of it. You can't even pass along the specifics, 'cause I'm the only person they could possibly have come from. I've got sort of a *quo prid quo*, that if I keep my mouth shut, they won't give me a negative job reference."

"I'm listening."

"No, it's got to be better than that, Gil. I don't know who's behind all this, but there are far too many bodies turning up around this case, and when Nussbaum canned me, he didn't look mad, …he looked terrified."

"Look, Shig. I could bullshit you and say that I would never tell anyone a word, but I can't do that honestly. If you level with me, I can't promise that nothing will ever get out. All I can promise you is that I'm your friend. That means I will never do anything to put you in jeopardy, unless I'm sure there isn't any better way. I don't throw my friends to the lions, Shig. But I don't let wackos wipe out half the population, even if some people I care about have to take a risk, too. I'll be there with you, Shig, up on whatever line you have to stand. But this guy has got to be stopped. If that is going to happen, somebody has to step up."

There was a long silence before Higawa spoke.

" . . . fair enough." He swallowed audibly, then continued, "Okay, the DNA prints had me confused, too. Nussbaum's set was legit. Made me go back and check my own data. They were fine, too, like I told you before. Had to get out the original sample to see what was going on. Didn't need fancy instruments to see the reason. With nothing but a binocular microscope, you could see three types of hair fiber. Two of them were a sort of silver, or gray color. One type matched your boy—that's the sample I tested. A second type was from somebody else—Nussbaum may have tested both, but that's the one he showed you. When I objected to withholding information about the first sample, I got reamed out. When he found out I was looking further into it, I got shit-canned."

"Then we're back to square one. Unless we know which fibers came from Stormer, we still don't know if he's the killer or it's someone else."

"Afraid so. But wherever you got the sample—the killer was there. And that third fiber . . ."

"Yeah, who was that from?"

"I don't know who the first two were from, but this one isn't from a 'who', it's from a 'what'. I made it as a polyester fiber, designed to look just like human hair."

"What are you telling me? Imitation hair?"

"Yes . . . as in a wig. Brown and slightly wavy."

"Oh great. We got silver hairs from more than one guy, we got brown wigs, we even got animal hairs."

"I don't know if it's any help, but since you brought it up, that animal hair from the earlier incident—I made it as horsehair, right? Well, that's used for wigs sometimes, too."

"Wigs. Thanks. So somebody in this is wearing wigs. Some of the data makes sense, some of it doesn't. But hell, even the parts that make sense are so damn late, and they don't seem to get me any closer to the answers."

"I guess that depends on what answers you're looking for."

Gil wondered what that was supposed to mean. He sure as hell had been struggling to find answers lately—not just in this confusing case, but in his life. Shig wasn't referring to that, was he? Gil didn't want to pursue the idea. He thanked Higawa, suggested some precautions to improve personal and home security, then hung up. His next call was to Lucille Sitra at the News.

CHAPTER 63

The man some called 'Drang' usually felt like the planet was his fiefdom. Today he felt like he was falling off the edge of the world.

He was so angry he was dizzy with the waves of rage that washed through him. His own flesh and blood had betrayed him. He held the proof in his hand, a note in Roger's handwriting that admitted substituting harmless tinted water for the potent poison he had so carefully accumulated. Wine into water, indeed! Roger had been playing a messiah type for so long, he was forgetting who he really was. The blathering idiot had almost ruined everything. It was just like him—weak soul that he was. He deserved the bullets it was necessary to pump into his craven back.

The false turns were maddening. First the detective escaped the bomb, now millions had escaped their pre-determined fate. All might be lost at this point if it were not for extensive and careful planning. The Point man never made arrangements for an action without one, sometimes two, back-up systems. So as frustrating as the situation had become, he now merely had to follow the carefully constructed contingency plans.

The Federation Headquarters were dark and silent when he opened the false wall to return to the basement valve system. In his depleted condition, it was a near superhuman effort to lug over the extra four canisters he had hidden in his chambers. Fortunately, he was stronger than most people. He considered that perhaps he was superhuman. What other human could do what he had done, or withstand what he had withstood, and survive?

He decided to move one container at a time and discharge it before getting another. The building seemed deserted, but someone could appear at any moment. He didn't want to spend long minutes moving all four, then be interrupted and need to abandon them before having a chance to start the lethal work. Bringing them singly, he could begin the extermination immediately, proceeding as long as the situation permitted him.

With only four canisters, of course, the spread of destruction would not be as large as he wished, certainly not as large as originally planned. Still the poison would do its work, and many would die. In the resulting chaos, others would let go of the trappings of civilized behavior, so the destruction would expand in a ripple effect. Society would fall apart like the house of cards that it was. Only the strong would survive.

He hoisted the first canister into position. Before connecting it to the valve, he drained out a few drops of the reddish liquid into a small cup. From a bag, he removed the whining puppy that he had taken away from the breeder girl, his seed. He pushed the pup's snout into the liquid, so that it was forced to lick at the few drops that wet its face. In minutes the dog was choking, sneezing, and drooling. As the animal went into convulsions, he knew this batch was properly lethal. It was from the same batch that had been given to the less dedicated followers. They had died on cue. No Jesus tricks here.

A quick twist of connectors was followed by a satisfying gurgling sound as the canister finally emptied its contents into the water supply. Finally, the real toxin had been released. There was no doubt this time and no way to stop it. His furrowed brow smoothed a bit at the thought.

While the poison emptied into the conduit, he walked back to where the woman and child were lying, bound and helpless.

He had plans for them.

Pilar looked up, as the grotesque man approached. She was beginning to think more clearly now. The drugs had almost worn off, though recent events still had her off balance. She realized that there had to be some tranquilizing vapor in the air of the temple, as well as the drink she had been given, yet still berated herself for going willingly into captivity. She had enough of being drugged. She also had enough of being passive.

Gil could not be dead. She refused to accept that. Maybe she was fooling herself, but she didn't think so. As much as she was a trained scientist, a Ph.D. Psychologist, she could not ignore an intuition that went deeper than thought. Just as her mother and grandmother had sworn that they sensed far away events, and knew about deaths the moment they happened, Pilar felt she could sense that her husband was alive.

As for the videotape, that had floored her. Yet it was not the devastating blow the killer planned it to be. Long ago, she had realized that human beings are not without weakness. After sharing the secrets of so many, she realized how common it was for each person to have a weakness, or just to have made some big mistakes. A man like Gil was special, but he wasn't a saint. The idea that he might succumb to temptation at some time was not unthinkable. After all, she was a Psychologist. How many clients had shared their moments of weakness, to her understanding ear? When she used that ability to make a penetrating analysis of herself, she had to admit that she had been focused everywhere but on her primary relationship in recent months. It would be easy to lay all the blame at Gil's doorstep, but not very helpful and not very honest.

The ability to step back and analyze her motives made it difficult for Pilar to become too outraged at Gil. There was hurt, of course—anger, too. But so many people she counseled eventually shared tales of affairs, either physical or emotional, that perhaps she had a more philosophical attitude about such things than most. Anyhow, she had to look at her part of the situation. Also, the truth was that she too had been only a breath away from straying into immoral territory and giving up her own values.

It would have taken little for her to go willingly into bed with this charismatic man, before she saw the monster he really was. She had been practically there. She recalled the pull of emotion; that tickle in her belly when he touched her, the rush of feeling when they kissed. She recalled how helpless she had felt as the potent mix of natural hormones, emotional needs, and mind-altering drugs had swept her toward sexual union with a man that had turned out to be a dark and evil force. The fact that she didn't actually complete the act, was more a matter of circumstance than virtue. She couldn't now assume the role of the virtuous damsel betrayed by a horrid beast of a husband.

In a way, the playing and replaying of the video had worked the opposite effect the killer had intended. Each time it played, the scenes became less shocking. In time, she noticed details that convinced her Gil was probably not himself when it was taken. His movements were not hot and hungry, but slow, languid, eyes half -closed, as if drugged or in a trance. Since the video's setting was obviously in the Federation Headquarters building, she could assume that the same drugs used on her had been employed to break down his resistance. The doubt that remained to trouble her, was whether it was a temporary drug-induced lapse, or more significant. Was this a single case of weakness and chemically altered behavior, or the beginning of an affair that would destroy their life together? Was it a brief encounter, or a love that would take him away from her forever?

Then she wondered how long "forever" might be, as the crazed man approached her again. Her expectation of a long life was beginning to seem less and less likely. The man held an object in his hand that looked like a cellphone. Is that what it was, or was it some new device of torture?

CHAPTER 64

Gil pounded the desk impatiently with his free hand, as he held the phone, waiting for Lucille Sitra to pick-up his call at the newspaper office. When she finally came on the line, he spoke in machine gun bursts, asking about the Second Avenue Subway debacle, the "Grand Design", and the investigations that had proceeded from various scandals during its construction. She was ready for his questions, with plenty of answers, including some details he hadn't expected about the construction companies involved. She had done her homework well.

There was a 'beep' to signal that he had another call, so he promised to get back to the editor with any progress he made on finding Grady Dickson's killer and thanked her for her research. He punched a button to take the other call, hearing only low static on the line for a moment. He was about to hang up, when he heard a now familiar hissing voice.

"Ssso you are still alive. I am impressed. You may not go down easily, but you will go down. In the meantime, do you want your woman? Ssshe is here. Sheee will play her role in the final conflict."

Gil wanted to yell at the voice, to rage and threaten him, but knew this was not the time. That would have to wait until Pilar was safe.

"Let me speak to her," he said instead.

After a brief pause, the next sound on the line was the voice of Gil's wife. She was hoarse, speaking in a gravelly whisper.

"Gil? I knew you were alive, I just knew it."

"Are you okay?" he asked.

"I'm all right so far. He thinks he can break me with threats and videos, but I'm okay."

"Videos. Oh God, Pilar, were they what I think they were? Were they of me, and . . ."

"Look Gil. I'm a big girl. If you still love me, we can work it out. But not unless you get me the hell out of here!"

There was a clunking sound and a growl.

"Stick with me, Baby," Gil whispered their old endearment, but the only reply was a hissed challenge, the maniac having taken back the telephone.

"No, you pathetic pig. You give her false hope. Only those who stay with me, shall triumph. Those who follow The Survivor will survive. But I expect you to follow your pallid beliefs to destruction. Yessss, I have annihilation waiting for you. Come get her, if you can."

"Where is she? Where are you?"

"Ahh, that is part of the puzzle, isn't it? But I am sssure you will find us. We are waiting . . ."

The line went dead.

CHAPTER 65

The red-tinged liquid from the Survivor's first canister thinned as it dissolved, moving through the larger conduits to disperse into the trunk lines and supply feeders. The color faded, as it mixed with millions of gallons that had once been pure and ready for human consumption. Soon it was invisible, the water containing it indistinguishable from ordinary tap water. That didn't mean it lost its killing power. Since a proportion of only a few parts of the poison per million would still be lethal, the concentration was still far beyond what had been calculated as necessary.

Some of the new mixture was dissipated in the quantity diverted to a car wash and the sprinkler system of a florist who was watering his rooftop greenhouse, but much of it continued on its deadly way. The first person to directly use the contaminated flow was Mary Guillet, a retired French teacher and translator, who stepped into a bathtub-full, completely unaware. The poison was initially unable to enter her body in a way that would cause harm. Her skin was an adequate barrier to delay the joining of her vital fluids and the lethal ones. But later she washed down her daily dose of Valium with a full glass from the bathroom faucet.

The Valium wasn't sufficient to make it a relaxed death.

At Trump Towers, a wedding was taking place in the Grand Ballroom. Invisibly, a slight additive joined the clear stream flowing over the decorative waterfall nearby. That water merely sluiced into a drain and went out into the sewer system. But the same additive was a part of the wedding punch, caught in crystal cups by hundreds of guests as it spouted from numerous spigots of an ornate brass beverage fountain. The first two servings were taken to the bride and groom in eight-ounce crystal goblets, specially engraved with their names and the wedding date. Drang had calculated that two ounces of water would be sufficient to assure death. The happy couple toasted the guests and drained their five-ounce cups. One hundred and seventy-eight of the two hundred and twelve guests followed suit. So, subtracting the eight non-drinkers that fainted or were otherwise overcome by shock, there were twenty-six people available later to help with the bodies. Not everyone was up to the task.

In Chelsea, at the Morning Glory Nursery School, Teacher's Aide Gayle Smithers filled a large pitcher from the kitchen tap, poured in a packet of flavoring to mix the concoction the little ones gleefully called "Bug Juice." She carefully filled twenty-four small paper cups. It was snack time for the evening group, the children whose parents worked late shifts. Morning Glory was the only local nursery school that catered to this group, instead of limiting their schedule to the usual daytime work hours. Gayle didn't like working evenings; it played havoc with her social life, but a job was a job these days. Besides, she really loved the kids.

When she rang the "Ding-Dong" bell for snack time, forty-eight grubby little hands, fresh from finger-painting went to snatch away the row of cups.

"Hold it!" Gayle bellowed over the sounds of giggling, squealing and jabber, "Wash hands!"

The splashing riotous play at the sink only superficially removed the layers of grime, but soon the little ones were lined up in a grinning column. Just as the teacher was about to give the signal to begin, the door burst open.

"Surprise!" shouted the chubby woman who appeared. It was little Robert's mother, Frieda, who was the parent helper for the week, and she was lugging a case of boxed juice drinks. The containers were immediately distributed and greedily dispatched, along with the entire contents of three packages of cookies. There were just enough of Frieda's drinks to give one to each child, so Gayle and Frieda had to make do with the "Bug Juice." The cups only held five ounces, so the women each had two or three before their thirst was slaked.

When the ambulance arrived later, the attendants noticed that in a last unselfish effort, Gaylinda had dumped the remaining beverage in the closest sink, before she was doubled up with cramps. Most of the children were unaware of the two bodies on the kitchen floor, as it was naptime after snacks. Creatures of habit, they had dutifully laid down on their mats and dozed off. The two adults had lain down too. They just never got up.

CHAPTER 66

"What do you think is waiting for us, down…there?" Stubby asked. The small team was gathered around a table where blueprints mixed with investigative reports, dirty napkins, cardboard coffee containers, and boxes of ammunition.

"Your guess is good as mine," Gil answered, "But this guy has thrown around some firepower already. He or one of his minions took down Stormer with an automatic weapon, and he makes bombs. He stuck one in Sedgwick's chest."

"Damn, it's too bad about Cage. He could have come up with something good for us to use on this operation," Frank said with a sad smile.

Gil raised his head at the comment, looked thoughtful, then stood and silently made for the door. He descended to the first floor, stopping by a cleaning closet to grab an old crowbar from a box of tools, then went to the basement changing room.

Walking along the rows of battered old metal lockers, he looked for a characteristic "C.S." that Cage had used to mark his storage, and the fateful badge number, 22622. He found several doors in a row with the numbers clearly scratched in the old olive drab paint. He hooked the crowbar on the padlock of the first locker, then gave a hard pull. It took a couple of tries before the tired metal flange gave way, the lock popping off and clattering to the floor.

The first locker was filled with perfumes and toiletries, jewelry and watches. Beach moved quickly on to the next one, which opened to reveal a collection of electronic equipment, computer accessories, and what looked like kinky sex gizmos. Gil hit the jackpot on his third try. In that locker he found a smorgasbord of weaponry and ammunition. The next locker held similar treasures. He nodded his head. It looked like Sedgewick would contribute a posthumous part in the payback for his own murder.

Gil let the hastily assembled team help themselves to the ordinance. They grabbed for weapons like holiday shoppers at a clearance sale. He wasn't interested in adding much to the two handguns he already carried but saw a Mossberg auto-loader shotgun. Out of curiosity, he hefted it. The ventilated rib barrel gave it a look of machined power. It was fitted with all the extras—modified choke tube, Speed Feed Stock, heat shield. Cage always seemed to have the best. Maybe a little more firepower might come in handy. He slid it into the crook of his arm, grabbing a box of mag shells just in case.

Helen needed to stop off to pick up her Kevlar vest, and Stubby had to switch vehicles, so they agreed to meet a block away from the Federation Center in half an hour. Gil chaffed at the delay, but knew they had to be ready for anything. They planned to meet at a well-known hotdog vendor's cart. The stand was something of a landmark, familiar to everyone. The vendor, Carlos Amado, used to be the City Drug Czar, before he got canned. He was doing politics as usual, but when the time came for a shake-up, somebody had to take a fall. Most folks couldn't understand how a high and mighty governmental type could make out with a hotdog stand, so they felt sorry for him. Sometimes Gil envied him. If the money was adequate, and apparently it was a lot better than you might expect, a simpler life didn't sound bad at all. He could imagine slapping dogs into buns and BS'ing with folks all day. It didn't sound so awful, when the alternative happened to be dealing with murderers and scum and putting your life in jeopardy by storming an enemy of undetermined strength. Not to mention the assault was being done with a small group of hastily organized cops, most of who hadn't fired a shot in the line of duty during their entire career.

Unable to sit still during the delay, Gil made a quick stop at the hospital, where he insisted on seeing Stormer, though they told him the wounded man was not lucid. Gil wasn't sure how lucid anybody was at this point, including himself.

They told him he could have five minutes in the little curtain-bordered cubicle of the Intensive Care Unit. A nurse hovered nearby, as he bent over the bandaged form, tubes and wire leads exiting at various points, beeps and bubbling and whooshing sounds forming a background of mechanical noise. In the corner, a uniformed officer stood watch. Gil read the name “M. Douglas” on the nametag but didn’t recognize her.

Stormer’s face was unmarked. He looked like he was sleeping peacefully, except for occasional flutters of his eyelids, as he would apparently try to rouse himself, then slip back into a coma-like state.

Gil stood over him for a minute or two, unsure whether to attempt waking him, when the man seemed to sense the detective’s presence. He weakly mouthed a word, or name. It came out something like “Randee . . . wyy?”

“No, it’s Gil Beach . . . Daniel Wiggins.”

“Randee? Markus? Why? Tell ‘em it wasn’t me . . . tell ‘em . . ,” He coughed weakly, as the tubes increased their gurgling sounds. The rate of beeps coming from the small green screen above the bed speeded to a staccato rhythm, as a bright yellow dot scribbled a jagged line up and down across it. The nurse went into action.

“You’ll have to leave!” she ordered. Stormer was clearly in distress now, but still trying to choke out words.

“Why’d he . . . want to . . . kill me . . ? . . . brothers!”

The nurse was now glaring at Gil. She waved for him to go, as she adjusted the machines and called another nurse to get the Resident physician. As they exited, a disembodied voice sounded over the intercom system, saying "Code Blue, Code Blue, ICU." Gil didn't mind leaving. Although he hadn't heard much, what he had seen was more important. Finally, the vague memory that had been bothering him clicked open. Now he knew who it was that Stormer resembled.

As he drove to the assembly point, Beach heard sirens everywhere. The radio frequency was jammed with announcements to halt all water use. A sound truck drove the streets blasting the same message from a roof-mounted PA system. Gil was reminded of a scene from one of those "after the bomb" type science fiction movies, where the streets were deserted, big brother voices made public announcements, and bands of armed aggressors roamed the city.

If so, his team would have fit right in.

The intimidating group waited grimly at the corner, looking dangerous. Passersby quickly crossed the street to avoid the heavily armed band. Dressed in rugged work clothes, with guns bristling, if it wasn't for the 'POLICE" logo on their backs, the team could have been a group of terrorists or bank robbers, rather than law enforcement personnel. Even those who suspected that the group was made up of cops, knew it was probably better to stay clear.

It looked as if somebody was in for a whole lot of trouble.

Chapter 67

As the building blueprints had suggested, the painted column in the basement of the Federation Headquarters turned out to be a hollow structure, hiding an entrance to deeper realms. The mural borders masked the edges of a hatch door that swung open to reveal a descending staircase. Gil led his team into the dim passage, with Helen right behind, Frank following, and Stubby guarding the rear. The ironic fact that in military terminology this made him in the "point" position, was not lost on Gil.

"Point, counter-point," he thought to himself.

Descending the narrow stairway, Gil was reminded of a book he had read as a youngster—The Princess and the Goblin, by George MacDonald—in which a young boy named Curdie ventured into the caves of an underground race of evil creatures, to rescue a princess. The book and its sequel had become favorites of his. Sometimes reality imitated art. Here he was, over thirty years later, acting out a real-life version of the childhood tale he had dreamed about as a youngster. It wasn't exactly a princess that needed rescuing; it was his wife—yet the theme held true. It was also an underground tunnel instead of caves, but that too was a fine distinction, and you might truthfully say that the creature he was after came about as close as you could get to a real-life goblin. Gil tried to remember if the story had a happy ending but could only recall the scary sense of darkness and fear he shared as he read the story of the boy hero's descent into the earth's belly. Leave it to him to have loved such a dark and frightening tale. He shook his head, clearing his mind of everything except the few feet ahead. It was not a good time to be distracted.

The walls became increasingly damp and cool as they worked their way down the stairs. The dim light from the entrance soon faded. Frank handed Gil a small mag-light. The beam only illuminated a few feet at a time, so it seemed like the passage had swallowed them up. It had no beginning and no end.

Eventually they came to a wider platform, lit with a weak bulb.

The footing was slippery. A heavy odor hung on the humid air, combining the smells of oil, decaying cardboard, and chemicals. A chain-link gate barred their progress, secured with a rusty padlock. Kinnear pulled out a big pistol he had picked up from Sedgwick's stock. Gil was afraid the Narc would play hotshot by trying to shoot off the lock. That looked good in the movies, but in real life was hard to get right. In a small space like this, it could even result in a deadly ricochet. He was glad when Stubby reversed the large weapon to grip it by the barrel.

"It's a Wildey 357," he grinned, "Weighs over four fuckin' pounds." Using the heavy gun like a sledgehammer, he gave several whacks to the lock, until the hasp gave way.

"Well, nothing like announcing our entrance," Terranova quipped. His words were prophetic. A blast of gunfire immediately echoed, bullets pinged off the chain link gate, throwing sparks as the four team members dove to the floor.

"Damn!" Helen complained, as she fell into the muck, "Another pair of slacks ruined."

Either the area was brighter, or their eyes had adjusted, because now they could see that they were in a large cave-like tunnel, an unfinished subway line for sure—one of the "Tunnels to Nowhere." Massive girders flaked off big chips of rust, like mottled leaves shedding from autumn trees. In places, suspended from the huge beams, the dripping earth water had formed hanging stalactites like an ancient cave. Piles of debris sat in murky pools of brackish water. Toolboxes, ropes, stacked metal rebar, disintegrating canvas tarps, cartons of pipe fittings and lighting equipment, all moldered, rusted, and rotted in the huge crypt—a burial place for many grand plans as well as pieces of equipment. Gil hoped it wouldn't end up a grave for some cops as well.

"They're shooting high," he told the others, "Amateurs always do that. They don't compensate for the kick, so they let the barrel rise. Stay low . . . spread out." Holding the shotgun across his arms cradled in the crook of his elbows, he imitated the crawl he had learned in boot camp. "I'm too old for this shit," he complained as he moved forward.

"Now he tells us," Kinnear cracked.

"How come they don't stand up in the open to fire, like they do in all those movies, so we can pick them off real easy?" Terranova asked. His words were loud enough to draw a volley of fire, which clanged off the other side of the steel column he was using for cover. Slugs ricocheted in all directions with nasty zings and whines.

"I got a line on at least one shooter," Helen whispered. "He's behind that pile of lumber over there." She pointed at a load of wood planks a few dozen yards away.

"Shit!" Kinnear cursed, "Somebody take the fucker out. I just caught one in the leg from the son-of-a-bitch!"

In the dim light, Helen could see Stubby clutching his thigh.

"I think it's time to stop playing nice," she announced, pulling something from her waist bag. It was the smooth ball shape of a grenade.

"Damn," Terranova exclaimed, "Is that all? You sure Sedgwick didn't have a nuclear bomb lying around for you to use?"

"Look, Frank. I probably could throw this thing," she said. "But since I haven't had time to practice, it might end up someplace I didn't want it to go. I'd rather somebody with a better arm did the honors. Capice?"

Frank looked over at Gil, who nodded agreement. Helen handed the round object to Terranova, who weighed it in his hand for a moment, took a deep breath, pulled the pin, and lobbed the grenade toward the pile of lumber. It was a good thing their opponents weren't expecting anything like that, because Frank hadn't waited a few beats before he threw, uncertain about the length of the fuse delay. It seemed like a long time before anything happened. The shooter probably could have tossed the thing back at them, if he hadn't been surprised and panicked. All they heard was an "OOH," along with the scratching, scurrying noise of someone scrambling backward—until all sounds were eclipsed by the blast.

Carefully, Gil moved over to Kinnear, who didn't seem to be seriously wounded. Apparently, it was a ricochet, so the force of the slug had been partially spent when it bounced into Stubby's thigh. He refused to go back or leave the group, showing that he could still move forward in spite of a limp, once he had tied up the wound with a sleeve ripped off Frank's shirt.

"That's gonna cost you," Frank grinned, "Italian special, cost me plenty."

"Four ninety-eight at Wal-Mart is more like it," Kinnear laughed with gritted teeth.

They moved down the tunnel, from cover to cover, in street fighting technique, trying not to look at the huddled forms of two camouflage-attired soldiers, torn and bloody, splayed out where the grenade had landed. Helen grimaced as they passed.

"Is one of them . . ?"

Frank made a quick pass of the mag-light over the bodies.

"No. One's a middle-aged black guy. The other's maybe in his twenties—practically a kid. For a group of dudes that call themselves 'Survivors', they aren't starting out too well."

Up ahead, they heard the rumble-bang of metal drums being knocked aside. A shadowy figure darted through a doorway into what appeared to be a metal-sided construction shack, recessed into the side of the tunnel. When they approached the structure, gunfire flashed and glass shattered, as whoever was inside shot at them through the unopened windows. Gil figured there had to be at least two gunmen. The team's return fire punched a pattern of holes in the thin walls. The air filled with sparks, dust, chips and smoke, while the thudding concussion of gunfire mixed with the bang of punctured metal and the zing of ricocheting slugs.

Soon there was quiet.

With the smell of gunpowder in the air, the team advanced slowly. Gil and Frank each took a side of the door, diving through on the count of three. The room was littered with debris, including dozens of empty rifle shells and a sprinkling of broken glass. Three bodies were huddled or spread out in postures of death on the floor. Puddles of red pooled around their forms. Seated on a chair in the middle of the area was a grease-painted figure, naked from the waist up, silent and still. The face was hidden behind a cloth camouflage mask, which blended with make-up at the sides, and thatches of grass tied around his head. His dirty chest was stitched with a pattern of small blackened holes; bullet wounds.

Frank walked over to the slumped form to tug off the mask. A face appeared, framed in tangled strands of long damp hair. The high forehead, which would normally have been covered by the stringy mop, was exposed, revealing a yin-yang symbol.

"I know this guy!" Frank exclaimed, pounding a fist against his brow, as if to jar the memory out. "This guy is Senator Delucia's campaign manager. Fred . . . Fred . . ."

" . . . Valario," Gil completed his thought for him.

"We got him," Frank crowed.

"It's not our guy," Gil corrected.

"Whadda ya mean? He's got the mask thing on, and . . ."

"Well for one thing, he's been dead for a while," the voice of Helen Joseph interjected from the doorway. "Those bullet holes didn't bleed."

Unlike the other bodies, this corpse seeped no precious life fluid from its wounds—a sure sign that the holes were made post-mortem.

"So who is he?"

"His name probably isn't the most important thing," Gil explained, "but he's got a couple of relatives who were in the construction business a long time ago. In fact, this tunnel was one of their projects. Unfortunately, they got caught siphoning off millions in overages, fake claims, uncompleted work, and that kind of stuff."

"How do you know about all this?"

"Well, sometimes two and two makes five. This guy Storm mentioned that his name got changed at Ellis Island. That's probably bull, but it made me think about how people's names are often variations on the originals. It's common to find a guy using the initials of his real name in his alias, or the first name made into a last name, you know—like Pete Bassilovich becomes Basil Petros. I had Lucille Sitra do some research into the archives at the Eastside Evening News."

"So you found some brothers named Fred?" Terranova added his usual wisecrack.

"He went by the name of Fred S. Valario. The S. was the important part. Turns out It stands for 'Sturmer.' The name 'Storm,' that our friendly Federation guru uses, is another variation on the same last name. He and Fred are two of the family members that made up the Sturmer Construction Company. The subway scandal closed down their whole business, but in the mess that resulted, the Sturmers dropped out of sight. They changed their names later, so the company's scandal wouldn't follow them. There were four men and two women in the outfit—all part of the family, by birth or marriage."

"Son of a bitch!" Kinnear swore. Gil wasn't sure if it was because of the new information, or pain from the leg wound he gripped with his free hand.

"I'm thinking one Sturmer is Roger, a.k.a. our pal Storm," Frank reasoned. "This guy Fred is number two. Is the Survivor character one of the others?"

"That's what I figure," Gil agreed, "The Sturmer boys included a set of twins."

"Not Fred and Roger?"

"No. The records suggest Fred wasn't even blood—but an adopted kid. He couldn't be who we're after. One twin was named something like Randy. When Storm shaved off his beard and mustache, I thought he looked real familiar. Which figures, since I see his twin brother all the time. Would you believe me, if I was to tell you that . . . ?"

The sentence was cut off by an immense concussion. The walls of the shack caved in like paper, as a massive explosion collapsed the entire structure.

This time the bomb worked.

The Survivor broke into a sinister laugh. He approached the smoking remains of the shack, pulled down the fatigue trousers he was wearing, and urinated on the rubble.

CHAPTER 68

The man, or whatever inhuman thing he had become, would have been upset to know that his explosives had again failed to do the job. No one died in the blast. He had placed his age-weakened charges outside the corrugated metal walls. Wide flat sheets like those panels have the characteristic of being extremely wind resistant. When they blew inward, like kites or airfoils, their broad surfaces acted as brakes to the force of the explosion, slowing and dispersing its power as they flopped onto the shocked detectives. The members of the team were all knocked silly, but the large lightweight panels landed across the tops of various pieces of furniture and boxes, leaving large open spaces underneath, where the small group lay stunned in various postures and states of consciousness. The metal sheets had acted more like protection than destructive matter. Gil was the first to come around, as the sound of liquid spattered against metal near him, carrying the acrid smell of urine. He lay still until the sound of footsteps told him the man had walked away. Helen was closest; he felt her arm against his shoulder. He turned, running his hands over her, to see if she was bleeding or had broken bones.

"Keep that up, and I'll have you up on sexual harassment charges," she wisecracked, "or up to my apartment, I'm not sure which it should be."

"Man, they don't even check to see I'm dead, before they start screwing around behind my back." A foot kicked a piece of wood away, revealing Frank's slightly crooked grin. "What happened? Is it over? Jesus, at least you could've waited till I was cold before you started feeling up my honey."

Gil wasn't smiling. He wasn't sure how far away the killer was, and he was worried about Kinnear. Frank reassured him. "He's right over here feeling sorry for himself. Got another boo-boo. Arm isn't working too good, but he'll be okay. I think we'd better leave him, though. He's too banged up to be much good, and he'll be okay here, if we keep moving forward. I guess it'll just have to be the three of us."

"Two of us," Gil corrected, "we aren't leaving a wounded man alone down here, unprotected. We don't know what kind of rear-guard the survivalists have. We don't even know where their leader is, except I think I heard him moving further on down the tunnel. Helen, I want you to stay with Stubby."

"What is this, Macho Man time?" she complained, "Women are nurses, men are warriors? Women stay with wounded while big men go to fight? That's bullshit. Give me a break!"

" . . . take care of myself," a voice mumbled from the darkness. It was Kinnear. "Let the 'Granada Mama' go show off," he grumbled.

Now Gil smiled, but the expression didn't reach his eyes. He was glad that the team was still relatively in one piece, but unfortunately, Pilar was still out there somewhere. He agreed to leave Stubby by himself, if he promised to stay hidden and was armed with a few weapons.

Gil pushed one of the metal sheets with his shoulder. It slid to the side with a rumble like movie thunder. Cautiously, he stuck his head out of the rubble. Dust coated his face, giving him the appearance of a dirt-caked soldier on a guerrilla operation. It wasn't that far from the actuality.

The three bruised detectives worked free from the jumble of the ruined shack, brushed themselves off and checked their weapons, before heading down the tunnel again. They left Kinnear with enough ordinance to hold off a regiment.

They had only gone a short distance when they came to a steel partition, walling off the next section of tunnel. There was a hatch in the rusting metal wall. Gil signaled the others to wait, while he moved up to the door, directing the light from his flash slowly around the edge. In a moment he found what he was looking for, as a glint of shiny wire reflected the light. It was a trip wire—another booby trap. He had enough of trying to disarm explosives, besides there was no time. He ran back, signaling the others to lie flat behind a large drainage pipe. He steadied his shotgun on the pipe, took aim, and pulled the trigger. The Mossberg bellowed, kicking back against his shoulder like a linebacker. That was followed immediately by a larger blast that sent fragments pinging everywhere. Amazingly, the metal door was still there after the blast, but it was all pushed-in, hanging open at a crazy angle.

Helen thought it was a sign of the men's confidence in her that they let her go first through the hatch. It was—they wouldn't have even taken her along unless they knew she was solid. But Gil also planned it as a risk reduction move. He figured that the first one through a door was more likely to make it unscathed, because of the surprise element. The next ones through could expect any shooters to be more ready by the time they followed. That's about how it worked out.

The gunman must have been waiting after the door was blasted, but as Helen dove into the opening he didn't move quickly enough to zero in on her and didn't pull the trigger fast enough to hit his target. A few poorly aimed bullets spattered above her head. Like the veteran she was, she followed her dive with a roll, then kept moving until she was sprawled behind a pile of crates. From there she could lay down covering fire for the others.

Gil thought of the concluding scene in Butch Cassidy and the Sundance Kid, as he and Frank jumped through the door, firing rapidly from their weapons. Fortunately, there wasn't a whole

South American army waiting like in the movie. Still, even with fewer people shooting, they didn't get through untouched. Bullets seemed to be flying everywhere. Frank caught one in his chest. The slug flipped him around and knocked him off his feet. Gil reached down to grab a handful of clothing, dragging his partner the few feet to cover behind a big black box. Helen dropped one of the shooters, as Gil flopped down next to Frank and pushed a dirty handkerchief against the wound.

"God, first it was Helen, now you can't keep your hands off me, either" Terranova chuckled, but Gil could tell he was hurting. With each laugh, his partner coughed, and a wheezing sound came from the wound in his chest. His face was pale and moist. Twenty-five or thirty feet away, Helen looked stricken. She signaled that she was okay, but worried about Frank. She had dived to the right, while Gil and Frank had gone left. She was just following proper procedure, but that put her on the other side of the room. She would have to expose herself to fire if she tried to cross the open area to join them.

The light was much better in this part of the tunnel due to overhead floodlights, so Gil could see the look in Helen's eyes, which told him everything he needed to know about her relationship with his partner. It was love all right. Gil waved her to make a dash for it, then started pumping out shots from the Mossberg to cover her movement. His first blast splintered a thin wood panel and the body of a Federation soldier toppled out from behind it. The twelve-gauge shells filled the air with enough lethal material to keep everyone's heads down and allowed Helen to run the few yards across the room, sliding in awkwardly beside them.

"Hi-ya Sweetcakes," Frank smiled weakly. "Never win the base-stealing trophy like that."

"Hi yourself, num-nuts." A volley of bullets whanged off the box they were huddled behind.

"Hey, will ya look at this?" she laughed, patting the protective barrier. "This thing that is presently saving our asses—it's our own damn safe. I'll be damned, if it isn't the lock-box from the Youth Bureau."

"Thanks for arranging it," Frank replied. There was a wheezy breathiness to his voice.

"Well, you just stay safe here behind it, Darlin' while Gilbert and I take out this scumbag."

"Not this time, Helen," Gil stopped him. "Stubby's injury wasn't too bad, but this is serious. It's a sucking chest wound. You've got to stay here with him."

Helen now looked at the bloody rag Gil was pressing to Frank's wound, and realized why he kept the hand clamped tight against it.

She nodded, slipping her hand over the soggy cloth that plugged the hole in his chest wall.

"Why weren't you wearing your vest?" She asked accusingly.

"Uhhh.. guess I forgot in the rush."

Helen shook her head in disbelief, then turned to Beach.

"I don't know how we're gonna get him all that way back."

"I don't think we'll have to. We came far enough that we're probably near the other end by now. We should be able to go up easier by going forward. I noticed an upward slope for the last block or two. I think we must be a lot closer to the surface."

Helen brightened, as she reached into a bulging bag she carried at her waist. She pulled out a portable police radio.

"Maybe we can transmit now. I'll try to call for back-up."

"Go ahead, Helen—but I can't wait. Pilar is down here somewhere. Five minutes could mean life or death for her, too. I've got to go after her. If you reach help, get Frank and Stubby outta here, then send back-up after me. I'll get Randall."

"Who?"

"Oh yeah, we were interrupted, weren't we? Our friend S.B. Randall, the friggin' Assistant D,A. is the former Randy Sturmer, brother and twin of Roger Sturmer, a.k.a. Storm. The brown wig fooled me for a while, but when Stormer shaved off the beard and mustache, I knew I'd seen that ugly mug before. It was the same nasty face I'd seen so often on the Assistant District Attorney, Borough of Manhattan. None other than 'Son-of-a-Bitch' Randall."

"I always knew he was a creep."

"Creeps I can handle. People that kill kids and my friends are a different matter. I've got to stop him before he kills my wife." Gil looked up at Helen, who looked back at him with a grim expression.

Both of them knew she was thinking, *If he hasn't already.*

"Give me covering fire," Beach told her.

When she started firing, he rose and walked slowly forward, shotgun leveled and belching destruction. Twice, Federation soldiers showed themselves to fire at him. Twice the Mossberg roared. Each time an attacker went down.

Chapter 69

The Survivor hadn't terminated the woman yet, but he planned to do it soon. He wanted the policeman nearby, when she was eliminated. He would prefer that Beach hear, perhaps even see her agony. She was no longer in the grotto area; he had taken her one level above to the long hollowed-out room where pipes ran supplies of steam, water, and sewage under the city streets. It was also directly underneath a huge gasoline storage tank that provided the fuel for one of the city's largest taxi fleets. Randall had carefully drilled an opening in the tank, using a static-free drill to avoid premature ignition. The hole was plugged with a simple mechanical stopper, designed for resealing soda or wine bottles.

As he heard the firefight move closer, he knew it was time to act. He moved to the tank. The woman watched transfixed, from where he had lashed her to the pipes, along with the child. He didn't acknowledge the girl as his offspring. To him she was now only another pawn to be played, a body to be sacrificed. The young one slumped, unconscious. She had passed out somewhere along the way, but the woman stared intently at Randall.

He hoped that she understood the significance of the massive metal tank with "Texxon Oil" stenciled on its surface. It seemed so, since her eye twitched when he reached for the plug to pull it free, sending liquid gushing out. Potent fumes quickly filled the atmosphere. The pressure from thousands of gallons in the tank shot out a stream of gasoline like it came from a hose. The stream dug away at the dirt wall where it hit, cascading down to the oil-soaked floor, widening into an explosive pool of flammable liquid. He loosened a plug from a separate pipe, to let a black gurgle of thick oil join the pool. The dark oozing stream worked its way down the length of the room, seeking an exit. Eventually, the viscous mix flooded over a lip at the hatch-like floor entrance, down the metal ladder leading to the lower level.

Gil had made it halfway up the ladder when the thick mixture of mud, oil, and gasoline showered down on him. The mix stung his eyes, nostrils and made his head swim. He grabbed for the next rung, now coated with slippery fluid, but missed. He lost his grip on the slick steel, then teetered for a moment before crashing to the floor below. His head connected with an outcropping of rock, making a dull thud. He hit the floor and lay still. A laugh echoed from above.

Randall moved back to the woman and child, though few would have recognized him as the man who once represented the State in criminal court. He was emaciated from fasting and coated with dirt, gasoline, oil, sweat and blood. He was also lost in madness, a feverish intensity giving his eyes the appearance of burning holes in his darkened eye sockets. It was ironic that the police officers now knew who he was, because the man no longer knew himself.

Or at least, he no longer saw himself as Randall. He only believed himself to be the "Survivor," the 'Point man' of the purging wave, the embodiment of Sturm und Drang—the final union of darkness and light.

A Psychologist would have recognized that the link Randall had maintained with the real world was irretrievably lost. Ironically, there was a psychologist present, though hardly able to maintain a professional stance at the moment. Yet she could still recognize the signs. Pilar knew that this macabre soul had slipped over the line into psychosis. She tried not to react to the loathsome touch, but a shiver went through her when he reached out to draw a yin-yang symbol on her forehead. It was a very different kind of shiver from the one she had felt when he touched her earlier. Intuitively, she now grasped that he was not at all who she had originally thought he was.

"You aren't Storm!"

"Of course not. My brother is nothing. I am the ultimate Survivor, who is appointed to revenge the violated and save the last remnants of humanity."

No wonder she had felt a change from the gentle intelligence and understanding he had exhibited in the first orientation sessions. It really wasn't the same person. She wondered at what point this man had played on the innocent attraction she felt to his brother, stepping into his place, to use and seduce her? Now she recalled times that he seemed to have inexplicably changed in manner and tone. She found some of her fear turning to the anger of one who had been tricked.

"You make it sound like you're a force for good, but you aren't," she challenged tearfully. "All you want is death and destruction."

Randall seemed unfazed by her criticism. In fact, he nodded in strange agreement.

"Yes. To civilization's yin I am the yang. To its ice I am fire. From the weak and the frightened, I draw strength. From the darkness I draw my light."

Now he looked at her with more awareness, as if seeing her for the first time.

"You are his woman. So look at me. I am your man's mirror image and anti-force. As you die, his power will become weakness. Your death will bring me a surge of new life. Your blood will flow to nourish the growth of the new age. Your life is forfeit for the victorious reign of the Survivor."

He removed his fatigue trousers and shoes to stand naked before his captives. Picking up the limp form of the girl's small dog, he reached for the razor he had set on a ledge near the girl.

"No, not Genny! No!" the child cried vainly.

Despite the poison in its system from having his snout stuck into it, amazingly, there was still life in the dog, so they heard a last wailing yelp as Randall sliced it from belly to neck. Holding the carcass over his head, he then squeezed and twisted it to release the fluids, which trickled in gruesome redness down his naked body. Even in his far-depleted state, there was stirring at his groin. He felt soaked in darkness and delicious evil. The critical moment was at hand.

"Let the final conflict begin. Let the enemies come. I will destroy them all. I lay waste in order to build again, I harvest so that a new seed can be planted. I am the darkness that the light needs to exist. Prepare yourself woman . . . for now it is your time."

He moved toward her.

CHAPTER 70

Gil groggily opened his eyes, to find himself staring into the dirt-smeared face of Stubby Kinnear.

"Wha? Stubby, what are you doing here . . . ?"

"Oh hell, I got tired of waiting for you guys back there. So what? I got a lame wing and a gimpy leg. I figured you could use me, anyway. You ain't exactly overloaded with talent here."

Gil looked around, recognizing he was at the bottom of the steel ladder, in a pool of gasoline and oily mud. The liquid had flowed well beyond this alcove, wending its way across the main floor, to puddle at places and produce potent vapors. Some of the volatile mixture pooled around metal barrels filled with chemicals, petroleum products, and other flammable liquids. He knew that with any kind of spark, the whole place would go up. Kinnear knelt over him, an automatic rifle in one hand, pistols sticking out of his pants like he had a part in a Rambo movie.

"Don't even think about using those," Gil cautioned, indicating the guns. His head was starting to clear a little. "With all this gas, one shot and we're history."

Kinnear looked around, more somber now, then nodded his understanding. Gil rose to his feet but told the other man to leave.

“Frank’s over by the other side. He took a bullet in the chest. He needs to get to a hospital. Go help Helen get him outta here, if you can manage, before we all get roasted alive.”

Kinnear started to protest, but as he raised to his feet, he grimaced and nearly fell at the pressure on his wounded leg. Frowning, he shrugged, then turned to limp slowly back toward where Gil had left the others. Gil removed his jacket, then tore his shirt into strips of cloth, which he wrapped around his hands for better grip, and on his face to reduce the smell. He started back up the ladder.

His left arm and side felt numb from the fall. His head throbbed sickeningly, dizzy from the fumes. He was bleeding from numerous cuts and scratches he had sustained in the running battle with Randall, the shack explosion, and his nose-dive from the ladder. Gas and oil continued to slop from above, the smell almost overpowering him. He could get a breath by leaning way back, away from the ladder, but that made his perch less secure, and left him even more vulnerable to anything delivered from above. So he gulped a couple of breaths and flattened himself against the ladder, then worked his way up two or three more rungs before stopping and leaning back for another breath. He stripped away the cloth he was using as a mask, because it accomplished little, and partially blocked his vision.

He had gotten about three-quarters of the way up to the next level, when a shadowy figure appeared above to make a throwing motion. Pain seared through Gil's shoulder, as a spear-like metal rod bounced off his upper arm, gouging a large gash in his flesh as it caromed off. He went for his gun, but stopped when he remembered the volatile fumes. There was another flicker of movement, then a large stone hit him. His vision went black, as the rock glanced off his already wounded head. Pain mushroomed sharply and he nearly fell again, but managed to hang on until he could see straight. Then he heard screams.

CHAPTER 71

Pilar had started screaming because she didn't know what else to do. She had heard voices and knew one of them was Gil's. When Randall started dropping things on him, she reacted with an age-old reflex—a shriek. It got his attention, but when he came back for her, she began to wonder if that was such a good idea. She had been working on the straps that held her to the pipes. One hand was slick enough with sweat and blood that she had worked it partly loose, but it looked like a case of "too little, too late." She pulled and twisted, even as she knew it probably would do no good to have only one hand free, while remaining bound everywhere else. The demented man advanced on her with a blade in his hand, slavering like an animal, grunting and whining, with an insane leer pasted on his twitching face.

"Randall!" Gil's voice sounded very loud in the enclosed space. His face and shoulders appeared at the opening. He grabbed a rock off the floor and pitched it at Randall, but the stone bounced harmlessly off a pipe a yard away with a dull clanging sound. Pilar took a sharp intake of breath, seeing her husband's battered face and body.

Randall turned back toward his pursuer, a deranged grin still in place.

"There is no Randall. There is only the SURVIVOR!" He laid his razor back down on the shoulder-height ledge, taking a gun from beside it. It looked like an antique weapon, a collector's item, but Gil was worried less about getting shot than the certainty of going up in smoke, should a gun be fired and its muzzle flame ignite the fumes.

"Don't do it . . . uh," he shouted, "Drang, Survivor, whoever. You shoot that thing and this whole place goes up like a bomb."

The insane grin widened, as he slowly nodded his understanding of the warning.

"If that is the case, so be it. It is my wu-wei. I have set an incendiary device to go off in minutes anyway, my dear adversssary, " he hissed. "But this way it will be more perssssonal. You will be joined in the final glorious union of fire and death. The wu-wei will proceed directly by my hand, the Point man of darkness."

"If you set that off, you'll die too."

"I cannot die. I am the Survivor."

Gil didn't have any bargaining chips left. The wacko had the advantage, and to add to make things worse, he was flipping out. This monster was beyond reasoning. The bizarre figure stood trembling in some kind of mad anticipation, with his naked back nearly pressed against Pilar, gun in hand, ready to go out in a fiery finish. Somehow, in his lunacy, he didn't believe he could die. There isn't much you can do to threaten someone who thinks they can't die. Gil saw Randall pull back the hammer of the pistol and start to squeeze the trigger.

Chapter 72

On the street above, Stubby Kinnear and Helen Joseph eased Frank's limp body through a narrow construction entrance. An ambulance screeched up, answering the call they had made with Helen's radio. Soon blue and white patrol units, as well as other emergency vehicles were jamming the street. The first NYPD Administrative Officer on the scene was Lieutenant Graham Scherf, who refused to allow anyone in the hole once he heard the dangerous situation described by Kinnear and Joseph. Soon he had the area blocked off, with neighboring buildings evacuated. Minutes later, fire engines joined the melange, using their smaller two-inch hoses like rope barriers instead of water conduits to cordon off side-streets. Two fire marshals conferred about ways to deal with free-flowing gasoline and trapped fumes. A firefighter volunteered to stay by the open entrance to the tunnel, an air tank strapped to his back and mask in place, radiophone in hand so he could watch for signs of action below and relay situation reports to the brass. Nobody used the word 'hero' but he gained a lot of respect for his courage.

Down below, time seemed to stand still, as Gil watched the gun being cocked, and Randall's finger start to whiten with the pressure of pulling the trigger. The detective found himself focusing on irrelevant details, like the way the symbol engraved on the man's forearm pulsed redly, with a band of lighter, untanned skin surrounding it. He could now see how the man in his attorney persona had hidden his tattoo, by wearing a large diver-style watch to cover the area. Veins stood out starkly on the fellow's forehead; instead of silver hair a shaved skull gleamed. The bare head must have made it more convenient for Randall to hide beneath a shaggy brown wig—or a silver one, when it pleased him. Now the ADA's longhair public image made more sense, as did some of Shig Higawa's lab findings. Horsehair and polyester wigs must be ready to suit each occasion.

A thin scream sounded in Gil's ears, though he couldn't tell whether it was Randall or Pilar producing the sound. For all he knew, it could be coming from his own throat. It seemed like this was all a strange impressionistic movie, peculiar celluloid images divorced from reality. The illusion of being in a film was reinforced, when Randall raised his hand, making a signal to 'Stop The Action' . . . or so it seemed.

The signal was the classic movie director's gesture of drawing a hand across the throat area, as he yelled, "Cut."

Yet something about the gesture wasn't quite right. The motion looked wrong, and so did the hand. In his battered state of mind,

Gil took a moment to figure out what was amiss. Then he saw that the man had too many arms. His left hung to the side; fingers splayed in reflex action, while the right one gripped the gun. It was an unexpected out-of-place third arm that moved across in front of the man's neck. This extra limb was white, thin and feminine. It clutched something metallic, shiny and straight.

Randall's eyes bugged out in surprise. Suddenly he gave a cough and blood spurted from his throat where a long gash had abruptly appeared. He stumbled forward, dropping the pistol as his hands grabbed at the ugly wound in his neck. When Randall moved, Gil could see Pilar was behind him. No wonder the hand and motion had seemed odd. It was her thin white arm that had moved across Randall's throat. The small pale limb wielded a blade, the razor Randall had set down to pick up his gun. He had placed it just within reach of the one hand Pilar finally managed to work free from its bonds. Now untethered, she used the same razor with stunning effect.

The creature that had been Randall went down. He fell forward to thrash in a puddle of gas and oily filth, blood pouring from his neck to add to the awful mix. As he fell into the wet depression, his legs gave a reflexive jerk that kicked over a small wooden crate. This enclosure fell open, discharging a smaller metal box, with a timer and glass tube-like affair, in which two thin wires were immersed in a clear liquid.

"It's a combustion initiator!" Gil shouted, hurriedly stuffing back the packing paper and closing the lid on the small crate. He then rushed to free his wife. "It's already been initiated. Once it completes whatever timing sequence it's on, a current will run through those wires, setting off the chemical in the tube. There's nothing we can do to stop it. He's sure to have built in booby traps that would prevent disarming. I've seen how he works before. Any minute it's going up in flames.

If we're still here, we'll go up with it."

He saw her staring at him and stopped momentarily.

"I don't have time to tell you how sorry I am," He blurted, "but if we get out of this, I promise I'll make it up to you."

There were tears in her eyes as she shook her head.

"We both have some making up to do. Like I said before, just get me the hell out of here, and we can work it out!"

"You got it!" he yelled, running over to Nina's limp form. It took a few seconds to untie her legs. He left her hands lashed together, though they were bound with a sour-smelling leather strap. At least that allowed him to slip her arms over his neck like a loop, so he could carry her unconscious, hanging on his back, like a human knapsack. Pilar was already working her way down the ladder when he swung his legs over the edge to search for a foothold on the slick rungs. Halfway down, his grip started weakening, a foot slipped and he nearly fell. He managed to hook an arm over a crosspiece, hanging for a moment suspended by one elbow, Nina's dead weight nearly choking him as the thong cut into his neck. Pilar reached up to position his feet on the nearest rung. He spit out a mouthful of gasoline and oil, gagging while he grabbed at the metal side rail to regain his balance. Soon they were slogging across the tunnel floor in the direction he hoped was the way out. They weren't aware of how close they were to extinction.

The explosive limits for gasoline vapor range from 1.4% to 7.6% vapor-to-air ratio by volume. That is, you need those proportions of gas and air in order to have an explosive mixture. The fumes in the chamber had reached a ratio of 5.3% gasoline, fairly itching to ignite in a frenzy of destruction. All the mixture needed was the proper amount of heat. Gasoline has an ignition temperature somewhere between 536- and 800-degrees Fahrenheit depending on the ignition rating. On the NY City Street above them, the Gotham Quick Taxi Garage kept costs down by using the cheapest regular gasoline available, so their storage tank which Randall had tapped, held 86 octane non-detergent generic gas. It would require about 750 degrees before it went up. Once triggered, the initiating device would have no problem reaching this temperature. It had already begun its sequence and could not be stopped.

Gil's assumption was correct. A booby trap device had been attached that would have been activated by any attempt to render the incendiary inoperative. Now the main device itself began to carry out its primary function.

Inside the ignition wiring, a sequential relay advanced one position to complete the circuit. Current raced through the wires in a microsecond to jump between the bare leads. That open spark ignited the kerosene inside, which burst the tube and spread to the paper surrounding it. The Kerosene ignited more easily than gasoline, at only 480 degrees, which was sufficient to set fire to the shredded paper packing. Still, since cut paper has an ignition temperature of only 446 degrees, the heat was not yet to the 750 degree level that would set off the gasoline fumes in the tunnel.

Glowing embers smoldered in the closed crate, gobbling up the tiny paper strips—a beast waiting to be freed. When Gil stuffed the packing back tightly in the container, he bought himself a few brief seconds. As soon as the smoldering spark found a pocket of air, or licked out of the box to where oxygen was waiting, the fire would burn with a hotter flame . . . hot enough.

In the charged atmosphere, an explosion would commence that would swallow everything in its path.

Gil and Pilar had reached a stairway, rusted metal steps climbing a concrete-walled passage. Beach signaled for his wife to precede him upward. Hiking Nina up on his back to adjust the load, he started up after her. Nina may have been a child emotionally, but still swollen from her recently terminated pregnancy, she weighed over a hundred pounds. He usually tipped the scales at one-eighty-plus. Adding her weight, every step was like doing a leg press of almost three hundred pounds. Steeled by regular workouts at the stadium, Gil's leg muscles were better than most, much better. Still, after only a few stairs, he felt the strain and had to concentrate on moving forward one stair step at a time. After ascending a full flight, his thighs burned while his chest heaved for air.

The passage widened into a small alcove and landing, with a door to another stairway. By the time they reached the next landing, the atmosphere was still thick with gas vapor, but seemed less laden. He was thinking they might make it after all, when a thumping explosion sounded from below. Everything, including the stairs, moved with a heaving paroxysm.

The air at their level was not sufficiently saturated with gasoline vapor to ignite, but the chamber below had erupted like an immense Molotov cocktail, leveling support beams, melting steel struts and shoving earth, rock, and man-made structures upward.

The massive movement then dropped its load back, carrying the destruction even further. Concrete slabs tilted and crashed inward; metal beams bent like wet noodles. This man-made earthquake threw the three people like dice in a jar, dropping them in a moaning tangle.

Once they regained a semblance of awareness, Gil saw that walls had crumbled and collapsed ahead of them. They were trapped in a space that no longer led upward.

If they were to get out, they would have to go back down again

Chapter 73

Despite the destruction, the force of the explosion also worked partly in Beach and his party's favor. For a short time, it burned off the explosive vapor and blew out most of the actual flame with the power of its blast, like a giant blowing out a candle. For a few moments the fire was almost extinguished. Yet a few fingers of flame flickered among the debris. Soon an unconsumed stream of oil and gasoline re-ignited. At first it burned sluggishly, since the explosion had removed much of the oxygen needed for combustion. Yet the hungry fire sucked new air down into the tunnel to feed it. The flames licked at clusters of barrels grouped in small clumps along the way, their peeling paint curled and bubbled, the contents heating ever closer to the temperatures needed to vaporize the flammable chemicals. The danger of the surrounding atmosphere had diminished but that threat was replaced by the danger of dozens of barrels waiting to blow up like bombs.

Returning to the tunnel floor was like a nightmare worthy of Dante's best images. They entered a burning, billowing netherworld of fire and death. Gil had to concentrate on supporting the unconscious girl, while Pilar scouted paths around burning rubble and pools of flaming liquid. Gil was looking down to find footing, when he noticed a jerrycan that turned out to be partially filled with brackish water. They soaked pieces of cloth torn from their clothes and pressed them against their faces, draping a wet piece of shirt over Nina's lolling head.

The first barrel to go up must have had a rusted bottom ready to give way, because with a whump and whoosh, it shot off at an angle like a malfunctioning rocket. The next barrel just blew to smithereens and set off another container that sprayed oddly green-tinged flames across a whole stockpile of moldering supplies. The flaming blasts missed Gil and his small group, but acrid smoke and billowing fumes began to fill the top of the tunnel. There was still oxygen at shoulder height, but Gil knew that they didn't have much time. Breathing in the noxious fumes would knock anyone out. Instead of running, he stopped to run his eyes back and forth, sweeping the side walls.

"C'mon, Gil!" Pilar shouted, "We have to go back the way we came."

"We'd never make it. Before we were halfway there, we'd be either gassed or fried."

"We can't give up now!"

He said nothing, but slogged over to a part of the wall that was lined with wood, already scorched and smoking. He was about to lay Nina on a large flat box but paused for a moment to look more closely at a peeling label. He tore off a portion of the paper, shoving part into his pocket before he set her down. Relieved of the burden, he immediately picked up a section of steel reinforcing rod, and started banging on the wall panels repeatedly, sparks and charcoal flying from the charred surface.

"What are you doing?" Pilar shouted, near panic. "Don't flip out on me now! You can't do that." Then in a slightly different tone, "I still have to give you a hard time over your play time with that busty bimbo!"

Gil stopped for a moment, then turned. When he saw the pugnacious twinkle in her eye, he almost smiled. Instead, he explained his reasoning.

"You can't have a tunnel this long with only two outlets," he explained, "I figure somewhere behind this board is an opening, or at least a vent. Look at the smoke."

He pointed to the top of the panel he had been assaulting. Pilar looked up, to see that smoke was sliding across the ceiling like a wave, disappearing through a crack at its top, like dark gray water running into a drain. She looked around until she found a length of two-by-four so she could join him in beating at the splintering wood. It looked like it was giving way.

Suddenly the panel burst toward them instead of away, pushing surprisingly in the opposite direction in the opposite direction they were pounding it. The wood section knocked the two of them backwards as it broke and fell against them.

An apparition stood on the other side. Curls of smoke rising from his burned and flayed skin, the ruined thing that had been Randall confronted them, the hiss of searing embers melding with hissing noises coming from his throat between moans and growls. One eye was no more than sticky glue running down his cheek, the remaining orbit red and fiery, sunk in a blackened hole of his skull. Somehow, he must have maintained a vestige of sight, because he glared at them like all the rage in the world was focused through that one remaining crimson eye. A deep slash across his throat witnessed to Pilar's previous courage, but apparently her strength had not been sufficient to the task. Though it had temporarily disabled him, the wound had only separated layers of flesh and superficial blood vessels without penetrating vital parts or severing major blood vessels. The bloody line around his neck looked like a huge, off-center grin that matched the berserk grimace he still wore, peeling lips stretched in a mockery of amusement. Wisps of hair smoldered, and in one scorched area of his head, a pearly piece of skull bone showed through. Mucus ran from his nose and mouth, mixed with dirty blood. It also seeped from ears apparently ruptured in the blast. His swollen and seared hands held a fire-ax, crusty fingers tight with rage.

With a bellow, the bizarre specter pushed through the opening. Apparently, he had gotten far enough from the main explosion before it went off, to survive. So far, he was true to his reputation as a survivor. Behind him a communicating passageway was revealed, which explained how he had managed to make his way to the opening. It didn't explain how he continued to have the malicious energy to move and pursue them. Yet he lumbered forward toward Gil, who lay unarmed, in a numb daze.

"Noooo!" Pilar screamed, which raised Gil out of his stupor enough to roll sideways as the ax crashed down. It hit the earth heavily at the space his head had been occupying. Gil got up as far as his hands and knees, but before he could rise further, another blow was aimed in his direction. He couldn't move fast enough to completely avoid this strike. Misdirected, it still glanced off his spine, sending a bolt of pain through his body. A four-inch gash was opened in his back. Blood spread down his shirt as he dropped to the ground, stunned and helpless. The ax rose again, arched back behind the demon's back and started forward to deliver the *coup de grâce*. Gil could do nothing to protect himself.

Yet, as the scorched apparition bellowed and heaved to deliver the final blow, there was an unexpected hitch in the forward movement of the blade. The ax stopped in mid-air. The madman grunted, trying to bring it back over his shoulder, but it was being held back. He turned his dark gaze to find Nina, awake and staring back at him, her face an odd portrait of what looked like terrible sadness. Her wrists were still bound by a leather strap—the one he himself considered sacred and had used so many times before. She had slipped her hands over the end of his killing tool on its backward swing. The strap was looped over the steel head of the ax, with one of the girl's arms holding on each side, her whole bodyweight hanging on it. The ax could not be lifted without lifting her as well. In the chaos of his addled mind, the tortured soul didn't recognize the irony. He was being held back by the same strap that had restricted him many years ago during the childhood travesty he had barely survived.

The charred monster howled, desperately wrenching at the re-straining bond. When he turned he gave a last great tug, the old leather thong finally parted. Maybe it was weak and rotten. Maybe like some human beings, having held too many weights, too many secrets, too many pains, it was too tired to go on. Or some might say that there was a spirit living within it, formed of its many victim's agonies; a spirit that wanted revenge. Because, for whatever reason, the leather gave way at just the wrong, or just the right moment—depending on your point of view. For when it separated, the mighty pull that broke it also carried the ax wielder backward with such force, he lost his balance. With a wail that mixed rage and despair, he fell backward into a deep pool of burning oil and gasoline. There was violent thrashing that roiled the flaming cauldron, then subsided. After a moment in the middle of the inferno a smoldering figure rose-up briefly, in a last struggle or final protest, mouth open in a silent scream before sinking out of sight.

"She couldn't let him hurt anymore," a small voice came from the girl. The girl's self-protective MP process was activated, allowing her to distance herself from the act. But the words were enigmatic. Gil wondered if they meant she had to stop the hurt Randall had inflicted on others, or did they mean that she had to put him out of his misery. Either way, she was probably right. The suffering of victims and terrible insanity of the madman both needed to end. Now, finally, they had.

Gil slipped one of the trembling girl's arms around his shoulder, pulled her to a standing position and moved forward. Pilar followed, wobbling along on unsteady feet. Almost dragging Nina, Gil stepped through the opening that was now channeling great wafts of smoke out and up to some exit above. Barrels of chemicals were now exploding in batches, and huge waves of flame were pulsing up and down the tunnel. The going was slow with the child dangling at his side, so Gil finally picked her up in his arms and pounded up the first un-blocked stairway that appeared.

One flight, two flights, three . . . as they reached a landing, whooshing flame knocked them flat again. With great effort, Gil managed to get to his feet and bent to help the others. Pilar tried to get up but found that she couldn't support herself. She had reduced strength in her lower limbs as a result of an old injury, and was further weakened by her ordeal. She found that her legs couldn't function sufficiently to meet these enormous and unusual demands. She crumpled and went to her knees. Gil swung his burden down, turning his back to Pilar. He grabbed an arm and told her to get up on his back.

"You can't carry us both," she moaned, tears welling.

"Shut up and get on!" he ordered.

Obediently she pulled herself up with her arms. As he lowered to the ground for her, she managed to hike herself up, piggyback style. Nina sat, still stunned, on the floor. Gil slipped one arm under her legs, the other around her back. He took several deep breaths, then with a loud grunt, slowly rose to a standing position, like a weightlifter straining to lift a record-breaking set of weights. Moving ponderously, he started up again, the sound of bursting barrels, and roaring flames at his back. Cords stood out in his neck, sweat poured down him, as he laboriously reached the next landing. The strain sent knives of burning pain shooting down his overloaded legs. He pushed up the next two steps, then two more, heart pounding great whacking beats through his chest.

"*Got to keep going, got to keep going,*" he chanted to himself, heaving himself and the weight of two other people up one more step, then shakily up another. He might have stopped there; given up. He felt like he had come to his limits. He wanted to lie down right there and die, rather than endure anything more. But Pilar lay with her head on his shoulder. Turning her mouth to his ear, she whispered a few words.

"Stick with me, Baby," she said, an echo of some deeply held sense of purpose and experience they had shared. Then, insistently, "I love you, Gil Beach."

There was little left in his body's arsenal, but from some deep reservoir, as much emotional as physical, he found enough to go on. Part of it was the conditioning of his regular intense stair-climbing workout, but the expenditure of energy was beyond what even he should have been able to do. He refused to acknowledge those limitations. He had something driving him that was more important than tiredness, or pain.

Whatever that was, it was enough.

A few minutes later, he flopped, gasping and retching on the street above, arms around someone worth saving, and held by someone he loved.

Gil was treated at NYU Medical Center, along with the others. They wanted to keep him overnight, but he refused. He found Pilar in a room on the medical service floor.

"I'm okay, Gil," she said as soon as he limped into the room. "But you look like crap."

"Yeah, I suppose. But I'm fine. Just cuts and bruises."

"Not to mention a burn or two," she added, as she gently touched a singed spot on his scalp. "They want me to stay a night for observation. I think mostly I just need some rest."

"That's for sure," he agreed, "You just take it easy. I've got a couple of final things to take care of."

"Oh Gil, you aren't going to be doing something dangerous, are you? I've had enough of that."

"No, nothing dangerous. There's just a couple of things unfinished yet."

"Please be careful, Gil. You've been working too damn hard. As soon as possible, I want to take a vacation—someplace nice and relaxed."

"You want me along when you take it?"

"Pardon me?"

"Well, after everything that has gone on, I wasn't sure you'd want to be around me anymore."

"Don't be ridiculous. You couldn't get rid of me if you wanted to. You're stuck with me, buster . . . for life."

"I almost lost you a couple of times this week," he replied, more seriously, "And one of them was my own stupid fault."

"We let a lot of things and people get between us, Gil Beach. If I'm really gonna be honest, I have to admit that I was as far from our wedding vows as you were. Maybe I didn't screw anybody physically, but that was as much circumstance as virtue. Our marriage was the farthest thought from my mind."

"Can you fix that kind of thing?"

"I don't know for sure, Darling. But I know there's a stronger bond between us than just some words at a ceremony. I sure believe in you, Mister. If you still believe in me, then the really important thing hasn't been broken."

"I believe in you, Pilar . . . I believe in US."

"Then we can make it," she smiled, reaching up and tousling his singed hair near the little bald spot in back.

"Stick with me, Baby."

"Like glue, darlin' . . . like glue."

Chapter 74

Senator Delucia was wowing them again. He glanced at his watch. It was nearly time to arrange an exit. He could work the crowd another five or six minutes, then signal Evelyn who was subbing as coordinator and stage manager of this appearance. Ever since he had screwed her a couple of times, she was like a devoted puppy, slavishly carrying out his wishes almost before he asked. When he tugged at his ear, she would give a high sign to the bodyguards, who would then hustle him out, as if against his will. He checked the guards' positions casually. The one he sarcastically called "Lurch," a huge farm boy-turned-bouncer, whose real name was Lowell-something, appeared to be examining someone's I.D. Then, surprisingly, the hulking bodyguard nodded and stepped out the side door with the man. *He shouldn't do that. He should never let me out of his sight.*

Delucia jerked his eyes to the stage exit, where the federal agents assigned to him as a presidential candidate should have supplemented his security staff. Two men stood there that he did not recognize—strangers. He started to feel a trickle of sweat run down his neck into his collar. This didn't feel right. Something was going on. He looked for Jeannine but couldn't locate her. She had been a little cold lately, since he had been slipping the pork to Evelyn, but she should have been used to that by now. She had no claim on him. He had given her a career, an exciting life, and some good times in the sack. He expected gratitude, and he expected her to be around when he needed her. Like now!

He looked for Sherri, his Legal Counsel, not finding her at first. He momentarily had second thoughts about choosing so many women as aides. They were handy for recreation and easy to control, but if it came to a physical confrontation, he would have liked a little more muscle in sight. But that's what the security team was for. Then he saw Sherri in the rear of the room, her face in her hands, another strange man standing over her.

What the fuck was going on?

The roaring applause had died down. He realized he was standing with his mouth open, looking like an idiot. The crowd started moving toward the exits, a dozen or more police directing the herd, acting as sheep dogs.

A small group of people approached him. They had the bored, tough look of cops. Except one of them, who looked a mess, hair singed away from the side of his head, scratches, burns and abrasions all over his face and hands. That man didn't look bored—he looked pissed-off. Then he recognized the man. He was Gil Beach, the crazy cop who had caused so much trouble. With him was an imposing black man that the Senator recognized as Police Commissioner Charles "Chuck" Franzen.

“Uh, hello, Chuck,” he tried the old charm, “Nice to see you. To what do I owe this pleasure?”

The other man did not smile in return.

“Hello Senator. I don’t think you are going to consider this a pleasure. I have the unpleasant duty of informing you that you are under arrest.”

“Now just hold on, there,” Delucia sputtered in protest, “Sherri, get your ass over here,” he called to his Counsel, who looked up blankly. “What the fuck, is this, Franzen? This is a big mistake, Buddy. You don’t just walk up and arrest a United States Senator on the basis of some loose-cannon cop’s insane accusations, like this moron. I’m a candidate for President of the United States, for Christ’s sake.” He glared at Beach. “I already told you about this nutcase.”

“Yes, you did,” the Commissioner agreed civilly. “You did a lot of things to interfere with a major investigation. That’s one of many charges you are now facing. You are also charged with conspiracy to commit murder, accessory to kidnapping, and a few other gems . . . Mr. Sturmer.”

“M . . . Mr. . . . Sturmer? What . . . wha?”

Franzen just looked annoyed. With a disgusted wrinkle in his nose, he turned his head, waving at Beach to take over.

"Yeah, we know your real name is Markus Sturmer, Billy Rae Sturmer's brother," Gil picked up the lead. "He took the rap for the construction scams of Sturmer Construction, but you were the power behind it all. You were 'Uncle Markus' to his boys—Fred, Randy, and the rest."

The look of anger drained from Delucia's face, to be replaced by an expression of stunned disbelief.

"You also poured money into the Federation of Natural Selection's operation, and made Boyd . . . or should I say 'Roger', the front man. Well, he's a basket case up at the hospital. When I last saw him, he didn't look like he was long for this world. The Federation is finished for sure. It was a nice cover for some of the other garbage you had going, but Randall went too far. Now he's dead. So is your other nephew, Fred."

Delucia's mouth dropped open, his face going pale. He turned from face to face, looking for something soft, some opening. He saw nothing but hardness.

"Unfortunately, they didn't die before they and the rest of you in that crazy Yin-Yang survivalist group cost the lives of a lot of good people, including some of my friends," Gil continued. "We know all about the secret treasury—the records were found in the Federation Headquarters archives. There are some interesting things still to be determined, I am sure, about your political efforts to continue the `Grand Design' subway plan, and the role of the Sturmer Construction Company. I would love to check out the details of your campaign financing while we're at it. From what I saw, I can finally understand why Randall plea-bargained that scum, Chee-Chee, when I had him dead to rights. The asshole was one of the biggest contributors to your campaign. But something tells me the murder and conspiracy charges will be enough to change your status from environmental standard bearer to inmate. Your career just got sidetracked, Senator."

"What? I . . . , I don't know what you're talking about. I had nothing to do with any such group," the desperation was now evident in his voice. "Yin-yang? What are you talking about?"

"Sir?" Gil Beach asked the Commissioner, "If I may?"

Franzen nodded.

Gil stepped up to Delucia, who raised his hands protectively, as if expecting to be hit. Beach grabbed the man's left arm, pulled it down, and unbuckled the large watch that the Senator habitually wore. It was very similar to the one regularly sported by the late S.B. Randall. As the watch slipped free, Beach jerked the man's arm around, so that the back of his wrist was visible. In the wide band that had been covered by the large timepiece, a mark was vividly tattooed. It was a circle with intertwined dark and light halves.

“No wonder you guys always wear big watches,” Gil remarked dryly. By the way, you should have read that motto inscribed over the nature center.”

“What motto?”

“It says that we should let the welfare of the world be the supreme law.”

“What’s that supposed to mean?” Franzen asked.

“Damned if I know. But it doesn’t mean that the welfare of Senator Mark Delucia is the supreme law, that’s for damn sure.” He turned away from DeLucia.

“If it means anything else, I think we can let the Senator ponder it for a few years, while he’s serving out his sentence.”

“Right. Oh, by the way, Beach,” Franzen said, “I’ve got somebody here wants to talk to you.”

“Oh, like who?”

The Commissioner waved across the room. A figure slouched across to them, shoulders sagging, head down. As the man got closer, Gil recognized him.

“Gorman, you shit!”

Before Beach could decide whether to slug the man, insult him, or just walk away, the IAB Investigator spoke quickly.

"I know you're pissed. You've got a right. When we found out the pressure to investigate you was coming from Delucia, we dropped the whole case against you."

"Yeah, sure you did. Don't you mean after you found out he was getting indicted?"

"Think whatever you want, but you're in the clear. On behalf of the Internal Affairs Bureau, I apologize for any difficulty we have caused you."

This was history in the making. I.A.B. doesn't give out apologies to anyone. Then Gil noticed how Gorman kept glancing at the Commissioner and realized that this apology was probably being delivered on his orders.

Up until then, Franzen had kept quiet, but when he saw Gil's look, he stepped over to whisper in the Detective's ear.

"Don't be too hard on him. He took your part in this thing, you know."

Gil was too worked up, to let go of his anger so quickly.

"While you're apologizing for the IAB, how about for yourself, Gorman? Do you always walk into somebody's house and eat their food, while you plan to screw them?"

"I suppose it looked like that, but it wasn't. We know the Deasons. They just suggested we come with them that night. The investigation had nothing to do with it."

"Yeah? Well, what was that little message you made sure I heard—the one about not looking or talking?"

"Oh come-on, Beach. That was just conversation."

"What do I look like? Like I just got out of diapers?"

"No, honest. I wasn't even on the case till later."

Gil saw Franzen nodding confirmation, but he still had a hard time changing his view of the IAB Investigator.

"Look, Gorman. If you were really legit, you wouldn't have lied about your job."

"Oh sure, just walk in and tell a bunch of cops and their wives that I'm IAB. Right! And maybe wear a sign that says 'kick me' while I'm at it. I always did like to set myself up."

Gil thought about that. "I guess you've got a point there," he grudgingly agreed. "Sort of like stopping in at the PLO to get directions to the Yeshiva."

"Or asking the Bishop to pick up your order of contraceptives."

Beach tried to keep a straight face, but a little splut of laughter squeezed out. Gorman's shoulders gave an involuntary jiggle as he tried to hold back a laugh. The tension had been getting too much, the confrontation was getting old, and they were both tired. As the men stared at each other, they began to crack up. Gil started to choke, Gorman began to sputter. Commissioner Franzen even started to chuckle, then he sneezed, which sent the whole group into a fit of laughter.

"Hey, look," Gorman finally managed to say. "Hate me, if you want, but my wife Peg, and your wife seemed to be hitting it off pretty good. How about we tolerate each other enough to at least let them do their own thing?"

"What the hell," Gil said, wiping his eyes in amazement. "I survived your investigation, a running gun battle, an underground firestorm, and a whacked-out killer trying to chop me into kindling. I guess I can handle having you at a barbecue."

Delucia was still standing nearby, looking like they must all be crazy. So was Helen Joseph, who was watching to make sure he didn't bolt. And the truth is, the idea that a street Detective, a Commissioner, and an IAB Investigator would be standing around laughing with each other, was about as crazy an idea as most cops could ever imagine. Franzen must have realized that too, because when he saw the looks they were getting, he straightened and assumed a more serious expression.

"Why is he still here?" he barked, nodding toward the Senator, "Cuff him and read him his rights."

"You got it," Helen responded, sliding a pair of handcuffs onto Delucia's trembling wrists.

"Tell me, Gil," she asked, as she snapped the manacles into place over Delucia's tattoo. "I still don't get the whole yin-yang thing. What was the deal with that? Something to do with the survival idea?"

"Not really. Partly, it was just misdirection, I suppose. But mostly it was camouflage."

"Camouflage?"

"Yeah, the Sturmer Construction outfit used it as a logo."

Gil pulled a curled paper from his pocket. It was part of the label he had torn from the tunnel wall. At the center of the label was a big S inside a circle.

"They used this on their trucks, equipment, everything. A couple of the boys even tattooed it on their arms, when they were drinking and raising hell. Made it kinda hard to go incognito."

"An S, like it stood for Sturmer?"

"Right. I found this on some of the stuff underground. Then I realized that all they had to do to disguise it, was darken in half of the logo."

Gil pulled a pen from his pocket and scribbled on the logo. Using the S as a dividing line, he filled in one half with black ink, leaving the rest white.

"Damn," she exclaimed. "Look at that. Now it looks just like a yin-yang symbol—half dark, half light."

"Well, it was all dark, as far as I can tell, all bad. And so is this creep you've got on your hands."

Helen nodded and pulled Delucia toward the door.

CHAPTER 75

As he watched the soon-to-be-Ex-Senator being led away, Gil, still in the auditorium, could hear the familiar words being recited.

"These are your rights. You have the right to remain silent, you have the right to . . ."

Then another voice spoke, right behind him.

"You have the right to a big hug," Gil was startled by the voice. He turned to find his wife standing a few feet away. She was still pale from the ordeal, but she was walking. There was a mischievous smile on her face.

"I didn't know you were being discharged," Gil apologized. "I would have been there."

"I know. No problem. I wasn't really supposed to be out yet, but I guess I'm like you—I don't like other people telling me when I can go to the bathroom."

"You got that right. But that's about the only way you're like me. We're different in a lot of ways."

"I suppose you're right. We are pretty different people."

"Yeah, though most of the differences are very nice," he said with a grin, taking her into his arms.

"Speaking of different people, Gil . . . ," she said softly, her voice changing key.

"I don't like that tone in your voice," he chuckled. "I know that sound. It usually means you want something."

"Ummmm. I can think of something I want very much," she leered, wiggling in his arms. "And I'll bet you'd like it just fine."

"There was one other thing," she added coyly.

"Oh-oh, here it comes."

"I was thinking about Nina."

"Oh, the MPD girl? Poor kid."

"Yes, you realize she has no family now?"

"No family? Yeah, I guess so. Wait a minute, you're not thinking what I think you're thinking, are you?"

"Right now, we're the only people she can trust, Gil. They're keeping her at the hospital until tomorrow, but then it's foster care, or an institution."

"Are you sure that isn't a better place for her? If you're right about her problems and all."

"Oh I know I'm right—but I told you, she's not psychotic. MPD is a tough problem, but it isn't insanity. It's treatable."

"And you want to treat her?"

"No, not me. There are folks who specialize in that. But I could give her support while she dealt with it. At least I understand the problem and I understand her. And you . . . you saved her life. She could feel safe with us. She doesn't have many places she can feel safe."

"I don't know. You're talking about a big responsibility, Pilar."

"I know. You're right, it is big. But if people like us don't take that kind of responsibility, who will?"

"Ummm," he said, looking thoughtful. His thoughts went back to what he'd said to Shig Higawa only hours before, about 'stepping up to the line.'

"We don't . . . have children of our own," she added in a choked voice, swallowing hard.

"I know, Pilar . . . I know that makes you . . ."

"We have a decent income, and we have a huge house to ourselves. I mean, we could just do it on a foster care basis for now, and . . ."

He reached out and put a finger gently across her lips, to slow the rush of words. She paused, eyes bright and eager.

"This is pretty important to you, isn't it?"

"Yes, Gil—very."

He was quiet for a few seconds, looking at her eyes. Finally, he pulled her into his arms, and spoke into her ear.

"Okay, with one condition."

"Oh Gil!" she blurted out looking thrilled. Then she paused to hold him at arms-length. "What kind of condition?"

He grinned mischievously.

"Well, I know we've got some extra space at the house," he said with a smirk. "but if she turns out to have more than three personalities, they have to share rooms."

Pilar giggled, punching him playfully in the shoulder.

"You mean it? It's okay with you if we take her in?"

"Yeah, if you really want to. At least on a temporary basis. I guess I'll survive."

"Survive? I know you will. But I didn't think you'd ever want to use that word again, after the way Randall distorted it."

"Well, it still bothers me, but I had a thought down in that hole, when we were trying to make it to the surface."

When he didn't say more, Pilar goaded him.

"Come on, motor-mouth . . . explain."

"Well, see, on the way up from that . . . that hell hole, I was ready to give in. I didn't think I had anything left, but I kept going. And then I thought I understood.

"Understood what, Gil?"

"Well, I guess why some people are survivors and others don't make it. I've heard about people that survived as P.O.W's and all. I even knew a couple. They had something different than the ones they left behind."

"So, tell me, what's the difference?"

"I don't know quite how to put it in words, but I don't think it matters how tough you are. I think the survivors—the people who keep going when others fall by the wayside, are usually the ones that have something to live for."

"You're sounding like a famous Psychologist."

"Yeah?"

"Uh—huh. Victor Frankl. He was a prisoner of war, himself. He founded a theory of psychology. If you care about names, he called it Logotherapy."

"I don't know much about psychology, but I know something about life. Lots of folks know HOW to live. But that isn't enough. To really survive, you've also gotta know WHY."

"How about you, Gil Beach? Do you know why?"

Although he was quiet for a moment, his face showed no uncertainty, other than that of finding the right words to express himself.

“Yes. Yes, I think I do. But don’t expect me to explain.”

“I’m used to that.”

“All I can say, is . . . that you’re the biggest part of it.”

Pilar just smiled and then nodded, taking his arm to walk beside him out of the room. She knew that was about as much explanation as she was going to get.

. . . It was enough.

www.ingramcontent.com/pod-product-compliance
Lightning Source LLC
LaVergne TN
LVHW021753060526
838201LV00058B/3082
9798887759968